Gayle Ridinger

THE SHADOW WIFE

ISBN 978-0-6151-4039-1

Cover: Detail from *"Where have you been, Awen, my druid muse?"* by Annabelle J. Verhoye

PART ONE

Four eyes, exactly the same, like vitreous blue French beads, watched him in the mirror. Twin sisters close to thirty, a brunette and a blonde, still quite similar looking even down to their few wrinkles, who wanted to look identical again. In those less than enthusiastic first moments, as Manuel the hairdresser freed their two oval, tell-tale faces, he realized that it would take him four if not five hours to do what they asked, his hands stained in their new red hair dye, his sister with their toes in her lap, in this remote gray corridor of the shopping mall, in a hair salon destined to close down like every business there before it. Since he was a fool with a family to maintain, he'd said, 'yes, all right, sit down.' They insisted: they wanted to be absolutely interchangeable. He reassured them amicably at first, then stopped talking. At every snip he took, the woman with the brown hair, which he'd unpinned from an Indian leather patch and stick, maintained a stare of radical conviction in this transformation process. The blonde one with the classy dye job, on the other hand, kept fidgeting with things in her deep plush handbag. After a while, she looked at him questioningly in the mirror. Then she started speaking to her sister in what sounded like French.

And the map's in there? Monique's concern was feigned. She simply liked hearing Sophie sound expert and resolute.

Not just the map—the notebook with everything! Sophie said she'd tucked it into the zippered inner compartment. Reminder pages on the child-care tips they'd gone over, recipes, how to operate the appliances, little Leslie-Ann's comfort preferences. And as many details as possible about what Monique considered to be 'the bull to be taken by the horns.'

The reshaping of their eyebrows took a long time. Once when Manuel's sister jerked too hard on the tweezers, the soon-to-be-ex-brunette complained. The hairdresser made a quiet comment in

Spanish and it didn't happen again. For the hour it took for him to paint and lift, paint and lift all their locks in that deep crimson they wanted, the two blue-eyed women just sat there—no glamour magazines for them—but long locked gazes, yes, these they did indulge in, finding somewhere past his mirror so many remembered things—or maybe people—that it began to drive him crazy, and every so often there were new outbursts in French.

The new dress for Leslie-Ann is in the car for you to give it to her. Don't forget. She's expecting it, said Sophie.

How do you know that when she hardly says a word? rebutted Monique. Sophie's daughter was only two and a late talker. Ah Leslie-Ann. For whom this was all being done, one could say. Because her mother wanted to live a comfortable, renegotiated life with her. Someday she would know this.

Still other things are suddenly coming to mind, muttered Sophie. *The water man comes tomorrow. Remember that I go to church with Leslie-Ann—the Catholic church—and so you'll have to go too, sorry about that.*

"Manicure, ladies."

Sophie watched the application strokes of red nail polish, and herself in the mirror turning more into, well, a show girl. Their new look—Monique's choice—was a shock tactic to keep others from suspecting anything. My, that's red-red, she thought. She suspected her husband wouldn't like it, but then again she'd been wrong about his preferences regarding hair color in the past. "Blow on your nails. Make them dry," commanded Monique, and Sophie puffed strenuously. For the moment it lasted, this extra blowing generated the equally superstitious doubt that Monique was really capable of copying her detachment or her quieter ways. She'd carried it off well when they were children, and even teenagers, but that was a long time ago.

They both closed their eyes while Manuel finished with the hairspray.

Again in French, Monique said, *Have you decided where you're going?*

I thought for tonight to the Ramada Inn over in Jersey, in Cherry Hill.

Blinking at the mirror, Monique took in her sleek bobbed hairstyle. The intense red color added to that sleekness, she decided. It was sleekness of an audacious rather than an understated sort, *voilà*. Then she scrutinized Sophie. No tears. Not yet.

CHAPTER ONE

Beginnings

Near the end of the war John Morton shot down the Vichy collaborator pursuing Danièle Foucher in the street with scissors. This took place in Paris, after the big Liberation Day celebrations had ended in the summer of 1944. The man was a barber who had been driven mad by the war's inverted tide and by his knowledge that Danièle Foucher had done favors for the Underground while helping out at her mother's café next to his shop. Spying her on the momentarily deserted street, the barber, whose less than flourishing business had been burnt down by those who despised him, tried forcing her at scissor- point to acknowledge some respect for old Pétain: maybe he'd gone wrong, but still he'd done all he could for France. Danièle Foucher spat.

That's when she received a fierce jabbing, as if she were not just cold and jeering to him but also made of marble, and he couldn't resist chipping something off of her. Respect! He wanted respect! The barber's identification with Pétain was strong: even his haircut came unhinged. ("He looked like a wildman-- a beast." Danièle said when she told the story—as *Danielle*—in America in the years that followed.) Then he shrieked at her the only curse that his desperation allowed him: "Someone—woman!—will force you to walk in another's shoes!" His fury mounted and his intentions became crystal clear. He would make her instantly into someone she wasn't; he would chop off her hair so people would think she'd slept with the enemy, that she'd turned traitor to her cause and to General de Gaulle. Believing the barber was trying to kill her, the closest American sammy on patrol, rescued her with his machine gun. The barber crumpled in two.

John Morton, that American soldier, asked and asked, "OK? You OK?" He made the respectful gesture of almost touching her cheek. Danièle half let herself feel giddy and half fought the feeling off. Grim but curious, he offered Danièle his different nature, his bit of undamaged belief. She would never have to look at that barber again, and because she was young, her old physical sense of freedom, to move her limbs and breathe as she pleased, came back to her. He told her his name. They moved away from the barber's body, which passersby were ignoring, to a covered entranceway, where they attempted a conversation. His tapping at his watch and her smiling and miming a glass with her fist established a first rendezvous for that evening. In Paris at that time there were plenty of girls and women who had gone up to the first Allied soldier that they'd seen passing –not one who'd done anything to help them in a personal way—just to plant the most passionate kisses on his lips. Danièle showed far more genuine interest, and sweetness too, by inviting him to her mother's café. Other times followed: she led him here or there, all over Paris. Laughing, he would say, "Where are you taking me?", perfectly aware that she didn't understand, and getting to know himself as a different person because of it.

Over the next couple of months, Danièle's few but direct words of English and John's natural bluntness would speed them, like so many others, down a short alleyway of romance. Soft concepts, glorious intuitions that broke through the language barrier, half-expressed strong feelings, and the night John risked being counted as AWOL, did the rest.

She scrounged up a bilingual dictionary and an English grammar, thanks to one of her mother's faithful old customers, and learned enough English to render their relationship three-dimensional; and then when their passion reached its zenith 'full scale.' To secure the right to stay together, they became officially engaged. They didn't have to wait long—not by the standards of back then—and suddenly one day their odd, deprived life as a couple in war-ravaged Paris was over; in the winter of 1946 John Morton carried off his war bride with steel nerves to a small town in New Jersey, where he went into the business of insuring people's lives.

Fast gunner, quick thinker, why shouldn't he be attracted to life's solid pay-off plans? Some years down the line, when his twin daughters, Monique and Sophie, were just into their teens, he apologized for how unimaginative he was, which only endeared him and upped his rating as their steady and dependable dad. It might be expected that over the years he'd had little to say about the Vichy barber he'd killed. Just a brief admission once: "I charged like a bull, war's like that. I'm only telling you this because it's how your mother and I met."

In rural Gloucester County, John and *Danielle* Morton eventually settled into half a two-storied yellow house, a 'duplex' as they were called, backed by peach trees and cornfields but in sight of the shiny Commodore Barry Bridge, which as it spanned the Delaware seemed to promise a wide, flying fairy-tale ride straight into Philadelphia.

They lived in half the space they could have, contenting themselves with a living room and kitchen downstairs and two small bedrooms and bath upstairs. Meanwhile, the same arrangement of rooms—also their property—went uninhabited beyond the hall wall and behind an identical front door adjacent to theirs, giving onto the joint front porch. That they lived like this had its origins in both idealism and family economics. "It's like using half your brain most days, but knowing you can count on all of it when you need it," John Morton said, when he first saw the for sale sign, its color starting to fade, plastered like a "Wanted" poster on the trunk of a large elm in the front yard. In the empty rooms they could host his mother from Gettysburg or her mother from France, or cousins, or should times get rough, a boarder; later, when they had children, the kids as of a certain age might want to live on their own, yet be just next door. Immediately upon buying it, John Morton got the idea of converting the space to business premises—and briefly did: his insurance company gave its temporary blessing to his idea of creating a local agency, which failed, however, to drum up much new business among the many peach and tomato farmers and relatively few store owners of rural Southern Jersey, despite all of John Morton's contagious good-natured faith in life's and Prudential's pay-offs; and so after only a year of Danielle's tiptoeing around their half-a-house barefoot when she heard a customer come in on the other side, John went back to covering the county in his car, and the space reverted—like the spare part of the brain that John had compared it with—to a quiet place of possibility.

Having lived most of her life in one of the most famous cities in the world, Danielle found it disconcerting, and yet charming at first, to be living on the outskirts of Clearsboro, a town consisting of two rows of wooden houses along a highway and with no clustered center. Once past this little line-up, there were only fields and stunted fruit trees. It intrigued Danielle the fact that the local farmers had to go from their house to barn to chicken coop in plain sight of anyone passing by, without any walls, bushes, or trained branches to shade them from view. No stone enclosing walls meant that there were no courtyards, of course; there didn't seem to be secluded places of any sort, actually, for enjoying one's privacy in the open air—unlike in any corner of France. Then there was her discovery that everyone over the age of 16 got around by car, tractor, or truck (except Danielle, the only adult to use a bicycle). Since John drove their car to work, and since Danielle couldn't stand sitting around the house all day, nor walking for miles in anything other than city streets, she got on her bike daily and made a large loop (*je fais le tour*, she said to herself) for miles, considering it her constitutional.

In the six years before the twins were born, she saw quite a bit of farmland cleared and built upon. The local population gradually became a mix of farmers and people with office jobs, whose small wooden A-frame homes, all alike, went up on brand-new lanes in the middle of nowhere, accessible only by car...or bike. John said these groupings were called *housing developments*. They were most interesting to her. They made her think back to the rows of identical military tents in the GI camp where John had been stationed. To be honest , her original impressions of those soldiers—so good-natured, disciplined, energetic, well-fed—often colored her opinion of her South Jersey neighbors, which whom she had similarly sporadic dealings. Now as then, she engaged in the activity of watching Americans, with the exception of John, from a distance. She caught daily glimpses of local inhabitants weeding in their back gardens, plowing their corn fields, or pushing on their front doors with their arms laden with bags of groceries purchased over in the county seat of Woodbury. When she got particularly intrigued by or sympathizing with what she was seeing, the words sometimes came to her which her mother had often muttered with a smile behind her café counter: *no one understands me but I understand everyone.* From John, Danielle learned the names and family histories of those she watched, information which he sometimes laced with confidential details from their life-insurance applications. No intimacy, unfortunately, came out of this for her. Not that the Southern Jerseyites were unfriendly—on the contrary, when local people happened to look up and see her as she biked past, they would almost always smile and wave. Americans were excellent wavers, she thought. They put pep and amicability into the gesture. There didn't seem to be any outdoor place where local inhabitants could regularly gather, however. There was no square, daily market, park, or café terrace—the places where they would have congregated in France, and so for quite a number of months at the start Danielle was at a loss for where she might make a friend.

She finally managed one day to strike up a sort of semi-friendship with Louise Vassalli, the farm wife who ran the family produce stand along the stretch of highway between the Morton's duplex and Clearsboro. Louise was striding towards the stand, wiping her hands on her apron, just as Danielle began to pass by on her bike. Her timing couldn't have been more perfect. At Louise's friendly wave, Danielle impulsively turned onto the narrow sandy strip along the road's shoulder. She bought a bushel of apples from Louise. Then she decided on some early peaches, it being June. By the time Danielle had started squeezing the zucchini, Louise was dishing up some intriguing county gossip and beginning to ask her a swarm of personal questions.

This mix of shopping and socializing at the Vassalli stand constituted Danielle's only efforts at friendship at first. It was fine by her that she and John didn't see other couples—or go anywhere really. John spent too much time on the road during the day to want to go out in the evening. "Let me get my land legs back again, honey," he'd tell her—tenderly, not resenting her occasional request. She didn't feel any real disappointment. Nothing about her life could feel anything like depravation to her, not after the hunger and bombs of Paris.

Besides, on Saturday John and she would drive to the library in the county seat of Woodbury, and she would get in her long chat with the librarian, Mrs. Olson, who found her English books of just the right level of difficulty, and who answered questions about American laws and ways that were beyond John's ken. Danielle mentioned these leisurely visits to the library, which she knew illustrated the easy well-being of her life, in the letters that she sent, along with money orders, to her mother and brother Dédé. They continued to describe Paris as grim, hungry, and *très très cher*. By contrast, she felt that she had no right to feel anything other than grateful.

Only once did she feel otherwise. This happened one July afternoon at the antique shop in Clearsboro. She'd been absorbed in contemplating the plain form of a child's highchair from the early 1800s, imagining that the family had sold it and everything else before migrating out West (she'd been reading about pioneers) when the elderly owner, Mr. Mills, came over to her. "Mrs. Morton? I thought you might like to talk to a French lady from Lyon who is the wife of an old friend of mine." He gestured toward the two people behind him, a man with glasses and baby-smooth skin, dressed in a light-blue linen jacket, and a tall tanned woman in a sleeveless white dress, which accentuated her slim waist, with matching white shoes. As Danielle and the other woman, Corinne, exchanged soft polite greetings, Mr. Mills made quick work of explaining who each woman was to the other as well as something about their smoothly unfolding new lives. Corinne's husband was a professor of Art History in Philadelphia, and she—imagine!, marveled Danielle, who had an intrinsic respect for artists—was a sculptor.

"Been to Philly with your husband yet?" Mr. Mills asked Danielle kindly.

"Not yet," she answered, apologetically because he seemed to want this visit to take place for her.

"Mind you, there are some rough neighborhoods you won't like."

"Excellent art museum," interjected Corinne's husband cheerfully.

"Right," confirmed Mills. "And it's full of historical sites from the American Revolution." He caught himself. "Naturally, you two ladies have probably had enough of wars."

There was a moment of silence which seemed like a tribute to the dead but was really just a stall in the conversation. While Corinne's husband made a quip about Mill's well-intended little faux pas, Danielle and Corinne exchanged guarded glances. There was something about Corinne's elegant tall presence, calm interest in the antiques around her, and impenetrable gaze in that moment that drove home to Danielle that the other woman had her ambitions, her creative streak to feed, her cultured existence to lead—one which was even more financially secure than Danielle's own. The war was something that she didn't think about, anymore than Danielle.

Would she be happier living in the city as Corinne did? Danielle wondered suddenly. It was the first time she'd allowed herself to imagine herself as less than happy, less than grateful. The question echoed in her mind a moment. Then she went back to her life.

That Danielle gave birth to twins in the summer of 1952 surprised everyone but herself. Not that she was expecting twins; there were no known cases in either her or John's family, and nothing about the pregnancy had made her or the doctor suspect there were two little girls, instead of one, growing on the other side of her tightly stretched tummy wall. She wasn't expecting twins yet found, upon reflection, that it was perfectly fine. Destiny was looking after her. With respect to her family and friends trying to rebuild their lives and fortunes in France, she had been granted an easy life of abundance. Lots of food and heating, lots of appliances, and now an instant family of four.

These passing thoughts were, of course, rapidly buried under the pile of urgent childcare tasks. John and she were caught up in a twenty-four- hour spin cycle whose cardinal points were the girls' feeding and bath times, together with the boiling of the dirty linen diapers and the sterilizing of the formula bottles. To help her as much as he could, and because getting organized to deal with this blessing of twin daughters was the aspect which gave him the most pleasure for now, John planned his visits to insurance clients in such a way as to continually be crisscrossing the county and stopping by his home. He'd arrive with a bag of groceries or just in time to change the baby who was waiting to be tended to.

Hard as it was and sleep-deprived as they were, they managed it together.

Hard as it was, Danielle began to discover things about her Monique and her Sophie, who were named after her two grandmothers. John approved of these French names without accents, acceptable and feminine-sounding to American ears.

The curiosity that Danielle had felt initially about the habits and ways of Clearsboro and South Jersey she now trained on her twins. Ironically, though she took less interest in them, the local people began to open up to her. The lady behind the counter at the post office, for instance, was full of advice on what mail-order catalogues for children's clothing were worth requesting. Then there was the minister's wife at the Lutheran church, where John had wanted to have the girls baptized, who brought a casserole dinner over when she heard from the pediatrician that Monique and Sophie were sick with croup. In short, for all the people who stopped her with her baby carriage to exclaim over the girls looking so identical, and go on *and on* about this, there were plenty of others who seemed to understand it was kinder to take little notice. She was just a mother to them. At last she felt settled in. And how much those two small warm bodies that she clasped countless times daily had to do with it!

In reality, a few adjustment problems still remained. Sometimes, during the after-service church coffee, for instance, she panicked and felt terrifically unsure of herself. Was it all right to change the subject that the other women were talking about? Should she forgo asking a question that maybe she wouldn't have the courage to ask in the future? It went far beyond the mastering of English. Sometimes things went haywire, and the American women would give her a queer look, and she would get the cold feeling that she'd never make a social go of it here. But these moments began to get fewer and fewer.

John started bringing home magazines, fine glossy ones with photos, with advice on child-raising, gardening, and making your home beautiful. When it was time to buy a proper dining room set, they followed the advice of these experts and chose a Danish Modern style. More usually, however, the magazines served to keep them up to date about parenting. Danielle often selected an article or two to take over to Louise Vassalli's. More than once Louise found what she read fascinating enough to want to phone a friend of hers. "Mary could use this," she'd tell Danielle, and then she'd read aloud to Mary the latest on the subject of spanking your child. There was a Dr. Spock who was very much against that.

Oftentimes Danielle came home aglow with satisfaction. Every minute spent swapping these tips was so well spent. Yet for all the pleasure Danielle took in these exchanges, she preferred to keep to the subject of the other women's babies and not say too much about her own. The others picked up their ears when she had anything to reveal—twins were so interesting, and she had to endure so many conclusions, musings, and pronouncements. It was best to say little.

In her mind, however, she cultivated and continually corrected her personal certainties about her two little fascinating creatures.

One of the first things she'd noticed about her girls was that although they usually had the same reaction to things, it rarely happened at the same time. From the moment Monique and Sophie had come home from the hospital, they'd slept, nursed and shat on two staggered schedules. Now, as their toddlerhood evolved, she grew to sense that this being on separate inner clocks left much room for chance and even fate to intervene. Her daughters, she intuited, might end up living very different lives.

There was something that, however, made her doubt her own thinking at times. It was the girls' "code talking," as John and she called it. Regularly, from the age of two onwards, the girls filled the house with gargly grunts, and syncopated yelps, and fricatives and labials in the oddest combinations... one little girl sending the other to retrieve a dolly from the couch or some such thing, in a language that only they could understand. At first Danielle and John found this special way of communicating was 'cute' to watch, but over time thought it so only so long as the girls weren't fighting. In those fights Sophie's and Monique's code-talking really alarmed them. Sometimes Danielle and John watched the twins on the verge of a cold panic because the girls didn't seem like human children but small enraged aliens, before separating the two. It was another story entirely when the two girl played pacifically together. 'Nuts to people who are down on kids,' John remarked to Danielle one Friday evening as they watched the twins on the living room rug with blocks, stuffed animals, and bits of cloth from Danielle's sewing bag. 'Just look at my girls putting together a city—a city! I think they've exchanged all of two words. I'd like to see politicians do that.'

Danielle thought that Monique and Sophie could communicate in an extra-ordinary way, if not exactly telepathically. "Perhaps twins have six or seven senses instead of five,' she mused.

Then she filed this impression away with all the rest.

At age four, Monique and Sophie were drawing smiling people with very long arms and claw-like fingers who could touch a mommy passing in the sky. Danielle kept the artwork in an album entitled "Sophie and Monique: New Jersey, 1956." She imagined taking these drawings down from the shelf in a distant future and finding something more revealing than innocence at its brightest. Of course, she knew that all mothers did that; there wasn't one who didn't feel a fantastic intuition of their children's genial, informed wisdom. But was a clever picture that her twins made a joint effort or in fact thought up by just one of them? Would the girls both be bright, or both of them average, or then again, one bright and one slow? It was time to start wondering about this. What about in fifteen or twenty years' time—would they be interested in doing the same things in the real world? Would they like the same sort of men? A mystery—all of it a mystery.

.

While a mother's strong impressions are seldom wrong, these still may take years to be verified, emerging out from under the capillary network of evident talents and shortcomings that children, unable to look past the skin-deep, stubbornly defend as their "nature." In this case, nothing significant happened to bear out either Danielle's sensation that her daughters shared a mysterious bond nor that chance and fate were molding her daughters into very different beings until Sophie and Monique started school.

The first surprise the Mortons had when the girls entered first grade two years later was that the elementary school insisted that they be placed in separate classes. John Morton received a little white appointment card, similar to the kind dentists give out, to go to the school in the second half of August. The principal, Mr. Johnson, pointed out the danger, over the coming year, of letting the twins set up their own, closed universe. He cited new studies, which though he presented them dynamically, remained a bit over John Morton's head.

Why should Monique and Sophie be separated at school?, John thought in considerable puzzlement. Why should keeping them in the same class "stunt their growth" (Johnson's words)? John was convinced that growth, change, and a healthy response to external events came naturally to all human beings, even when they were twins. Besides, the girls were speaking in code less and less of late; another year, and they'd probably have it out of their system.

Convinced that he was being persuasive, Johnson was not surprised when at the end John Morton gave him a you-take-care-of-it smile, the sort that his customers used with him when they were ready to sign their new insurance policy. Johnson would never know that John's respect for expertise and "democratic authority" (which dated back to his GI days) suddenly got the better of him and make him yield to the principal. John's unshakable trust made him cheerfully view his own yielding as open-mindedness—a quality that made him happy to get out of bed every morning.

"If you ask me, the people at that school don't think they can tell you two apart," he joked to his twins when he got home. "I mean, I don't see your math teacher, or whoever, using my tickle test." Then suddenly—for surprise, too, was always part of it, he lunged with wild hairy hands and his light baritone laugh for the daughter closest to him, judging from her shrill reactions and more acute cry that she was Monique.

"Daddy, no!"

"Daddy, no!" echoed Sophie, in a fainter version, when in her direction, too, he waved his crabbed fingers.

The game usually continued this way: Daddy would look at his own fingers, feigning horror. What could such splayed savages be trusted to know? "You girls are just teasing old Dad." And he would call Sophie 'Monique' and Monique 'Sophie' and pull them both down with him in a wrestling hold, or a "bear trap", on the living room rug.

Today, however, Monique wouldn't allow it; she crossed arms in a huff and pulled her brows in an intense scowl of furious annoyance, definitely copied from her Gaelic mother. Then she stomped her foot. "NO MORE!"

"All right, girls," said John, with his peacemaker tone of voice that had a warning edge to it. If one could cut the coddling intent from his words like an outer layer of lard, that would be for Sophie, whereas the dark tone of discipline was meant for Monique. Monique seemed to need a bit more rearing in. She had always been slightly bossier, slightly more articulate, and slightly more discriminating than her sister; she was therefore treated by their parents as the slightly elder (even though it wasn't true; for Sophie had emerged first, and the doctors said it was always the older twin to do that). This investiture as symbolic first-born probably explained why, in that final shopping week before school opened, when they made shuttle missions in the car to buy paper, pencils, lunchboxes, clothes and shoes, Danielle glanced in the rearview mirror at Monique and popped the question, in French: *did she realize what it would mean to be separated from her sister at school?*

"Yes."

"*Vraiment?*"

"Yes," Monique repeated in English, that frown of hers making slits of her eyes; it was a solemn frown today, directed both at things out the window and at things in her head. She could maintain a frowned "yes" like that for weeks, or months on end, experiencing it as a tunnel entered into. Monique was like that. Sophie, on the other hand, had never frowned, not even as a baby. Infancy had revealed other differences besides this; what would have Danielle done without them? There was that blue vein on the bridge of Sophie's nose, for instance, or the faint dot of a beauty mark on Monique's right eyelid. Before they could talk or walk these tiny individual imperfections— which make any child unique and a twin all the more so—were what she had relied on. Things changed when they started saying their first words. Danielle didn't have to look for a telltale mark in a moment of doubt because she could now tell them apart from their tone of voice-- firmer Monique's, more monotonous Sophie's--although, strangely enough, this was true only in English; their singsong French was interchangeable. When they spoke French, Danielle tended to keep them straight on the basis of the frown Monique made and because of Sophie's frequently wandering attention.

Sophie never seemed to concentrate hard on things. In the car, Danielle asked Sophie if she realized that first grade started tomorrow.

"*Demain?*" echoed Sophie, consulting with Monique about the meaning of the word.

"You have dinner, go to sleep, wake up and that's tomorrow," elaborated Monique.

"After breakfast," said Sophie.

"After dinner-sleep-and-wake-up, I said. Aren't you listening?" said Monique.

"After breakfast," repeated Sophie.

It was indeed after breakfast that two emblematic events –lasting just a few minutes but of such guiding importance as to function as lines of tension for years to come—took place.

From the elementary school auditorium, with its polished wooden floor and basketball hoops, Monique filed out with the herd of six-year-olds, each with yellow name tag, who now belonged to Mrs. Collins; while Sophie was caught up in a crowd of blue name tags, swarming around Mr. Jeffers. Once in her new first-grade classroom, Sophie noticed, while playing "Name Your Neighbor," that Christine, the blond girl sitting to the right of her, had no eyelashes; she was immediately eager to tell Monique about that. By recess, of course, she'd stored up numerous such discoveries. Mr. Jeffers was fascinating; his suede shoes squeaked and his right arm muscle rippled under his short sleeved shirt as he pulled forward the easel board. Was Monique's teacher, Mrs. Collins, as interesting? Sophie wondered.

When the long bell for recess stopped ringing and viscous streams of children emptied into the hall, Monique found Sophie by the wall outside the bathroom door, doing the impatient knee dips that someone else might have attributed merely to a full bladder but which Monique knew meant happy excitement. Sophie grabbed Monique's arm and they went sailing through the doorway and into the tight tiled corner by the first dwarf sink.

"You like it?"

"You?" asked Monique.

Sophie stared at Monique's mouth, anxious for more words to come from her lips. If sharing was so hard, if Monique had so little to offer, what catastrophe were they bound for? Sophie made bewildered sounds at her sister. "Ssskkeee. GabEEkwahwha, LOOOOOOO?"

"So what now?" Monique said impatiently, refusing to answer in code. She trained her attention on the white ceramic tiles, her eyes traveling with them in their orderly rows, up and down and over and back.

"Let's trade."

"What are you talking about?" Monique repeated, scowling. Sophie had peeled her blue name tag off her dress and stuck on two fingers like a used band-aid. "I'm not going to go swapping places just like that."

"Don't you want to see the other class where I am?" Sophie asked.

"No."

Heat came to Sophie's cheeks. Already, the hurt she felt was depositing itself in the same dark pit as the other sensations of this morning. And it all made her heart beat very fast.

Ten minutes into recess, Monique scraped a knee on the playground and was sent to the school nurse, who sat at this hour at an empty desk behind a glazed door with a red cross on it. Mrs. Young, who was freckled and friendly, because of her Southern accent had a yawning way of talking and a big bite of a smile that reminded Monique of a frilly fan graciously opening and popping shut. She told Monique that every occasion was good for a learning experience. "How would you like to take your own pulse?" she asked. While Mrs. Young swabbed and painted red the cut in her knee, Monique pressed her index and middle fingers on the blood vessels in her wrist, as directed.

"I don't feel anything," she said after a minute.

"You have to apply more pressure. If you were playing the piano, no one would hear your note." Mrs. Young beamed. She molded Monique's fingers into a different position and pushed down on them, and they suddenly captured the faint, quick surge in her flesh. "Oh," said Monique with pleasure, smiling now, too. "Oh dear, I lost it."

And Mrs. Young's freckled hand, with the lady's watch and wedding ring and the clear, respectable polish on her short, tapered nails, made another game-board motion on top of hers—and like magic Monique felt the beating again. She kept her eyes averted into a ceiling corner, the better to train on what was going on inside her.

Mrs. Young wrote down her pulse rate and blood pressure and temperature on a form with Monique's name on it (special numbers, thought Monique, watching), which she pulled from a file cabinet. "I see you're a twin," the nurse said, glancing at where there were typed words at the top.

"Yes," said Monique on a sharp breath, crossing her arms tightly across her chest.

Mrs. Young didn't know why Monique had tensed up, but she assumed that she could guess and be on target, the way adults do with children. "Relax. There's no shot, no needle now. You just go off and play and learn."

Then she closed the file. And Monique's proof (that if her pulse was hers, then her heart was hers, and she herself was hers) became history... a mute cornerstone.

CHAPTER TWO

Oct. 20, 1962

Dear Grandmother Morton,

Thank you for the toy safes you sent to Monique and me for our birthday. We keep them on the dresser in our bedroom. We hope you come to visit us soon.

Love, Sophie

Dear Grandmother Morton,

Thanks for the safe you sent. I keep my allowance in it. My numbers are easy (but secret). Come and see us soon please. How about at Christmas?

Love, Monique

Dear Mother,

You won't believe the scene the other day. Monique had memorized her safe combination and torn up the paper into tiny pieces. Sophie wanted to try opening her sister's safe but Monique wouldn't let her. Sophie started waving the slip of paper with her own combination, offering, "Look, Monique, here's mine, you can have mine." Monique stood up on a chair, covered her ears and shrieked, "Secret! Secret! Secret!" Then Sophie grabbed Monique's safe and threw it two or three times on the floor (till I stopped her), attempting to break it open like an egg. Don't worry, it's still in one piece, though. That's life with kids! Danielle had to take Sophie into the other, empty side of the house and make her lie on the sofa bed (new! - for you when you visit) and sing to her in French for maybe an hour. Monique and I could hear a hysterical sob escape Sophie like a hiccup every so often through the wall. Monique's one tough cookie, though. She's not letting Sophie into her safe and that's final. Nothing beats the high drama of twins, I'll tell you. Thank God we got two in one sitting and are done with having any more. By the way, your psychology books on twins help and don't help at this point—same as Dr. Spock. Anyway, we look forward to seeing you in a couple of months.

All our love, John and the girls

*

At Christmas that year, when the girls were ten, the empty side of their house finally filled with visitors, which was the way John and Danielle Morton had been planning it since buying the duplex. All the relatives that the Mortons kept inviting, and who so seldom came, converged on them at once.

Grandmère Marinette and Oncle Dédé flew into New York from Paris on one of the first commercial airplanes to substitute transatlantic ocean liners, and then came down to Philadelphia on the train. Grandmère Marinette had on a well-fitted tailored suit and pumps with little gold buckles, of the sort the girls had never seen before, as well as the big fat amber-beaded necklace that she was wearing in a photo she'd sent of her and their uncle in their café off Boulevard Saint-Michel. As for Uncle Dédé, he was as tall and gaunt in person as he appeared in the picture with that crate of bottles by his feet.

Danielle had hoped that her work as interpreter wouldn't be too wearing, but this was not to be. By New Year's Eve, she was so frazzled that she made disconnected jokes in the wrong language for the people listening to her, and drank champagne with a desperate thirst, and, sitting on the rug, watched *Singing in the Rain* on television with tears in her eyes, mouthing the words, drawing up her knees, and tuning out all the company around her. Who could blame her? She had nine extra people to be hospitable to, four of whom were children under twelve, seeing that Grandmother Morton had driven over from Gettysburg with Uncle Robert, Aunt Cindy, Brian, Pam, Marie, and Scotty.

John Morton's brother Robert was an insurance broker like him, and for reasons which neither he nor his brother explained but left buried in their past, Robert was considered by the Morton clan to be not as successful as John. He, too, had fought in Europe, but then had come home to marry only a girl from America, who'd spent the war years reading the papers to keep track of his division and studying stenography. The fact of his having put up a bit of money, almost all of which was now paid back, towards the purchase of this duplex was evidently important to him, and tied up with his sense of achievement, if his daughter Pam was to be believed. ("My dad helped buy this place," Pam sniffed at Monique as she toured the two sides of the house. "You wouldn't have it if it weren't for him.")

Monique and Sophie could have helped their mother some with translating during Christmas, but they didn't. They ran off to play with Pam and Marie on their unmade beds. Every so often their father stuck his head in the doorway to say, "Girls, go help your mother." "Do what?" they asked with invented innocence, and John Morton exasperatedly said, "Do whatever, young ladies!", and up they would stand from a ruffled pillow, or from their Indian crouch by their dollhouse, and obediently go and ask their mother what they should do. And then, hearing that all they had to be was good, they ducked around an Aunt Cindy struggling to describe her house to Grandmère Marinette, and got back to the other two girls in a jiffy.

At night, the four girls crowded onto the same quilt and lay with their feet where their heads should be, their toes sticky against the headboard, pretending to be lady teachers pacing the classroom floor in high heels. Pam, who was two years older and always breaking new ground for her cousins, described, in a raspy whisper, dreams which she'd heard from thirteen- and fourteen-year-olds. "And you know what happens then?" she croaked proudly. "Men and women throw themselves on top of her"; or, "someone wants to cut off her breasts with a big, guillotine blade." "But why would they want to do that!" Sophie exclaimed, clutching small Marie's hand. Shh! Shh!, Pam scolded.

And then there were the special outings: going to Woolworth's, each of the four girls with a Christmas dollar from Grandmother Morton and the right to choose whatever toy or paint set it would buy; or driving to Woodbury to have lunch in a diner along the brick main street, where Grandmère Marinette and Uncle Dédé were supposed to try American specialties-- baked beans, corned beef or bacon-lettuce-and-tomato sandwiches, pecan pie and the like--and where Uncle Dédé cheerfully disassembled his sandwich into its original parts on his plate and ate them with a knife and fork, in the same order as one would in France; or attending a matinée of the new Disney film, *Pinocchio*, at which Grandmère Marinette laughed with an excited, girlish titter that didn't seem to belong to her any more than she did to America. But the absolute best part of their stay was when they all attended the church nativity play that the twins performed in.

Monique was the star; she was Mary in the scenes where Mary talked. Sophie, on the other hand, was the silent Mary in the final scene where the Three Wise Men came to the manger.

Monique loved her ride on the wooden rocking horse, fixed on wheels and pulled by a Joseph genuinely named Joseph, who as boys went was kind of cute, especially when he told her so seriously that it was their duty to go to Bethlehem to pay their taxes. Her truly favorite moment, however, was when she got to hold her belly (under the cushion tied round her waist, hidden by the choir robe) and moan, "Oh, oh", to suggest birth-pains. Joseph took her hand then. She could smell the straw and the animal smells of the strange night as she pulled out from under a blanket her baby doll Jesus.

"There, there," she fussed, kissing and quieting him the way she'd seen a mother do with a baby in a store the other day, then laying him in the manger.

She liked the audience looking at her and clapping for her both as the Virgin Mary and as Monique Morton. It was a fine feeling!

Too bad that this pleasure was spoiled for five minutes at the end when she was forced to acknowledge that the audience took Sophie in the final silent scene to be *her* Mary. That's what Sister Donna wanted. There was nothing she, Monique, could do about it.

Still, it was so unfair that she wanted to cry. Instead, tucking one hand into the other's hanging sleeve, she felt her own pulse and was comforted.

Onstage, Sophie was not only cradling the bald baby doll Jesus but also sending magic thoughts out to her family in the audience. Maybe they would magically hear the "I love you" she was transmitting their way; or maybe they'd just watch her really hard and magically feel the tingle of the Holy Spirit that Sister Donna, the play director, had described. She was positive *something* would happen anyway. Magic was everywhere in her life at present. At school, she predicted an instant before Mrs. Williams called on a pupil what name she would say, and almost always she was right (Magic! Magic!). At the dinner table, if she just counted in her head to five-- to five and no other number-- she could always get her glass of milk finished. And then there was that boring Sunday afternoon this fall, when she'd had nothing to do till dinner but to sit through "The Amateur Hour" on TV, until she hit of the idea of sending magic thoughts to her friends and relatives. Hadn't Uncle Robert actually phoned a few minutes later and put Pam on to say hello?

She had no lines to say. She was Mother Mary, who could not die but who rose directly into Heaven. Magic. And double magic for this being wiped out like a soap bubble, immediately, thoroughly, at the sound of applause.

"Come on, I want to try it," said Monique. It was a few weeks after the Christmas play; it was the day Grandmère Marinette and Uncle Dédé were leaving to go back to France. Monique waved two floppy hairbows, one pink and one yellow, at her sister. Sophie was dumbfounded. Trade places? Now? But on the first day of first grade, Monique had said no to her, a refusal set in stone!

"All we have to do is, you know, plan it," said Monique. "Let's find our white sneakers."

It seemed to be just a lark to Monique, or a dare—though at the same time she was trying to pass it off as a joke, saying, "Gee, won't it be super if we can fool them."

"How are you going to be me?" Sophie asked then. "Let me see."

"Go look at yourself in the mirror. Now pretend you're sitting in the car. Close your eyes. Imagine Dad and Maman are driving us to the Dairy Queen. Open your eyes. Look out the car window and watch the Vassalli farm go by."

Sophie blinked; and blinked. So Monique started blinking, too, to show how well she could bring off her imitation.

"Good, eh?"

Sophie nodded.

"So which will it be -- yellow or pink?" asked Monique.

But they were interrupted by Maman's impatient call from the bottom of the stairs: *"Monique! Sophie! Alors? C'est l'heure!"* Danielle Morton wore her red coat and mink hat. Not hearing their voices or moving feet, she clapped her hands hard, exclaiming again, this time in despair, showing the strain she felt under the burden of seeing her mother and brother off at the Philly train station.

"Yellow," whispered Sophie.

As they ran downstairs they clipped their bows on.

"Remember," grunted an excited Monique through her teeth, "we say we have to go to the bathroom. Right before Dad gets to the gas station by the toll bridge."

Sandwiched in between Grandmère Marinette and Uncle Dédé, the two girls knew that they were supposed to keep out of the way;

the grown-ups wanted to chat or fall silent as they pleased. Of course they always wanted to do that but, as Dad explained last night, when adults are gearing up for a big goodbye, they tend to insist on it. This was unfortunately at loggerheads with Monique's plans. She didn't want to keep quiet, she wanted to act up. She wanted to whine—and get Sophie to whine—as if they were five years old again, and get their parents so fed up, at the same time that they were involved in their goodbyes, that they wouldn't see Sophie and her switch bows and names.

She repeatedly complained that she was thirsty until her father snapped at her mother 'to give that kid a drink!' and her mother, not having anything else to offer her, dug a breath mint out of her purse and told her to 'make do with that.' She waited a bit before attempting her second stint, because it was a far worse thing to do: she began to mimic her grandmother. Grandmère Marinette was marveling in French at everything she'd seen on her visit -- with the unconvincingly happy voice of those bracing themselves for the violent collapse into a lesser world, which was a "goodbye". And as the poor woman listed all those things that it was-- *vraiment!-- hard to believe,* Monique irreverently mouthed in unison with her every *vraiment!— hard to believe,* concluding on a snorted giggle that made Maman turn round and glare with suffering eyes.

John Morton was oblivious to this. "We can't say that a lot of good things haven't happened since 1944, can we, Marinette?" he called over his shoulder boyishly.

"*Comment?*" Grandmère smiled uncertainly and turned rouged jowls towards her daughter, who translated in a volleyed mumble, happy that in an hour she wouldn't have to do *that* again for a good long time.

Directly behind in the back seat, Sophie heard Maman add a sigh at the end. Sighs made Sophie want to see people in happier circumstances. So she conjured an image of Maman with a splendid carefree grin—a very unsettling sight, not very Maman-ish at all, but probably it was because this Maman lived in Paris, and not in New Jersey: she had never set foot in New Jersey, and Monique and Sophie had never been born. Sophie could see her very clearly coming and going down the boulevard by Marinette's café.

Something really important wasn't clear, however: who did she love? Could anyone know this? A moment of doubt—Sophie's imagination came to a temporary halt while she considered this. No, no one could. She could conclude that this Maman-who-lived-in-Paris was very much like one of her fancy dolls, for dolls could change countries and wear different dresses and not worry about where the money came from for them, and could not love—though you might suspect they do when you're very very young. And Sophie ached, because Grandmère could stick this Maman under her arm and take her back to France on the plane with her, whereas the Maman in the front seat of the car at this minute couldn't do anything about going to France.

Then Monique kicked her.

"DadDY! I-have-to-go-to-the bathROOM!" Monique sang out, purposely like a little kid.

"DadDY, I-have-to-go-to the bathROOM," echoed Sophie, in the aftershock of a daydream cut short, while rubbing her shin.

This request brought on new sighs from their mother, deep horse-like expellations at the anxious thought of a delay. But since she didn't out-and-out forbid him from doing so, John Morton stopped at the next gas station. "If you're not quick, I'll have your butts!" he roared at his twins.

The windowless ladies' room went brilliant. At the same flick of a switch, a fanned-in whiff of chemical pine covered the urine smell. Sophie lifted her coat, pulled down her pedal-pushers, and plopped on the toilet seat. "Do you really have to have a pee?" asked Monique, "or is it just because we said so?"

"I dunno."

"Don't tell me you're chickening out."

"Well, I don't feel right," Sophie admitted.

"It's a game, silly! We're pretending like in the Christmas play." Monique put her hands on her hips and added bossily, "Remember to speak French. Maman once told a lady she can't tell us apart when we speak French. Now open the door. You go first."

Sophie-as-Monique heaved open the heavy white steel door. An instant puff of January wind rose, and her hair lifted from her ears. Thank goodness that inside the car it was toasty. The thick padded coat arms of her grandmother and sister buttressed against her own made all her goosebumps go away. And yet her skin continued to tingle—why? Also, for some reason she felt fidgety. All this because she was Monique now?

Maman felt a dull whack of a foot against the back of her seat and complained, "Monique!" A surly, ironic "pardon!" came from Sophie-as-Monique's mouth. She found that she wanted her words to cut through the air as sharply—as swiftly--as swiftly-- as her foot.

"You say that nicely to your mother, go on," commanded Dad.

As she repeated a whispered sorry, and felt stoically innocent for having only done what she couldn't help doing, Uncle Dédé squeezed her sister, saying that she was a good girl, sitting there quietly and looking very pretty. *Très, très jolie*. After a moment, he withdrew his arm and let his smile, which exposed half-rotten teeth, dissolve into the close-lipped expression he had chosen to be known by. When Uncle Dédé released her, Monique-as-Sophie slumped. Involuntarily, she felt floppy all over. Being Sophie seemed to slow her thinking: she found she had to put her own thoughts on hold while she listened carefully, and then in silent replay, to what Uncle Dédé, Dad, and Maman said. Only after hearing these words twice and even three times did her own reaction swell up. It was a tolerable state of affairs as long as too many things weren't said, for then her head filled with a cacophonic chorus, and to be invaded this way really disturbed her. In front of the train station, with everyone getting out so Dad could go park the car, and Maman and Grandmère arguing, Maman refusing her mother's folded wad of dollars and francs, and two taxis setting down other people, and Uncle Dédé heaving suitcases and teasing her sister, who was setting the smallest hand luggage on the curbside, while Dad kept up his warm baritone protests: "Really, Dédé, wait for me, you don't have to do that", she was tempted to return to being Monique and talk loudly over this great din. She strained to remain Sophie.

And no one knew that she was doing this. No one had a clue. Wordlessly, in a strange way exhausted, she hung onto her mother's arm-- Maman, who was sobbing openly now, waving in her fist Grandmère's wad of bills, as the train started to move.

On the ride home, the sleepy twins lay head to head in the now spacious back seat, cheeks flattened against the blue car vinyl, a messy mass of long hair cascading over part of each other's face.

"Your bow's bothering me," said Sophie-as-Monique. She plucked out her own and her sister's, and threw them in a jumble on the carpeted floor hump. In that moment the air stopped tingling. Her arm against her forehead gained back a bit of heat. She languidly rotated it.

At last, the girls slept.

John and Danielle Morton talked for the rest of the ride home about her old companions in the French Underground. Bearing in mind that her mother and brother had just left and she could be wondering when she would see them again, John thought this talk might not only distract her but bring her comfort. When a person imagined his lost friends and acquaintances out somewhere in the world leading productive lives, he was bound to be consoled, John thought.

"Any idea where they are now?" he asked.

She knew that her friend Martine worked at an office job and had a few children. She'd heard that Serge and Françoise were still in Paris, Pierre in Limoges, Nicole somewhere in Switzerland. She said all of this haltingly. John's assessment of his wife's mood was off and by the end Danielle was just barely answering, "I don't know" or "Who can say?"

There was silence.

"What's the back seat doing?" John asked brightly.

"Still sleeping." Danielle's two words, insignificant in themselves, provoked in her a sustained sighing fit. She sighed to keep herself from thinking. Inside her there was a door to a cavity of pain and nostalgia that would remain closed if on the heave of each sigh she turned the key in its lock.

Behind them, the girls made a hairy monster, with a double, open fish mouth, four arms, and two sets of sneakers.

When they reached home, Danielle got out and walked to the front door without glancing back.

"Monique!" John Morton bent down to do the job left to him, shaking Sophie. "Sophie!" he called to Monique.

"I'm not Monique," mumbled the real Sophie, forgetting.

"I don't care who you are," said their father, prepared since their birth to be wrong. "Just wake your sister and get inside."

Their parents' bedroom door was shut. The twins heard low urgent voices, then silence. A bit of whispering. Silence again. They went to their own bedroom and prudently closed their own door.

"They didn't care. They didn't even notice," said Sophie, piqued.

"Big deal." Monique couldn't help feeling satisfied. It was weird to pass for Sophie, a completely different thing from being the Virgin Mary.

"Now I can't sleep. I can't read or play either. I can't concentrate," said Sophie.

"Big deal, Sophie. Come on, stop complaining." She, Monique, had just to be patient and sit on her bed till her feeling right in her own skin came back.

"I hate you," said Sophie.

"Will you be quiet?!"

"What are you doing?" Sophie wondered why Monique was pressing two fingertips against the inside of her wrist.

"I'm remembering my safe combination," she bristled.

"Your safe combination?"

"What's it to you?"

CHAPTER THREE

Dear Monique, I just wanted you to know that I think you are different from other girls. You are special, Monique. Will you go steady with me? -- Jim.

One November morning in 1966, when she was in eighth grade, Monique went to her hall locker in the three minutes between English and World History, and found a folded yellow note sticking out from the slats of the air vent. At the sight of her own name printed on the outside in pencil, her heart made a jump-start; this caused hot flashes of readiness to run down her arms and legs. After which, she was left marveling. Marveling at the strange intimacy that the boy (for he printed like a boy) had assumed in deciding to write to her. The humble vulnerability of that small, lightly penciled Jim offset her dismay that the note was "only" from Jim Toth.

Yet she had felt a tug of interest in him at times. She liked his questions in class, and even his small, weak eyes when they debated something; but his face had a white pallor to it that no other boy's had, and the fact that in mixed gym class his chest seemed to jiggle with flabby breasts, like a girl's, and also the fact that his last name (she had already tried writing Jim Toth, Monique Toth, Mrs. James Toth) sounded like a cross-blend of moth, wooly monster, toffee and loathe-- all of these, and especially the pallor, made her shudder (the very idea of kissing him) when she'd read the note and had to think what to do about it.

Taking out the note again before lunch and giving it her serious frown of full attention put her back under the magnetic pull of his sensitive and sincere compliment-- her being different from other girls. How could she be rude or abrupt when he thought that? And so when the last bell rang for the day, she flitted quickly down the hall and out, making her way home with the half-panicky, half-euphoric determination of a teenager with a lot more thinking to do. She confided in no one. By evening she was well within one of what her mother called her "tunnels", a reassuring one of murky indecision; if she didn't reject Jim she didn't simply pair off with him either. She answered him in pen, saying that she was really surprised by his note, though in a nice way. He replied in pencil: she didn't have to say 'yes' right away. He really admired her and was prepared to wait.

How happy that made her! She even, in truth, had the impression of having triumphed—though she didn't understand how exactly she'd managed to pull off this ideal arrangement, whereby she could maintain Jim's interest without committing herself to anything in particular. Still, here she was, enjoying a warm bowl of so-so soup, this intimacy at an arm's length.

This went on for a week, maybe two. Jim Toth was patient, but there was a limit. If days passed without his being able to stand by her at her locker or sit close to her in the lunchroom, or if they happened to spar amicably under their teacher's eyes in class, he would write her another yellow note. And she would read it as willingly, and in the same blind rush as she had his first one, basking in his voice but waiting for that wave of disgust.

Then just before Christmas vacation, when all five eighth-grade teachers were at home in bed with flu and their five homerooms were combined in the auditorium under the guide of one substitute, Jim Toth discovered the existence of Sophie Morton. He thought he was following Monique through the door and, quickening his step, was able to lean over her shoulder a moment and smell the pretty smell of her hair. Sensing heat (his breath, his body, his psychic effort), Sophie turned. Because he looked so nice—nice and expectant as a boy sheepishly smelling flowers—she smiled.

"You aren't Monique Morton, though, are you?" intelligent Jim asked.

"I'm her twin sister Sophie."

"Twins. Wow." He beamed.

Jim Toth's best friends, Bill and Chuck—with whom he formed a confraternity known as "the smart farm boys," couldn't understand his fascination with the Morton twins. It was getting to be a real bore hanging out with him during school hours. They couldn't believe how he went out of his way to catch a glimpse first of Monique and then of Sophie (or vice verse), the important thing being that he make both these glimpses in the space of the few minutes between classes. He claimed it was really neat to see one twin gesticulating and laughing while simultaneously a few yards away the other twin—the same face—was, for instance, downcast and serious.

"I bet you're hitting the books on this," moaned Chuck. "Twins. Let's see, I bet it's genetics first."

Jim did look at some science books, but the history books were what got his imagination going. The Dogons in Sudan considered twins the embodiment of human perfection. Certain Indian tribes in North America used to believe that their being born violated natural law and one had to be killed off. He was astonished to read, moreover, that in yet other cultures it was the parents, not the twins, who were punished: they had to isolate themselves and undergo purification rituals. Jim Toth couldn't lay eyes on either Monique or Sophie without thinking of these ancient ways of perceiving twins, the way adults who love art can't look at certain faces in Italy or France without recalling scenes in old paintings.

When he tried out this new knowledge on Monique, she slammed her books down at his feet, which astonished him. She fumed that he was a know-it-all. She was "perfectly aware of all this, thank you!" Oblivious to the other students jostling by them in the hall, he responded to her displeasure by switching smoothly from history to egg fertilization, though it interested him less. Did she know that the longer the fertilized egg takes to divide, the more likely identical twins were to have complementing characters? He didn't mean to badger but, really, she ought to see the fascination (well, he actually meant the beauty) in that!

"Congratulations. Go steady with her." Monique thought, *I was stupid even to look twice at him.*

Though that smile on Jim's face neither twisted nor dropped, he wondered why she was seething. Had he really hurt her feelings by talking about her sister? Could she be so jealous? An intelligent girl like her should be able to see that in fact that the existence of a twin enhanced her, made her infinitely more fascinating than other girls. "Hey," he reproached affectionately. "Hey, Monique Morton, don't give me that."

At dinner that night Monique made her sister pass her the salt and green beans on the sheer weight of her threatening glance. "What's going on?" Dad asked, noticing.

"She thinks I'm stealing her boyfriend," replied Sophie, in reference to an angry conversation that she and Monique had had in their bedroom an hour before.

"That is not what I think," corrected Monique. Jim Toth was *not* her boyfriend. "There's this guy in my class named Jim Toth. His parents own a sod farm. He likes me but I don't like him," she explained to her father.

"But I can say hello to him, can't I? Why can't I talk to him?" sputtered Sophie.

"Did I say you couldn't talk to him?!" replied Monique, exercised. "I just said—and how many times do I have to tell you— that if he thinks he can tell me what I am thinking and feeling, it's your fault. I don't know what you do or say to him. All I know is that before Jim Toth people left us alone. Sure they noticed, and maybe said something, but we weren't this big deal—we weren't this incredible scientific category called Twins. Jim Toth's different," Monique concluded curtly. "I *don't* like being read like a book or dissected like a frog. Jeez, it gives me the creeps!" She glared round the table.

"Why don't you just talk back to Jim Toth in French? That'll show him," suggested Dad good-naturedly.

Monique rolled her eyes.

"The other kids would think she's showing off, Dad," explained Sophie. "She can talk and act French in the school play, though. That's OK."

Monique had become quite the actress. She had a part in every junior high school play, the one in the fall and the one in the spring. Very often she was the mother of some other character because, as Mrs. Yeats the English teacher and director explained to her once, she was not only a bit tall but had a loud commanding voice. Also, there was the fact that she could do accents—not just French but also English and German. And she could imitate people's tics as well as what Mrs. Yeats called their master gestures. Learning lines came easy to her. She'd read a page of script a couple of times, then face her dresser mirror and say her part. It rolled off her tongue. Though it was funny—she herself noticed this—that she forgot her lines completely when a play was over and done with. At the end-of-the-year school fair last year, Mrs. Yeats asked her to deliver her best Mrs. Malaprop monologue, but Monique couldn't come up with it. The words were gone. She got red and flustered, said something about not feeling well. It was an exceptionally hot day in June, and she was already uncomfortably sweaty and thirsty after performing the Guatemala dance she and five other girls in flowered peasant skirts had learned for Social Studies class, so Mrs. Yeats believed her. Monique made sure after that to tell the other kids in the theatre group that she positively loathed doing bits from old plays. "Enough! Give me something new!" she said. She liked herself best when she spoke with this intensity and used hand gestures. She didn't like the mousey, watchful look Sophie gave people. It was as if the two of them were identical lamps, only she was turned on and Sophie switched off. But wasn't that a nice way of putting it! She congratulated herself. Mrs. Yeats was giving her A's on her compositions.

Besides Ursula Muller, whose family was from Austria and whose father was building a top floor to their house with his own two hands, Monique was the only one in class who liked writing those compositions. Ursula got A's too. Sometimes Monique thought that their English teacher expected more—even too much—from them for being Austrian and half-French, in a way that she didn't with the other kids who were completely American and in any case third or fourth generation Italians or Poles. Still, it seemed a definite advantage to have a grandmother in Paris, about whom she could choose or not choose to talk about.

"My buddy Pete from the Army asked me to go fishing with him on Saturday," John was saying to Danielle as she handed two of the ice cream bowls to Sophie to take to the table and picked up the remaining two. "I'm not much of a fisherman, but I said yes."

Danielle raised her eyebrows at him. "I can't imagine you. Sitting quietly waiting for a fish to bite? Without singing old songs with Pete?"

"We'll do that too," said John sheepishly. "Anyway, I thought I might take the girls along and give you a break. Pete said he was bringing his daughter."

Monique gave a short shriek. "There is *no way*! Fishing's got to be one of the most boring things on earth."

"I'll come, Daddy," said Sophie quickly.

The next Saturday, after spending two hours on a folding camp stool by the edge of the reservoir near Culls Hill, John pulled two small sunfish out of the water. Sophie, on the other hand, pulled out something far more important than a fish from the water. Immobile alongside her father, having insisted she preferred to remain standing, Sophie pretended to watch his fishing line and floater but actually she was eying him. She smelled his nice after-shave and noticed how well he was shaved and how smooth and handsome his chin looked. The red-and-blue striped shirt collar, showing above the neckline of his light jacket, made her think of the similar piece of fabric she had run under the sewing machine that week in home-economics class. The wrinkles on either side of his mouth looked a bit deeper—maybe it was an effect of the daylight. But then again, his eyes also seemed more recessed, more set in their dark bluish shadows. She wasn't sure she liked that. Maybe it was on account of the black baseball cap he was wearing and that visor covering half of his forehead.

All of a sudden he lifted the cap off his head, wiped his sweat with the back of his hand, and passed the cap to her. "Honey, can you put that somewhere for me?" he asked, his eyes on his now bobbing line.

She saw that Pete's daughter Margie, who was her age but whom she barely knew because Margie was part of the 4-H club like most farm kids here, while she was not, had stuffed his cap into their wicker picnic hamper, before wandering off somewhere. She didn't think her father's cap belonged there and after a moment simply stuffed it in her pocket and resumed her position by her father's side.

"Lost it. Damn," John said, pulling his rod to and casting off again

"Not a great morning," grunted Pete.

And then as her father turned his head towards his friend, Sophie saw it. A thin silver line starting at Dad's left temple, surrounded by brown.

"Daddy," she breathed, as if a viper were climbing his leg. "Daddy, you've got gray hair."

"That's the way it goes, I guess, honey. Your dad's getting old."

"No, you're *not*," Sophie said firmly. Her heart accelerated. "Let me get them." Her fingers worked at her father's temple. "There are only two." She plucked and tugged at the two fine white threads till they snapped. She flicked them on the ground. The uneasiness inside her quieted. Her dad looked perfect again.

*

It was a Sunday night and the two sisters lay in silence in their bedroom. Sophie dreaded the stuffy, royal way Sunday evenings dragged on. First the telephone call to Grandmother Morton and once a month also to Grandmère Marinette. Then it was time to get their weekly lunch money and allowances settled. A light supper, then off for a bath, followed by the Mutual of Omaha documentary on television. Above all, Sunday meant going to bed early, too early, and always with a library book, because it was their official reading time as established by Maman and Dad. Monique was happy to read in bed, but Sophie didn't like it at all. She buried her head under her pillow. Eventually, sleepiness began to fan over her. But it wasn't a very pleasant sensation. It was as if someone in jest were covering and uncovering her with the heavy velvet robes that this day was made of.

Then she remembered the matter she wanted cleared up before school tomorrow.

"Jim Toth doesn't write me notes—even though *I* think he's nice."

"He will if I tell him to." Monique spat a little laugh. "He writes me stupid ones at least twice a week." In truth, the notes were far from funny. Last time he wrote, '*Even if you go by me pretending to be Sophie, I know it's you, Monique.*' She'd stared at those words of his. Friday at lunchtime it had been; her stomach had begun to hurt. He now used red ink. Why did he keep at it? It made her seethe. The page in her diary for this Sunday contained JIM TOTH in giant letters, underlined six times to express her maximum dislike and encourage her to come up with a coping strategy.

Monday during her lunch hour, she purposely stole into the junior high school gym. It was clear from the desolation of the gym that no student was supposed to be there, but she didn't let that bother her; there was something that she just had to check out. She ran fleetingly over the echoing floor, keeping close to the wall, and slipped into the girls' locker room, still fluorescent and steamy and smelly from the last gym period. She plopped down on the skinny bench closest to the white-tiled showers and the full-length crome-edged mirrors. Her face, as it was reflected back to her, was narrow and pasty, and the beginnings of her thighs under her dress hem were ugly, spreading cylinders of flesh. If she wasn't horrified it was because she'd already received the shock of her P.E. teacher's Polaroid photos of the class in bathing suits. She was here now on account of those pictures. They'd been taken here against the adjacent stretch of wall. After the group shot, they'd posed individually too, front on and then in profile. *To determine our figure weaknesses, girls. And to see how to correct our bearing and posture.* It was the younger, bleached blonde instructor, Miss La Salle, who insisted on remedial calisthenics; who liked doing tummy tucks and leg swings with them, her own copious rear end doing its energetic grinding on the mat in front of them, as she grunted numbers. Miss LaSalle had sorted out all the photos of her classes and written a personalized exercise program on the back of each. "Wait a minute" was her comment as she handed Monique hers. From the batch of a different class she'd pulled that of Sophie. "Look at both your profiles." She left Monique to gaze at them a

moment, then added importantly: "Look at your craning neck."
Miss LaSalle clucked her tongue.

A shoulder butting the mirror now, Monique pulled her head and
her belly forward in the direction of the world. Yes, that's how she
usually stood. The truth, therefore, was that Monique looked
hunched over, whereas Sophie was erect. Monique's dismay was
suddenly laced with satisfaction and relief. *This   is   Jim   Toth's
secret!*, she thought, happily cranking back her shoulders and chin.
He couldn't read into her soul... he'd just looked at her slouch.

*

"Gad, things are quiet around here," said John Morton one
evening a few months later. Danielle was up in their bedroom on
the phone, he gathered, offering the marital advice of the
Continental sort that some woman from the Garden Club wanted.
As John imagined them, the whole lot of the local Garden Club,
which had been founded two years ago by Louise Vassalli, wanted
to see intrigue spring up like an enchanted thicket around their
marriages. "Gad," John said again. His wife had snickered recently
that this coming to her for counseling, because she was European
and more worldly, was the Club's latest fad.

He called upstairs twice, not that she answered-- nor did he
expect her to. It was so French to make fun of something and then
do it in earnest.

"Gad."

So he was left on his own in the living room. His all-time
favorite Beethoven symphony was playing on the hi-fi, and, true, he
had his newspaper and, for afterwards, Bruce Catton's book about
the Battle of Shiloh, but there was no one to read a snatch of this to;
and John Morton liked serving up to his family giblets from history,
because these had nothing to do with the know-it-all-in-the-can
scenarios that he swore by in the insurance business. He knew that
his clients saw these scenarios flash in front of their eyes as he
spoke to them. They were going to die someday, and when they did
their children would need an inheritance. A fire or thieves could

take away everything they owned. History contained fires and family deaths naturally but also a hell of a lot more. He liked the unpredictable stuff and didn't mind the perverted bits any more than he did red pepper on his food. The main thing was to share this tasty stew. So he was left pretty dissatisfied that no one tonight would gather round for any.

His mind started to work. As always, when his family wouldn't come to him, John Morton let his mind run all over them-- seizing and picking, slapping and smoothing with vim and vigor--nothing scientific, none of it a distilling process, just a rough hands-on experience. Tonight he tackled the conglomeration of everything his wife meant to him. There was something he had yet to make sense of. If Danielle was a woman who had emotional reactions to partings, holidays, and commemorative events in general, and if telling her something was Important could usually make her cry, what in hell could explain her reaction to the Memorial Day parade in Gettysburg last week?

It had been a spectacular morning of marching men in old uniforms, from both World Wars and the Spanish-American one, as well as the son of Civil War General Longstreet from the Battle of Gettysburg, who at noon would give a speech in the National Cemetery. John had been moved by the entire parade, which they'd watched from the deep cool veranda of his great-aunt's porch. Of course, there was fake musket fire and lots of children in Union and Confederate caps. Gettysburg was a tourist attraction (and even a tourist trap) after all, and there were a number of commemorative events even now, a year and a half after the Centennial celebration. Maybe there were even too many—he was willing to admit it. But this didn't prepare him for the sight of his wife twitching about the mouth as if there were bitter camphor pellets inside. And then Danielle said that she just couldn't relate to this, that the only war that was real to her was the one she'd lived through it, and that if she were to see a tricolor stream of jets over Paris and a parade of men dressed up as Allies or Nazis, maybe the horror and glory of that, yes, *that* truly earth-shaking and history-making war would come back to her and make her cry but not this three-day battle, bloody though it was, between Americans in a cornfield.

He had never heard her talk this way.

This chance discovery of how she really felt was disconcerting to an extreme. Indeed, since a justifying support beam of any international marriage is that husband and wife can fathom the fundamentals about each other, it was very serious. For the first time in 17 years he had ominously begun to look at her at times and think, "ah, yes, the French." His was a sort of adultery and it frightened him.

The retracting metal bolt in the girls' bedroom door upstairs clicked back and forth loudly, then he heard a bump. When all went still again he went to the bottom of the stairs and hollered, "Sophie! Monique!" Another bump. He knew he'd have to yell out at least one more time to bring one of them to the banister. "Bother with it," he murmured, returning to his Lazi-Boy recliner, which he cocked back just a tad—for the moment that one tipped backwards, one felt like a pilot shooting off on an adventure.

He reassumed his meditation on his wife, concluding that Danielle was caught—unhappily—between who she'd been and who she was now. He wondered if she would get over this soon. He concluded that he himself vacillated—happily—between what he'd been and what he'd never been. This really was something he'd first experienced in his boyhood, wandering the battlefield while he was still living at home in Gettysburg. He'd walked for miles along the crisscrossed wooden fencing on Seminary Ridge, stomped through the Peach Orchard where the Confederates had attempted Pickett's charge, and climbed the boulders and down into the deep crevices of Devil's Den. He'd popped out from these rocks every so often to stand among the visitors listening to a battlefield guide— oftentimes one of his uncles or cousins—who showed them how to survey the landscape and see imaginary armies from this vantage point. And he would see the soldiers and the seminary nurses (one had been his great-great-aunt), but also the spot where he'd lost his favorite baseball, and further on, even his own roof. The shuffling behind the high boulder to his left, say, was being made both by a rebel sharpshooter and by his buddy Willy Weaver gone rock-climbing. You just tuned in on one or the other with your heart and soul. It was wonderful to flip back and forth between the past and the present. Why couldn't Danielle see that and be happy?

He glanced up at the ceiling over his head. "Gad," he breathed. At age 41 it wasn't time yet for him to linger in memories for too long at a stretch. He fumbled for his Bruce Catton book, which had dropped to the floor beside him (an hour, just an hour a day of such reading and he was all right) and dexterously opened to a page.

From her bed Sophie cradled her swollen girth and listened to the sounds of her mother in her own bedroom preparing to go out. Over to the Vassallis again. Maman didn't even call it the Vassallis' place; she just said, *you know where*. Across the room Monique was on her bed reading, the amber lamplight striking her book like magic to Sophie's eyes. She hadn't completely outgrown her love of magic even though she was thirteen and having her first period.

Maman was downstairs in the kitchen now. Sophie could hear up the stairs the jangling of the charm bracelet as her mother took it from the spot by the sink where she liked to leave it, so that she'd see it often and remember to wear it on outings. There was a brisk pulling to-and-fro of the folding closet door in the front hall. Maman replaced the scrapey thin hanger. Her murmurs answered Dad's murmurs. They were all sounds Sophie was used to, sounds of their mother confidently "closing down shop"—Sophie imagining their house as a factory, where Maman made things or directed their making. And now, after she walked out the door, Maman would be fashioning different things with her time, in a not completely knowable fashion.

The front door closed and Danielle was gone. And when her shoes left the front walk and she was treading on grass, silent as well as invisible, Sophie lay suddenly back on her bed.

"I just felt a big spurt."

"Don't be gross, Sophie."

"I'm telling you how it is, that's all." In their parents' bedroom, the phone rang. Dad must be saying Maman wasn't there and to try the Vassallis. "Who knows when yours will start."

"Maybe I'll be barren and have a nice flat tummy all my life."

"You're the same as me," said Sophie stubbornly.

"Cut it out. All women menstruate."

Sophie made a groan of discomfort and thrashed her legs on her bed. Aware of how her sister's sympathies worked, and that Monique would respond best to a question asked matter-of-factly, she waited until her cramp had passed, then said, "Monique. There's the seventh-and-eighth-grade dance... You know?"

"So?"

"Are you going?"

"I doubt it."

"Can't we go?"

"You go."

"No, I mean... why can't we both go... with Jim."

"Give me a break."

Sophie extended an arm across to Monique's bed and took light hold of her elbow. "Then with who?" Sophie's thumb rubbed the flesh on her sister's pointy tip of bone. Monique was instantly aware that with Sophie touching her like that, their two bodies made a unified flesh machine. Siamese twins. She shrank into her own skeleton by closing her eyes. Then she pushed her sister's arm off.

"Don't be dumb," said Monique. "Please." She got up to flick off the light on the stand dividing their beds. Sophie made her sounds of contentment, clearing her throat and sucking up a small stray sigh. The question still stood: *If not with Jim, then with who?* After a few minutes of waiting for Monique's answer, Sophie began to doze.

It was another Sunday when the front door heaved and the strip of bells that Danielle had hung there so as to hear when her girls were leaving or entering the house, let out a jangle. "Maman?" called Sophie, not taking her eyes off the Mutual of Omaha documentary. Monique heard the high heels in the front hall coming closer and turned. The televised gazelles, showing the same graceful sway and serenity that their mother had left them with, made the sight of Maman now all the more shocking. Her face was wet, her scarf knot pulled out, and bunches of her teased hairdo had been twisted into arrows of despair. "Danielle," John Morton murmured, standing up.

Slowly, as if broken or old, Danielle Morton rested her hand on the back of the couch. Monique turned off the television, as their mother's mouth convulsed on one side. There were one, two, three, four, five involuntary twitches until Maman said: "I have learned many things tonight." Her hand gripped the back of the couch like a terrace railing. From her jaw line, tears fell with audible softness on the carpet.

"From who? From that Vassalli woman?" Dad said.

"*Voilà.*"

Then Maman went into the kitchen and unleashed her fury against her neighbor and once best friend by banging cupboards and bottles (it sounded like the gin bottle from the buffet and the tonic water from the refrigerator). As she fixed herself something to drink, she muttered about what had happened in French.

"Oh my," sighed John Morton. "Danielle?" When she continued not to come to him, he got up stiffly and went to the kitchen. "Danielle?"

"*Merde,* have a drink!" she said to Dad. Then the girls heard something about a wife working too hard to revive her marriage and in the end enticing not her husband but a girlfriend's husband—and this apparently, said Vassalli and other women, was their mother's fault.

"You take this seriously, Danielle?"

The girls saw their mother stalk into the living room, her face contorted, her eyes bloodshot; a bucketful of water in the immense sob she was gagging on.

"Danielle?"

"Yes, seriously," she answered, her eyebrows and shoulders rising in the apologetic stance of someone breaking down completely. She was gagging, gagging. "They-*they*-said I don't know when to stop. I push. I manipulate. I got them worked up, they said—got them thinking about things that they shouldn't have. If only I hadn't starting being so French. They thought they knew me. They think that maybe I should pray more. Yes! Even that.

They spoke in that nice but nasty American way. With tight mouths. Plaw!" Her own mouth screwed up. "'*Sure you're not interested in Jan's Herb yourself?*'", she mimicked.

John did not ask about Joe.

"They are idiots, *des imbéciles, des bêtes.* I don't know why I am so upset. I ask myself. It's strange. It's so stupid and awful and now it's over. They were my friends. I have no friends."

Sophie picked her lip anxiously, sympathetic to her mother's breath-stopping sense of isolation, whereas Monique was all admiration for her mother's combativeness. The twins had never heard her talk like this. It was a shock. To them, she had always shown a perfect-glove fit to America. She was immune to homesickness. As for John, who had laid stock by her angry words and alienation last Memorial Day—yet who had so far seen nothing come of it, he could only wonder why she had ever cultivated those fat farm women's friendship. Granted, he could see that she'd had little choice as to her company, living where they lived, but what on earth had possessed her to fiddle with these women's sense of the ideal and the romantic? Jeez, you shouldn't do that with anyone.

Abruptly, without a word more, Danielle went to the bathroom with her gin-and-tonic, plonked it down by the sink, threw cold water on her eyes, picked up her drink again, and, sniffling, went upstairs to bed. Because she hadn't said good-night to her family, her bedroom felt strange to her. She propped up the bed pillows as if she were a hotel maid. She sat on the covers without turning them down.

Then she began to talk aloud to herself. Snatches of French and English. "Who am I?... *Je ne me reconnais pas.* What's happening to me?" She felt numb and half outside her body. She saw those faces from an hour ago. Those women believed she was diabolical. They wanted her to believe in a lie. She felt a pain shoot through her numbness. She had adapted too much to them! They did not know who this Danielle—Danièle—was, didn't know the woman living in this house. They saw some other woman; John Morton had some other wife for them. She rocked back and forth with a mighty ache in her chest.

The next thing she thought was that she would never accept being buried anywhere other than in France.

She said this aloud, too. She hissed it. She whispered it.

How many things she'd said in her almost perfect American accent all these years! How many sweet suggestions, snappy commands, droll remarks, dry information, directions to strangers. Only to feel tonight, nice voice or no voice, that she'd never truly belonged.

Now her brain began to tingle with the voices of those women. She re-heard things from the recent past. "Oooh, *that's* nice!" twanged Jan in her Carolina accent, tickled pink that she could play a neat practical joke on her husband, by writing him the anonymous love letter that Danielle had suggested. She, Danielle, had offered a lovely, subtle weapon of re-conquest and the only thing snickering Janet saw was a half-smutty prank.

"I don't want to see you again, Janet," Danielle said through her teeth.

She reached over to the bed stand for a long sip of her gin-and-tonic. A glance at her closet door brought back to her the first of a number of things her mother used to say when she was a child. That old request that she hang up her clothes properly in her side of their armoire. Then the exhortation to come straight home after school. The impatient reminder to go downstairs to buy some bread.

"Yes...," breathed Danielle, finishing off her drink and then lying back and closing her eyes. She could vividly see her mother standing with her in their kitchen in Paris. There was a large sheet to fold between them. She was about twelve—anyway it was before the war. They walked towards each other and touched the sheet ends together, but the match wasn't perfect and her mother said to do it again. Her mother was very exacting. Certain things had to be just so.

I will be more exacting too, she moaned softly.

The next day Danielle didn't get up. She couldn't. By morning there was just too much in her head, reams of old conversations with all sorts of people; literally, it upset her balance and kept her horizontal. By noon, her eyes roaming across the ceiling of her bedroom, she was reliving the first conversation she'd ever had with Pam McKinley, the gaunt wife of the local bank president, who liked to sit with crossed legs and a cigarette in a corner behind the apple strudel at the Thursday morning coffees which Louise Vassalli hosted the year she was elected Vice President of the PTA. Pam cultivated her ironies and her problems. "Aren't we ladies of leisure this morning! Go on, indulge—have another cup of coffee, too." Pam batted her eyes coquettishly. "I'll have you know that *my* coffee keeps me from getting drowsy on my Valium."

Danielle's pillow was getting hot so she turned it to its cool side. She was grateful to think about all these things, even the silly memories like the one of Pam McKinley. She smiled into space. Now she was remembering taking her bike off the train with Dédé behind her, in 1942-- out in the country by the woods where they hunted for mushrooms during those hungriest months of the war. Why did it come back to her now? Perhaps because she was getting hungry for lunch and that had been one of the worst days of hunger that she'd ever lived through?

It was shortly before she joined *le maquis*, the Underground. She was nineteen and Dédé was twenty. It was sunny and the woods were swarming with a crowd of other Parisians just as famished as her brother and her. There were young *zazous* too—and how good it was to see those cheeky boys who kept their hair long to ridicule the closely-cropped Germans. She and Dédé didn't find much food. There wasn't a mushroom left anywhere. They returned to Paris with a couple of dried ears of corn from a field. Maman had had better luck that day. She'd sold one of her stashed bottles of whiskey to a German officer. When they got home they feasted on eggs and coffee with sugar in it.

It was because of an egg that Danielle entered the Underground. Amazing, wasn't it? It was the egg that Maman saved and gave the next day to Madame Dominique, one of their oldest customers, who always traded away her food ration cards for cigarettes and didn't get enough to eat in Maman's opinion. Madame Dominique was there when the German officer returned to confiscate all the rest of Marinette's hidden whiskey and declared her cellar off-limits. Afterwards, lighting another cigarette from the end of the first,

Madame Dominique drew aside Maman for a private talk. That was how it all began. *Sistème D* was what all the *zazous* chanted, "D" for *défiance*. But now, smiled Madame with Maman's approval, it will be a "System D" for Dominique, Danielle, and Dédé.

Danielle recalled the big key ring Madame gave her with keys to cellars in their neighborhood. Dédé wheeled storage crates to them, in which escaped British pilots or French Freedom Fighters were hiding. Maman told people that seeing that the Germans had confiscated the café's cellar, she had to store her empty equipment somewhere, didn't she? Naturally, their family took care not to occupy any cellar for long. Right before curfew, Danielle would go back to these cellars and spring the sweaty, filthy men from their pine chests. She got a match-lit look at them. Their eyes were crazed blue, impassive gray, merry brown, and they all had beards. They towered over her when they stood up. While the French shook her hand, the English didn't touch her. How quiet those men could be. Like tall walking shadows. Disappearing down the street in the change of clothes she'd given them.

Someone knocked on the bedroom door. Someone exercised the right to open it.

"*Oui,*" she said faintly.

"Danielle, you OK?" asked John, sticking his head inside.

"*Oui,*" she repeated, even more weakly.

When the door closed again, she rolled frantically from side to side. She was tempted to believe that the snatches of conversations in her head constituted her life story. Of course they were all jumbled up, but did it matter so much? Couldn't they still show her who she was? She might start trying to pick out the most important words and memories—anyway, the most beautiful and the most painful.

The dark of her brain kept registering voices: *Who does she think she is?!* Jan Pierce's saying this to Louise Vassalli last night and meaning Danielle.

The insult of not being directly asked that question to her face. As if she were invisible to them.

Downstairs, a worried John Morton began to put together a family dinner.

The next day John went to see Louise Vassalli. He decided that he just had to. In the big breezy fruit-stand he found no one but her sales clerk, a young girl with bad teeth, so he crossed the gravel parking lot to the Vassallis' "Ye Olde Christmas Giftshop," a red converted garage to the right of the house. A huge black Great Dane bounded by him, kicking up pebbles like an eager pony. One year during the town's Sidewalk Fair, Sal Vassalli had told him the owning a Great Dane had been, along with having children, on his wife's "must-do-in-life" list. The dog banged the aluminum screen door with his paw and Louise appeared in one of her shapeless dresses, her arms looking heftier than ever.

"Hello, Louise."

"Hi, John."

"Danielle won't get out of bed." He raised his eyebrows admonishingly.

"Why don't you come in, John?"

"I'd like to know what happened. What got said."

"Come in and sit down, John."

Her jaw jutted. When her two boys had been mischievous toddlers, her jaw had frequently slipped out and then back into place; sometimes it ached and ached—so much so that the doctor had to give her a shot by her earlobe—but then she'd stopped gritting her teeth during heavy house-cleaning, and especially stopped washing the floors so often in the house and in "Ye Olde Christmas Giftshop", and her jaw had quit bothering her. Still, that strong jaw line did seem to alert people to her determined nature.

She could have told John Morton that what had happened was between Jan Pierce and Danielle—and before that between Pam McKinley and Danielle, as recounted by Pam at the last coffee, though one never knew with Pam—and in any case it all had nothing to do with her. But she didn't. She was too curious to hear what Danielle had told him and knew that he wasn't going to give her that account if she pleaded ignorance and disinterestedness from the start. She dusted the gold ornaments and old-fashioned stuffed bears and china dolls on the lower shelves and said, "What's funny is that Danielle never used to talk about France and how things are done there. It was like pulling teeth to get her to describe how tall the Eiffel Tower looks. You know that, John."

(As she said the word "describe", it suddenly occurred to Louise how much John knew about her, thanks to the lengthy family history she'd given him during that insurance interview last month.)

She continued: "When Jan said she was going to visit her mother in Delaware and was thinking of sending Herb a postcard or two to surprise him and maybe make him miss her—because things were getting dull between them—Danielle asked why she didn't send him letters instead. Daily letters. Telling him what she did in part and only hinting at other things. Like a famous countess and marquis in France a long time ago. We all got fired up about it. Danielle said that Herb would either write back or come and get Jan at her mother's. He came to get her. She noticed that he asked her a couple of cryptic questions but on the whole he was very sweet and also brought flowers. As soon as the two of them got home, Jan called me and then, of course, we were all on the phone to each other."

John Morton grunted. "Gloating, I bet."

"No. But it's nice getting someone to do or say something, or be a certain way, without his realizing it. Danielle said it wasn't necessarily a man-woman thing. During the war, the Underground got a lot of information out of collaborators with these techniques."

"Manipulation, it's called." He didn't believe Danielle had talked about the Underground in such a way. Louise must have gathered this from some movie.

Louise didn't take offense. She stuck to her explanation as if it were a stallion that had a lot of gallop left in him.

"I don't know why this should all seem news to your ears. Danielle must have told you something, John."

"Let's leave Danielle out of this."

"Leave Danielle out of it?" Louise Vassalli asked, astonished.

"For God's sake, Louise what happened then? Get to the point!" He glared. "Please."

Louise Vassalli took a strategic pause to deliberate on what she would dust next and what she would say. She retrieved the foot stool from its place under the cash register, kicked off her pumps, and climbed with her stocky, nyloned legs up where she would reach the framed Currier and Ives prints and plastic holly garlands. "A little mystification in a marriage goes a long way. Danielle, however, insisted it had to lead somewhere. That's the whole of the problem. Jan continued to want advice and step-by-step instructions and Danielle gave them to her—when, if you ask me, John, she should have had the common sense to refuse. In the end, Herb got so jealous that he exploded. Do you know what an inner explosion does to a person? Try to imagine, it, John. I mean, poor Herb could see how much his friend Bernie was noticing Jan the more he, Herb, told him about her little surprises. He thought she couldn't be scheming to make him love her better-- a person only schemes to hide something. That's what he wrote in his letter."

"Letter?"

"The day he walked out. After poisoning Jan's Great Dane." Louise Vassalli's eyes watered. "Why can't Danielle say she's sorry?"

"Well you know, all she did was give some advice."

Louise remained impassive.

"I say, Louise, this is going too far."

"The least she's got to do is to realize it's her fault."

She did not tease from him any reply. But she did catch something John muttered on his breath. *Damn Vichy barber*, he said. Her finger-pointing reminded him of that deranged collaborator in Paris in 1944, the loony bird who'd cursed Danielle for not walking in another's shoes.

Louise Vassalli puzzled over it for days.

*

"We two can still go to the dance," said Jim Toth, leaning against the wall of the lunchroom on the Friday of the following week.

"It won't be the same," said Sophie.

"That's all right." Jim shrugged.

She couldn't tell anything from looking at him. Nothing of how he felt, or what he'd like her to say.

"You could pretend I was Monique."

"Pretend?" He frowned. "Naw."

"I could pretend-- and you could know it was me."

"Naw," he said, considering it.

*

John Morton shuffled from the telephone in the kitchen to the bottom of the stairs.

"Sophie! Phone!"

Some boy.

After what seemed just a minute of talk on the upstairs hall phone, he heard scuffling and thumping in the girls' room. "Why did you do that?" Sophie wailed, then she went into the bathroom and her sobs were muffled.

Then the telephone rang again. Again, no one else in the family could be bothered to answer it so he had to.

He lumbered to the bottom of the stairs.

"Danielle!" When his shout had settled like dust he tried again. "It's important. IT'S YOUR MOTHER."

He hoped Marinette would work a small miracle. It had been ten days since Danielle had last made supper. Or since he'd been able to count on her speaking to him in English. A few days ago he asked her to go to the supermarket but she said she couldn't. And last night, she came into the kitchen when he and the girls were eating to say that she knew it was a good idea for Monique and Sophie to take piano lessons, as they'd discussed, and that she should call up a teacher, but that she was sorry, she just couldn't. All this was making his work harder. Instead of writing up his insurance claims after dinner, he was doing the dishes and, over his shoulder, coaching the twins on algebra. Well, not tonight. He switched off the light in the empty kitchen and returned to the living room. Monique was there in her pajamas and slippers.

"What's going on?" he asked. "I heard Sophie crying."

"She's crying because I got hopping mad at her for throwing away my violet eye-shadow yesterday because she thought it wasn't 'our color.' I'd spent half my allowance on that eye-shadow at the five-and-dime last week! I gave her a slap. You can punish me if you want but I'm glad I hit her."

"Monique," John said warningly.

"Listen, you don't know half of it, Dad!"

"Half of what?"

"She's always wearing my clothes. She copies most of my homework. And I'll have you know that she made Jim Toth believe at first that the two of us would go to the school dance with him! When I'd said absolutely not, I wasn't going!"

While Monique was complaining indignantly, John was thinking about what Marinette might be saying to Danielle. They'd been on the phone for a while now.

"Dad! You're not listening." With a dramatic shrug of her shoulders, Monique walked off.

"You don't have much reason to belly-ache in my opinion," John called after her.

She didn't stop. She went into the kitchen.

He called to her again. "Your sister loves you. That's a beautiful thing!"

Silence. This addled him. He walked to the kitchen. The refrigerator was open and Monique was pouring herself a glass of grape juice.

"Let me tell you something else, young lady." In his eyes was an intention to inflict punishment. "You don't know how good you have it."

Then Danielle swept into the living room behind him. He turned and saw that the hem of her droopy purple robe was dragging and she was white. Her hands pressed hard against her cheeks. "John!" She stopped, and looking right at him in a fixed glassy way said again, "John!"

"Gad, Danielle, what is it, honey?" With bated breath, he wrapped her in his arms. In his soul he thought someone must have died. Danielle didn't take her hands from her cheeks and so her bent elbows cut into his chest.

Sophie came running down the stairs. "Uncle Dédé's had a motorcycle accident!" She explained about the truck which had sideswiped him while he was returning with café supplies.

John pulled Danielle's arms open so that he could hug her better and felt her against his collarbone. "Where is he?"

"In the hospital in Paris," said Sophie quietly. "In a coma."

"Do they know if he'll come out of it?"

"No!" Danielle raised her head on a sob and her hair tumbled in her face. "I mean they don't know." She gave an enormous snuffle at this uncertainty, this blessing. In the silence all sorts of imaginary happenings were plausible.

Lowering his chin so that it nestled gently in his wife's hair and his breath would go directly and softly into her ear, John Morton asked, "What do you want to do, Danielle?"

She couldn't tell him.

"Grandmère is going to call back later." Sophie's eyes pleaded for forgiveness for breaking the bad news.

"So O.K. All we can do is sit by the phone," Monique said very quietly from the kitchen doorway, coming over to pat her mother's shoulder methodically.

John stroked his wife's back. "Is there anything that you want *me* to do?" he murmured softly.

She couldn't tell him that either. She wished he would figure it out for himself. After all, she was the woman who didn't know herself.

John said that as long as Dédé was in a coma there wasn't anything she could do that would make any difference to him.

Monique said that it would take two days or longer to get to Paris.

John told her to shut up.

Of course, if her brother were conscious, or her mother thought it the best thing to do, she'd be immediately off to Paris. But he wasn't, and she didn't, so Danielle felt the decision to stay put was made for her. She tried not to remember that she'd been elbowed off the local landscape or give into the desperate feeling that she was just biding her time. She waited for her mother's next phone call.

She felt much less useless at night. On a bed that felt like a raft afloat in the dark between the continents of Europe and America, she joined her brother, saw him on his dusty gray motorcycle with a crate of just-bought bottles strapped behind him, saw him ride down Boulevard Saint-German with its big nodding trees, leaning to one side as he turned into the narrow Rue Dauphine, then over Pont- Neuf and the open Seine. And when he was on that motorcycle, she would also see his side-parted bangs, which he pushed out of his eyes constantly, flying up with a jerk and leaving his white forehead bare to its fate of an eggshell on pavement.

Though she continued to stay in bed most of the time (the bedroom by now her sickroom, with John sleeping on the living room couch) Danielle got up at four in the morning all of that week and went down to the kitchen where she sat in her robe in front of a bowl of *café au lait* and waited to see if her mother would phone with news. It was an ideal hour—ten am—in Paris. She imagined her mother going at six in the morning to the hospital, a brand-new one built with American dollars but still with large open wards and screens between the beds, Maman said. She came too early to see the doctors, who weren't making their rounds yet, but she'd become friendly with a nurse from a town near hers in Brittany. This nurse told her to have hope. That the doctors wanted her to have hope. Maman said this the first time she called. Despite this hope, Maman's days were long. By half past seven she had opened the café. She couldn't afford to keep it closed. She had the additional expense right now of paying a boy to do the heavy work that Dédé had taken care of. If Marinette had news for Danielle, she would leave the boy in charge of the café for a few minutes around ten o'clock, when there was the usual lull in business, and climb the stairs to her overhead apartment to phone. Though Danielle didn't expect a call every day, she got up before dawn religiously, feeling that she had to do *something*, make some constant little sacrifice for Dédé.

Round about mid-week, she looked up from the stove and the heating pan of milk to see Sophie shuffle in the room with tussled hair and half-closed eyelids.

"*Maman, ça va?*" Sophie asked in a husky morning voice.

Mixing the milk into the coffee with a spoon, Danielle claimed to be fine.

After rubbing her eyes, Sophie watched her mother raise her bowl to her lips. *Why* was Maman up so early? she wondered. Was it a bad sign, did it mean she was getting worse? Sophie was half convinced there was something physically wrong with her mother which she wasn't being told about. That the terrible thing that had happened to Uncle Dédé might have caused something bad to happen to Maman on the inside, too. Already, before hearing this news, Maman had been weak, too weak to make dinner, because of what her friends had done to her.

Danielle urged her to go back to bed but Sophie insisted on keeping her company. As she was pouring milk over Sophie's cornflakes, the phone on the wall rang.

News at last from Paris. Small signs that made the doctors believe Dédé would recover.

Twelve hours after this conversation, Dédé emerged from his coma. He could see, move his limbs, talk. A miracle. Too bad that he couldn't remember much and only dimly recognized Maman.

Should I come? she asked her mother. *No, don't. There's no need for you*, said Marinette. Danielle heard this as a *we don't need you*, and bobbed on her raft that night in a heavy storm of tears. Still, before dawn she did make her ritual crossing: she reclaimed the Dédé with whom she had biked into the countryside, reclaimed him in the same May landscape of fields and poppies that they'd crossed at the ages of nineteen and twenty, gazed at him not as a brother but as a man—understanding in her bones how for years afterwards he had matured with the seasons and sunshine and rain of France that she'd missed out on.

*

Sophie put sweaty palms to her flushed face and watched over the heads of the parents by the punch bowl as the gymnasium lights dimmed and an adolescent tension smoldered into being. In the scratchy pause which replaced The Beach Boys, Jim Toth took her hand. Around them other couples came together for a slow number. Sophie imitated what she could see Debbie Hemming doing, and cupped Jim's shoulder. As they shuffled in their boxed steps, she stared at his chest and jacket lapels, feeling charmed with her narrow line of vision of him; and how well it went with the music; and she liked it all so much so that she leaned the side of her head on his shoulder, feeling him in turn settle in against her crown. She didn't know what he wanted to convey to her in doing that, but she melted all the more.

"Are you waltzing?" Jim's breath made a spot of her hair hot. They turned a circle.

"No."

"Neither am I. I guess we've invented a new dance."

She raised her head to have a look at the others, but he gently lowered it to his chest again.

Sophie's eyelashes swept open and shut against his shirt.

"Hi!' Debbie Hemmings called, tapping Sophie's elbow, which roused her. "Hi, you two!"

With her hair up, and dressed as she was in these party clothes, she wasn't necessarily Sophie; no one seemed sure enough to address her by name. The lights dipped lower and turned deep blue, and as Simon and Garfunkel sang their love-starved way through the seasons, Jim rubbed Sophie's back the way he saw Robert Borton doing with his date. Sophie's firm downy neck, free of her mane of hair, invited the thought of Monique, the back of whose neck he'd never seen. With little success he continued to fight against seeing Monique as the original and Sophie as the copy. He continued to imagine it was because he'd seen and talked to her first, and noticed how mentally fast she was in class, what an actress she was, what intense glances she gave...all of which appealed so much to him, all of which were lacking in Sophie. Of course there was no harm in Sophie being how she was—if she had no twin, if she didn't share identical looks with Monique, she'd be a perfectly fine girl...maybe he'd even want to go steady with her. For now, it was what he wanted, however. Absurd as it was, he was going to wait till high school and then find a way of talking to Monique in some quiet corner at school. He'd give himself all of ninth grade to try to convince her to like him again. He was obstinate by nature, his mother said, in the way of one of his great grandfathers on her side. There was a family story about how this granddad had struggled with a stubborn water stick which—and here was the lesson for him, his mother said—continued to point downwards to the same arid spot of land.

At eleven pm, when he and his father drove Sophie home, Jim walked her to the front door and pressed his mouth respectfully and a mite contritely in the middle of her forehead. Monique was watching from behind a cracked bedroom shade on the second floor. Monique didn't think she was snooping or being deceitful. She just wished she could hear their dialogue better.

Sophie was in fact asking *was there anything Jim wanted her to tell Monique?* In answer, Jim's lips flattened once again against the button-sized spot on her forehead. She closed her eyes, then opened her eyes to his gently murmured 'goodnight.' A few minutes later, hitching up her blue, silky prom dress and leaping up the carpeted stairs, Sophie rushed in on her sister in the bedroom. Sitting Indian-style, Monique was nonchalantly munching a bit of cheese, and there was a wax-papered stack of saltines spilling across her bed blanket. To Sophie, everything in the room under the annoying overhead light had harsh bluish edges.

"So how was it?" As Monique licked the corners of her mouth free of cracker crumbs, Sophie's evening disintegrated into a nebula that no one could call proper memories.

"So?", Monique prompted.

"I-I", Sophie faltered. "It was fine. I'm tired."

She walked to the bathroom and found that the toilet and vanity sink were unfamiliar. She had to learn them again. When she had, they too added to the impression that the only real evening had taken place here at home. She buried her face in her towel, pressing her eyelids and cheeks dry. The instance of dark brought back the prom to her. She pressed the towel on her eyes again and squeezed out another black cloud-puff sense of it. Then it was over; she couldn't bring any more of it to mind. Her back slumped against the cold ceramic tank of the toilet. Now that she was home with

Monique, she couldn't make it linger—though she did know it was hers.

She wiped off the rest of her makeup with cold cream and in the mirror looked haunted. A chance glance revealed the new contents of the trash can. A torn-off bit of plastic wrapping. Monique! It had happened. Tonight while she was gone!

She padded back to their bedroom, where her sister lay with her knees drawn up. She didn't let on that she knew, in order to enjoy the moment of solidarity better.

"Jeez, will you turn off the light? It's always the same thing." Monique used her tone of aggravated hatred.

Sophie flipped the switch. Monique gave an immense impatient sigh, the kind that signals one's outlook to others but does nothing for oneself.

Sophie was swallowed by that sigh.

*

Her mother forewarned Danielle: *He's different. He's a bit stupid now*.

At first she refused to belief it. Dédé had suffered a terrible trauma but he was on the mend. He wasn't paralyzed, he had no organ damage. Already that was saying so much! And he had woken up *from a coma*. Countless others die or stay in their vegetative state forever. What good fortune, what happiness it had gone otherwise. Dédé was saved. This news revitalized her. She wasn't spending the day in bed anymore. She was getting dressed, making meals, running the washing machine, even went for bike rides—along back roads where she wasn't likely to encounter anyone.

You're going to notice he's different, her mother insisted during the ten days the doctors kept her brother in observation at the hospital.

On the morning of the special day when she would get her chance to speak over the phone with him because he was going home, Danielle took a walk through a peach orchard and a few fallow corn fields. She was a mile or so away from any road. There was the buzz of a saw felling a tree. Or of a reaper. The earth stank. The smell was strong, and somehow it pulsed in her ears like barked words as well as in her nose, making her dizzy. Feeling that she'd had enough, she re-crossed the fields to her bike, which she left along the dirt tractor path leading to the road. As she pedaled her way home she sang a song to herself, the one that she and Dédé had learned in school and that she had taught her twins. It brought Dédé to her in sharp focus, clowning as he always had while he sang, imitating a duck or a fat man. It was this Dédé who was going to call her from Paris today, this brightness and luster that she wanted to hear.

And though she knew this couldn't be, she was all the same devastated when over the phone at 3 pm her brother had nothing to say but *"Oui, c'est sur!...c'est sur...c'est sur,"* mechanical exclamations that were as boyish sounding as they were empty.

Her bed was not a raft that night. It was a miracle that she slept at all. She, the woman who didn't know herself, had a brother who would never know himself *again*.

*

John Morton came in from having put the car in the detached garage, and found that not only was dinner arrayed on the table but Danielle was wearing a dress. He hadn't seen her in anything other than nightgowns or slacks and t-shirts for weeks. He thought for a moment about what to say, then made do with an "I'm home."

"Monique says she has a stomach ache." Danielle whisked the butter dish out of the refrigerator, like a woman who'd never done anything but cheerfully bustle through life. "And Sophie, who says she's on a diet, is upstairs sewing a hem for me."

"Just the two of us eating?" He sat down at the table.

"That's right."

John chewed a bit of stewed beef and then Danielle added in that bright way again, "Where are your sheets, John? I've been meaning to ask you. I want to wash them."

"You didn't find them because I'm, uh, not sleeping on the living room couch, Danielle. I'm—you know—over there on the other side."

"John? Since when?" The awful brightness went from her voice to her eyes. The light of new emergency, thought John.

"A couple of weeks, I guess, though maybe it's been longer. I was glad to give you our bedroom, Danielle, but sleeping on the living room couch wasn't working out for me. I needed some peace and order, honey," he added contritely. "Evenings I've got claims to write up."

Silence.

"Maybe I should go back to France, John."

He took this calmly and replied reasonably, "I thought we were past that. Dédé's out of his coma. And the twins have got school."

"I'm not talking about a visit. Or them."

"What *are* we talking about, Danielle?" He kept a handle on himself. She wasn't really going to take such revenge on him for going to sleep in the other part of the duplex, he told himself.

"I don't belong anywhere, John. You see that."

He felt a mix of relief and concern at this wild statement. "If you're talking about Clearsboro," he began kindly, "I think you can come to like it again. Forget the stupid Garden Club."

"You know, John, ten or twelve years ago, when the girls were babies, it was different. I thought I was all right here. I was younger and fresher then. I want to go back to France, but I'm worried. Paris knew the younger me too, not the woman I am now." Her chin began to quiver while she spoke.

"You see? There's no reason for you to go back," he urged gently.

She drew a deep breath and pressed down on the table edge with both open palms. "I...hate this country."

"Well, I can't change it for you, Danielle." He took another bit of meat. *Let her mediate on that*, he thought. Then he added, "But I *can* make you a proposition."

She looked at him, waiting to hear it.

"Would it help you feel better if *you* slept on the other side of the house? Do you want to trade with me?"

"Maybe yes."

"And maybe no?" He envisioned this physical rearrangement of their life. It could be immense, he realized suddenly. Though he himself was just camping out for a while, she was capable of moving into that half of the house for good. It would be used for a purpose that it wasn't supposed to have, a purpose that went through him like a knife. "Tell you what? Let's just sleep on it, honey. It's a pretty silly thing, really."

She arched an unyielding brow. Perhaps they weren't talking about the same thing. "Sleep where?"

*

"Where are the girls?" Danielle rolled her head to the left, but didn't get up from her supine position on the beach blanket—a coarse olive-green one that John had kept from the army. Her heels dug into the soft warm sand and the ocean surf pounded and splattered, gray and white under the sun.

"They're jumping the waves." John righted his billowing newspaper and squinted at the people sitting next to them, reassured by their company. It made the Jersey shore seem the way it was in the proper summertime, still six weeks away. Today was a treat. Things would be put right in this family again. After two nights spent sleeping in the other half of the duplex, Danielle had agreed that they could forgo this odd sleeping arrangement. Thank God, they were back together. Separate beds on a permanent basis were intolerable. They led to Divorce, which John feared and rejected. That was for other people. Two of the men he worked with were divorced. Handsome men with lady friends, men who cared about how aged their whiskey was or how their suit jacket was cut, as well as about getting up to New York to see a show. Men who didn't see, or so it seemed, that the essential business of life was forming a family and handing what you knew and possessed down to your children. "It's a nice day for the beach," he said to his wife.

She didn't answer. Her eyes were closed again.

"Well, isn't it?"

"Oh yes."

Her tone bothered him but he stuck with his optimism. For a while they were quiet. They let the Atlantic talk.

They'd organized this beach day at the breakfast table; it'd been one of John's sudden ideas. There was the usual tension between the two girls ("Will you stop copying me? I know you don't like corn flakes. Choose your own kind of cereal!" Monique huffed at Sophie), and Danielle herself was getting weary and dreary just thinking about the ironing and vacuuming awaiting her this Saturday, when John intuited the general need for a tonic.

"It's only an hour and a half ride to the ocean and we never go," he said. "I don't know what we're waiting for." He smiled broadly.

"We're waiting for a gift horse to look us in the mouth," replied Sophie, smiling back at him and alluding to one of her father's favorite lines.

At a moment like that, Danielle was aware of her husband's decency and its sex appeal. He was a good man and had always been so. From the day he rescued her from the barber's stabs and onwards without exception. She wasn't interested in abandoning John. She got the feeling, however, that he was afraid of this— which was ridiculous because she certainly had no desire to move elsewhere in this country just to stop being Mrs. Morton and become Mrs. Somebody-Else. She'd yielded to him on this question of sleeping arrangements because his efforts to convince her filled her with tenderness and because her malaise was lodged too deep in her soul for this issue to matter. They'd been sharing the same bed for a week now, and, frankly, she liked having John with her on the raft at night. Sometimes, when she held his hand, the raft traveled slowly in time with his breathing rather than her own.

"What time were you thinking we'd have lunch?" he asked suddenly, stuffing his newspaper into a beach bag and yawning.

"I could get out the sandwiches in about a half an hour, is that all right?" Turning on her stomach now, her abdominal muscles tensing, Danielle felt herself the fully attentive sort of mother and wife again.

"Sounds fine to me." He blew her a kiss and stood up to survey the horizon.

He still had a nice trim waist line, she thought. She saw him pushing the mower up and down the part of the front lawn which sloped down to the roadside ditch; he made small regular marching steps and his white undershirt clung to him as he sweated. "Where are the girls?" she asked.

"In the water. They've got the air mattress."

Out in the gray ocean Monique had had enough. She was cold. She was tired of sharing the air mattress or making sure her sister hadn't had it knocked out of her hands. She wanted to be on the beach, wrapping herself in her towel and getting another look at the family to the right, with that boy who looked to be about fourteen or fifteen and was a bit slight in build, with a large head and high forehead—a sign of intelligence, just her type. She was glad she was wearing this particular two-piece swimsuit. She wadded in place, thinking about how she'd better take this air mattress back to shore with her and guarding against swells of waves behind her that might rise too high at any time. Before she could figure out how to ride the new one arising now, it peaked thunderously over her head and knocked her down, the air mattress still in her clutches. "That's it for me! I'm getting out," she yelled to Sophie, who was too far out to hear her. On the next foaming thrust, she paddled furiously, belly side down, slipping once and then again off the air mattress. Without ever ceasing this strenuous effort, she made her way to shore.

Sophie bobbed in place, her eyes on her twin sister trying to reach the beach. Unlike Monique she did not get anxious when the sea was rocky. She always positioned herself out beyond the break-line of most of the monstrous waves, and if she felt a great pull of backwards rushing tide, she simply lowered herself until she was completely underwater, thrusting up again when they'd passed. Up and down she bounced, up and down buoyantly, never touching bottom. Watching her sister gaining the shore on her raft, Sophie performed this effortless act. As she watched Monique, she once again felt "it"—the sensation that first came over her on prom night: real time and place were where *Monique* was. The stronger this sensation became the more she herself felt queer and depleted.

I am doing the watching, she thought confusedly, *and Monique is doing the next bit of living, getting out of the ocean, running to Maman and Dad. Her hair is slicked back and she is rubbing her face in her towel. Her blue eyes are red from the salt water, the way mine are. If it weren't for the two-piece swim suit, it could be me standing between Maman and Dad and eying the sandwiches that Maman is unwrapping.*

After a while this inward narration stopped. The vastness and the silence of the water enveloped her senses. There was a profound rightness in her being where she was—free-floating, separated from the rest of the family on land, and letting real life happen to Monique. *I don't even have to---,* mouthed Sophie, bobbing in her ocean. *She's so like me that I don't even have to--.* On the word 'to", Sophie rose skyward by several feet. Then her body lowered itself into the wonderful warmth and peace of helplessness. *'To'* launched her again.

On shore Monique stretched the back of her bathing suit down over her butt, and turn briefly to look up the coast towards Atlantic City, shading her eyes. Sophie's gaze never swerved from her sister. *She's so like me, she is me.* The ocean lifted her and set her down euphorically. It had a will. There was no need for her to give the tiny jerk upwards with her hips as she had been doing. She let her body go completely limp, kept only her head righted. The sun was over the mainland and scorched her eyes. The land did not want her to look at it. Her parents on the land didn't, either. The land and her parents wanted her to close her eyes and point her face blindly at the heat, which sank into her like a blessing. In the stronghold of the sea, she began to realize that the effortlessness was no longer a soaring but a sinking; that the will of the water was such that little by little she was being not set down but pulled down. She would, however, continue to bob on its surface as long as it was in some way effortless. Wonderfully wonderfully effortless.

And then the rest of the truth could complete itself: *She's so like me that I don't even have to exist.*

"Where's Sophie?" Danielle asked, sitting up abruptly. "Where is she?"

"I don't know," Monique said. "We were over there before." She pointed at a spot in the water where now there was no one.

The alarmed eyes of all three swept back and forth over the new crests of tide. They couldn't discern a buoyant dot on the horizon anywhere. The ocean was blank and seamless. Then John Morton was on his feet, yelling into the wind, "What the hell?!"

He charged at his gray solid enemy with GI legs. Danielle and Monique heard another "helllllll!" from him, muffled by the wind like a war whoop by a mountain. He dived into a flip of water, tucked under another, arms pulling forwards, torpedoing frantically, launched into battle.

His girl. His war with fate.

CHAPTER FOUR

Sophie blinked herself awake in the hospital. She blinked at the white ceiling, at the brown door, at the two white people with brown hair standing by the bed and the one who was sitting. "Sophie, sweetheart!" John Morton began jubilantly, before Danielle shushed him. Sophie blinked endlessly, wordlessly, and as Monique pressed the call button on the metal bed panel, Danielle tried to rub worldly interest into her daughter's still hand. A plump nurse abruptly came between them and Sophie; the woman touched the girl's forehead, stuck the silver end of a stethoscope on her chest, assessed that gaze which sputtered like a candle and didn't want to stay lit. The blinking went on so long and became so rapid that Sophie seemed on the verge of a seizure. The nurse told the family to leave the room. The three of them saw a doctor arrive, an orderly came along the hall with a new monitoring machine on wheels, and a second nurse carried in a tray of I.V. bottles. They did not hear Sophie's voice.

Out in the hall John talked resolutely about how, now that she was awake—three hours after the accident, the doctors could run their tests, see what happened. He paced in front of Sophie's door with his hands locked behind his back. Since the moment he'd beached his daughter like a thin, slick seal on the sand and sent his air into her lungs, he'd remained fixed on the idea that she'd suffered cramps—that spasms in the gut had made her go under and nearly drown. During the ride in the ambulance, he'd treated with derision the paramedic's comment that she didn't appear to have been bit or stung. Of course not!. Cramps, cramps were the cause. *Overwhelming, weren't they, honey?* he'd say to her. *You had to fight them while treading water so far from shore and you just pooped out, didn't you, baby?*

"Aren't there any chairs?" complained Monique.

John glared at her. "Tough it out."

"Please, John," breathed Danielle. "Stay calm. Sophie's alive. We're sure now."

"Of course she's alive. I got to her in a minute's time. I never had a doubt. Not ONE DOUBT."

"It seemed forever before I saw you emerge from the water with her." Danielle blew her nose. The new tears filling her eyes would spill down her cheeks in a moment and after dabbing them, she'd put the tissue to her nose again, as she had for the last three hours. In her chest there was a burning to match that of her eyes. "I felt I'd lost her. The ocean was her grave, and I was grieving."

John clucked his tongue at that. He didn't mean to, it just happened.

"I'll stand here another two hours if you want, Dad," said Monique with a rising edge to her voice. "I'm glad she's all RIGHT, and I care that she's ALIVE. OK? "

Batting a hand impatiently at both of them, John moved down the hall towards a window.

Danielle cracked open the door to Sophie's room. "They're still huddled round her," she whispered on a sniffle. Monique grunted.

Eventually Sophie stopped blinking. The new intravenous drip she was put on was less responsible for that than the doctors believed. As she herself experienced it, the truth was that Sophie stopped blinking when she decided to accept the new strangeness she perceived about her. She looked at her parents and sister— looked at their bodies, that is, and took pleasure in those dense forms. The world seemed a flat place except for these bodies, which stood out from the background containing everything else the way food on a tablecloth does in a still-life painting.

She didn't let on, however, that she was viewing reality in this diminished way, and the doctors in their tests did not pick up on this. Danielle, who spent the next two nights sitting by her side in a happy and grateful vigil, didn't notice anything either. As for Monique, she didn't take much interest in Sophie's hospital stay once her sister was conscious again; she found most of the doctors' talk incomprehensible or boring. She wondered when they would let Sophie come home. Her sister looked like a slender hurt animal—a battered baby colt perhaps, on account of the long face and big eyes that she and Monique had. Though every time Monique entered the hospital room, the sight of Sophie, weak and pale against her pillows, made her grave and sorry, she was completely over the alarm to the point of terror that she'd felt for those five or ten minutes on the beach, as her father dived into the waves. It was as if suddenly there was a wall of silence cutting off the signal her sister would otherwise be receiving from her. For a long moment Sophie was lost—for a long moment Monique asked herself if she would come back. Then when two heads surfaced on the horizon, she knew suddenly and for sure that Sophie was alive. By contrast, her mother, who was sobbing behind her, receiving comfort from two lady- sunbathers who held her by the elbows, blurted out that she was sure to be dead. But it was Monique who was right. When Dad reached the shore with Sophie, Maman put her head to her chest and heard her heart beating. *Tu as raison, Monique!*

There was not only a wonderful miracle that Sophie hadn't drowned; there was the additional wonder that Monique had known this in a special way—Maman in her joy connected the two things.

Now that the emergency was over, and they had to make this tedious hour-and-a-half drive to the hospital every day waiting for the doctors to sign Sophie's discharge form, Monique mulled over this part about herself. Did she really have a sixth sense about her sister? She didn't want any such spooky power. And she certainly didn't want Sophie having it either. Once, she remembered, Jim Toth had launched into a monologue about telepathy in twins. She recalled interrupting him to scoff that she knew all about it, when in fact it wasn't true. Now she half-wished she'd let him spew on at the mouth.

In the insurance report to his own company that John Morton filed that week on Sophie, he termed her brush with death by drowning "a serious swimming accident." One that warranted not only a hospital stay but also a considerable period of convalescence at home.

"Let me be very clear about what I mean by convalescence," said her neurologist on the morning of her hospital discharge. "First, bed rest. Second, monitoring—she'll have to come back in for check-ups because of the coma. Third, tutoring at home. No school for her till Christmas."

"Even if she's supposed to start high school with her sister in September?" John objected gingerly.

The neurologist, Dr. Craunick, shrugged his shoulders and smiled. He was a balding, black-haired man with thick lips and a very thick gold wedding band. He'd told them he and his wife had six children. "Her sister will go to high school for her. She'll know all about it when she starts attending. Probably in January but we'll see."

To look at her, Sophie was happy to get home. She was happy to walk through the living room, take a look out the kitchen window at the grass of the back yard, climb up to her and Monique's bedroom, open her chest of drawers, and finger her folded clothes inside. She had a smile pasted on her face. Fortunately, at lunchtime when she took her medicine, that fixed smile faded and she looked normal again. Because of that medicine, however, she felt an overwhelming need to take an afternoon nap. This became a regular thing. To tell the truth, this was the one real change that her parents noticed about her. Monique, on the other hand, was assimilating Sophie's new habit of glancing away in the least bit of conversation they exchanged. *Boy, this is news*, Monique thought to herself. And it was. For thirteen years, Sophie had always basked in the light of her sister's attention, and when Monique couldn't be bothered, she had always mooned at her sister. Now, it was as if she mustn't look at Monique too hard. Or rather, it was as if she earnestly wanted to do so, only it gave her a funny feeling and she had to stop.

For her lessons, Danielle and John Morton re-opened a room on the other side of their duplex. There are few arrangements made with more zeal than those drawn up for a convalescing child, and Danielle threw herself into the new routine with enthusiasm and optimism. Starting the following week, in accordance with the neurologist's instructions and even though it was still August, Sophie's tutor, Miss Fletcher, came daily to their house at nine o'clock. She stepped up to the front door with splendid, unhurried composure and her dark hair swept up anew in a French twist as miraculously free-standing as cotton candy. There was an ironed smartness to her clothes to take pleasure in. Surely, Danielle thought, from this self-respect and amour propre flowed some of the magma of wisdom. Sophie would come willingly and quietly out on the porch with her mother, who unlocked the door of the other side of the duplex and held it open till Miss Fletcher caught it. "Everything fine today?" she'd ask, nudging Sophie up the stairs ahead of her. And Sophie's head would nod immediately and she would take the steps two at a time and seeing these things Danielle felt reassured and went back to her side of the house.

Things went this way for a week. Sophie seemed a bit perkier. At lunchtime she listed for her mother the subjects she had studied during the morning—true, without doing into detail, but the tone was right. After her nap, she usually struck up a new conversation about her likes and dislikes of the day, as if during her rest she had mulled over the taste of her meals, the light and temperature outside, the colors of the clothes she was wearing, how she liked hearing her father mowing the lawn in the early evening yesterday....all little things. All good signs of recovery, however, to Danielle.

But noontime on Friday Miss Fletcher put an end to this illusion, when she made the offhanded, parting comment that "when Sophie seems confused and forgetful like today, it's hard to get much done."

"In what way is she confused?" asked Danielle with wide-eyed surprise.

Miss Fletcher murmured that she preferred not to go into a lot of detail, for there was time for that on Monday, but she did leave Danielle with a single diplomatically-put certainty which was just enough for her and John Morton to meditate on over the weekend: *teaching Sophie,* she said, *was harder than it should be.*

Danielle spent all that Friday afternoon in an anxious state, fighting the urge to phone the neurologist at the hospital and tell him what the tutor had said, even before she discussed things with John, who was making the rounds of his insurance customers and wouldn't be home till six. There were both painful moments of tenderness, as she thought about how fine and healthy Sophie had been before her accident, and other moments when she felt sorry

for herself. Why were the people she loved—Dédé and Sophie—
being damaged? Why did she have to live a life that held such
grief? A question, this last one, which invited other, even more self-
flagellating thoughts (which had been on hold but which now
gushed forth) about not being happy in America.

"No, I'm not for phoning Craunick," John said slowly—just
home and not particularly happy about finding himself immediately
involved in such an emotional discussion with Danielle. The two of
them rattled plates and silverware in the kitchen on purpose to
cover their low voices and together set the table for dinner. "Not till
we hear what this woman has to say. Better yet, I'm going to call
and ask her to write it up for the doctor."

When Miss Fletcher heard that her report was for Sophie's
neurologist, she took it *even* more seriously, if that were possible.
She zealously suggested meeting John Morton—in the parking lot
by Vassalli's produce stand of all places—a little before the lesson
on Monday morning to give it to him and talk things over. When
John arrived, she was righting a folder of papers on the hood of her
car, looking every bit the scrupulous teacher who does her own
homework. The first thing she asked him was if Sophie's brain
could have been deprived of oxygen under water long enough to
cause damage.

John Morton was bowled over. "So don't you think you can
teach her?"

Miss Fletcher's throat and chest under the necklace she was
fingering marbled up red. "Sophie is learning, Mr. Morton. I'm not
saying that." She read from her notes without lifting her eyes at
him. Except for her pink-spotted throat, she reminded him of a
tough, triumphant police detective.

His heart sank at what she had to say. Sophie was less capable of
abstract reasoning than was the norm; in fact she could only
manage such thinking in spurts. There were Xs in Miss Fletcher's
teacher's book by the few exercises that the girl actually did
unaided. Yesterday, in addition to her usual daily notes, she'd
written, *"Sophie is repulsed by theories. Diverging viewpoints also
tend to 'silence' her."* Miss Fletcher noticed how when she had to
answer complex questions anxiety rolled around inside her eyes.

The girl's only tolerance seemed to be for history facts and math formulas. *"She doesn't like to be asked about things that require inward reflection and the formulation of an individual opinion. It's as if it really bothers her to see or analyze differences between objects or people. She keeps returning to the similarities."* This fueled Miss Fletcher's conviction that she was slightly "disturbed"... or, since the cause was a drowning accident, "injured."

Frankly she would recommend that Sophie see a psychiatrist for testing; she hoped that the doctor would not feel that she was over-stepping the bounds of her expertise by saying that. It was just her heart-felt conviction, based on years of teaching. Her second bit of advice was that Sophie continue home tutoring certainly for the full year and perhaps even for the rest of high school. Naturally, she was willing to continue with their lessons, Miss Fletcher reassured John Morton. She concluded by asking that he and Danielle try observing Sophie in the way she had been doing. This reopened the floodgates of his panic. When he'd made his humble promise on that and was back in his car, he gripped the steering wheel at a different angle from usual and swore softly and tersely. Damn! Was Sophie going to be all right? He squinted oh so very hard at the road in front of him. He had a desperate desire for life to flow untroubled. Was there really something wrong with Sophie that wouldn't heal on its own?

When Sophie had her next check-up, Dr. Craunick changed her medicine. He skimmed through Miss Fletcher's pages without making a comment. But when he smiled and shrugged as he stuffed the report back into its envelope, John's concern got the better of him. "What do you think, Doc?"

The neurologist absent-mindedly turned his big gold wedding ring on his finger as he decided what to say to the anxious Mortons, after he'd sent Sophie out to the waiting room. "Don't you see how your daughter's eyes have brightened up? How she's walking straight and tall? Sophie's making good progress towards a full recovery. I want you to think about that. Nothing else." His warm handshake conveyed conviction.

"So?" Danielle murmured to her husband as they walked with Sophie out to the hospital parking lot. She glanced at her pretty, long-haired daughter out of one eye. She had always had good posture, as far as she could remember.

"I feel better," stated John. "Don't you?"

"Yes," she said in a small, wavering voice.

He took her by one hand and Sophie by the other and gave them both a squeeze. "I thought that was a productive visit," he said. Actually, it was running through his mind how astonishingly quickly doctors and teachers could agitate or calm a parent down. *It's their ball game. We have no control over how they're going to make us feel,* he told himself. "The new medicine is the main thing," he concluded aloud.

The new pills did make a difference. Sophie seemed less tired and stopped taking her daytime naps; also, as Miss Fletcher told Danielle at week's end, she paid closer attention to her school work. Even though she still couldn't summarize what they were covering in what was now being called Social Studies, or put together a proper book report, she was getting much better at memorizing facts. Miss Fletcher said that she was optimistic that she could pass ninth grade.

No schoolmate came to see Sophie except Jim Toth. It was an unlucky coincidence that she'd had her accident during the summer between junior high school and high school, when kids tend to lose track of each other. In place of the compact junior high school in a cornfield just a few miles down the road, in a couple of weeks they would be taking a twenty-minute bus ride to the sprawling high school inside Woodbury city limits, along with over a thousand other kids from all over the county. In that sandy-brick school building, constructed in the popular style of the 1970s like a blond giant spider, with a long corridor and class rooms along each leg, most faces would be new and encounters with old classmates relatively few. Come September, Monique wouldn't recognize anyone in her new homeroom class. She'd run into Debbie Hemmings, however, who'd ask about Sophie, having heard somewhere that she'd broken her leg, or maybe it was her hip, and so couldn't attend school. Monique would let her think that it was a bad facture. (*Metaphorically* it was; her old English teacher would like her saying that, wouldn't she?)

School wasn't in session yet, however, when Jim Toth visited Sophie for the first time. He happened to be in the Clearsboro pharmacy when Danielle was filling Sophie's prescription and heard her ask the pharmacist if it were better for her daughter to take this pill right before or after eating, since all the doctor's note said was "at meals."

"Is Monique sick, Mrs. Morton?" he inquired politely, as she was closing her change purse and leaving the counter.

"Jim? Why hello." Danielle squinted at him, unused to conversing in public with anyone other than a shop-owner, clerk, or fellow bystander; she hadn't made any new friends in the last couple of years. "It's not Monique," she informed him. "It's Sophie who's had an accident, Jim."

"Oh gosh. What happened?"

The boy was as tall as her. The boy who had taken Sophie to the prom. A bit puffy-faced behind the glasses that he had to wear now. He didn't finch when she said "drowned" nor when she said "coma." In fact he continued to meet her gaze even after she'd finished explaining, waiting for more, and giving her the idea of being a judicious boy who could accept a lot of bad among the good things in life.

"Could I stop by to see her?" he asked.

"Of course," she said gratefully.

Several days later he rang the doorbell in the middle of the afternoon, holding a small wrapped cardboard box. Drawing back the beige living-room curtains, Danielle waved to him to go round to the backyard where Sophie was weeding the lettuce-and-tomato patch for her father. Danielle's next look, out the kitchen window over her sink, was at the backs of the two of them, both in white T-shirts and dark shorts, crouching down in the dirt beyond the little white fence John had erected to keep the bunnies out. As the young couple stood up, Sophie had Jim's box in her hands. Launching him a look of admiration and appreciation, she pealed off the flowery wrapping paper and ripped it open. Seeing her blink in perfect puzzlement at its contents, he laughed and gestured to her to sit in the grass with him. When she too was sitting Indian-style with the box in her lap, he reached over and lifted out of the first box a still smaller glass box with gravel and water in it. Danielle at the kitchen window was just realizing that it must be an aquarium when he overturned it on the grass and Sophie clapped in excitement. Jim pointed to a moving something that was the size of a brown wet stone.

He had brought her a water turtle.

She named it Daisy. Jim said it was female and that it might snap at her. But the turtle didn't try to bite Sophie. It just receded its head into its tiny shell and flayed its four legs when she protectively moved it to some smoother bit of lawn or judged it time to get the turtle back to its water again.

"You can't hug it and it doesn't talk," Jim said quietly. "But I like turtles. Knew you would, too."

"Oh, I do!" Sophie replied with delight. She watched Daisy turn her head from side to side just once, then stop immobile in place. She tried to imagine what the turtle saw. Dense forms? Maybe like the ones she saw when she woke up in the hospital room? Her face clouded suddenly. "A turtle can't run away, can it?"

"A turtle *run?* Did you really say that?" Jim chuckled in a way so as not to hurt her feelings, and Sophie smiled.

"You're not going to keep that smelly thing in our bedroom!" was Monique's reaction where she got home from her bike ride shortly before dinner time and saw the glass box on their dresser. "Put it in the living room, or put it on the desk in the other side of the house where you do your lessons. It can watch you," she said to Sophie, adding just as sarcastically, "Poor turtle—you want to kill it? That's not an aquarium. It looks like a finger bowl."

"Daisy doesn't need to stay in the water all the time," Sophie said matter-of-factly, lying on her stomach on her bed. "She doesn't like it."

Monique raised her eyebrows and covered her ears theatrically, then went downstairs to find a parent to complain to. She was not going to have a bedroom with a smelly, free-roaming water turtle in it. As luck had it, she encountered her father, just home from work and still in his tie, standing by the kitchen pantry and snacking ravenously on pre-dinner pretzels. A big chunk made a bulge in his left cheek as he chomped and glared at her as she went through what he termed her bellyaching routine. "You've given me an idea," he said between bites. Then purposely, he popped another pretzel chunk into his mouth and told her about it in an incomprehensible jawing.

John's idea was to get Sophie a bigger aquarium and another turtle. He asked Sophie for permission to take Daisy with him to the pet store so that he could get companion of exactly the same species, only male. Sophie called him Lollipop. Monique rolled her eyes at this infantile choice of names. Sophie spent at least an hour daily observing the pair—she as silent as the turtles were mute—while they scuttled over their rocks and up on their plastic island with palm tree, or glided through their few inches of water. Mid-afternoon, she usually brought the aquarium downstairs, set it on the kitchen table, and munched an apple while Daisy and Lollipop did their miniscule things behind glass. Coming in one day, to get distilled water for her iron from the cabinet under the sink, Danielle asked Sophie why she didn't run a little experiment if she was so interested in turtle behavior. For instance, why not take Daisy out of the aquarium and leave Lollipop by himself, to see if he looked for her?

Sophie's round blue eyes shifted towards her mother. "That—that'd be mean," she replied in a wondering and bewildered way. Then she picked up the aquarium and went into the backyard, where she took both turtles out and let them wander where they pleased under her vigilant eye, while she sat in the shade of the young maple and beech trees at the rear edge of their property—the tangled underbrush of which was trampled by squirrels and full of poison ivy, Dad said. If Daisy or Lollipop headed in that direction, she would diligently pick them up and move them closer towards the house. When she deemed that the turtles were ready to sun themselves on their rocks, she put them back in the aquarium and lay down herself in the grass in the sun. If there were clouds in the sky, she'd open her eyes every so often to see how far they had moved or what they resembled. Once in a while, too, she would raise her head to give a glance at Daisy and Lollipop and feel like the over-sized mother of a tiny, silent family. The way she did when she approached their tank with their food—raw hamburger or minced up fruit—and saw them flapping their flippers excitedly.

One balmy afternoon at the start of September, before Labor Day and the opening of school, she raised her head from the grass and saw Jim Toth coming around the side of the house towards her. She gave him a big smile and waved with both arms.

"Well, well, I see there's a friend for Daisy now," he said, satisfied, hands on his hips.

He didn't think to sit down and she was eye-level with his uncovered knees. She noticed for the first time the mannish thickness of the blondish hair on his legs. He bent over, his bangs sweeping to one side over the tops of his glasses, his small eyes glinting. "How about a bike ride?"

They went for four or five miles along quiet roads through sun-drenched fields and orchards, and along sun-dappled woods, tracing what would have seemed airborne like a huge rectangle. Oftentimes they pedaled at the same speed, their chins and chests pushing forwards at the same time. Jim had told her to put the turtles in their aquarium and to leave it in the grass. "They should get as much natural light as possible," he said practically. He was treating Sophie as he would a favorite girl cousin on the mend after a bout of something awful—there was a case in his recent past to remind him of this. The sight of Monique, or dealings with her—*that* alone could send the old jolt through him; for though Sophie was Monique to a T, Monique had a stirred up character that worked upon him like a storm on an electric field. When he gave the snapping turtle to Sophie, in fact, her joyous face had an intensity which was usually completely lacking in receptive, calm Sophie, and something which made him feel queer for a moment, as his heart leaped back to the intoxicating days before and after his first bold note to Monique. It was a good thing for all three of them, he reckoned, that he hadn't encountered her on either of his two visits to the Mortons' place. He idealized the next time he would see

Monique. It would be in the churning crowd of unknown faces at the new high school. She would let him talk to her. He would have to talk into her ear so as to be heard above the din. His lips and nose would brush her long brown hair. There would be that special pertness about her, her head would retract, and her restless blue eyes, which were always scheming and yet at the same time drinking down what the world had to offer, would fix on his shirt sleeve as she listened to the words, his magnificent words. That was all he could picture. But he had some days of vacation left yet to perfect things.

It was a gusty afternoon of rolling clouds and strong wind, which was their friend when Jim and Sophie cycled eastward and their enemy when they went westward. At six Sophie turned into the pebbled driveway and called goodbye. Flushed and panting with happy exhaustion, she lowered the bike's kick stand onto the grass and jogged, sore and heavy-legged, around to the rear of the house to collect Daisy and Lollipop.

The aquarium was lying on its side, with all the water and half its stones spilled out. A foot away lay the capsized island with its plastic palm tree. Sophie didn't see the turtles. She backed around in a small cautious circle, then in a wider one, examining each swatch of surrounding area with eagle vision. The turtles were nowhere. *Gone.* The world had taken them away. Shock swelled in her, stopping her heart, her breath, her mind. It overflowed into a wave of vomit. If she didn't black out, it was only because she willed herself to get down on her hands and knees and feel her way across the rest of the lawn, her fingers hunting between blades and clumps for her friends' shells in place of her eyes, which filled with tears and perceived only smeared green light.

A few minutes later her mother opened the kitchen door to call her to dinner and found her doubled over on her knees, her forehead on the ground, sobbing for dear life. She tried to get Sophie to sit up but she remained attached to the grass like a crab. Danielle understood from the knocked over aquarium that the turtles had escaped, and after giving Sophie's back another rubbing, stomped herself around the yard in her kitchen apron on the outlook for the runaways without finding them. It must have been the wind that afternoon to upset the lightweight tank almost without water, she imagined. Or was it an animal? A loose dog chasing a rabbit? A squirrel? It was hard to say if the turtles were really gone; maybe they were in the poison ivy patch. She got down on her haunches and whispered in Sophie's ear that Daddy could check there. This hope, combined with Danielle's strong underarm pinioning, got Sophie into the house.

After dinner, John changed into a long-sleeved shirt and pants, put on gardening gloves and rubber boots, and got out a rake and a flashlight, since it was going on eight o'clock and the shadows under the trees were long and deepening. He gave the flashlight to Monique, who had fled after dinner to the living room couch with a book, and ordered her to follow him into the yard. John stepped gingerly in among the springy plants as Monique shone the light, illuminating circles of red-tipped ivy leaves. He gently poked and ever so slowly raked, trying to strike but not harm two small dark snapping turtles. "I'm going to have to do this tomorrow at six," he said in an irritated voice aimed as far as Monique could tell at Nature, guilty of having let it get too dark for him to see.

When Monique turned to check, Maman was standing with her arm around Sophie behind the screen door of the lighted kitchen, watching them. Maman kissed the side of Sophie's head. What will happen, Monique wondered, if we don't find the turtles tonight, which is likely? Will Sophie whimper all night? Will they have to give her extra medicine?

"Let's give the front-yard ditch a try," Dad gruffed.

She followed him wordlessly through the soft cool grass, shining the flashlight here and there, like a dancing spotlight. The duplex and the low shrubs nestling up against it became a stage backdrop. She directed the flashlight at the sky.

"Monique, I can't see!"

Exactly. Blackout.

Then she pointed the beam into their roadside ditch. Scene Two. She was participating, she thought, in a drama completely out of proportion to the events. She would jot this down in her diary later. *Life will have lots of these times*, she would write. She intuited already that being in plays at school was not just fun but useful.

John didn't find Daisy or Lollipop in the ditch either. Consequently, he got up at six as he'd foreseen to continue the search. Danielle heard him in the shower. She wanted to get up and help, only she was exhausted from not having slept. The mere idea of sitting up and planting her feet in her slippers again made her dizzy, and she shifted her weight towards the warm center of the bed. She'd worried off and on through the night over whether she had done the right thing by giving Sophie something to make her feel drowsy—on top of her real medicine. Fortunately, Sophie was breathing regularly when she'd checked on her that last time at four a.m. Turning on her side now, Danielle clutched her pillow, her face covered protectively by her left arm, movements which always made her feel firmly aboard her raft. Her eyelashes repeatedly brushed against the inner side of her forearm, as she began to wonder what she would say to comfort Sophie that day. She knew that John wouldn't find the turtles. There were no words of comfort for sudden disappearances, she knew that from the war. When customers had brought to their café fresh news of loved ones or neighbors taken that night from their homes by the Germans, her mother's eyes had got bright and hard, and—Danielle remembered this vividly—she'd swallowed hard in sympathy and make a grimace at the enemy's demented barbarism, going immobile for a moment, spellbound—you could see she had the disappeared person in her mind's eye—before stoically taking a rag and wiping the counter. There were no words to help another accept the abrupt loss. Sophie had only lost a couple of water turtles, and yet it was the same thing in miniature. There was the baffling problem of words. There were no words, but since she was her mother she knew that words must come.

Sophie surprised them all when she finally woke up from all her medicine, round about noon. She didn't greet her mother and sister in the living room but went straight out to the backyard. She picked up the aquarium abandoned in the grass, collected the pebbles and the plastic palm-tree island, and brought them inside to the kitchen sink. She wiped the glass tank with a dishtowel and placed it on the counter. Danielle, who was watching though the doorway, heard her say murmur, "There."

"Sophie?" she said tentatively.

Sophie turned and replied in French, *I understand now, Maman. They escaped.*

They escaped?, Danielle echoed.

They've gone somewhere better.

Oh, thank goodness, Danielle thought.

Turtles move faster than Jim Toth thinks, Sophie added with satisfaction. *Wait till I tell him.*

There was the earnestness of a much younger child in Sophie's words which made them heartbreaking.

Unconcerned by her mother's silence, Sophie took a box of cereal out of the pantry and fixed herself breakfast for lunch. Although her spoon clanged regularly against the sides of her ceramic bowl, she didn't give a glance to what she was eating. Instead, she gazed steadily at the yellow wall with the hanging set of copper-bottomed stainless steel pots that the family had recently acquired with H & G stamps, chewing in a mincing way, her head bouncing every now and then as if in time to a silent song.

Danielle went wordlessly over to the aquarium, still there on the linoleum counter between the sink and the refrigerator, its glass smudgy and in need of a cleaning, and looked inside it. Not a drop of water, yet the little palm tree stood erect in a corner and around it jutted miniscule rock promontories. Sophie had remade it, the way a mother remakes her child's bed. Tenderly, Danielle imagined a mother whose child was away on a trip, glancing in every morning at his empty bedroom, certain that he was happy and not concerned that he was in danger or difficulty. Perhaps Sophie as a woman would turn out to have such faith and serenity, Danielle mused. And who knew what other undamaged talents she would reveal having? There was such potential in Sophie—she believed this once again. It fortified her belief in Sophie's future. Naturally, she'd need a bit of help from the family on occasion—and here Danielle made a mental note to make sure Monique did her share—but her sweet girl was going to be all right.

On Labor Day Monday, under a hot sun, John pulled the chain on his lawnmower and with a noisy gnash of metal teeth the engine chortled, then raced into its whine. He adjusted the visor on his canvas hat and hoped for the best. The grass had grown high enough to be unsightly—he just had to cut it, Daisy and Lollipop or no Daisy and Lollipop. After a week they couldn't be lurking in the lawn somewhere…but you never knew with kids' things, did you? He was mowing in a circle around the pink myrtle tree in the bit of lawn in front of the other side of the duplex (and so as far away from the scene of the crime as possible) when he felt a great whack on his left shoulder and his wife's "DOING?!" penetrating the racket the mower was making. He gagged the engine, took off the hat, wiped his brow with the handkerchief which came from his pocket, and barked back at her, "I know! I explained to Sophie! The grass needs to be clipped!"

He'd knocked on the girls' bedroom door half an hour before. Sophie was alone, sitting on the rug with the books she used with Miss Fletcher strewn around her—her doing homework was a relief to him.

"It's OK, Dad," she said calmly, when, hat in hand and his forehead glistening anew, he told her plainly what he had to do. Early yesterday morning her Lollipop and Daisy had turned up in a dream. She had fed them. And just before waking up, she glimpsed them wriggling on a flat green horizon. A dream like this helped.

"That's my trooper," John said huskily.

When he had shooed Danielle away, he mowed the back yard in long strips that looked like lines of immobile ocean waves. He maintained a very regular gait as he pushed his mower—something of a march, actually; it was his trademark, as one of his local customers had termed it. He hit something hard once but the blade continued to rotate and he kept going. Two hours later, he bagged the clippings and tied the string on the black plastic garbage bag—body bag?—without a look inside.

By October, Monique started to feel Sophie's accident was *her* opportunity. The lump generalizations about "you two girls" this-and-that ceased, and, moreover, she was allowed to do lots of new things on her own. Her parents let her go out whenever she was invited—to a movie in Woodbury, to a bowling alley, to a cast party, for a drive to a park, even when that meant getting a ride from juniors or seniors just a couple of years older than her. She was the *active* Morton sister. And since it was now an uncontestable family fact that Sophie was the weaker twin, Monique could even concede that she, Sophie, was the nicer one. Monique didn't care one iota about niceness. She was the *strong* Morton sister. Every page of her diary radiated confidence—the confidence of a very young woman who has only to shake off sleep and inertia in the morning to experience limitless concentration, uncomplaining effort, and tireless scheming. Diary entries of plans and hopes alternated with those recording successes. High school was great. She jotted down how she and seniors Linda and Steve won the inter-school Debate Club tournament, and, allowing herself the luxury of calling classmate Susan Miller her "Enemy", gloated over how she'd managed to get herself—a freshman—assigned the second female lead in the school play.

How could such a successful, well-adjusted girl suspect that her mother, Danielle, would draw her into the bathroom off the kitchen, where their family went for private talks, and want to know for the neurologist if she, Monique, had ever had an episode like Sophie's down at the beach? "You know," she said in French, "we have to consider your genes."

"And please don't cry, Monique," Maman added, detecting a tearful shine to her eyes.

"I'm not!" Monique registered shock at this, too.

"Maybe it's just the vanity mirror light. But why do you have to shriek? I wonder about your character. The smallest thing and you feel put upon. I worry you're going to make yourself sick sometimes."

It was enough to make any teenager scream out in her mind.

"It may be you'll change *ma petite*." Danielle unlocked the door, though she still had one more important thing to share. "In any case, remember that one of these days you'll be asked to help your sister. *Prepare-toi.*"

Monique narrowed her eyes at her own reflection and did not follow her mother into the hall.

*

Her first year at high school had not quite ended when Monique came to understand that what had happened at the ocean to Sophie was not exactly an accident.

Back in the fall, Linda Pierce from Debate Club had started inviting Monique to her house after school. They took the bus home together (Linda lived by the Garden State Parkway to the east of Woodbury), and Monique stayed on till her father finished with his last homeowner interview and could pick her up. The two girls sat on Linda's bed, fine dust swirling around them in the brothy sunlight, and Linda, who liked to gather her hair in a loose, instantly releasable ponytail, confided to Monique—once, then again, and still again, taking a shining to the pronouncement—that Steven Austin Scofield was everything, the sun and the moon to her. Her brow smoothed out and the tasty potency of her feelings could be seen in her face; her voice, meanwhile, remained as somber as that of a magistrate—the way she sounded when she was smearing their debate opponents. Monique was very impressed by Linda's love and by the tenderness with which Linda and Steve held hands and laced fingers in front of her at school. And when Linda struck this chord of love worship, which was usually a prelude to dark words about how terribly uncertain their future seemed, with graduation and college lying ahead, Monique thought about the sort of love (that paled in comparison) which had come her way—first, in junior high school, in the form of notes and that bit of mushiness from Jim Toth the Loth, and now in senior high school, with the grabby, fast kissing she got on stage from Jeffery Goldman, a senior like her friends.

She was playing a lively French parlor maid to his tall randy butler in the fall play. The stage business that the director, Mr. Stearn, invented called for her to have her rump swatted and for Jeffery to give her a loud kiss.

"Bigger. I want that bigger," called the grey-haired, hefty-sized Mr. Stearn from the audience.

And so Jeffery would kiss her again. And again.

She learned to expect to feel, three times a week during rehearsal, Jeffery's breath (clean and sweet, fortunately) in her nostrils, then the friendly bush of his moustache, and the sting of his moist kiss. At first, in her naivety she took this exclusively for acting. It would take his confession and extemporaneous smooching at a party—much longer than anything on stage and of marvelously enhanced familiarity —to wake her up to what was going on. She couldn't say that she was in love, and yet kissing Jeffery—both the high school senior and the stage butler—had become something so natural that she, well, became addicted to it, started to count on it. Anything that Jeffery did to further their intimacy felt physically right to her. She let her body decide. One day after school Jeffery took her home with him on the Woodbury bus. The house was a squat white cube divided into four rooms, each of which was tiny. Jeffery seemed to be the master of the place in his father's absence, judging from the passive, expectant air with which his mother and sister looked at him and the dinner fare that, in the brief conversation that Monique heard, they asked his permission to make. Most amazing to Monique was how Jeffery had the authority to close and lock his bedroom door on his mother and sister and pull her, Monique, to him on the bed, roll with her so that he was on top, press and rub against, taking off her shirt and his own, kissing and groaning as loudly or softly as he pleased. Her senses began to reel. Every so often she would catch full sight of his tanned hairless chest and arms, as toned and smooth and muscular as those of a Greek statue. Handsome male arms that lifted a lacrosse stick and unloaded groceries on supermarket shelves three evenings a week to earn money for college. He had freckles on his nose—a Jewish boy with freckles. When she managed to forget that beyond that closed door were his mother and sister thinking God knew what about her, Monique had a momentous afternoon. Both of them were bare-breasted and still in their jeans. To take off another stitch of clothing would be to mar the perfection, to ruin this afternoon. Over and over and over Jeffery pressed his denim-covered sex into her soft groin with its hard bone, their hips rotating in unison. His breathing came as fast as hers. It seemed so loud to her, when between waves of pleasure that she had never imagined existed, she noticed it and his exhilarated glassy look. When after an hour, they unlocked the bedroom door and quickly walked out of the unlit, apparently empty house, she felt as if she were making a jarring return to a cool indifferent planet.

"I do so like a good chocolate," Jeffery said in a simpering falsetto with French accent—one of her lines from the school play. Then putting his arm around her shoulder as she giggled at him, he diverted her to the blue sedan parked in the driveway. He took a set of keys from his pocket. "Ta-dah!" He swung them in the air, grinning like a boy who knew how to get his own way *always*. Without asking anybody's permission, he drove her home.

Monique ran into Jim Toth on the front porch one of the times that Jeffery dropped her off. It was around six o'clock and already dark, but her skin tingled as if it were summertime and she felt as if she must be all aglow. She was finger-combing her rather messy, wild long hair, and gathering it in a ponytail, when the porch light switched on and Jim Toth stepped out of the door in a heavy hooded jacket. He'd been to see Sophie again, she presumed. His face was still that blubbery white color that she'd disliked in junior high school and which the overhead light made seem even pastier.

"Hi," she muttered.

"Hi, ya." He stopped in place, eager for conversation.

Noooooooo, she thought. He was so bland and sexless. He didn't seem like a man inside a boy's body, as Jeffery did. The thrilling and abiding power of her afternoon with Jeffery pulverized the flash impression she had of the afternoon that Jim Toth had spent with Sophie and made whatever relationship he had with her sister seem all the more measly and insipid. For although her own carryings-on with Jeffery couldn't compare to what went on between Linda and Steve, who were true lovers, the experience had made her—to her mind—a woman and set her in a higher league, light years beyond these two.

"I get the feeling that Sophie doesn't know too much about our high school," Jim Toth began.

"Oh, I'm sure you fill her in."

"Why don't you tell her something, too?"

Then before Monique could tell him to mind his own business, he added impetuously, "Believe me, she'd listen eagerly to anything you have to say," and gave a small nervous cough. "You know how important you are to her." This was said in a way that made it clear that he was referring not just to Sophie but also to himself.

"I didn't know you two had such heart-to-hearts."

He met her eyes. "She's told me a few secrets."

Monique could have had those secrets then if only she'd asked. But she would have to wait because she let her love of sarcasm and impatient feeling of superiority got the better of her.

"I guess that makes you a member of the family," she said icily.

He didn't flinch. A mix of superficial and deep feelings got the better of him, too.

"Secrets that not even you know about," he boasted. "See you around."

Both the Saturday and Sunday performances of the fall play came off well. Everyone's timing was right, no one forgot lines, and the audience laughed more than any of the cast had dared to hope. Danielle, John, and Sophie sat in the third row, their faces half-illuminated by the stage apron lights. For Monique the audience really did seem like 'a sea of faces', and the stage like an island. The floorboards were yellowish brown like sandy tropical soil, and she crossed and re-crossed them like a happy islander, her face bathed in an intense light as she and her cohorts went through their antics. For over an hour she strut about in her black and white maid's uniform and wiggled her bottom; she feather-dusted her employer's nose out of distraction; she rolled her eyes when Jeffery tripped. She got kissed, kissed, kissed. No one imagined how real Jeffery's lust was. She made many funny, grotesque faces at the audience but in the flood of light, her family was indiscernible; the sea had swallowed them. Blackout. She had always loved and still adored blackouts. The gloriously suspenseful silence and then the first hearty claps, following by a rain of applause. Full lights up on the next act. Through his toothy grin, Jeffery muttered, "I want you." The farce bounced along to its silly, giddy conclusion. Three curtain calls. The satisfaction of being recognized by strangers, who increased the speed of their clapping; the happiness of making a curtsy like a noblewoman of centuries ago, of joining hands with the other players; the wonderful sense of belonging to a special little troupe that had delivered on its promises.

"Good show, good show." Mr. Stearn waved his hand in the air backstage. "I want to thank you all."

The cast party was held at the house of Mary, the quiet and well-organized stage manager. Along one wall of the paneled basement rec room was a table of food and along another lots of fold-up chairs. Couples sat in each other's lap, rock music was playing, and a few of the costume crew were already at their dancing. The lights dimmed to some blue and red spotlights angled at the ceiling. The boys still had a smudge of mascara under their eyes and their hair was damp. The girls, most of whom were in sweaters and jeans, had kept their piled-up hairdos in the style of last century. Monique sat in Jeffery's lap. He was nibbling at her neck, giving her "hickies." He asked her two things, one very big and one flattering and small. The big thing was if one night before Christmas vacation, after he got done with his shift at the supermarket, he could come round to her house. He had noticed that the other side of the duplex was empty. He wanted her to be waiting there to quietly let him in. He wanted to spend the night with her. This left her dizzy and disoriented, and fortunately he didn't try to pry an answer out of her. He just kissed and nibbled harder. After a moment, he asked the sweet thing: if she could cut her hair or wear it up like this all the time.

"You really want me to look like this always?" she replied, languidly as a pretty ingénue.

"You look terrific, babe. Your eyes really stand out." He kissed first the right one, then the left one. His moustache brushed her eyebrows.

"But I like my long hair!" The languidness left her. She wanted to play the vixen now—there was more fun in that. She gave him a short playful slap. "Oh, you mean thing. I like washing my hair, combing it out, brushing it…"

He gave the coil on top of her head a little hard twist. "Darling," he breathed, as theatrical as her. "*Why* stay a twin forever?"

On Sunday she took scissors to her own hair and gave herself a pageboy cut that came out so badly (at the back especially, where she had to work using two mirrors) that she was forced to ask her mother, in an estranged voice, to come into the bathroom to even out all the hacked and chopped ends and salvage her appearance.

"*Why are you doing this?!*" Danielle fumed in French. It was not easy to rectify such butchery. She muttered and sighed a lot (her sighing seemed to increase in daily frequency as the years went by), and at one point added mysteriously—but just as angrily, "*You grow it long again. We'll need it long again. Long, you hear me?*"

As soon as the principal damage had been righted, Monique grabbed the scissors back from her mother and stormed off to her room.

"Be quiet, lady!" she yelled in English, before banging the door shut.

Her reaction, of course, was to her mother's tone and not to the words. She didn't hear the words anymore than any ruffled teenager did. Monique lay on her bed dry-eyed. She looked passably all right in the mirror once again, didn't she? Her moment of panic, right before she'd called her mother, was already forgotten. Regret was rare in her—or, better, it was a selective emotional circuit. She was so worried about wrongly leaving things *un*done or *un*tried (like cutting her hair…or—maybe—secretly spending the night with Jeffery) that she de facto desensitized herself to her actual mistakes. Had it been a mistake to take scissors to her hair like that? But the question was impermissible. She did things….that were successful or unsuccessful. AND THAT WAS THAT.

The end result was a limp brown pageboy-style hairdo without bangs, clipped straight across her earlobes. There wasn't much similarity to the soft Gibson-girl look that Jeffery wanted. No one in a thousand years would call this haircut becoming. It made her face look as long and narrow as a stick. It made her eyes look like bulging frog eye sacks. But because Monique was Monique, no one made a negative comment—not Jeffery, not her father or her sister, and not even Linda and Steve. Everyone kept quiet—except Jim Toth.

He stepped in front of her in the hall at school, and in his odd excited way told her that he never would have believed that she could change so much. And if that weren't bad enough, he added that he imagined that she'd done this for Sophie's sake.

FOR SOPHIE'S SAKE?!

"You're crazy," she managed to hiss, pushing by him in anger, her eyes stinging from the hint that she had changed for the worse.

That was the moment Jim Toth enthusiastically let the truth slip about Sophie's accident.

"She'll never think that it's better for her to die again. Because you've made yourself so different. Brilliant, Monique, brilliant!"

His voice echoed inside her head all that day. *Better to die? Better to die*! Were those tremendous words Jim Toth's or Sophie's? Monique felt confused and sick. Part of her was convinced it was just Toth, interpreting things as he pleased. But another part of her gave credence to that terrible moment at the shore when she couldn't sense Sophie anywhere in the world. Her sister had most likely been on the verge of dying then. But being about to die was one thing and wanting to die was another. Monique couldn't accept that. Twins don't think in such a way. And besides, Sophie liked life. She'd loved and cared for those turtles; she liked sewing with Maman; she got all concerned about Dad's few grey hairs; she went on bike rides with Toth.

Stupid Toth.

On the other hand, there *was* that awfully peculiar look her twin sister gave her at times—from her bed yesterday for instance. Monique was standing in the middle of the room talking about something, and Sophie's eyes were fixed on the small space between her knees. The weirdest thing was that Sophie sometimes stared at that tiny space avidly, as if she wanted to squeeze into it. Monique thought of a leech, digging into the side of her knee and being carried around, spectator and passenger, to her day. Honestly, at times like that her sister felt like an awful and morbid burden.

But could she really think it was *better to die*?

At most, Monique thought, Sophie was asking her to lead the way, to proceed her in life.

Which, yes, got irritating. And maddening.

But still.

She wouldn't think about it anymore.

If she could.

On Saturdays after tournaments, Monique was allowed to go out with Linda and Steve. They usually started off with a walk along the Delaware River in Federal Park. When dusk came, they would drive along back roads until they found some housing development under construction; all of the carpenters and masons had stopped work by that hour and they would find a cul-di-sac of empty lots and one or two houses just being framed. Steve would park his mother's car and then open and pass the bottle first to Linda beside him, then to Monique in the dark back seat.

It was dandelion wine today, a nippy afternoon in December. Steve and his big brother had made it together one evening. Talking about homemade wine led them into a discussion of what their families did after dinner. Linda's dad was building a canoe in the garage, and Steve's mother was weaving a rug on a hand-loom she'd bought.

"I don't have anything so interesting to tell you," said Monique, ruefully and meaning it. Her dad did the dishes and went to sleep pretty early-- even nine-thirty or so, when his snooze interrupted his reading in his easy chair. Her mother left the dinner table for her bedroom with a full wine glass, and went upstairs to bed at the same time as her sister, "so as to check on her."

"How old's your little sister?" asked Steve, the bottle at his lip.

"She's not little."

"Who knew you had one," said Linda. "My, my, secretive baby Monique. I suppose we should feel grateful that you even took it upon yourself to tell us your mother is French."

"My sister," Monique took a breath, "my sister had an accident a little over a year ago, and now she gets schooled at home." She realized she might as well get the fascinating part over with: "We were born at the same time but we're not the same."

"Twins, are you?" Steve pivoted round towards Monique behind him.

"Identical actually... Just not at all the same," she replied stoically.

"And you say she had a terrible accident." He whistled lowly at this close call.

Then Monique told her friends what she had half-gleamed last week from Toth. For the first time, she tried this truth out—if it was truth:

"To put it bluntly, she tried to commit suicide."

You see, you see, it sounds so crude, Monique thought to herself, her heart skipping a beat. Too crude for her. Too crude for Sophie.

Steve and Linda were both scrutinizing her. Like the most serious and cautious of judges. This came by instinct.

"I take that back," she amended gravely. Then with plaintive vehemence she added, "It's just what I've been led to believe."

Sophie Morton lay in her bedroom, which contained the bottomless hole of her sister's absence in the other twin bed. Monique had asked to be given her own bedroom in the other side of the duplex. She was now sleeping on the other side of the wall, in what was technically another house. It being only about nine o'clock at night, she tried scratching at the wall, but no response came. From across the hall, she could hear her mother lift her pelvis from her mattress and roll to one side with a sigh of release after passing the gas of the day. She could hear her father downstairs straightening his newspaper and see the shaft of lamplight that his not-to-be-disturbed reading sent up like a warning arrow across the banister of the stairs.

In the other half of the duplex Monique sat in the darkness at the desk near the stairs and kept a quiet vigil, aided by her watch. The suspense and heart strain would last for another good hour and a half. Nothing could start before 10.30. She'd made that very clear to Jeffery. Tonight was the night. The *one and only* night, she underscored to him.

When he got off his supermarket shift, he was going to drive to Clearsboro, leave the car parked in front of the pharmacy and walk down the back road to her house. He was going to throw a few pebbles at this front window, and she was to go quietly downstairs and let him in the rear door to this side of the duplex. They would creep ever so quietly to the most remote corner of the bare living room and lie together on the carpeting. Jeffery had thought of everything. They would spend *the night* together!

It was the first time that she had done something so big behind her parents' back. She had never been told that she couldn't sleep here with a boyfriend yet it was certainly forbidden. She felt as if she were putting a hole in a wall that she had never noticed but that had always surrounded her. The experience was scary and yet she didn't feel weak—she felt strong. She had super vision, super hearing, and super energy. Deceiving her parents like this gave her the giddy impression of being grown up. *Doing something that a part of you is determined to do and that another part of you is uneasy about is what it means to mature*, she decided.

She heard her father's heavy footsteps on the stairs beyond the wall, as he went upstairs to the bathroom. The little pink clock on the desk, the one that told Miss Fletcher and Sophie when to stop their lessons, read ten minutes after ten. A powerful sensation that she didn't quite understand began to dominate over her excitement and anxiety. She shifted in her chair and clasped and re-clasped her hands. Her breathing began to get labored. When she thought about the fact that pebbles would be thrown at this window and that she would obediently go to open the door, her need for air became even more oppressive. She stood up and went to the window. The tops of the trees were visible in the light of the half-moon but not the road. She put her forehead against the pane. She still couldn't breathe right. She wasn't in charge, she wasn't in control—Jeffery was, and though it had been this way from the start, from the first kiss, it bothered her, irked her, *rankled* her now.

She went back to the desk to read the clock. Half past ten.

She wasn't in love with Jeffery.

Five minutes later there was a tap, like the sound of a small hail stone against the windowpane. A second, lighter strike. A third.

When she went to Jeffery's house, they locked the door of his bedroom and she lay on his bed, waiting for him to take her clothes off. But this was her house.

A bumpy rain of pebbles. A whistle.

At her house she wasn't in love with Jeffery.

Her father moved through the other hallway. He turned on a lamp. It lit up a bit of the front yard. Fortunately (she looked out her window) he didn't see Jeffery. Her father left the light on. The wall that she had never noticed around her was now patched, thanks to this spot of light. There were no more pebble throws. She reckoned that Jeffery must be walking back to his car. Tomorrow at school she would tell him that she'd fallen asleep.

She sat for a while longer at the desk, her right hand checking the pulse in her left wrist.

Herself again.

CHAPTER FIVE

After five years of silence, Louise Vassalli stood once again in Danielle Morton's foyer, feeling as embarrassed she had known she would be and offering a job to Sophie. "And since I hear that both girls have their driver's license now, I thought she could do it... She seems so, uh, adept."

Danielle said nothing

Perhaps she was just waiting to hear what she meant by 'adept,' thought Louise. She wasn't going to let the awkwardness of this occasion get the better of her. Still, she hadn't envisioned that even Danielle's house would seem hostile. The rooms along the hall yawned at her, their invisible contents also sullen and indifferent, when objects were usually eloquent and well, friendly, to Louise. This made what she was doing—standing there and offering a safe, steady babysitting job in the midst of hostility—feel like a more daunting task.

Joy Adams had asked about names of possible babysitters last week in Louise's store. Making the small open-palmed gesture of well-heeled suburban women when they feign helplessness, Joy had said she couldn't continue to rely on her parents for all this childcare. She ran the town's best antique shop with the financial backing of these parents, the proprietors of a horse farm whose white fences ran on for miles and miles. Behind their white mansion with black shutters was the converted carriage house where Joy and her four children lived. She was blonde, divorced, and knew now to maintain an agreeable, light tone of voice even when she was complaining about something. "I'm really up against a wall as to babysitters," she'd said. "The fourteen-year old I had come yesterday had my kids watch her wash her hair in the sink." Louise had given Joy's problem her friendliest attention, and that's when the solution of Sophie Morton had had its spontaneous generation. Louise didn't believe that she had a job lined up for the summer like most 17-year-olds. If her sister Monique was already getting a head start by working a few hours after school at the convenience store down the road where Louise had seen her last week, Sophie was apparently the recluse of always. The girl needed a sense of purpose, independence, a bit of responsibility, and her own money. And all of that Joy could give her.

Danielle was coldly civil. She would have found an absolute stranger more human than Louise. She found it hard to throw off the impression that her ex-friend had been purposely living her life in secret, in order to snub her better, these last six years. She did not ask Louise to sit down or to follow her into the kitchen; the two of them just stood at the foot of the stairs in the small narrow front hall, Louise jingling her keys as she launched into a description of the job offer for Sophie.

"Ah-ha, I see," said Danielle with non-committal poise. "I don't know what Sophie is going to think about this, but I will ask her." She demurely climbed two steps and called up the stairs in English to Sophie. "Could you come here, dear? You have a visitor." Her voice was an imitation of what she imagined wealthy ladies in their Philadelphia mansions used. Bright, a tad distracted, and sugary.

Plopping down on the bottom step, Sophie mumbled a shy raspy 'hello.' Though she still resembled Monique (whose hair was long again) to a tee, Sophie looked pale to Louise Vassalli, and peculiarly introspective as the housebound tend to be. She listened impassively to the facts about Joy Adam's children, aged 10, 8, 5, and 3, while her mother stood by ready for guidance or interpretation in the finer cultural register of their other language. Louise had expected them to be far more wary than this, and relieved, bulldozed on with an outline of the daily schedule of things that Joy was asking of Sophie. *Louise has aged,* thought Danielle. With that strenuous smile, yellowy teeth, creasing and moving mouth wrinkles, and red lipstick, she looked like an old mime.

"So, Sophie?" concluded Louise with a glance from daughter to mother.

"I guess I can," said Sophie with a shrug.

"Oh good!" burst out Louise, like a little girl. "I'll tell Mrs. Adams that you want to start next Monday after school." She turned towards Danielle uncertainly, "If she wants to start next

Monday, I'm saying." Again, Louise Vassalli got the sense that Danielle despised her and was dead opposed to this.

In reality, Danielle felt incapable of opposition. Indeed, from the moment she'd opened the door and looked into that face that, for the first time in five years, had wanted to gaze back at hers, Danielle had been overwhelmed by Louise's right to be there. Louise Vassalli had an inalienable right to come into this American house in which she Danielle lived. Its closets in place of the old familiar armoires, the bug screens on those pull-up sash windows instead of open-air *French* windows, and its 'master bedroom,' all instilled patterns and habits which were Danielle's for as long as she continued to live in this country, but which were Louise Vasalli's *forever*.

All this was somehow caught up with Louise's right to restart in neutral the old pathetic motor of their friendship. It was as if *savoir-faire* had been transferred from herself to Louise Vasalli. She had lost her effervescent "right touch", after being made to pay a price for possessing it, and it belonged to Louise Vassalli now. This was the paltry end-result of these past five years.

"I do believe there's something Joy would like me to add," said Louise, a happy artisan applying the finishing touch. "It would be good for Sophie to come on Sunday and see the house, meet the kids, and, you know, get familiar with her car-- it's a big long station wagon, but you're only doing local driving on back roads so you'll be fine.."

That light in Louise's eyes just wouldn't go out. She touched the doorknob, possessed it for a moment before withdrawing her hand and waiting for Danielle to open it.

"Bye then. Be seeing you," she enthused.

When she was gone, Danielle asked Sophie if they'd done the right thing. Sophie didn't know what she meant.

Her eventual agreeing that it had been good to accept the job didn't sound like conviction, but Danielle let it pass.

And Sophie began.

On Sunday, she drove their family Ford to Joy's carriage house and met four running kids, who were talking and joking and jeering among themselves but who stopped-- an arm or shoulder caught by Joy for a moment-- for a good-natured hello. The youngest mooned at and fixed on Sophie's face, but it was just a habit of toddlerhood. The others hardly looked her way for the next hour. They were used to being a close-knit pack, a blur of reaching arms and legs and "I'm hungry Mom"s.

Joy showed Sophie the house. Since Sophie knew that she didn't have to get to know the kids but only drive them, she didn't take much in about the tour, except that the boys had the blue bedroom and the girls the pink one. At the end Joy led her back to the kitchen, which had copper-bottomed pots on the wall like in Sophie's house, only these were so immaculate that they glowed like rosy winter suns impaled on hooks. They sat at a table under whose clear plastic surface were pressed thousands of tiny seashells, which distracted Sophie while Joy was penciling in her car route on the unfolded county map. The two smaller children's summer day camp was just down the road, and the pool in a detached residential area on the other side of Woodbury. Joy insisted that Sophie was to chauffeur the kids around in *her* car only. "You leave your Mom's Ford here. That way I'm paying for the gas and any fender benders." They went outside to the Plymouth, and Joy had her sit in the crimson red driver's seat and work the lights, wipers, hood release, and ignition. "Remember not to trust the mirror when you reverse. This thing's longer than a tank... Anyway, it's not too bad a job, right? You'll just spend the afternoon in the car."

Sophie used the smile and nod that Maman had told her to be sure to make. She wished that her own hair were blonde instead of brown and that it would stay flipped under, like Joy's.

Joy, who considered this chauffeuring to be a waste of her time and a frittering away of her own prime years, smiled back.

Over the next few months, driving the four Adams children around in the long, sleek Plymouth station wagon gave meaning and shape to Sophie's day. From the first day, she noticed a special thing. Starting up the Plymouth's engine, she had a flash image of herself as Joy. Not only, but every time that she glanced in the car mirror, she half expected to see Joy's face instead of her own, and her heart unfailingly skipped two beats, one in excitement and one in disappointment. It was a momentary flicker of belief in magic—because at seventeen, she had a normal adolescent assumption that the future held good things. She understood that what she had on loan from Joy now would be hers in the future.

People who watched her drive by seemed to sense this somehow. For one thing, Sophie didn't look at all like an untried adolescent. Sophie behind the wheel looked *wedded* to that car, born to drive it and make it go places. Jim Toth, for instance, saw her cruise by that summer, and waved timidly, as if afraid he had the wrong person, from up there on the trailer bed of his father's sod truck, his legs hidden by the stacked mound of grass carpet, each jelly-roll swatch an even swirl of green and brown.

Each time she encountered Jim's sod truck, Sophie never failed to roll down her window and call to him, her fingers opening and closing, as if pressing all of time, the past with the present and the future, in her fist for an instant and then releasing it. "Jim! How are you?" she sang out, as those four kids in the back seat jumped in place, their arms flaying towards one and other in an incomprehensible sequence of jubilance and offence-taking.

He always took this greeting to mean that she was both eager for him to come see her again and reproaching him for not getting in touch sooner.

"I'm fine, Sophie," he called back. "Yourself?"

She had time to nod and that was that. The Plymouth flashed its turn signal or in any case sped onwards.

Contrary to his intentions at the start of high school, Jim hadn't had much to do with the Morton girls over the last two years. Sophie losing the turtles and Monique cutting her hair and getting hot and heavy with Jeffery Goldman, had left him feeling...well, disappointed in them. Sophie was sweet, though, to wave to him regularly this summer, and he warmed to her friendliness, albeit in a more disinterested way than before. He knew he could stop by the Morton house again, Monique or no Monique, and say 'hi' to her, the way she wanted him to, any time it suited him. Once or twice he even considered which day might be best, or what time. But he never actually went. It had something to do with the sight of Sophie at the wheel of that station wagon, he knew that. With her back erect, her glances into the rearview mirror at the children, the sunglasses she slipped on after she'd finished calling her hello, Sophie was a perfect Mom of the upper-middle-class sort. As Jim saw things from his father's sod truck, preparing to lay instant lawns for precisely these people, these were women with no more life-shaping decisions or hurdles in front of them. They came out to the sod truck for a quick hello in their crisp shorts and perfect makeup, and he could see as plain as day that they had been briefly on their own out in the world and had already returned, in their protected environment, to the essentials of life: children, love, and food. That Sophie looked fifteen years older when she was behind the wheel of the Plymouth station wagon, that Sophie looked like *them*, paralyzed Jim Toth with a shyness that he'd never felt with her before.

The end result of this realization, that Sophie was as perfect and remote as Monique was rebellious and irate, was that Jim stuck the Morton twins in his mind's freezer compartment that summer.

At his age Jim's mental freezer space was most ample. And though he was beginning to shove large-sized things into it (gearing up for college), it was great to know that he wouldn't have to make a meal of anything stored inside for a good number of years to come.

*

Louise Vassalli gestured at Danielle Morton to come across the road into her fruit-stand parking lot when Danielle was pulling the mail from their mailbox.

"I guess Sophie's found her calling in life," said the fairy godmother of the arrangement.

"I suppose it depends on what you mean by calling." Danielle took care not to arch a brow. (Louise had been so nasty about that, the night of five years ago). What was Louise insinuating? That Sophie's calling was to work someday with children? Or that she was going to be normal after all, because she was already a perfect little wife-and-mother-imposter?

"Danielle, she's earning money! She's making something of herself."

"Fine for now," said Danielle tersely. "Till she goes to college."

"*What* college?" Louise queried, incredulously.

"A teacher's college," Danielle invented.

"Shippendale?"

So there was one, thought Danielle.

"Sophie will need to take the S.A.T. exam. Anyone who wants to go to college has to take it," Louise observed.

"True enough. We're preparing her for it." Louise would be sure to understand that this meant Miss Fletcher, though it wasn't true.

"Shippendale State Teachers' College is a couple of hours, across the river in Pennsylvania. You'll want to, er, look up just how high Sophie's score has to be."

When Miss Fletcher left at lunchtime, Danielle had a talk with Sophie. Tired from her lessons, Sophie lay resting on her bed, and Danielle gently combed her fingers through her long hair as she described what she reckoned to be the life and job of a kindergarten teacher.

"Isn't that nice? Wouldn't you like to do that?" she asked in French.

Sophie nodded.

"I want you to be happy. I want this for Monique, too," Danielle added. "I want this more than anything in the world." Despite her uneasy truce with America, she managed most days to concentrate successfully on her daughters, especially on Sophie. When she felt like she was being a nurturing mother who knew how to prod her teenagers along in the direction their talents lay in, she once again enjoyed the amenities of her American lifestyle—the mall shopping, the big fast clothes dryer, the convenience stores at every intersection, the air-conditioning. Yet cyclically she also felt like a failure; she went through sleepless nights wondering, confusedly once again, if she was living where she should be. In the city, in the country, in America, in France? Was there a place that could make her, the woman who didn't know herself except as a mother and a wife, feel finally at home?

Often at the start of the second or third of these restless nights, Sophie would knock gently on her bedroom door and stick her head in, saying softly and apprehensively, *Maman, I can hear you. What's wrong?*

Sometimes Danielle attempted to tell her what. Other times she sighed. Once or twice she replied hoarsely, *Please go.*

Sophie was irremovable. *Maman, are you all right?*

Maman?

The moment filled with poignancy. The knowledge that she had almost lost this daughter, and the vulnerability that she felt, became enormous. It enveloped everything but Sophie's earnest *Maman?* She wanted her to be all right so much, that Danielle eventually was.

*

Monique, prepare-toi.

The look of being in her tunnel, then: *Oui, Maman.*

*

John Morton didn't like the plan of Monique taking the S.A.T. for Sophie and argued with his wife about it. Their conversation soon became a vortex of contorted logic and every now and then John would pull out, exclaiming, "I feel like I'm being railroaded into something that's wrong." In essence he felt that Danielle was mixing her own reasons for feeling unhappy in America with certain facts concerning Sophie in order to justify a highly unethical if not criminal plan.

Naturally, he agreed with Danielle that their nearly drowned daughter, who had never seen the psychiatrist that they'd promised to take her to, who would never understand even the most elementary notion of physics or the most plug-and-crank ones of political theory, who had trouble focusing on people at times, who repeated your words as if memorizing them, who never got heated up over issues big or small-- this daughter couldn't "stay at home like an invalid," as Danielle put it. But Danielle's remedy was as appalling as this prospect, in his opinion.

Danielle insisted: Sophie was lucky to have an identical twin sister, who had at last long hair like hers again, who would fill in for her, take over her life for three hours, and thus make possible the future that Sophie merited. After which she would go to some two-year college, teach small children, and receive a salary. "There is a S.A.T. test in Bridgeport the Saturday following the one in Woodbury, which the kids from our local high school are scheduled to take. We'll get a doctor's certificate for Sophie and sign her up for the Bridgeport date."

John scowled at his wife in disbelief.

"We won't tell you if it's Monique or Sophie going out the door," she added. You won't have to know....*D'accord*?"

How could she sound so unruffled, he wondered? Where did it come from, this hard slab of inevitability on which her plan rested? "Don't humor me," he scoffed. "Of course I'll know, Danielle."

She heaved a very large sigh—decidedly bigger than her usual daily variety. "Then go somewhere, John. Go fishing. Go see your mother. Go to the garden center and buy flowers for the yard. Go to the library. Go—."

"Enough," he interjected, holding up a hand. "You haven't convinced me. Let me make that very clear."

She could tell from these words—he was being so cowardly but ethical, wasn't he?—that she had prevailed.

"I'll be in Gettysburg," he grunted.

Monique drove herself to the testing center set up in a high school in the northern part of Woodbury, and followed the paper signs and guide arrows, whose accruing commands and suggestions put a person in the mood for serious business, till she reached the right classroom. The man in charge of the nationally administered exam asked for her name and receipt stub but did not ask for any other sort of identification. Since Jim Toth was sitting in the same room, she took the precaution of sitting in the front and slumping in her chair—very definitely Monique—the way next week she planned to be very definitely Sophie by sitting in the back by the window with her shoulders squared and spine arched. She found the examination hard. She picked her brain all morning, silently repeating multiple-choice word meanings to herself, goading and galvanizing (*come on, Monique, you shit head, what is ob-se-qui-ous?, get with it!*). On the math part, she made tense but usually successful retrievals from her baroquely branching mnemonic ordering of geometry formulas. Her lips were usually still moving in their ceaseless reformulations when at the end of each timed section, the supervisor deflated the room's expansive silence with, "Put your pencils DOWN, please; pencils DOWN." After the click click click had finished going from desk to desk, he said, "All right, now TURN the page." She found a column of fresh blue dots to blacken, like a lane rope disciplining the swimmer as she goes for another lap. Around her, chairs creaked and fellow test-takers would clear their throats as if re-mustering breath or muscle control in a long-distance competition. At one pm it was over, and blurry-eyed from the fatigue of too much suspicious rereading, she pushed past the hall fire-doors, abandoning the classroom and the quiet, feeling that she had undergone a leveling process and completely in the dark as to how she'd scored.

At home, Danielle sat with Monique, watching her eat her lunch of cold cuts, *l'assiette anglaise,* and trying to pry information out of her. "I guess it went all right, Maman," was all to come from Monique's lips. Sophie breezed into the kitchen with that showered look with which she went to Joy's. She worked for her on Saturday afternoons now, too. Fishing some peppermint candies out of the kitchen jar, Sophie stashed them in her purse to distribute among Joy's kids. It was clear to Danielle that she was thinking about her afternoon and not about Monique's morning. Both girls left the kitchen with a brief, "See you." Sophie went out to the driveway to wait for Joy and the kids to come and pick her up. Monique went upstairs and took a long three-hour nap. Danielle washed the dishes and felt a vague uneasiness over how things were going. Monique was doing her best—everything that she had asked of her—and yet were these plans going to work out? John was against her. She wasn't used to this, and it hurt her. She wondered if John's disapproval of her attempts to make Sophie's future happy could be considered a milder version of the lambasting she'd received from Louise Vassalli. Was she going overboard with her efforts this time, too? Did she have some character flaw that made her arrogantly presumptuous in her forging on ahead? ...She might be drifting through life even more than she'd imagined.

John Morton returned home around 10 pm. He found the house quiet and dark, except for the small amber-toned lamp on a corner table in the living room. Danielle was on the couch with a book, one bare foot tucked under her, the other leg crooked and raised so that she could lay her cheek against her knee. It was that peaceful time which comes of an empty evening. When he came in, it was as much an effort for her to stop reading and stroking her smooth leg as it was for him, given his embarrassment over the day, to open his mouth and ask something about it.

"The girls?"

"Upstairs."

After a pause, she asked if he'd had anything to eat.

"Pretzels and ice cream." His lips twitched with a joke: it was a family tradition in Gettysburg to skip dinner on Saturday night and instead eat enormous bricks of Neapolitan. "You know I'm glad I went. It was wild. They'd put the big white house next to my brother's up on steel beams and were carting it away when I drove up. A whole house going down the road, pulled by a tractor trailer. It's not something you forget. My brother and sister-in-law don't know what the government will do when it comes to their place." He described Robert as being uneasy, his wife Cindy as worried. There was talk of another house nearby that was going to be burned for fire department practice. John shook his head. "Must be awful. Memories, home improvements, beautiful wood work—gone forever."

"They get their money," said Danielle.

She seemed unduly detached to him. He wondered if it was because of the book she'd been reading. Or perhaps the big day hadn't gone off well.

"Actually," he said, "the government pays pretty good money."

She recognized one of his American ways of self-comfort. That the National Park Service wanted to restore the Gettysburg Battlefield to the way it had looked before the bloody three days in 1863, and in doing so eradicate the history of a dozen families, was a bureaucratic decision of misguided idealism which echoed any number of past grandiose plans in France. But try telling Americans that—there was no lesson there for them, no sir. *Ils sont fous les américains.* Crazy, crazy.

Staring at him, she burst out with a "So!"

"So?" he blinked.

She stood up. "You're not going to ask me how the exam went for Monique this morning?"

"I—I'm pointedly not going to."

"Never fear. I wasn't—and am not—about to tell you. But I think you'll want to be in Gettysburg next Saturday too, John."

"You don't say."

Something about how he said that softened her and she put her hand on his shoulder. There must be a way around his disapproval. There must be *something* she could do. All these years spent together, yet she didn't often understand what was going on inside him. Why not imagine something charitable? There had been times, she remembered, when he had been utterly disoriented because a profound reason or cause of something had risen from its submerged position and thrown daily life off balance; when for example his own procrastination had caused him to miss a deadline at work and lose a chance at a promotion. His way was to refuse to acknowledge it...unless it was a matter of life or death. "Big deal," he'd say. "Nobody died, did they?" Perturbed all the same and in need of reassurance.

Charitably she gave his neck a little kiss.

He patted the back of her head affectionately. Two pats. She counted them.

That was all the comforting either one could manage tonight.

She sat back down on the couch and returned to her reading. *Madame Bovary*, in English of course, because where was she ever going to find the French? John went upstairs to bed, where he nursed the worry that he was losing his fighting spirit. After about ten minutes of such anxiety, he threw off the covers, got down on the carpet, and did some push-ups. It made him feel decidedly better.

Gettysburg Saturday, however, remained written in his date book.

To reap her sister the right modest score and at the same time master her own fear of failure, Monique managed, the following Saturday in the Bridgeport testing center, to imagine, and share in, her sister's unshatterable inner calm. Though she considered as an emotional handicap Sophie's inability to entertain lively ideas, it was only by imitating this stillness that she was able to approach the exam in the right way. Still, it turned out to be much more of an ordeal than she'd supposed. Granted, she knew it wasn't going to be as easy as tricking their parents in the car on the way to Philadelphia with Marinette and Uncle Dédé when she and Sophie were ten. She knew it wasn't enough to brush her hair into the limp ponytail that Sophie favored these days and put on one of Sophie's pant-skirts; but neither did it turn out to be a matter of "acting dumb" on every other test question or letting loose what were like tight braids of thought in her mind. It was not going too far to say that she was obliged that morning to interpret a role in a profoundly interior dimension that no audience could see or fathom. In a sense she forced her way into part of her sister's brain. It was a tour de force, which left her exhausted, barely able to drive home. She was supremely glad it was over.

About six weeks later, the results arrived in the mail. Danielle was the one to open the envelope. She gave a shriek of joy and relief. "Monique" had excelled and "Sophie" had done respectably.

The future remained an open-ended affair.

CHAPTER SIX

When in the fall of 1972 the girls were settled at their respective colleges, Monique on fellowship to Oberlin, Sophie an hour and a half away at Shippendale, John Morton became an overtly sentimental, embarrassing father. He gushed over the phone. He said things like 'gosh, we really miss you, sweetie' and 'it's hard to believe our little girl's gone,' even though his girls, nonplussed, made their end of the conversation as neutral sounding as possible because they were in front of their new roommates. Afterwards, with the phone receiver back on its hook and the girls back to their studying, he reverted to his authentic self. Life was acceptable, even easier, without the twins. Yet while he had adjusted without trouble to the fact that Monique was gone, it was harder to do the same about Sophie. He worried about her; he knew Danielle did as well. That she considered her two roommates, Beth and Amy, "nice and friendly" was about all he and Danielle could glean.

Only Sophie knew how much pleasure it gave her to watch Amy and Beth personalize their corners of their 'triple'. The miracle of other people's homemaking was something she marveled at. She copied the girls' decorating tricks. They didn't mind, and perhaps they didn't even notice, because so many other students on their floor were doing precisely the same; on her strolls down the hall past open doors, Sophie saw fellow students pulling down bed mattresses to the floor, hanging up Navaho blankets and posters, setting their desks at an angle to catch the window light, creating incense tables and electric teapot stations. A few of them were sitting cross-legged on the floor in chat sessions. And outside on the green commons there were Frisbee games already going. None of her self-motivated peers needed her—no one needed anyone else, but still they came together and made friends. Just hours after arriving, she was already feeling both admiration for them and an increased need for home.

Not for her parents' duplex. She wasn't stricken by an anxious need for *any specific* place. It was more like a driving instinct to settle into a family-like relationship as soon as possible. When she looked out the window at the Frisbee players in the afternoon sun, she felt awash in, disoriented by, her own sea of need. Oh, yes, the sooner she found and established family again, the better.

If she didn't "nest" in the way of other girls weakened by the same instinct, if she didn't take up with some guy—if she didn't start sleeping around by Christmas (like Beth, or so Amy said), it was probably because her mother began driving over to see her once, and even twice, a week.

Some classes were going better than others. She was very interested, say, in phonics, and enjoyed the mini-internship conducted at a local elementary school, helping slow readers. Subjects like human biology, juvenile legislation, and even sociology, were torture, however. Pellets of spoken subject matter shot past her ears and for five or ten minutes of the professor's lecture she would understand nothing. In these intervals she concentrated on her fellow students' arm or leg positions, or on the professor's funneled but large expenditure of intensity. She *meant* to take notes and make sense of the ideas, but found the atmosphere too stirring. All around her she sensed a beautiful dedication to learning, to capturing truths. Her classmates' faces made her think of the absorbed and mesmerized faces of Jesus' disciples in the illustrated Bible they had at home.

Danielle concluded that something was *definitely* wrong the day that Sophie over the phone couldn't give a single example of what she had studied in her classes earlier that day. Danielle, who had only a vague idea of what might help, made a new trip to the public library. On Saturday, John noticed a fresh pile of books on their dining room table. Not the usual subjects that Danielle had been delving into since the girls had gone to college—the history of the French Underground as viewed by American histories, say, or medical encyclopedias that discussed her brother's brain damage, or behavioral disorders in identical twins—not these but...how strange, he thought...volumes of college-level sociology and biology?

"Keeping up with the girls, Danielle?"

She smiled cryptically and rather sadly.

"Is… Sophie having that much trouble?"

"Mmmm."

There is a special airless hopelessness that comes from disappointment in one's children.

"I'm going to drive down Thursday to Shippendale," Danielle said.

"We could go Sunday together."

"Thanks. But you know that would be pointless."

"You're not thinking of tutoring her, I hope."

"I don't know precisely what I am going to do. First, I'm going to get a better idea."

"You're saying that you're going to quiz her?"

"Oh probably that too." She sighed. "It's a funny war."

"Let it go, Danielle. Let Sophie come home."

"Not yet. She needs to find her proper life first."

"You can't *cram* and *stuff* her into a niche, even one right for her. Let her come home, Danielle."

"I'm sorry I can't listen to you," she said in a quiet but exacting voice. She meant "can't", not "won't."

Danielle drove across the bridge into Pennsylvania with a vibration under the skin of her arms: there was always an electricity to crossing borders, no matter how often she did it. In an hour and a half she reached Shippendale College and found the visitors' parking lot. Hot cheeked from the ride, Danielle unbuttoned her coat and yanked the bag out of the car trunk. With halting steps she made her way to Sophie's dorm, those textbooks in the plastic sack like giant potatoes.

"Oh wow, you're here," said her daughter, dressed in a tracksuit and sweat socks. "*Mais qu'est-ce que tu as là-dedans, Maman?*"

When Danielle pulled out the books—again, they felt like groceries—Sophie showed no visible reaction. "Guess what, Maman?" she continued in English. "I phoned Monique. Even Monique finds it hard to write term papers."

Danielle sat on Sophie's bed and caught her breath. "It was big of her to admit it, don't you think?" she joshed. "I have not been offered such confessions."

"She—she also said she wants to get away from us over Christmas."

"No news there. She's told your father and me that her roommate has invited her to Arizona."

"Do you know what I'm thinking, Maman? I wouldn't do what she's doing—going to the house of strangers in Arizona at Christmas. But that's probably because Monique wants more than me."

"Monique wants a lot that we'll never know about."

"Yeah." Sophie blinked. "So why did you bring those books, Maman?"

"I thought we could look at them together. But where are your roommates?" Danielle glanced at the other two well-made beds. "I see you've added more posters and pillows."

"And photos, too, Maman—look." Sophie was very pleased to guide her mother through a tour. Danielle thought that she would somehow make a life for herself, even though she wouldn't—couldn't—accomplish what Monique would. Sophie cared about making this room cozy, and that was a good sign. She would manage to stay up with the rest of them, on the surface of things. And only on the surface. Her mother's heart permitted Danielle to find this vision both frightfully inadequate and spiritually potent. In any case it did nothing to alleviate the effort and work that she put into the next three hours of tutoring. She made Sophie get out her course books, and after a look through them decided to start with biology; she was relieved to see that the table of contents was almost identical to that of the book she'd brought with her. Her aim was to make the contents of the first five chapters catch in her daughter's mind. It was as immense a struggle as she'd feared. And yet, by limiting herself to spoon-fed chunks, and initially not worrying too much about her success rate, Danielle did manage—reading aloud with an increasingly heavy and involuntary French accent and with many *"tu vois?"* exhortations—to cover topics like cell-organization and the similarities and differences in evolutions between man and the apes, and get Sophie to answer basic questions. By the end of the statistical presentation of gene-sharing and close description of DNA functioning, Danielle's tongue was sore and her mind in dry heaves from the strain. Out the window, the sun was setting. She was getting hungry and imagined that Sophie was, too. Her daughter was resisting complex sequences again. "Think, Sophie, think!" But no. Sophie went on smoothing out, like an idiot or a priestess, the ripples that reality kept making. At last fatigue and impatience snapped Danielle's tolerance in two. She shot up from her chair and blurted:

"Il faudra trouver un mari très riche, ma fille!" At this rate she'd better find a rich husband as quickly as possible, thought Danielle.

"Je le sais bien, Maman."

"You *know,* you?" Though Danielle feigned irony, a queer feeling shot through her. What made Sophie presume that this was the necessary scenario? What if Sophie sounded complacent because she embraced a destiny *she could intuit?*

It would explain a lot of things. To start with, it would explain why she didn't want to change her study habits. It could also be the reason why she was so calm, so accepting of circumstances. That would make Sophie endowed with something that she Danielle would give anything in the world to possess. *Sophie divined how her life was going to be.* Though there probably isn't a mother on earth who hasn't thought—hasn't fantasized—this about her child, Danielle's daughter wasn't little anymore; she was nineteen. It was unsettling to get an inkling about such a daughter.

Later, as Danielle drove home to New Jersey, she mulled over this half-conclusion of hers. She did not naturally ascribe good or bad luck to people. But a grain of good luck lodged in her daughter Sophie now. It lay dormant, not troubling anyone. For now Sophie remained the one who diligently painted and decorated the surface of life. And who struggled appallingly in most college subjects.

By the end of the week, driving back and forth daily to Shippendale, Danielle had hired two tutors for her.

*

Months passed. In spite of Monique's absence, Christmas was uneventful. Sophie frequently talked on the phone with her roommate-tutor Beth, who only lived thirty miles away. Danielle heard enough "Do-you-really think-so?"s come out of Sophie's mouth to feel confident that, without Monique, Sophie would discover more and more good things about herself. John's holiday thoughts went to his family in Gettysburg, and Danielle's to hers as well. She called Paris and spoke to her mother and Dédé. There was a pause between everything she said and every reply her brother mustered, which could not be explained away as the sound delay of international phone calls. It was too long and hollow a gap, and it made her ever so sad. She knew Dédé would never get better, but now she feared he might be getting worse. If only she could sit down next to her brother and squeeze his arm while she talked—to prompt his reply when it was his turn—the gap might disappear, she fantasized. Her mother didn't have time to stimulate him or even take him back to the doctor, for she had the café to run. And yet somehow all this wasn't big enough a push to send her to France now; Sophie needed her too much. Her eyes began to water as she hung up, and she had a brief cry, fixing on the gauzy white light trapped in her bedroom curtains.

Spring came long before Easter. They talked less frequently over the telephone to the girls. Monique didn't seem to have many friends, beyond the Peggy from Arizona who'd taken her home for Christmas, but claimed that she didn't mind and that she was really getting into running. She said that completing her four-mile daily jogging loop through the countryside provided the same little dose of elation as a heart to heart talk. For Monique, everything seemed to be going smoothly. Her parents never came to know that the first college term paper she wrote was marked "*unacceptable: see me*"; but after a horrendous night of wondering whether her perceptions fell short of university standards and if the genius that she and a couple of respected high school teachers believed she possessed was no better than B-level mediocrity, she rewrote the paper without going to see the professor and received a scolding for not coming but also an A-. There were other initiation rites naturally.

One night, for instance, while sitting on a mattress at a dorm-floor party, she felt a girl behind her massage the middle of her back with her foot. The situation caused tension in her jaw yet was also a novelty. She managed to keep her limbs loose and voice natural. Though it was a relief when the girl got up and walked away, her curiosity for the ambiguous—even the physically ambiguous—did not escape her.

A month before Spring Break she auditioned for and got a part in a theatre production of "The Apple Tree" that a guy named Ruben had arranged to put on at three state prisons as his Senior Project. Ruben was little and had a soft voice for a stage director. When you looked at him you noticed a lot of curly black hair on his body but not much on his head. The night he came back to her room with her after rehearsal, he rubbed oil into his fingertips very sensually and massaged her slowly for a hypnotically long time. When it got to be 2 am and her roommate hadn't come back, he slipped into bed with her and before going to sleep they made love. She didn't tell him that it was the first time she had had full sexual intercourse. It was all right as experiences went, though their bodies would have locked into place better if hers hadn't been a bit slippery from the oil. They remained a couple for as long as the show lasted, and, over Break, held hands in front of the prison inmates at the end of performances. When classes resumed, they stopped seeing each other so regularly. It was all very painless, open-ended and *unstructured*—so unlike with Jeffery in high school. Some weeks later, she went to bed with a trombone player named Gary, then because that didn't work out, spent a Saturday night again with Ruben. She wrote other term papers, which didn't seem as difficult as the first one...nothing seemed difficult now that she had found her physical and mental rhythm.

She received less notice in college than she had previously. She wasn't a twin, star student, or top actress here. She simply studied hard and cast her mental nets in as many waters as she could manage. She discovered the meaning of scholarship. By the end of the year, two professors in two different disciplines had encouraged her to undertake an honors project.

Though she had few friends and too many sexual partners, it was a quiet, happy period in her life.

It was at a time when John and Danielle weren't hearing much from the girls that they made a special trip to Gettysburg. As John had promised his brother Robert, they arrived early and stood supportively by as Robert's recently-sold house was being dismembered. John made comments galore about the quarry hole where the house next door had stood, and about the burnt remains of what had been the third house on the street, but it was difficult for him to express emotion about the ripping out and gutting of the sturdy gray "Cape Cod" that was taking place in front of them. Historical Society officers, flea market operators, restoration contractors, private individuals—they were all busy prying loose and carrying off its dark oiled woodwork, cabinets, floors, fireplace mantle, banister, faucets, and closet doors. His sister-in-law joked softly about the good quality of all that had been for years under her care. For a while her irony was welcome; they smiled in pain like people made to laugh by a funeral oration. Finally John said with a pat on his brother's back, "Well, Bob, I guess I've had enough." They walked back to their cars, eyes on their feet, John's hand on his brother's shoulder. Robert said that his daughter Pammy was waiting for them at the Battlefield Visitors Center, where she worked on Saturdays.

"There's a mini re-enactment of Pickett's Charge this afternoon. They do re-enactments at the drop of the hat now."

"Aren't you sick of them all, guy? After what you just saw done to your house?"

Robert snorted an embarrassed laugh. "You got up at the crack of dawn to come here. And you've never seen any of these re-enactments. I feel like watching Pickett's folly, that stupid dash across the field. I'm in the mood for that today. What does your wife say?—what do you say, Danielle? Want to see a bit of the American Civil War?"

Although Danielle thought it was a strange thing to do, she didn't say so. '*Ils sont foux les américains*' passed through her mind.

They followed Robert and Cindy in their car to the parking lot of the war museum and cyclorama. From the last time she was here, when the girls were little, Danielle remembered the great semi-dark corner of the museum's best room, where the tiny topographical lights of the panoramic map blinked white or red as the Battle of Gettysburg advanced through its fated three days and its fixed twenty-minute voice presentation. As they waited among the tour buses, she watched the 're-enactors' mulling about. She tried to gauge that kind of people they were, why they chose to dress up like this, all of them with the same double-breasted spill of gold buttons on their gray or blue army jacket. There were blond ruddy men with handle-bar moustaches and vintage wired spectacles. There were short dark-haired men with the glassy stare and hollowed cheeks of the real veterans in old photographs. There were big hefty fellows, whose guts overhung their belts and anchored them clearly in the over-fed twentieth century, making a travesty of their heart-felt masquerade. Above all, there wasn't a man without a rifle. Though a few in this growing crowd were in high spirits, most gave the impression of being ready to perform methodically and smartly. As if it were, by their standards, a proper and old-fashioned war for obedient heroes, she noted critically. She spotted a handful of women in long dresses and bonnets, and a few middle-school kids outfitted as drummer boys. These at least looked like normal paraders, the sort she'd seen on the 4th of July.

An unshaven man with a megaphone, walking backwards and waving his free hand, beseeched the bus-boarding army in the parking lot to follow the signs once they were let off along the Emmitsburg Road by the Peach Orchard. "Folks, we want to meet up past all those small white monuments, those obelisk things, at the High Water Mark. Got that? *That's* where General Pickett was aiming to break the Union line with his desperate charge. The monument we are concerned with looks like a big stone book, open to a page of history you could say." Past him and onto the buses lumbered flag bearers, cavalry, artillery men, a general or two with shiny swords and long gloves, medics with a field stretcher, and camp followers with cameras.

By the bus for the "Confederate Infantry", Danielle noticed a tall gaunt man dressed not properly as a Rebel but in jeans and a gray vest and with a black Stetson hat on. Straddling protectively a duffle bag between his feet, he listened attentively to two men, who told him something very quickly. She was noticing how unconvincingly American that cowboy hat looked when he drew out of his pocket a tell-tale chalky blue package of *Gauloise* cigarettes. When he had one lit, he bent over and pulled out of his duffle bag a piece of paper and waved it at the backs of those two men walking away, calling loudly and belligerently, "It's not just!" in a heavy French accent. This made the slighter of the two men turn suddenly around and double back on his steps

"I hear you, Frenchie. I told you I hear you. You've never had any trouble with your gun in Customs before, but you could have explained better about it being a relic not a weapon. It's certainly not my fault you had it confiscated."

The Frenchman took off his hat. Long stringy black hair fell nearly to his shoulders. "I have no gun, man. The battle is about to start, man."

"I know, stay calm. You remember Mike from the last time you came? Mike's such a good guy, Frenchie, that he's found a friend who'll be lending you a rifle. Now you still got your uniform and your hat, don't ya, so relax." The man gave him a 'good ol' boy' box in the upper arm, and went his way again.

The Frenchman took out another Gauloise to smoke and looked directly at Danielle, who was standing a couple of yards away, reciprocating her interest. She surprised him with her French, coming over to him to say that she didn't find it logical to expect re-enactments to go any more smoothly than real battles.

He grinned. She calculated that he had to be at least fifteen years younger than her. Out of curiosity she asked him his name. He said that it was Thierry.

Why do you come to these war games in America, Thierry?, she inquired.

His eyes lit up. He described the experience as fantastic. Everything had been *formidable* till today. How could Customs take his antique gun away like that? He explained that he was from Tours, where he'd become friends with an American exchange student who had invited him home to Colorado a few summers ago and taken him along to a "living pioneer town." After this marvelous experience, in a place where for a while you lived beyond your time and culture as men should be able to do, he'd found out about and started coming over annually from France to American Civil War reenactments. Danielle didn't understand what kind of job he had, or if his family in France was rich; he gave her no proper clues as to what kind of Frenchman he was and she'd been out of the country too long to know on her own. He was a curious type, she decided, and maybe even an oddball. That he was young, however, made her inclined to like him. Thierry continued to harp on his confiscated rifle, his ridge of cheekbones set in motion on every puff. How was he going to get back his fine old gun-- which he'd just had cleaned and re-oiled? *Merde*, why should the police bother him like that when there were plenty of criminals with illegal weapons to go after?

Although Danielle was beginning to weary of the subject by now, she said that one could live in a country for a very long time, like herself, and still feel that that Americans-- or whoever the natives were—were crazy.

He agreed. She asked if he was going to participate anyway and he said he was. She said that she and her husband could give him a lift down the battlefield road to the rendezvous point. He politely declined.

"Bon. Allez. Au revoir," she said.
"Au revoir."

She watched him circle with his canvas bag around the big parked chartered buses. She lost and caught sight of him several times. He did not look her way

She didn't expect to see him again.

She didn't expect that only an hour later he would be there in midfield, his hands over his beetle-bent body to protect his head, shrieking and stomping his feet in a small clearing within a quivering fleshy knot of sooty-faced men.

"What the fuck's he doing?" she heard. One of the men who'd spoken with Thierry by the bus ran past her on the left, followed by a Park Ranger and a sheriff.

"Frenchie! Frenchie!" the same man hollered. "What are you doing with real bullets? A guy's been shot!"

She was alone. John had dropped her here and gone off to the sharpshooters' re-enactment at Devil's Den. The migrating, muttering crowd, half of whom were in costume, suddenly cut Thierry off from view. She could hear him shouting at their idiocy in the language that he and she shared. He was pelting them with as many of his incomprehensible words as he could. He yelled that he'd been tricked, that he'd been had by the man who sold him what was supposed to be a gun with blanks. *Where was he? Assassin! Le vrai coupable!*

There was no movement, no reaction to this by the crowd. A police car with its blue thimble lights reveling on top cruised off the battleground avenue into Pickett's field and stopped alongside the ambulance, inside which the doctors and medics were attending to the wounded man, who apparently had been shot in the shoulder. After ten minutes during which nothing new happened, the bonneted woman standing in front of Danielle lost interest in the goings-on and left, pulling her drummer-boy son after her. This allowed Danielle to catch sight of Thierry again. He was handcuffed and being frisked. He had lost his dark Stetson hat and his hair seemed even longer, more unwashed and Parisian. He looked even younger than she'd first thought. *A victim of an ugly prank. A misjudged youth. Un français.* She felt for him. When the ambulance turned on its siren and nosed its way to the avenue, she was able to edge her way closer to him. The police were leading Thierry to the squad car. *"C'est pas possible! Pas possible!"* he yelled.

She came a final step forward. "Thierry," she said kindly.

His eyes stopped on her; his oaths spilled her way now, they were for her.

To the policeman who had him by the elbow she offered her service as interpreter.

"Don't worry, Ma'am," said the cop briskly. "We know he's hopping mad."

"You don't understand. Someone sold him that gun without him knowing about the bullets."

"I imagined that's what he was screaming about. A pretty strange story. But the judge will decide."

Why couldn't a strange story be true? A chill went through her. *And what was the meaning of 'strange'? Who did strange things—strangers?*

"*Ils sont des cons! Il sont foux!*" Thierry was drooling. The seed of his words splattered the road as a cop nudged him into the backseat and slammed the door.

Tears came to Danielle's eyes, and she bit her lip to keep from speaking. She just had to sit down somewhere. The rift between "us" and "them" reopened inside her and made her chest burn. She went blindly towards the monument shaped like a big stone book and slumped against its base. Re-enacters were mulling around aimlessly and uncertain about what to do, their charge across the wheat field having ended before it really began. No one noticed her for the half hour to took John to come back for her.

When he saw Danielle's estranged, teary face and heard the news—from the same unshaven man with the megaphone as before—that a Frenchman had been arrested and charged with shooting a man, he steered her out of the crowd and off the battlefield. Without taking the time for full goodbyes to his brother's family, he drove her out of Gettysburg. She sat limply next to him, watching the road and the bare rolling hills. He didn't raise the subject of Terry's arrest with her. He was convinced that she was thinking something along the lines of '*I hate this country.*'

But Danielle was not silently raging. Nor was she in the throes of crippling nostalgia. She was feeling very cool and mentally alert, at grips with a potent question. *Couldn't the dirty trick that was played on Thierry happen in France? No, it couldn't. But who was she fooling? Of course it could happen. It would be different, however. She would take it differently.*

They reached Route 30. John turned on the car radio; he tuned it, listened to it, retuned it, and listened receptively.

Too bad he couldn't do the same thing with his wife.
She was coming to a decision.

*

She didn't wait long-- just three or four days-- before she called Sophie at Shippendale to tell her—to command her: *"Bon, ca suffit. On rentre en France."* France at last. She and Sophie off to Paris for the entire summer. Only Sophie. She didn't want Monique. She didn't want all the words that Monique could utter. Anyway, Monique would want to work at the Medical Library summer job she'd lined up for herself. John couldn't take off that kind of time from work, so she was spared having to tell him that she didn't want him along either. Fortunately, he didn't make a fuss over the money it would cost, but he was not at all happy. He didn't like her going, he said, because he couldn't be sure that she would come back. The rest of their conversation went more or less as she expected:

"Why is Monique's taking the exam for Sophie all right but someone's fooling with Frenchie's gun so heinous?"

"It's a gun, John."

"A gun? For you, it's only because he's a foreigner. That's what makes that trick so savage. You told me so yourself. Be fair, Danielle. What if you'd seen me-- or me you-- as "just a foreigner" on that Paris street? "

"We are destined to return to that."

With a finger she solemnly traced a circle in the air. For a moment his old fear came back to him of Divorce, of her leaving him for good—for didn't she with that gesture want to say that they had come 'full-circle'? Or did she mean something else? He compared the two scenes from 1944 and today. There had been a gun (his) the day he met her and there was a gun in the picture now too...

"Oh hell," he said with profound irritation. "We aren't destined to anything."

Maybe it simply was that the circle Danielle traced referred to a different starting point from the ones John imagined. In any case, irony had it that at the end of the summer, Danielle came back to America, peace of a sort made between France and herself. It was Sophie whom the family "lost" over there. Just like after her accident, Sophie returned home and yet in a sense didn't return.

The accident this time, however, was a wonderful thing.

Sophie was in love; Sophie wasn't the same.

PART TWO

CHAPTER SEVEN

Matt Gagliardi arrived in Paris in that state of shocked fatigue that comes from a sleeping car pounding through the countryside for hours in the dark. He walked the noisy length of concrete platform as if it were a hushed pathway; it led from that train and its Italian dirt to the studio apartment off Avenue Daumesnil where for three or four indispensable hours he wouldn't have to use his voice or think about anything other than what gave him pleasure to think about: the goodbye scene in Venice. His mind returned to it, and returned and returned, without breaking the secret code that would make understanding possible but destroy the sweetness.

Paris was chilly at the end of August, the sidewalks still damp with an old rain. He got to the tiny apartment in full possession of the moment of saying goodbye to Lorenza as the vaporetto docked at the station. Annually he'd made this pilgrimage, since their meeting in a museum the spring he'd made his end-of-med-school tour of Italy. He had a recollection of all eight of their goodbye scenes, of the light and time of day and what, of all things, he was holding: once, he remembered quite vividly, he was grasping his own knees, and feeling as if he were out at sea, as he sat in the low old couch in her icy living room with its medieval sloping floor. Another time, he was clasping a dripping, empty mussel shell at a canal-side trattoria table. Again he heard her say in Italian, coaxingly at first, "Matt, I think this is too hard to keep up." ...She was such a strong and rigidly principled woman... and yet she could yield all of a sudden, too. All he had to do was insist—and somehow engage, more than her love, her empathy again. Lorenza could make all sorts of concessions when she started empathizing. He'd overheard her taking phone calls from friends and even students while he lay quietly next to her in bed. In those moments she seemed to wrap her voice, like the arms of a Queen of Humanism, around the thing that was affecting the other person adversely and, as if this wrong were only a naughty child, find some way to make the other feel better, even urging him or her to take measures that she herself would never consider. In the case of their relationship, it was important for this empathy of hers not to turn to pity; he tried his best to keep her feeling charmed and intrigued by him. He liked saying goodbye on a light note. This time, they exchanged a joke-"I can't look at a cauliflower without thinking of you"-"What about me, with my pantry full of all your rice!" -and this lightness prepared the way for the rebound in a year's time. As always, they waved at each other, waved the other off into a future which already lay like an unkempt garden between them. During the train's charging pull away from the shimmering lagoon, he felt—well, the word was satisfied—satisfied with how much, upon reflection, he hadn't said to her. There was a preservative power in saying less.

He unlocked the low, temperamental door of the small studio in Paris' 12ème that as of a year ago he co-owned with two old drinking buddies from medical school. Both of them, Mark and Phil, had "seen the light" (this was their little joke) and followed him into radiology, a specialization that vaunted astonishingly high salaries (at the right private clinics), good hours, and almost no interaction with patients. After a trip to Paris together one spring, they'd decided to buy a place for them and their families to use on visits. They were buying a lot of property actually—whims that doubled as financial investments; Mark had recently bought a golf course outside Philadelphia, and Phil a stable of race horses in Florida—while he himself was drawn to business ventures. At present he was toying with the idea of sending his youngest and jobless brother Pete to Italy. This week he'd talked to their cousin Mario, who'd moved from Naples to Padua and was a printer, about opening a small graphics and publishing center there. He'd heard the industry was really taking off, and Pete, an English major who could write a nice story when he decided to, could try his hand at those clever pop-up books for children that were so hot in Europe right now. Though talking to Mario made for a real reason to come to Italy again soon, he hadn't mentioned it to Lorenza. Not telling her put another twist in his spiral of secrecy.

Throwing himself on the beige sofa--the whiff of things French filled his lungs as he sunk his face in the pillows for a moment--he thought, yes, a *spiral of secrecy,* that describes it. In the dark behind his shut eyes, he descended a dark circular stairway. He knew it was a fantasy—a fatigue-induced day dream—but he stayed inside it because it felt like self-exploration. Along his descent, there were nooks and niches. Lorenza was in one of those. In a "place" that he could ignore—had *always been able to* ignore—for long stretches at a time. Incredible, wasn't it? He rolled over on the sofa and thought about what he liked to take for granted. He had to admit that the hours spent in bed with her were unfailingly a time of homecoming. Yet when he left Venice at the end of his stay, she receded into her niche within his spiral of secrecy. She remained uninvolved in his life, cast no real influence. Except for a residual smudge of sweetness, he could almost swear that for eleven and a half months a year he didn't recall that she existed.

For a while he continued to lie dawdling on the beige couch, fixing out the window on a black balcony railing. He watched the cracking apart of the solid gray sky into puffy clouds that then spurned each other. Into one of these gaps squeezed a smallish sun. At some point Matt nodded off. After his sleep he scrounged himself up a lunch of a fried egg and buttered noodles. He turned on the radio for a while, tracking the richness of the French voices closely, the way leave-takers do. He had four days more in Paris before heading home to the States and his medical duties.

In the afternoon, after a visit for no particular reason to Notre Dame, he went to what he bragged in America was 'his café.' The old woman owner and her giant son with that dumb stare, oily front cowlick and white tennis shoes in all weather, appeared to have family visiting them.

There was a woman who looked to be in her forties, fine china-like in her cheekbones and wrists, and wearing an expertly-flung and middle-aged silk scarf around her neck: her eyes were blinking blue almonds, exactly like those of the café owner, Madame Marinette. Matt saw the same nose on the dumb man's face and concluded she was daughter and sister to them. She in turn had a daughter of her own, whose long brown hair swept the small of her back and whose choice of a drink seemed to be a glass of green milk. As he sipped his beer at the table adjacent, the granddaughter glanced his way, switching her hair. *My word. That's Lorenza's expression*, he thought. It wasn't just the identical look of pleasant curiosity, either: no, she had Lorenza's build—those slim thighs, thin arms, small breasts, and even the same sort of hair, though longer. The similarity was all his to enjoy. The girl couldn't begin to guess what he was marveling at, nor where, in what inner forest of private unsharables, his thoughts were taking him. He ordered a second beer and made small talk with the girl in French. She confirmed that Marinette was her grandmother. He noticed a sudden blank, undiscriminating glance or two, which would be explained by the fact that this girl—Sophie, she said her name was—was so young. Twenty! He knew from his tours of museums and the bit of Art History that he'd studied that a portrait or a statue usually exalted certain features of the real-life original even while it failed to conserve others; perhaps for that, this young woman who looked like Lorenza appealed to him. Certainly, he hadn't looked twice at a woman this young before. In his thirties now, with a romantic past filled with accusations from ex-girlfriends of not "giving of himself enough," which were counterbalanced by the security that Lorenza annually restored in him, he remained convinced of his own receptiveness to sweetness. If inundated, if loved in some unimaginably new way, he might even consider...loving selflessly in return.

"Les 'Etats-Unis," she was saying.

"Hey," replied Matt in his native flat accent. "You're American?"

She talked a little about New Jersey. About living across the Delaware from Philadelphia. "Sorry, I'm tired," he said on a yawn. "Just got in from Venice. Have you ever been there?"

He came back to the café to see her at breakfast. Sophie appeared through the rear service door by the stairs which led up to Grandmère Marinette's third floor apartment. Croissant in hand, he rose from his little table while she greeted her grandmother and uncle.

"How's it going this morning?" he asks. His smile seems enormous to her: she can see almost all of his teeth, and an impressive count of teeth like that, she thinks, comes of more than a simple good mood. She tells him it's her birthday.

"It's really your birthday?"

She nods, full of odd feelings. Now that he knows this, he knows so much, doesn't he? He can, well, he can calculate her zodiac sign now, or ask her how old she is, or discover that she has a twin sister or more. It's my birthday, she thinks, and I've given him a present.

After they chat about how much hotter the summer is in Philadelphia than in Paris, she excuses herself to go to the toilet, and when she returns there's a small foil-wrapped chocolate by her cup, which he's bought from Marinette.

"Thank you," she says.

"Just a little something," he replies. "And so now how's it going?" Along with the question come the same smile and eyes— such small narrow slits those eyes are, covering most of themselves and yet giving of themselves too, she thinks.

"It's a nice day," she says. That bit of chocolate tastes good. She wonders what is going to happen next and feels seized by the sort of cheerfulness that might just as easily come of a good chess move when, glancing at their empty cups, he asks her if she happens to be free for a walk this morning.

"Oh yes, I'm free," she says candidly.

A birthday walk, he calls it.

The old woman, Marinette, watches them go with a pleasant 'au revoir, Monsieur.' With her granddaughter she exchanges an unreadable look. It's gusty and still cool on the street. The wind picks up and twirls the small bits of litter before herding them in a driving line along the curb. Sophie's hair shoots up, flaps, whips, and she has to stop and tuck it inside under her light raincoat.

"How's it going? OK?"

"More than OK" is her reply this time. She wants to come up with new answers for him, not repeat herself. She feels that he's saying a world of lovely things to her every time he asks that good-natured question. As if he had her well-being at heart, and would like her to feel better and better, happier and happier, in his presence.

While they are crossing the gardens of the Tuileries, he tells her how close he and his brothers and sister are, how they try to stay united now that their mother is fighting cancer. She hovers on the subject but doesn't drive a hole into his experience, doesn't pry the can open, as it were. Like Lorenza. She tells him about having a twin sister, their growing up, their being at different colleges. He does not find Monique's existence remarkable, and she doesn't wonder about this being natural or unnatural but sees it simply as a sign of how well they understand each other. She chooses the details of her life with the lady-like technique of managing a fork and knife in a restaurant, wishing all of a sudden that he'd take her hand or something. She imagines her hand under his often enough that when it briefly happens a half an hour or so later, she feels much relief in her pleasure.

They have ended up at the Louvre and tour galleries that each on his or her own has already seen this week. Sophie walks back up to the small ivory explanatory cards, the ones she's already seen and forgotten, connecting what she's read and forgotten once again to the paintings; taking a slow step back—again— she pauses in the informed stillness where all the pleasure comes... Yet it is a different pause from before because Matt and she are side by side, and this silent acquisition of time and space is also of each other. She eyes him, then the paintings, then him, then another painting, her senses charging on a voltage of color and perception and curiosity.

He asks if she'd like a sandwich. She almost tells him that there's a good chance she'll never be troubled by hunger again, but, instead, she eats with him (like a goddess not needing it) because she wants to see him chew and swallow, wants to watch that up close, sitting next to him. Every so often during lunch he raises her hand and smiles and says, "How's it going?" He's asked this so often by now that it appears to be a tic but also a way of making constant fresh approaches—as if his question could get her to confess things which would in turn lead him to confess things of an increasingly romantic nature. When he asks it in a comic voice, it comes off so well that she laughs, and he grins and says, "Boy, I wish you'd do that again." And so she laughs again, and he's nourished here in this moment with her, she feels, in a way he couldn't be anywhere else because she feeds his smiles back to him...making them bigger.

They show up at Marinette's café at aperitif hour. Matt wolfs down the tartines Sophie's uncle puts in front of them, enthusiastically plucking up even the crumbs on the plate, and then drinks the *ballon de rouge* in two gulps, talking happily and disparagingly about New Jerseyites with Danielle, coping with his straight black Italian hair that he parts on one side and that keeps going into his eyes as he swings round-- once, then again-- so as not to stand with his back to anyone, talking more now than all afternoon put together, certain of every quip and gesture.... closing his mouth for a judicious moment only when it comes time to ask her, in front of Maman and Grandmère, if he can take her out to dinner somewhere. After she has said yes, Sophie turns to her mother behind the counter and starts telling her in French what she thinks of this, then realizes that this won't do, for Matt understands French. The vigilant eyes of Danielle and Marinette display discriminating interest now in the beginnings of romance. Maman tells them to have fun.

Another day passes. Matt and Sophie hold hands as if that were the only proper way to walk down the street. Over a *steak-frites,* Matt tells her that he is leaving Paris early in the morning. He tells her more about his radiology practice in the States. He confesses he's not on leave or in early semi-retirement, which is the romantic impression that he's given, but just on a short vacation here. Her eyes hunt for a safer place to perch than on his. That is the extent of her surprise. That also is like Lorenza. He thinks about how things have gone so fast and well between them. Too simple and easy perhaps? But there's something she has that attracts him greatly; he pauses to reflect if this is another similarity to Lorenza but decides that it is uniquely hers. She has a knack for coming out of a silence as if from an important dream. This both relaxes and stirs him. It hints of other talents, a tangle of the spiritual and the erotic. She is young and yet to reach her prime, and he wants to continue this relationship. He can manage more than a tuck of sweetness once a year; he can tackle "the real thing" that his buddies Mark and Phil don't think him capable of.

They spend the rest of the evening necking on a park bench, necking in the corner of one café, and then necking in the corner of another....The waiter, a stern older man, pecks Matt on the shoulder and tells them that he's lost all patience. They almost don't understand why. They rise together in a perfectly executed and unrehearsed choreography of offense-taking. Matt pays; she puts on her raincoat and slowly raises her mane of hair from out from under the collar. In this brief physical separation—the first in three hours—provoked by the surly waiter, Matt says that he's got to go back to his apartment and pack. It's after midnight and his flight is in five hours.

It's a short walk to Marinette's building, during which he ascertains that she is definitely not upset--the way (needless to say) that Lorenza would not be. For an instant, maybe because it is so late, he half-expects that the two of them will feel compelled now to talk about pointlessness-- even hears suddenly in his mind a few of the words he uses yearly in Italian with Lorenza; instead, Sophie fishes a pen and a slip of paper from her purse and begins writing. He watches the words New Jersey, upside down, being formed.

"Wait. We don't need to do that yet,' he says, a glance at his watch. He can afford to spend another five or ten minutes with her. "We have time!"

She repeats his words "we have time." She's repeated various phrases of his over the last few days. Yet what a powerful effect her echoes have on him! It's as if they gave *his* words a longer life, granting them precious extra seconds in which to complete their sense. He has enjoyed this, and now the thought that he'll have to do without this enchanting magnification, makes him want her so much and so rashly that he considers missing his plane.

"I'll call you," he promises, "as soon as I land." Then with a brisk, embarrassed "Bye now, bye!" he walks away quickly. If she says something, he doesn't hear it. For him to be able to leave, it's crucial that he have the last word.

Matt Gagliardi and Sophie Morton began to see a lot of each other in the States, starting in September of 1973. Almost every Saturday, and for two years straight, after Sophie and her tutors had struggled for the week with her sophomore-year courses, Matt drove from Philly to Shippendale, and the two of them went for little trips all over southern or central Pennsylvania, spending the night in a motel. There came a hiatus both years at Christmas time, which each spent with the family (in Sophie's case just with her parents, because Monique continued to decline to come home), but for New Year's Eve they were together again, for Matt drove to the Morton's house in New Jersey, had lunch with her parents and her, then took Sophie to the theatre in the city.

Remembering how loquacious Matt had been over aperitifs at her mother's café, and not knowing how much out of character that was, Danielle was surprised that first New Year's Eve to find him so private, and pleasant but uncommunicative. He was the kind of young professional that you can tell feels at ease and open to all subjects but prefers to ask questions—quite intelligent questions-- rather than volunteer his experiences or (even though John kept pouring drinks) risk any personal stand beyond the admission that he'd discovered in time that while he liked medicine he didn't like dealing much with patients directly and so had gone into radiology. He seemed in love with Sophie, but there was something about him that made her wonder and hope that he'd offer enough of himself to Sophie in the future. John thought he was probably being vague on purpose, to avoid seeming full of himself, though conversely he gave the impression of someone who underneath all that politeness felt justly rewarded by life.

"You know, I started seeming shabbier and shabbier," John said afterwards to Danielle.

Though she'd read in the newspaper that specialists like Matt could make half a million dollars a year—counting their investments, she thought he was overreacting. "Why should his being successful be bad for Sophie? Thank God he is. Any other sort of man, in Sophie's case, would really be a worry. And don't you say anything to her. Don't tell her what you think."

"Why would I go telling Sophie anything?" John replied peevishly. "But there's another thing. He's twelve years older than her. Why should he want such a young girlfriend?"

"You're so square-headed. You can't accept that love has a thousand faces. What's twelve years, anyway?," Danielle shot back. Though they'd been getting along all right since her return from France, she and John had moments of insufferance for each other, and even episodes which got appallingly melodramatic, real snarls and sharp moans and the like. They'd never done any of that in the past with the girls around. The oddest thing was that the more histrionics there were, the easier it seemed to forget afterwards. It was a rapid and painless erasing. For Danielle, it was a question of pouring herself a glass of wine and retreating into another room where she closed the door. The nastier and more hysterical the clash had been, the more it seemed afterwards that it simply couldn't have taken place. She felt peculiarly calm, calm enough to imagine herself going and finding him and giving him a sisterly kiss, profoundly calm the way one gets after a mental hurricane, at the end of a turbulence that troubles the psyche with upheaval but leaves the body with its lazy right not to change an iota about reality.

Occasionally in this same peculiar calmness she wondered, "why didn't France do anything, show me anything or anyone, to keep me there?" She meant both this past summer and after the war. How easy it had been to leave her country in 1946. How impossible it felt at the end of her visit last August to remain there. The body with its lazy right not to change an iota about reality. But it had been more complicated than that.

She had helped her mother almost daily at the café, and with them poor Dédé, serving tables with shaking hands and an immobilized neck, taking orders with his empty eyes. Paris was not Paris when she was in the same room as her brother. Yet even when Dédé wasn't around, she did not feel the rightness she was in search of. If on the one hand, her fellow Parisians treated her as a native, and all the buildings and streets were so wonderfully familiar, and she herself felt well-disposed towards and curious about the new faces and personalities around her, she was disoriented by the acronyms of the new political parties, *la droite* and *la gauche* movements, the different procedures at the post office, the odd slang words, the American jeans in the stores and the strange prices in post-war francs. She had expected to shed her feelings of distance, her sense of solitude and of living in a suspended present. Though these lessened, she found herself feeling less competent and functioning at a slower pace. Sometimes at the end of a tiring day at the café, she wished that she could do her socializing according to the American rules of superficial politeness which she knew by heart, and which after years came more spontaneous to her than those of French. And having become inclined during those many years in New Jersey to expressing unchecked emotions in French, she found that she wasn't always as wary or self-concealing as she should be in her conversations, especially with strangers

She did have one exceptional day of well-being, however. That was the afternoon she went to see Françoise, her old comrade from the Underground, now living in a concrete apartment tower out in Créteil. Danielle had planned to take Sophie with her, but because the visit fell on one of those four days when Sophie was falling in love with Matt Gagliardi, she had to go alone. The splendid thing that she would always remember was Françoise's long self-confession, witty, ironic, and relentlessly honest. A torrential stream of words that left no aspect untouched of the last thirty years: miscarriage of a child by an American soldier of her own, surviving the next few years in the old neighborhood, marriage to a baker, secretarial job, feminist marches, lover, her son Jacques. The two of them sat in a small, sham imitation of an aristocratic parlor, so proper and fanatically petit bourgeois that she feared at first that the afternoon would be a disaster. Instead, what a candid outpouring Françoise gave her from the heart!

And yet she couldn't convey to Françoise—or to her mother or to anyone in France—her love and hate for America, the half-conscious roots she'd put down there, the habits that were now hers and the thinking that was now half-hers. She could tell them—

because she was capable of sincere self-confession herself—but they couldn't really understand. They could say they did, but *she would know the difference.*

This knowing the difference was the bane of her life.

*

It happened on a Saturday shortly after their second Easter together. Matt was visiting Sophie at Shippendale as usual when he went down the dorm hall to call his sister from the pay phone and learned that Mama had died in her hospital bed at dawn. Diane in her thickest voice wanted to know when he was coming and he assured her that it would be immediately. It wasn't a long call, neither one of them wanting to break down, not yet. He walked once around Sophie's room, his mind and heart racing after his mother, while the cry "Mama!" —the way he used to say it—came and faded and came again in his head. Without thinking twice, he asked Sophie if she'd come with him. They exchanged a look, and perhaps she just said "yes"—he barely was registering anything at this point, but she straight away got her purse.

"We'll have to stay a few days. There's the wake... the funeral," he said.

She thought aloud, "I should wear black."

"Oh good heavens, babe, just take some pajamas and a change of clothes." He guided her by the shoulder to her sliding closet door; he felt the mesh of his persuasive maleness with her convinced femaleness (and he was desperate for such comfort in his love right now) and he knew, as his hands touched her lightly around the waist, that whatever he needed to ask her now she would take it upon herself to do.

For the next three days Sophie let the grief of the *famiglia Gagliardi* fling a black veil over everything for her. She and the close-knit Neapolitan clan that was Matt's family met for the first time in the funeral parlor's viewing room, a square windowless vault with an apron of ceiling-to-floor drapery, where she returned their hugs under the coffin-directed spotlights, introduced to no one but immediately recognized by all. She understood they'd been expecting her. As the girl in love with Matt, she willingly participated in this sorrow, didn't she? Ah then, that very slightly softened the blow, very very slightly dulled the loss, and barely perceptibly lessened the burden of accepting the silence and stillness of Frances Gagliardi, who was where no mother and wife who is loved should ever be: very very far away and never coming back.

This small intermittent consolation she brought covered the span of the three days. They themselves alluded to her innocuously romantic presence. One of Matt's brothers murmured, "I'm sorry you never knew Mama. She would have liked you." Matt's sister said, "She loved the idea that Matt met you in Paris like that". And Matt's father, who had been mute most of the time, in the car during the procession to the cemetery turned abruptly to say to her, as if he'd received the supernatural communication at that precise moment: "Up in Heaven she sees you. She knows. She's happy."

Sophie Morton had never comforted—or been found to be comforting to others—in such a way before. As she lay down to sleep each of those three nights at Diane's house, she had the odd sensation that she'd become more adult during the day. She guessed that this might be on account of the new, though indirect, brush with death. In any case, as she closed her eyes each of those three nights, her only thoughts were for Matt's family, who she was trying to second-guess and comfort with her best emotions.

Matt's father, for instance, sat again, squat and reddish and with a lumpy beer belly, in the front row of chairs at the wake, staring at his own fat entwined thumbs. Sophie had heard that he was an uneducated mason and that he had whipped Matt and his brothers and sister as children and had even smacked his wife across the mouth in the kitchen with relatives present, but what she *saw* the first day she saw him and now every night were his shoulders: how inconsolable and alone a person could become in the shoulders. On her way back from the coffin, Matt's sister Diane slipped into the chair beside him and patted his arm. She was a legal secretary and, Matt said, a feminist who had never gotten over their father's refusal, or inability, to send her to college. In the silence of that room, Sophie watched Diane's open hand come down gently on her father's arm. Then over her own right shoulder Sophie felt a warm male breath —not Matt's, though he frequently used the same words: "How are you doing? OK?" This was followed, on her left shoulder, by a squeeze... which made both her and Matt, sitting beside her, turn, for the Talker and the Squeezer were his brothers. And since Tom and Pete looked earnest, which is not a very common expression in young men past the age of thirty and underscored the terrible specialness of this long tiring ritual, Matt felt prompted to whisper to her as well: "OK? OK, babe?" Though her reaction was quite small—a nod and nothing more—she felt happy.

In precisely the same way that the three Gagliardi bothers flanked her then, they flanked her at night before she went to sleep when she craved something felicitous to think about. Matt, Tom and Pete. And every so often, the fleeting, sympathetic addition of Diane, which shot warmth down her arms and made her shift into a final position in bed, the one that admitted sleep. Matt, Tom, Pete, and Diane. Sophie spent so much time thinking about them and feeling for and with them that she made profound discoveries about their smallest ways of coping and their most emotional memories. Having sat, for hours running and over three days, next to or behind them in their composed row in this church-like place, she had the privilege of seeing the fine-stranded workings of the brotherhood that united them.

By the time Frances Gagliardi had had graveside dirt thrown on her coffin and been lowered into the ground on a sunny spring afternoon, Sophie Morton felt solemn love for the entire clan. If authentic life wasn't this, the display of the Gagliardi family's most sincere emotions, intact under the inky film of their irritations and despair, what was it, she reasoned?

On the drive back to Shippendale, Matt asked her to marry him. And she said yes.

CHAPTER EIGHT

The big event in 1977 was held not near the Mortons' place but—seeing that the groom was footing the bill—200 miles to the north, in a white Catholic cathedral cleaving the elevated, deteriorating neighborhoods of Orange, New Jersey, where some Gagliardi cousin served as parish priest.

For the length of the northbound foray through the green woods of the New Jersey Parkway, Danielle, in the chiffon dress expected of the bride's mother, radiated curiosity. A bright inquisitiveness had become her existential trademark since her return from France. The result was that she went to this wedding of Matt's and Sophie's distant and unsupervised arranging (so strange it was not to have double-checked Sophie's choices—but of course Matt did that now) in a state of receptivity that neither John nor Monique, riding with her in the car, believed to be sincere. John said all the dour things he usually said when obliged to meet or mingle with anyone too wealthy or charismatic. He harped on about Matt introducing himself to Sophie in Marinette's café. "Is that anything to base a marriage on? Why should a rich man have to get himself a date that way?"

"I met you over a dead man's body in the street," said Danielle.

He groaned.

"We could have attended the rehearsal dinner last night instead of letting Sophie down," she added.

"Are you forgetting that Monique was flying in then?"

"I don't forget anything, believe me."

"Damn it, Danielle!"

"John, watch the road!"

Monique spoke up. "Why don't you two get away from each other for a while?" This was precisely what she and David were doing this weekend. David was her most important love as yet. He had urged her to go to the wedding: it wouldn't be as bad as she thought, he said; she should get a proper look at who her twin sister had become after almost four years; and he thought she should go "because when I was a kid, we had to go to all our cousins' weddings, even when it meant crossing four states, in that, our mother said, it was the last time we'd probably see them again. She was right." It had made her feel very tender towards him given the circumstances. He was trying to soothe her and at the same time persuade her: that was one of the nicest things about David. "If she's really hateful or awful, that'll be it. You can let the ghost rest."

"It'll cost a lot to fly there, David."

"Everything costs, honey." He tickled her chin. She ran her palm down his cheek. "Anything but regret goes on a credit card," he said jovially. Good cheer was a precious commodity to the two of them right then. A month earlier they'd found out that David's M.A. fellowship was taking him to England, far from any of Monique's still-open possibilities. In the space of four weeks, they'd been through many phases, the strangest of which were surely the days of ignoring the catastrophe altogether, compensated by the hours suffered through as if poisoned-and-waiting-to-die. Meanwhile, as happened with these things, the paperwork and correspondence necessary to make the fellowship take on life, got done. The looming separation seemed a blind bluff for two intellectual lemmings doomed to leap off. Yet there was something beautiful all of a sudden too, for until that final leap happened, they felt so much eager desire for each other that every night, every opening of a half hour in the day, was a frantic celebration of present possibility. As the date approached for Sophie's wedding, it seemed increasingly impossible for her to leave David-- now-- for three whole days. At the last minute she would call her parents and the airline and--.

"You're just scared of going to that damned wedding."

"I'm not scared."

"That's CRAP, Monique."

Suddenly they were fighting. She'd never seen him like that, so altered by this weird little conviction. It was as if he were afraid for himself, that he needed to be sure she was capable of flying off on her own mission in life, without him. That she wouldn't even go off to her sister's wedding put him in a panic.

It was a bad bad fight. Monique sat on that Chicago-Philly flight, consoling herself with her free drink, wondering if this immense hurt was making her feel more child-like or childish. What had till that morning seemed a heart-wrenchingly solitary weekend trip began to shape up into a dry, tearless, investigation of the world she had been determined to forget: the world as lived by Sophie.

Her blunt question to her parents in the car was also as dry as dry could be.

Her father's reply was utterly predictable. "Your mother's got to make peace with the woman she might have become." He shook his head. "Somehow, someday."

"What about your own need to make peace with who you could have been?" Monique asked her father.

"Bof," interjected Maman lackadaisically.

They drove on. The road felt like a groove. They listened to the radio weather report. "It's so gray, so ugly and rainy for February." She'd heard that her sister and Matt were planning to wait a year after his mother's death, in keeping with Italian tradition, but the appeal of getting married on Valentine's Day had apparently been too strong. "What a wedding day," Monique sentenced.

"Sophie's going to have a beautiful life," Maman rebutted. The phrase hung like a challenge over all three.

"Is that based on something? Other than his money, I mean?" said Monique, in truth, quite unthinkingly.

Maman twisted round in her seat to scrutinize her rubbing her knee caps through her pink satin dress. "You're jealous," she murmured. Then to Dad: "Oh stop making that sour face, John. Will you please tell me WHY you think Sophie's not going to be in the position to be happy?"

"I don't take any of it seriously."

"What is there to take seriously or not seriously?" Maman muttered in a starchy way, as if with starch she could iron out her initial doubts about Matt in Paris. "You and Monique are impossible. As soon as we get there I'm losing you in the crowd."

"Losing you is the word all right, only it takes years," Dad murmured. "Now let me concentrate on the road."

"Look at Monique-- she's all concentrated on something herself." The three of them exchanged a glance—and burst out laughing.

"You know, I had to marvel," said Monique openly then. "I had to marvel at Sophie writing a note at the bottom of her "S. & M." engraved wedding invitation begging me 'to be decent and come.' I mean, it was as if she were implying that we hadn't seen each other or been much in contact because I wanted to spite her, not because we went to completely different schools and lead different lives. Why 'be decent,' otherwise? I mean, I laid the card by my bathroom sink and said to myself in the mirror "I'm not out to get my twin sister; I'm not cruel."

"Of course you're not cruel," said John Morton after a moment.

"We're going to a wedding. Why are we talking about such things?" asked Danielle.

"Because I don't know how I'll even say hello to her."

In the end the only thing that occurred to Monique to do was to wave. Sophie, who was getting out of her bridal limousine in front of the church, waved back. After four years of winters spent in different cities and summers on different continents (because Monique always found some language program abroad to enroll for), Sophie had grown more graceful from how Monique remembered her. Her blue eye shadow today was a bit dark but otherwise her make-up was a professional job of contouring; her bridal gown, which left her shoulders bare, was quite becoming. After Maman embraced her, she made two excited jumps in place, her white gloved fists against her cheeks. It struck Monique as a display of "I'm so happy!" copied from somewhere. "Dad, here, over here!" Then already, because that was the way it had to be this afternoon, she disappeared, her brown hair a beehivish puff of beveiled Gibson-girl couture, into a room off the vestibule with Dad and four or five bridesmaids in the Valentine red gowns that made of her the Queen of Hearts.

The nuptial Mass that followed was noteworthy for being traditional to an extreme—no personal readings, no individualized cycle of songs, no words from Matt and Sophie at all, except the vow and the "I do." The February light waned to darkness in that hour and the stained-glass windows dulled to the creamy opaqueness of shell and lead. A cellist in a yellow spotlight lent the two at the altar the musical voice of his instrument. The poignancy was such that guests strained to see Sophie and Matt blink or gaze at each other as a couple should who are worthy of such an authentic voice. The implements of their rite matched them remarkably: the candles were long, as was the bride's face; the brass incense burner, as it swung, as round and dominating as that of the groom. Fate had given Matt Gagliardi the regular features, high forehead, and imposing and molded physique (though he was on the short side) which typified military pilots, male models, and naval commanders, even more than they did investment-minded doctors like himself. Monique, noting this, was tempted to believe that if he were as intelligent as all that he must surely know of the physical stereotype that he fulfilled and feel cramped by it. And Sophie? For all his integral intensity, Gagliardi couldn't overshadow Sophie, not with her billowing yards of gown. Slipping on her eyeglasses (rather weak and unnecessary actually, but part of her professional identity), Monique bore her gaze down upon Sophie's white shoulders during the gospel reading. On this occasion where a woman must be silent, Sophie was the hour's enigmatic prophetess: *let me marry*, her stance said, *and I will show you all.*

When they were pronounced man and wife, his two hands cupped her cheeks and held her in a wedding kiss till she gasped. But it was what they both wanted, for they drew away laughing.

Things dragged after that. The rice-throwing and hugs on the steps outside seemed endless. Monique pushed her way back into the church. Mimeographed sheets dedicated to "S. & M. Day" littered the benches, the leather prayer-rests, the floor. The gaunt photographer, wearing two cameras round his neck and working in a black turtleneck as stagehands do, was taking light-meter readings for the posed altar shots. Out of nowhere, Cousin Pam came and stood next to Monique. She had a shocking number of neck wrinkles, a dark tan, and long lacquered nails, which flashed their scarlet before Monique as she patted an infant over her shoulder. "Hi, Monique. It's nice to see you. Have you seen my little fellow here?" She turned and the baby's sleeping face was visible for a moment. You know, the doctors thought at first that they saw two embryos and I was going to have twins, because of it running in the family, but thank God I didn't. Gee, gosh. Come over here to the side with me a moment, can you?" There behind a pillar Pam opened two blouse buttons, lifted a brilliant white padded flap on an immense purple nipple, and nursed the baby, who she described as their "miracle child." Monique didn't know if she was alluding to fertility problems, to a difficult birth, or to something else entirely. Pam's miracles were not hers.

"Married?" Pam inquired.

"No."

"Well, now that Sophie is…"

"Family shots!" barked the photographer as the others burst boisterously back into the church. "Where's the bride's sister?"

"Here." In her tinted, gold-wired glasses (though she usually wore contact lens like Sophie, she'd purposely worn the glasses to distinguish herself) and with her own brown hair twisted into an old-fashioned yet smart chignon for the occasion, Monique climbed the marble step and took her position next to a beaming Sophie, whose cheek muscles were starting to twitch from the uninterrupted strain. When Sophie hugged Monique tightly around the shoulders, the two blades came together under the skin. It was unpleasant. Sophie squeezed even more zealously, so that Monique rose off one foot.

The photographer bellowed, "Will you two stop that?" and to Monique, "Are those glasses really necessary?"

"Are these questions really necessary?" said Matt, sounding like a good sport. The issue was dropped. "Matt," said Sophie, hopping a step back, "this is Monique." The cameraman artiste, who pressed the button just as the groom broke rank, barked, "Sir, please!" Monique's brother-in-law stretched out his immaculate hand sporting his new gold wedding band. Time stopped. Monique leaned past Sophie and gave him a small cocktail-party hug: "Congratulations." "Bear with us now, won't you?" he murmured as if her putting up with the ritual ins and outs of this day meant the world to him. Now that she was close up to him, Monique noticed his regularly mowed curly black hair, and also the flesh under his suit which seemed as firm in its swells as his character. Yet this vague air of discipline was in contrast to how he looked at you.

Few white men have almond-shaped eyes like that, she thought, eyes that elongate and tighten as they shift, hinting at something enigmatic on the inside—eyes which she'd only ever seen on women or on Turks.

During the restaurant banquet Sophie left her place and came to put her lips covetously into her twin's hair. "Can't we just be sisters, Monique? Get together sometimes, call each other?"

Monique pulled away, laughing, feeling so unfettered that she could be generous: "So call me, Sophie."

Matt Gagliardi, who was chatting with Maman and Dad about the large Victorian house that he'd had renovated, looked up and said: "Call you Sophie? Monique, why on earth for?"

During the rest of the afternoon, Monique had the impression of a harmless alliance forming between Gagliardi and her, thanks to which (why not hope for it?) Sophie and her sentimental paws might be held in check. Not the sort of husband she would have married, of course, but she was comfortable with how she pegged him: professionally established, rich, and full of himself. He had that telltale aura of a man who took it for granted that everything depended on him even on occasions when nothing much did.

Monique did not care for this unperturbed male self-esteem. She took it as a sign of trouble; she had dedicated diary pages to a couple of similar men—if older undergraduates really deserved to be called that. Still, she was in no mood to judge today (she had flown in and would fly out just as fast), and, indeed, wouldn't have, if Matt's small squat father, surly with drink, hadn't surprised the room by standing up at his applauding table and ripping his gray silk dress tie off his shirt. "Here it is, Matt!" he shouted. "Get over here, will you!"

And then Gagliardi Sr., with more paternal, vainglorious impatience manifested in his vexed low brow, had Matt's two jockey-sized brothers take him (apologetically) by the elbows. Sophie, too, deserted her place, retreating without really knowing what she was doing towards her parents and Monique, saying in an amazing state of apprehension, which none of them understood: "Not the tie. We agreed there'd be no tie."

With the same aristocratic, preparatory roll of the shoulders as a bull fighter, Matt shook his brothers off, but he did not look at the Mortons' table, as they were expecting. His aunt, a tiny waistless woman as wide-faced as a Matrioska doll, waved his father's gray dress tie in the air and beckoned at Matt to take it. "Matt!" bellowed Gagilardi Sr., standing again. The tie was passed hand to hand till it reached Matt, followed by a pair of manicure scissors. "*Dai, dai, su!*" Gagliardi Sr. butted his head to the left with an encouraging, broad, metallic smile, his bulbous nose going even more purple. "*Dai, dai!*" The pint-sized aunt's hands drummed the table, and she had the same smile.

It was impossible to read Matt's impassive eyes as his father began to whistle and applaud expectantly.

If Diane hadn't said, "Make him happy, Matt, will you?", Matt would have probably held out and stonewalled his father successfully. But there was something that made Matt Gagliardi hurriedly, without explanation, and with lowered eyes, snip off tiny bits of the tie at every banquet table, saying only, "Here's for you now" and "Here's for you as well."

"That's no way to do it, Matt!" bellowed his father, for Matt wasn't asking any of the guests to pay for those snippets, ten or twenty dollars. "*Per buona fortuna.* Matt!"

As he came and went from those ten or so tables with a loose and easy stride, Matt Gagliardi's nose and chin rose slightly into a position of superior concentration. Swiftly he went back to his place at the head of the table, where—still not glancing at Sophie (this intense way of ignoring her, as his brand-new wife, made strange, prickly electricity flush down her bare arms)—he spoke with a waiter, to whom he also handed the scissors. After a moment a new bottle of champagne was presented to his father. The old man cawed over that as well.

Sophie's lips parted. She started to pray that the old drunk would be quiet, addressing not God as much as the priest who had married Matt and her with words so fine that she was still wearing them like a mink stole. She felt in all her senses—in her ears, in her mouth, behind her eyes, up her nose, and, yes, it continued, down her arms under the mink stole—that he was being crass, small-minded, the ruin of the party. How could Matt's father have been so dignified— in short, so inspiring—at his wife's funeral and so terrible now at her wedding?, Sophie wondered, hurt and bewildered. She wished she could be in the Ladies room dabbing her eyes with cold water and telling her sister, "I thought they were going to be nice people."

A table away, Monique was musing that she didn't presently care enough to figure out Matt Gagilardi, but that maybe this might change someday. Then David's voice and body rustle and skin and smell flooded over her, and she married and divorced him in a swift violent moment that left her too tired to answer the question from the Gagliardi sister seated to her right.

John Morton, meanwhile, was thinking that the wedding reception should come *before* the marriage ceremony, so that one had time, with one's stomach full of wine and food and one's mind crammed with coarse impressions of strangers who were suddenly supposed to matter to one, to digest this in church during the music. Why, when he looked around, wasn't there anything but a party at its end, and a collective anxiety over the need to drive home? He made an effort to imagine Sophie in a year or two. It was his quiet toast to her, seeing no one had asked him to make a public one. He presumed that Sophie would be assigned her place in this soap-operatic Italian family and have her kids and be watched and needed constantly and so never have the time to feel so light and insignificant as she did when she nearly drowned.

It was time for the band to play its last number now, and Sophie and Matt went table to table with the odd little statuettes, sets of white-ceramic wrestling bear cubs, chosen as their wedding favors. As Sophie set the bears in their half-Nelson down on the white tablecloth in front of her mother, Danielle, in a meditative champagne stupor, saw before her eyes two soldiers, one tackling the other, his enemy, on a Paris street. "*When there's no war,*" she thought, with the intuition of a mystery solved, "*these energies have to go somewhere.*" But the champagne was there to save her today from dwelling too much on the analogy between bears, soldiers, and married couples.

*

By all appearances, he was alone in his airport-vicinity honeymoon suite with Sophie. He sat on the sofa and fixed his eyes on the window.

"Matt?" She was in the bedroom.

"I'm in here, babe. I'll be with you in a minute."

Honeymoon or no honeymoon, Matt Gagliardi was incapable of foregoing a couple of restorative minutes for his own secrets.

"*You're a little Matt boy, neither short nor stout,* " Sophie sang softly. "*Here is your handle, and ooh, here is your spout.*" She had made up another loving ditty.

He was phoning Lorenza to tell her he had gotten married. The telephone in Venice rang once, twice…then, oddly, it stopped. He waited a moment, as people do, thinking something can come of that silence on the line, thinking that he could say those words— serious words encoded in the language and governed by the edicts of civilized society…then realizing that he couldn't stand it, that he couldn't accept that the words "I am married" might communicate extras that he had no control over, he pressed the phone hook down, got the dial tone, and tried the number again, of a very different mind now, refusing to change things as they stood between Lorenza and himself, existing as those things did only every so often and in an occasionally visited spiral of emotion. He couldn't give up any particle of sweetness that belonged to him; he deserved—yes, *deserved*—this. At the same time, he wanted to do right, give his marriage a chance. Where was the inconsistency? There wasn't one. Sitting on this couch—this love seat—he was a man who a few hours before had been braced in place, together with a woman, on a wheel as it turned wildly, spinning them into the future. It was a good if shocking thing to be so well braced. He hadn't suspected anything or anyone other than himself could provide such sustaining force: so this was what it meant to be married. Well, all right!

He was relieved that Lorenza wasn't in. He left a message, "*Ciao, sono Matteo,*" a hello without a reason. He felt the physiological ease-up he was hoping for and went into the bedroom to lie next to, and help to further undress, his new wife.

CHAPTER NINE

Following Monique's return from her year-long fellowship in France and Germany to a precarious assistant professorship at Northwestern, Sophie began leaving *"how I feel today"* messages on her sister's answering machine. Monique listened but never *re*-listened. As Sophie told it, there wasn't one of the traditional time-fillers for rich wives (exercise class, Garden Club luncheon, charity fund-raiser, hairdresser) missing from her schedule: each helped to glue it together with greater inflexibility. In Chicago Monique responded freely to the recording with rolled eyes and irony, and wide-angled sarcasm on her grouchiest days, when her resentment at solitary life in her puny utility rental (which was broken up only by the occasional dinner invitation or weekend babysitting stint—a politically smart act of volunteering on her part—for her mentor, the Chair of Renaissance studies, and his French wife), when this resentment reached its peak.

Sophie usually left her recorded bit of "voice diary" for Monique right before her gossip session with Maman, where she recycled the material of her monologue, improving it even, and earning numerous "you said that so well"s from her mother in French, all of which enhanced the self-approval that had entered her like a vitamin pill since her marriage. And if chatting with her mother or leaving messages for her sister did her good, getting together with them was bound to be even better. A chauffeur from the service Matt used was usually available to drive her in the direction of the Delaware River and the thick scrim of trees that was New Jersey on weekly "pop in" visits to her parents. She liked to close her eyes to Philadelphia and Chester (yes, this was what she was paying for), and in that way saw nothing but farmed and unfarmed nature, an endless green strip sewing Swarthmore and the dappled shade of its grandiosely limbed oaks to Gloucester County and those puny fruit trees in their white, overdone sunlight.

Matt's sister Diane was often in touch with her that first year, and they were soon caught up not only with seeing her family but also his. She'd say to Matt, "Oh, your sister called to invite us…" and he'd answer, "Sure, babe", and she'd write it in her datebook and close the book afterwards, and if she were putting a soft lid on a kind of satisfaction at being in demand and well-loved. She spent frequent afternoons at the shopping mall, avidly surveying aisle displays in department stores; it could take as little as a few minutes and as much as three hours before she felt a rush of recognition at the right small gift for the next relative she and Matt would be seeing. Sometimes her mother asked her if she was looking for a job as a kindergarten teacher, for Maman wanted her to have something to show for having received her certification at Shippendale. But Sophie couldn't conceive of finding the time to look after a class of children; as much as she loved children and was already half dreaming and half discussing with her husband about having one of her own, something physically stopped her from *working* with them. Of course, a commitment like that would make it impossible for her to carry on with her leisurely and loving shopping and preparations for family get-togethers. Recently she'd taken an Italian cooking class. She was reading a book on entertaining and decorating. She'd memorized the birth dates of Matt's family, and followed their horoscopes daily, together with those of her own relatives. Wondering how others were feeling, and what you could do to make them a little happier for a moment, was the most important thing she could do in a day. This was, she imagined, precisely what priests and nuns dedicated themselves to when they weren't meditating on God. The fulfillment she felt was marred only by the fact that her twin sister kept her at a distance, and that her father-in-law was so uncouth and ignorant; it was mighty hard to wish good things for him!

Though Matt went from the hospital to his practice to his financial advisor (whose advice had reaped them a windfall twice on the stock market, Matt said) and often came home as late as nine at night, he kept Friday afternoons free; towards cocktail hour she had a chance to tell him the latest about everyone in their families and when they would probably see them, as they sat on the sofa, her legs thrown over his. He'd give her a big relaxed smile and nod (*continue* to nod slowly on and on, too—his married way of showing approval), and say, "My sister said that, did she?" or "Yes, I think your mother would like that." Sometimes he did something a little strange—he lifted her chin gently and turned her face to one side and then the other, his right eye squinting a bit more than his left one as he gazed. The first time this occurred was the day she'd come home from the hairdresser's with her hair dyed a soft shade of blond; she'd noticed that most of the wives in Matt's circle of doctor friends had their hair this color (as had Joy Adams, the lady whose kids she used to drive around), and supposing it to be significant and probably even important—in addition to becoming—she had turned into a blonde herself. "*Well now*," said Matt that day, taking in her new look. She couldn't tell if he was pleased—intimately pleased, as one wanted a husband to be—with the result; she did, however, understand that he appreciated the effort she'd put into looking more like the other wives. He could have been assessing, he could have been looking for a deep meaning connected to female hair color, one which only he knew about. He didn't explain, and she didn't ask.

For her, this maintaining a silence on things—on many things, actually—was one of the beauties of their relationship. Sophie was convinced this first year of marriage that they could read each other's minds. Or anyway that she could read his. Occasionally she made a mistake, and he raised his voice, but neither one of them was perfect, she reasoned.

One Friday evening, as he buoyantly brought their gin- and-tonics over to the couch he said, "You know, I think we aren't reciprocating enough." Drawing a long sip, he added, "All this entertaining could be a financial strain on them. We need to invite the family here more." It was like Matt to be vigilant of weight and measure. So they organized their first double-family holiday party at Easter (though Monique didn't come); then held a catered birthday celebration for his brother Pete. Celebration possibilities abounded.

Out in Chicago, Monique received uncritical word from Maman of the birthday party in her honor, of the fabulous presents and Sophie's hand-lettered "we love you" proclamations in the doorways of the lavishly decorated parlors of her gabled, chocolate-brown mansion. These details of excess were fed to her at a delicate point of her year: it was a moment when she was feeling a little damaged, wondering if she would be overworked forever and left to languish in a precarious T.A. position, with no hope of obtaining a professorship. This worry was turning into a blight on her research into the evolution of positive traits in female characters in European literature; already she had so little time for writing or meditating on the subject. Indeed, it seemed all she had time for (in the bathroom, in the middle of the night, entering a freshman class) was marvel and wonder at other people's accumulating riches; how awful it was to realize that the rich in question were people her age, her peers, *her equals*. Old schoolmates, cousins, new friends in other fields, they were all buying houses, big cars, expensive insurance policies, portfolios, and goodness knew what else. What stung her most of all, however, was how well off her sister—did she want to admit it to herself?: her *twin* sister—was. For the first time in a very long time she felt a peculiar if weak affinity with Sophie. Shouldn't she naturally have money and naturally have an easier time of it in life, if the only other who was identical to her did?

It was with this twitch that her adult curiosity about her twin sister began to bud and grow, after a childhood and especially an adolescence of haughty disdain. Meanwhile, another year or so passed without her having anything but the briefest phone contact with Sophie. Matt and Sophie began organizing reunions, animated family get-togethers *not* tied to any special occasion. First came the turn of the Gagliardi clan (three generations), then that of the Mortons (four generations on the American side, minus Monique), then a blended 'do' of both (John and Danielle barely tolerating by evening's end—despite Diane's mediation—the boorish drunken company of Matt's father). When this phase of group entertainment had run its course, its logical substitute was the kind of discreetly self-congratulatory party that the well-to-do end up resorting to, to celebrate buying the Porsche or getting back from India, weekend affairs which were lavish and long enough for close relatives to work the envy out of their system and feel in an uncomplicated way pampered and participatory.

Sophie accepted the fact that Monique never responded to the invitations. She never dared hope her sister would come. She realized that Monique was doing something important, that she was studying strong women with character—or was it strong women characters?—anyway she was engrossed in a research project that would show how brilliant and strong she herself was, and so be rewarded with one of those prestigious professorships she'd mentioned once. Sophie didn't want to be a bother or distract her from her work in any way. Yet she, too, was under a deadline, or at least her body was.

November 4, 1980

Dear Monique,

I tried phoning today but you weren't there. Guess what? I'm pregnant! The doctors think it's a girl. Not twins, though!! I'm so happy. I think Matt is, too. He doesn't say much these days...between explosions (ha-ha!). I wish he'd just relax—the way he was when I met him, or when we first were married. He's unbelievably uptight now. A change has come over him this last few months. Maybe the baby will make him relax, what you do think? I mean, yesterday, as we were coming out of the Mall, he told me to give him the credit card I'd used to buy baby things. "We've got everything we need and double. This is getting out of hand. I can't have you spending like this every week. Come on, give it to me!" He pulled it from my fingers as I was getting it out, and this in front of people. I was stunned. Why did he have to act like that in public?

Later we ordered carry-out Chinese and things were fine.

When did you say you could come for a visit? Did you say? Please, Monique, come.

Love,
Sophie

Sophie waited a week and then her excitement got the better of her. She mailed Monique a plane ticket and a note which said that the time had come ("It's now or never—with the baby due!") to inaugurate the indoor-outdoor pool. She also phoned at dinnertime. It was an evening when Monique had a guest, a visiting colleague from Rutgers, who was a restrained quiet guy who tried to loosen up by sounding wry about everything, and he took the call while she was draining their spaghetti: "It's, ah apparently, your...sister?"

Monique's face registered surprise. "Sophie? Did you have your baby?" she said into the phone.

"Oh, you did get my first letter, then!" Sophie laughed. "I've got another five months to go, actually." She explained about the airplane ticket she'd just sent, about the celebration of her pregnancy and the newly completely pool.

Monique heard the warmth of a woman of leisure pleased with her own organizational abilities. Sophie did not try to lure Monique out of her thicket of privacy; she didn't care that a man had answered the phone. She told Monique that Maman and Dad were coming as well. Monique's curiosity about Sophie and this weekend grew on her.

"It has been a long time, hasn't it?" she commented soberly. Perhaps, she told herself, there was no longer any real reason for keeping her life so totally separate from Sophie's.

"Ages!" cried Sophie happily. "Please say 'yes'."

To Monique that happy voice resonated with so much easy living. It made her make up her mind. She agreed to make a visit to Pennsylvania. She agreed to re-enter Sophie's world.

The new marble-rimmed kidney-shaped pool and its pink terracotta patio, enclosable at the flip of a switch by rising glass walls, was behind the house. The house was more immense than

Monique had been willing to conceive it as being; passing through it to the backyard, she went by large windows covered with stained-glass panels of flowers of a miraculous size. Sophie—a quite believable blonde, not the platinum sort she'd pictured when Maman had told her—was lying on her side on a poolside chaise-longue, wearing a swimsuit under a yellow tent dress which made the protrusion of her belly even more obvious, and her chin spotted with acne. She pulled herself up and hugged her sister, complaining of an acid stomach. Behind her, still in his raincoat with the overnight bag at his feet, their father wore an intense grin—a demonstration of his transformation from grumpy father-in-law to Matt's approving older friend. All in purple, from polo-shirt to thongs, Matt was following the rise of the humming walls with his hands, and said to their mother, "So you like it, Danielle?"

With sealed but upturned lips, Danielle batted her eyes: that was how she'd decided to allot approval to her son-in-law when he asked for it. Over the next hour, pleasure would continue to seep into her eyes, while her cheeks got hot from the cocktails and wine. She liked the alcohol; she was very happy to let the consolatory ritual of retreating to her bedroom after dinner at home with a glass of wine gave way to unchecked giddiness. She was vibrant and eager for conversation; no one would ever think she was the shadow of her former self (more or less at peace but a shadow of the courageous sparkling girl she'd been all the same). She gave Monique her hug, Monique who she hadn't seen in over a year. She commented that she looked thinner, that she wasn't wearing glasses any more; she asked Monique if it had been hard for her to tear herself away from her work and come, and Monique gave a strange pinched giggle and said enigmatically: "That too." At that point John came jovially over to them to say, "Come on, Monique, don't be a party-pooper. Smile!" She did but with averted eyes, surveying the lovely blue pool. Danielle took her daughter mentally to task. Why didn't she understand that there was a jolliness to partake in, that it was all right to expect bodily comfort and easy conversation this afternoon and evening. It was very simple. You gave Matt and Sophie your energy, sympathy, and such emotions as you had that that allowed you to temporarily participate in their concerns....and in return, *mais c'était très amusant*, Matt and Sophie (but especially Matt) involved you in discussions about, say, a certain eighteenth-century painting they were thinking of buying, or whether it was really vital for Matt to attend Sophie's LeMaize class.

Monique accepted her first cocktail of the weekend. It was the driest, most potent Martini she'd ever tasted. She carried it –as see-through as water in the stemmed glass—when they all moved into the library, and setting it on one of the shelves she explored the wall-length bookcase. Could it really be a first-edition Céline? And that an original Pirandello? Matt passed by with the Martini shaker. "Is—?" she started.

"Yes," he said on a short laugh. "Not a fake." He crossed his eyes comically. "I give guided tours. But only on Sunday night, when I'm sober."

The steel shaker swung away from her. He had started humming 'to everything there is a season.' She took a sip of cold chased by fire—and knew that this weekend was going to be stimulating not for the talk but for the drinking. She herself didn't drink to forget but to feel, feel more and more, until that snowballed into understanding—but did anyone do differently? She drained her glass. Through it, the fleshy blur of Matt Gagliardi's arm moved and Monique heard Sophie on the couch exclaim, "Matt!" Setting her glass down now, Monique watched that hand of his goose her sister again. "As long as it's you and not your father," Sophie cooed, then turned back to Maman on the couch beside her. Matt Gagliardi rolled his eyes. After which those infidel eyes narrowed to their usual expression of composure, and he moved on with his Martini shaker, humming where he'd left off.

What could that act of mooning the whites of his eyes at Sophie's back mean, Monique thought, except that he was less happy with her these days? Monique herself used to make mug faces at Sophie's retreating figure all the time. She knew that feeling of caustic impatience from the inside out.

After such a mean little revelation as that, she was not surprised when the evening was marred by overt unpleasantness at dinner. Though it didn't last very long, it came out of nowhere and of nothing. Sophie began complaining about Matt's father. She'd already done so earlier poolside. Now she declared that if old Gargliardi had been drinking, she wasn't going to let him hold the baby after it was born. Sophie threw Maman a look, which Monique caught. "My parents and sister as witnesses," she added.

"Sophie?" Matt's voice was as low as hers, but he jerked so hard on his cloth napkin in his lap that it flapped. "You know, I really think that's enough."

"I'm not kidding, Matt."

"*Enough*, dear."

Monique couldn't remember ever having seen this particular kind of frightened anguish on Sophie's face. Her sister usually couldn't find anything fundamentally odious about anyone. Matt's father, moreover, might be lewd and uneducated but he wasn't the devil.

"I get scared of your father, Matt. He--."

"SOPHIE, DO I HAVE TO REPEAT MYSELF AGAIN?!"

With a slap on the table, he fixed on her from under those mysteriously elongated oriental eyelids of his. Monique could see that his mind was locked into some master logic that regulated his self-control. His face relaxed. He even managed a smile at his plate. Under his re-found affability, however, his anger still remained, his mouth its retaining wall...and there was definitely a sting of salt in what he said to his wife about how to carve the roast beef.

As Monique watched, intolerance throbbed inside her too for a moment. Thanks to all the drinks she'd had, this intolerance pushed her in the direction of action. As loudly as possible, because it seemed to her in her state that the truth should be spoken at a great volume, she told Matt Gagliardi that the cork to the hundred-dollar bottle of Chateauneuf-du-Pape that he'd just opened smelled funny. It did: she'd learned a great deal about wine during her fellowship months in France. Either he didn't hear or was pretending not to. He and Dad were grinning like reptiles

"That's some bottle, eh, John?"

Then she pointedly put the cork by his plate. He got red as his burgundy.

"I'M REALLY NOT INTERESTED, MONIQUE." He would not allow her evaluation. "I guess we've all had enough."

Any further annoyance once this had been said could only explode with extra force. After dinner Sophie waddled into the library with her parents and Monique. Matt joined them about ten minutes later. He and Sophie stood at their brass bar sink and he asked her in a voice de-boned of ire, "Do they all want whiskey?" All three Mortons called out that whiskey was fine before Sophie could answer. While they nursed their drinks, Matt zapped on the television news, and as he sank back against a pillow, he hitched his bermuda shorts, those dark shaggy legs of his jimmying up and down.

"Think I'll get comfortable, too," Dad said, excusing himself to go put on his pajamas.

Danielle watched him leave the room and felt significantly less protected from potential ugliness in his absence. What was going on that was so different this weekend? Why couldn't Matt tolerate anyone contesting his opinions now? Why was Matt hostile to Monique? Monique could be abrasive, but what if it weren't Monique at all? She considered everything she knew about Matt. He was a driven perfectionist. *Why* he was so driven, what ideal motivated him, she did not know. She chastised herself for having forgotten the sobriety of her original opinion of him, and for having though recently that he was, above all, a bon vivant. This luxury, this house, had nothing to do with that sort of sensual and hedonistic approach to life. He was a man in control—or who thought he was in control. Such people went far in life; they achieved things she never would. Perhaps their intolerance and ire helped guarantee this. Sometimes she was audacious but that wasn't the same. She was a powerless middle-aged woman married to one man and two countries. And for good or bad, she was forced to do what Matt Gagliardi did very little of—what Pétain's barber had wished on her: to walk around in other people's shoes.

Upstairs in the left tower, John Morton made the mistake of opening one of the windows in their guest bedroom for air. The next instant the alarm siren went off. He knew enough about such things from working in the insurance field to realize that he had probably triggered it. The initial piercing snort of the burglar alarm was followed by a fierce, modulated blare, while outside lights crisscrossed the lawn like fat fingers.

Instantly on her feet, Danielle strained to make out some sound of John amid the mechanical wrath engulfing them. Monique stayed where she was, her feet and her hands crossed, while Sophie hobbled to the French doors, drawn by the search lights, and Matt Gagliardi bounded out of the room with an irascible, "Oh, COME ON!"

Finally, the aggravating sound-and-light show ceased. After an initial moment of peace, the three of them heard John on the stairs saying, "That's bad design!" Entering the library in his robe he commented, "I don't think Matt's too happy. He said he was sure that he had told us the alarm went off automatically if you opened a window after dark."

"No, he didn't," said Monique coolly.

"He said there were reasons for having an alarm system here. This isn't my home, it's his. Matt knows what his world's like. He's right."

"Just how did he say this to you" Monique asked her father.

A bell jangled, in the wall it seemed. "Oh, don't touch the phone. It means he's using it. He's probably calling in to the hospital," said Sophie.

"Or maybe," said Danielle swallowing a burp of whiskey, a sign of fatigue she knew how to heed, "he's explaining the siren to the local police"

"He's right," repeated John.

"He's not right," snorted Monique. "He's angry." Her words were full of her own resentment. She was matching Matt Gagliardi. "And why's he angry?!"

No one answered. Sophie, who as Matt's wife should have had something illuminating to say about his temper, made what sounded like a small whimper.

"I find him incredibly touchy. I detect a lot of penned up rage," Monique said briskly.

"Don't, Monique," hiccupped their mother. "Don't invent trouble."

There was silence.

Then Sophie said falteringly, "Now that you say that--."

"*Merde*," swore Danielle, shutting her eyes.

"*Go on*, Sophie," Monique insisted.

"He loves me," Sophie began. "He loves his family, he loves you. He's a good man. But…but now that you say that, it is getting worse. It comes out of nowhere."

Danielle opened one eye, the left one. John had just raised the volume on the TV and was watching a war documentary.

To her mother's one open eye Sophie mustered up a small smile; she knew she was confessing something wrong with her marriage that five minutes ago hadn't seemed to exist. Thank God that her mother and sister were here to listen, ask questions, intervene.

"Well?" prompted Monique impatiently.

Out of Sophie came a voice of recall of things that hadn't before had words, that had happened but hadn't been admitted. In her normal voice she would never have admitted that her marriage was based on what was not there; that is, on second-guessing and anticipating, on the absence of antagonism. Monique folded her arms across her chest as Sophie talked about the time Matt had told her his father would beat his mother years ago.

"He was just getting to the part about his father giving his mother a smack across the face," said Sophie fervently, "when he stopped and we looked at each other. Because he had just sounded like himself when he yells at *me*. So then we sat down and quietly looked at our hands, and I said, "Dear God, help us" and Matt kept his head bowed. We both got scared."

Danielle arched her eyebrows. "Then what happened?" she asked tersely.

Sophie snapped out of that earnest mode of being and seemed to know exactly why her mother sounded uptight for she answered, "No, no, he didn't lay a finger on me. Never has. But he does get, I'd say, nasty with me sometimes. It's not that he says things. But, I mean, he doesn't let me repeat his words anymore. You know, for clarity, or to get things right, or, you know, because I like his words, how he sees things. Instead, he repeats mine. Only it's different. What's it called? He mocks me."

On the television, Vietnam choppers whirled their blades as a retired general, who had fought in Korea and World War II as well, agreed with the interviewer that the specific nature of the enemy had to be accounted for. Old soldier John Morton's eyes were heavy with sleep.

"So do something about it, then!" Monique exclaimed. In Sophie's expression she could read "you're the strong one" as well as "don't overestimate me." She felt a chill down her spine. For more than anything else that weekend, more than any arrogant rudeness from her brother-in-law or weird breakdown in the general good will, *that look* ...for the oldest of reasons...made her sorry she'd come.

CHAPTER TEN

Matt Gagliardi was a man able to shrug off his own unwise or nasty actions. He did the same with his occasional itch to give someone a punch or a smack. It was interesting how he did it: he closed his eyes for a moment and thought, "Nothing's happened" or "I've done nothing." Even when he saw another's negative reaction, it didn't seem connected to what he'd done or said...He never did anything that was evil or bad, because whatever it was that was evil or bad would *feel* bad or evil in the doing, wouldn't it?

He did recognize that he had a tendency to simplify, to separate off the chaff from the kernel, eliminate a good deal—at times perhaps too much—in favor of the essential, as he'd been trained to do in the medical and business worlds, and as he'd always been inclined to do by nature. For this reason he knew that he was not an angry man, for anger to him was the frustration of not being able to simplify. He could furthermore confidently foresee that if his feeling that his wife was loyal but inadequate continued to grow, it would eventually serve—once his frustration and sarcasm were played out—to simplify their relationship. Indifference—and not rage—would follow. He felt moments of indifference already. It passed for a normal attitude in a husband, at least when it was dressed up as tolerance.

His father, on the other hand, had been for years a man with a temper. It was a very strange thing how on the brink of one of his attacks of distorted fury his father used to regain his full manhood. Matt remembered the magnificent line-up of his chest and jaw, the bulging arm veins, his triumphant eyes and that sense of his power to strike out and change the world that seemed ready to shoot out from under his leather belt, glowing (Matt guessed) between his kidneys. And then his father would actually do something—strike a door with a fist, or more often and vile, flay his mother with the side of his hand. Ugly and berserk it was, and Matt sometimes had to push his father back, or box him.

His father stayed wrathful until the day his mother discovered she had advanced stomach cancer. It was spectacular how his mother's starting to die dried up his father's ire, his father having found something easy to respect—death. And as his mother waned, his father was overtaken by adulation for Matt's medical abilities. Though his father had always admired and been proud of him, now he slipped into a more infantile attitude of worship. It substituted his rage, filling the hollow part of him. He nodded like a burly vassal in some medieval Italian painting, at every scrap of advice Matt gave. As a physician Matt was the highest human judge of when life could be saved and when there was no hope. When the end came for his mother, his father wanted all four of his children by his side, but Matt most of all. Gagliardi Senior's look and attitude conveyed that though he'd lost his wife there was still comfort to be had from his eldest born. "*Matt's taking care of it,*" he reassured callers and visitors in those chaotic and painful days of funeral arrangements, burial, tombstone, death certificate, and will, blithely oblivious to the fact that it was his daughter Diane as much as Matt who handled these things.

Two years later, Matt saw that his father not only still clung to this attitude of naïve adoration but seemed to regress childishly in other ways. He did not merely expect Diane to drive over and take care of his laundry and his meals; he also wanted her to help him decide what to do that particular day and complained crossly when she didn't. Also, Matt thought, he had begun to reason in smaller and smaller terms, the way children do; in a man of seventy, it was perplexing. Last month, he told his small circle of buddies, the retired Italian-born masons like himself with whom he played cards and drank wine, that he wasn't going to his cousin Tom for help this year at tax-filing time because he *didn't trust anybody anymore but his son Matt*. The latest development, Diane confided to him over the phone, was that their father was becoming lackadaisical ("worse than a six year old") about personal hygiene, and now had to be repeatedly urged to shower or trim his nails. "There are a stunning number of porn magazines lying about the house," she added acidly. "One of these days I'm going to throw them out."

"Watch him but leave him be," was Matt's response, uttered with a 'doctor's orders' air of authority. This answer left her free to think that he judged their father in a similar way to her—and that was convenient to him. As long as she sensed that he, too, thought their father was letting himself go and acquiring squalid interests, she'd be motivated to provide him with updates, wouldn't she? He didn't let on—had never let on—to how tolerant his feelings about their father were. True, Papa had embarrassed him tremendously at times—most memorably at his wedding reception. The whole family had witnessed it. What Matt kept a secret, on the other hand, was his tenderhearted urge to pardon him. Except for his father's wife-beating, Matt was inclined to forgive all his flaws and weaknesses. This blanket forgiveness came out of a precise incident from his childhood. He must have been about ten when his father had staggered home drunk late at night; the rest of the family were asleep in bed, but Matt was awoken by the most pathetic retching sounds coming from the bathroom located next to his room; he pushed open the door just as his father was lifting his head from the sink. Matt didn't expect him to take notice and was surprised—keenly electrified, too—when his father, with ruffled hair and a viscid strand of drool still hanging from his lower lip, said lowly and distinctly, "I'm a stupid idiot, Matt. I didn't have to drink so much. I feel like shit. I am shit." A jolt of love—so strong that he would never forget it—went through him when his father said those terrible things about himself. In that foul-smelling bathroom he had only eyes and ears for his father's candor. He found something to admire—an honesty which he himself would never be much capable of.

So, if Diane got up on her soap box to rant about their father's disgraceful behavior, Matt continued to disregard it. Nothing could touch the humble integrity of his father's rare self-confessions.

But there was yet another reason why he wanted their father left undisturbed.

In the few weeks before his daughter was born, Matt had his father come stay with them, despite Sophie's hostility, so that the *capo maestro* could build them a fieldstone patio. They would fence it and it would be a play area, a present from *Nonno* to little

Leslie-Ann. This physical transmittance of heritage, expertly set in cement by a grandfather belonging to a vanishing breed of Italian artisans, was an important thing to Matt.

He made a point of getting home at an hour when his father, sand-splattered and red-faced, was still in the midst of his work and could explain what he was doing. Every day he heard the smattering of English and Neapolitan dialect that functioned as technical talk for his father and his peers, and he took in the older man's contented pride. Once, cheerily waving a small bluish chunk of fieldstone in the air, his father imagined aloud how Leslie-Ann would have her birthday parties on this patio and how Matt would play songs on the guitar and perform those magic tricks he'd learned as a boy for her and her little friends. Another time he reminded Matt to take Leslie-Ann often to see their relatives in Italy. When he talked like that, Matt had the impression that his father had delegated the good part of himself to Matt to embody and represent. Feeling entrusted with his father's best self, he was even further inclined to take his father's defense. Did it matter so much that his father reached for the Puerto Rican cleaning woman and gave her big breasts a good squeeze? He was a dirty old man, wasn't he? Then, Matt repeated, *let him be*. The woman wasn't even a member of the family. She could laugh it off or resign. That was Matt's quick and brittle opinion on the subject.

Another fine thing about his father now was that when he was around Matt didn't have to worry or look over his shoulder when dialing Venice. He was covered in the warmth of his father's admiration even then.

Once he had said to Lorenza (and the words stayed with him later): "But I haven't made a major life change. I've gotten married. That's all!"

He was convinced that the power lines of his pure personality were hung high high above that sort of thing.

No, nothing changed at all. He planned to make his usual visit to Italy in the summer.

But then Leslie-Ann was born.

The child had the most incredible dark brown eyebrows. There wasn't an emotion that Leslie-Ann, 5 days old, couldn't express with them. At home from the hospital she crowded fingers—those of visitors, too—into her mouth and took all offered palms in her grip. Light from windows fascinated her as with most babies, and she paid homage to it, turning in its direction continually; yet she had to be bounced during her nursings, to prevent her from falling asleep.

Inside a protective arm-cradle, Matt carried her into all the rooms of the house, explaining their use and contents. From the start he did not use baby talk, but the voice of a happy teacher. No one, above all Sophie, had ever heard him talk aloud in such a way before. "Look, Princess, this is the room where all the toys for you have been put...And here is where you'll have your first bath, it's being planned for you already now, I can hear them...Then here, in here, I know there are a lot of books, intimidating, aren't they for now?, but in that corner is my electric guitar, all thin and bony, while in this corner, there's my acoustic guitar, all nice and hippy...And let's duck in here, Princess, this is where we cook and where in a few months you'll start having your breakfast. We could put the high chair there, right by my chair, what do you think?"

John and Danielle Morton visited the following weekend, and while Matt made business calls from his home office and the baby slept and Sophie rested, John went to the grocery store for them. As he left, a thunderstorm was gathering; the sky filled with thicker and thicker black bulges, till it looked like the insides of a washing machine overstuffed with filthy, billowing clothes. Fortunately the baby in her bassinet on wheels did not wake up. Danielle, who was keeping vigil beside her in the library, had taken a pencil and some note paper out of her purse and was making a sketch of the storm outside. She hadn't drawn a picture in years. She'd never drawn for her children, for instance. In fact, as she remembered things the last time had been during the war, when she'd swapped stick-figure directions with the foreign pilots in their cellar. She had only been twenty then. And not—as she was now—one of the third and oldest generation, the one that dies, the one that muses about what little objects will survive them. This drawing of the storm, this scribbling, for instance, would be worth something to Leslie-Ann someday, wouldn't it?, because it it'd been drawn by her grandmother the first day she'd come home from the hospital after being born.

The doorbell rang. As she went to answer it, Danielle knew it was probably Sophie's sister-in-law; they were expecting her. "Wow, Mrs. Morton. Just in the nick of time," said Diane as the rain hit the roof and windows like a spilling truckload of pins. When she slipped off her coat, Danielle saw that in honor of the occasion she was wearing a Sunday dress and pearls. "Where's our precious girl?"

In the library, Diane picked up the stirring Leslie-Ann and sat on the couch with her, her knees rocking back and forth to keep the baby quiet as she very carefully inspected every part of her at close range—arms, toes, backside, ears. Danielle wondered if she was going to peep inside Leslie-Ann's diapers as well. Finally she stopped and said, "Beautiful. Perfect."

Sophie appeared, yawning in the doorway, and Diane turned. "Hello, don't you look good though, for a woman who's recently given birth!" She jumped up, gave Leslie-Ann back to Sophie, then thrust her arms around both of them in a long enthusiastic hug. "I couldn't have asked for a more wonderful niece. Or your mom," Diane turned towards Danielle, "for a finer granddaughter. So how are you feeling?"

"I'm tired. It's awful. Sometimes I feel drugged."

"Oh dear," said Diane warmly. "But I guess every mother says that."

"I don't know," fretted Sophie, lowering her head to kiss her daughter's forehead distractedly. Even when she rested, she remained frightened at the prospect of having to rouse herself for breast-feeding every two or three hours day or night. "What if I can't get up when it's time to nurse her? What if I don't manage to force my eyes open?"

"Diane's brought the baby a present, Sophie." Danielle hoped to get her off the subject.

But before Sophie could say something, suddenly Leslie-Ann's mouth puckered and she started to bawl like a little goat, her little fists hammering the air. Sophie struggled to keep a firm grip on her when her legs started thrashing and her waist gyrated. "She's in pain. Do you think she's passing gas? I never know what to do. Maman, what should I do?" Without waiting for an answer and in contradiction with her own words, she swung Leslie-Ann expertly over her shoulder and vigorously patted her back. After a minute the baby began to fret more than cry.

"See? You remember all the tricks," said Danielle. "Of course they don't always work." Though the humor didn't seem to register on Sophie, Diane gave a little laugh.

John arrived home with the special powdered tea mix for infants. "Rain's stopped," he announced. "Hi, pixie." He waved at Leslie-Ann bouncing over her mother's shoulder as Sophie paced the room. "Looks like you got a present." He nodded at Diane's still unwrapped gift.

"It's just a baby outfit. Sophie can open it when she gets time later," said Diane quickly.

"Will I have time?" asked Sophie, rather despondently. "Where is Matt? Why can't he play some music for her? Matt!"

"Matt!" called Diane after her.

"Matt!" called Danielle.

No answer came from any part of the house.

John offered to go see what he was doing in his study.

"Tell him that Leslie-Ann needs him," Sophie said, lifting the baby up and putting her cheek up against Leslie-Ann's cheek. "Daddy's coming to play the music you liked yesterday, sweetheart. Remember the piano and the soft soft guitar? Piano then guitar, my girl." She repeated this another couple of times, watching the baby's brows for signs of distress.

Matt didn't come and John didn't return. Sophie began looking so disheveled from holding and rocking and burping the baby that Danielle took over. Sophie lay down on the couch. "My turn is next," said Diane. "No, wait. Footsteps!"

John Morton appeared. He was by himself.

"Matt?" asked Danielle in dismay, swaying the baby on her hip.

Sophie lifted her head from the couch and looked at her father in bewilderment.

"I knocked several times. Finally he answered me, though he never did open the door. Said he was still busy. That four adults should be able to care for one small baby."

Sophie sat up, her eyes growing still wider and more disoriented. "Did you tell him the baby needed him?"

"Yes," said John shyly. "He said it wasn't the baby but the baby's mother who said she needed him."

"SO?!" Sophie froze for a moment then collapsed on the couch again, her face in the pillows. The others kept quiet. She gave a stifled sob. Turning her head to one side to breath, she said in a broken voice, "It's as if he'd slapped me."

Still no one spoke. Danielle, for one, didn't feel right about responding in front of Matt's sister. Finally, Diane herself put an end to the awkwardness, offering to go change Leslie Ann's diaper. As soon as she left the room, the phone rang. It was Monique in Chicago, calling because she knew her parents were visiting. The two sisters had a short disconnected talk, which got interrupted because Leslie-Ann returned almost at once, crying her head off and ready to be nursed, and Sophie couldn't simultaneously hold the baby, work the buttons on her nursing bra, and manage the receiver. She passed the call to Maman.

"God, she sounds whiney," said Monique to her mother.

"You don't know, you're not here," corrected Danielle. Behind her, Diane had started singing Italian lullabies. To make the rest of what she had to say seem like true reproach she switched to French. Monique's presumption in passing judgment on her sister was inexcusable. *"You don't have a baby. You don't know what it means to be a mother."*

When she got off the phone, feeling miffed with her mother, Monique went to lay down on the bed next to Mike, the Rutgers colleague with whom she'd started a long-distance romance, and watched him still having a go at the anthology of contemporary French poetry she'd lent him. She moved her right leg onto his left one, and said from inside her feeling of sensual smugness, "I hope Sophie isn't going to let herself go to pieces."

"Ah," said Mike, who continued to read.

"My mother sounded frazzled, too." She glanced idly at the ceiling.

"Glad you're not there?" He turned the page.

"*Oui.*" She snuggled closer, throwing an arm over his chest but careful not to interfere with his reading. She thought about her own reading; and all her thoughts flew once again to Christine de Pizan who wrote her amazing allegory, *The Book of the City of Ladies*, in 1405, as a 25 year-old widow with three young children. Five hundred years later, in a new English translation from the French, the work was causing a stir in Monique's field. She herself was now working on the similarities between the narrator Christine, who indicts men from a position of superior benevolence, and the character of Portia in Shakespeare. How intriguing it was to see the same traits emerge in strong women, fictional or real, across the centuries. When she was immersed like this in the work and life of a woman of genius, Monique felt a radical mix of admiration and identification. Her sometimes-vacillating courage in life was enhanced. She saw affinities. She saw the importance of being lucid, self-assured, and entrepreneuring. Frankly, her mother and whining sister weren't doing the female sex credit.

She was on the verge of explaining this to Mike over dinner but didn't. Though he hadn't ever taken much interest in her family, or in her having a twin, she didn't want to encourage him to start now. Besides, it was Saturday night, their big erotic opportunity of the month. After a bottle of wine he was one horny boy. It was only eight-thirty, and they were already back in bed. She undressed with her eyes closed, exclusively responsive to touch. Pellet shots of pleasure bounced to her toes as he put his hands between her legs. Her eyelids parted briefly then re-closed. It seemed there and then like an involuntary blink, caused by all this electrifying stimulation. Yet for some reason in this dark now she saw her sister's deep walk-in closet. She didn't really want to be there, by the closet in the master bedroom suite in her sister's house, but curiosity drove her in. It was lined with countless shoes, one of which had tumbled on the floor and threatened to trip her; but no, it wasn't a shoe but a thin hard album. She kicked it open with her big toe: it was Sophie's high school diploma, the sum of her accomplishments. She kicked it again. For it wasn't just Sophie's closet...Since it was Sophie's closet, it was also hers.

Then Mike pressed into her with all his weight, and she, Monique, flew out of that cavernous closet, out of that illogically large house, over the heads of the cocky, mysteriously irascible husband and unknowable, demanding baby, into her own bright, valuable, safe mosaic of a world.

from Monique's diary

"Though Sophie started phoning me regularly again when Leslie-Ann settled into a routine (which was about a year ago), I never could have guessed that she would worm her way back into my life as much as she has. At first I was glad to hear the tidbits about Leslie-Ann—she's my niece, after all—and to know that Sophie was learning to feel comfortable with motherhood. But that phase didn't last long. A few months ago, out of the blue, she called at midnight on a Friday. I happened to be in, alone, and awake. In a very rushed and quivery voice, she said that Matt was on a business trip to Italy, and as always when he was away she 'was feeling strange.' That sent a chill down my spine and I clucked my tongue in feigned disbelief. She explained she meant that when he was away she felt as if she had more air to breathe and life to live. I told her not to get weird on me. That I couldn't understand what she was talking about nor did I want to. "But no, Monique, you have to," she insisted—very calmly, not pleading. There was no stopping her litany. I had found myself inundated in a similar way the day before, and this came to mind. As she recited the week's examples of awful things that Matt had done, I could hear the parallel laments of one of my graduate students, a woman who had made her hard life—a child out of wedlock and two daytime jobs— her permanent excuse for not turning in the next part of her Master's thesis; the previous day I had abruptly decided it would

be the right thing—that a woman of genius like Christine de Pizan, or the others I have become so familiar with, would find it the right thing—to listen sympathetically for once, and I let the perennially worried woman complete her list of set backs. We discussed them for a few minutes, and she was full of gratitude. This recent exercise in receptive listening, together with a strange dream the previous night which I really must write down one of these days, kept me from hanging up on my sister."

June 19, 1982

Dear Sophie,

It was so marvelous to get the last photos of our precious little granddaughter. She is a beauty and must bring you immense joy. I still remember the day my blue-eyed twins came into the world...every one of their birthdays brings it back.

We want to thank you for your invitation to come spend a week this summer at your lovely home. I've talked this over with your mother and we think that while we would love to come, you and Matt are under great pressure right now, trying to set your marriage back on track, and the last things you need are two houseguests. Our hearts and thoughts go out to you at this delicate time.

We will phone in a few days to sing "Happy 1ˢᵗ Birthday Leslie-Ann". Next year I'll be sure to pull her ears in good luck, you tell her that.
God bless you.

Love, Dad

From Monique's diary

"*Weeks have gone by and Sophie continues to phone. I impose certain times for these phone calls, but if something better for me to do comes up, I make it clear that it's her tough luck. Meanwhile, irritation of a more profound sort creeps over me. I can't help it: I can see obvious remedies to her ills. 'Have you thought about...?' This simply encourages her floundering in new directions of grievance, which all lead to the same conclusion: Matt criticizes everything she does for Leslie-Ann. L.A.'s first birthday could have been nicer, her clothes aren't up to sniff, she isn't watched attentively enough, and so on and so on.*

I notice that often she doesn't refer to him as 'Matt' at all but just calls him 'my husband.' This probably comes from being around other wealthy unemployed wives—I've personally observed how this is part of their automatic everyday lingo, a way to sound powerful and pampered at the same time.

In any case her griping became something more yesterday. My hunch is that it is a turning point. Sophie said: "He's getting heavy-handed about 'safety precautions.' First the alarm system on the house, you saw that. Now he wants to put a sonic band around the baby's leg. And he wants to move us into some high-security high-rise tower closer to the city."

"Like Rapunzel," I say. (It actually takes her a moment to understand what I mean.)
Then I grill her, well, on the essentials.
"That old thing...you know, the brutes in his family."
"No, he hasn't touched me," she says.
"Does he force sex on you?"
There's a silence. I record it here. Then she says, "No."

Because I have to finish writing tomorrow's lecture I say then:
"Sophie, what are we talking about this time, then?"
Her answer? It's "He constantly puts me down, Monique. I don't know why he started to but now it's like he can't stop. I fail to meet his standards."

I picture my sister looking mute and dumb at the AMA wine-tasting gala she describes, I see her not knowing how to contact the County about their property tax assessment and having to be coached on even the smallest and most banal parts of the telephoning. But he must have foreseen having to deal with her inexperience—he must have known he'd have to teach her a lot of things. And besides, I think to myself, he's rich. I want to send him a telepathic message to get himself a personal assistant. On my lips is the advice to Sophie to 'answer him back, put him in his place for being so rude,' but my sister blurts out this most peculiar thing: 'I don't think you understand. He makes me feel wrong. That every bone in my body and even every unsaid thought of mine is WRONG.'"

*

His elbows propped on the large mahogany desk in his home study, Matt pressed his fingers hard against his eyes. He'd just had a conversation with Lorenza in Venice, but instead of feeling refreshed, and even sexually alert (as often happened), he was alarmed and disoriented. Lorenza was thinking of making a drastic change in her life—taking a year off from teaching and joining her sister and her enterprising Scottish brother-in-law in Northern Africa, where they were leading tourists on excursions through the desert. She had to tell them if she was coming with them in the next few days. Of course, as an unattached woman in her thirties she had every right to do as she pleased; and this initiative, moreover, like all the others she'd taken and then explained or described to him in these past ten years, seemed right, existentially perfect for her. Nevertheless he was in a state. For the first time he felt she might disappear beyond his reach, taking all the sweetness with her. Why couldn't she stay in Venice?!

He opened his eyes. "I'm all right. Nothing's happened," he thought immediately and automatically. The room and the wall of framed diplomas and photos returned; he rose and went over to scrutinize the picture of his wedding day. Those stupid momentous smiles on his and Sophie's faces. How would he get through these next days before he talked to Lorenza again, he wondered? He was on the verge of panic—his heart rate had picked up and he was getting cold around the shoulders—and he was forced to resort to closing his eyes for a second time.

"I'm all right," he said to himself vigorously, and his old engrained way of mentally defending himself started functioning again.

*

Sophie was sniffling as she told Monique that Matt was spending the evening with an old school friend, in town on a business trip, who he did not intend in any way to introduce to her or vice versa.

"Why does it surprise you?"

Monique was piqued about Sophie phoning only three days after their last conversation. While she was holding firm to her intention to be more accommodating with her sister and students, she didn't feel like being thrust into the role every fricking day of the week. "It doesn't surprise *me*," she continued. "There have been signs all along that he was such a jerk. It's high time that you thought your relationship through again from the start."

Dumbfounded silence.

Finally Sophie asked hesitatingly, "You mean...um...back to when we met in Paris?" Couldn't the romantic beginnings at least be left intact, she wondered?

Monique told her what she suspected. It was very likely that at the start Matt—being a restless hot-shot doctor with plenty of opportunities—had viewed her, Sophie, as a plaything, and had already been entertaining the idea that it would be nice to marry a plaything, too.

Sophie was taken even more aback. Not just at what Monique was saying, but at how she was saying it. Oftentimes in the past when her sister had talked in that heated, convinced way, she had been trying to persuade her that something was true when in fact it wasn't. "I lead a very comfortable life, you know," she said stiffly.

"That's—that's calling a spade a spade," sputtered Monique on a laugh; the other things she had been ready to say seemed pointless in the face of such candidness. That money could keep one—for a while or forever--from taking unhappiness too seriously... how often was that the pepper in the works of world literature that she studied?...At her age she could just begin to intellectually see that this consoling power of money became greater and greater the older one got, and so (though she wasn't there yet, didn't believe this herself yet) she could accept the idea that if her sister felt that security, she shouldn't let it go.

Yet the phone calls continued. There was a new incident. Matt had spanked Leslie-Ann hard, with his father's boisterous approval, for having bolted out in front of a car on the street. Her bottom had welts, and she'd cried hysterically; Sophie hadn't been able to calm her down for anything. There were also mean moments when Matt got so angry—for an unflushed toilet or invitations accepted without his being consulted or check amounts not written down—that he got nasty: "Bitch", he said now, "you fucking bitch."

As this phone reportage grew protracted and habitual over time, Monique began to forget that she really didn't know her brother-in-law; that her view of him was something on the order of a Cubist portrait, an assemblage of distortions. She held the phone receiver against her ear and let Sophie provide the jumbled, sharp-angled pieces of this puzzle.

"Today," Sophie said, "he called me stupid in front of a lot of people."

"What did you do?"

"I was supposed to do something? It was in the supermarket line with Leslie-Ann sitting in the cart behind us. I turned to him and missed placing the milk on the conveyor belt, and he called me stupid again, only more quietly."

Monique pictured the scene vividly. Why this scene and not one of the others Sophie had recounted? Maybe it was because this one struck an instinctual response in her. It was a scene she could enter. A supermarket was a neutral public place. She saw her sister frozen with shame and embarrassment in that supermarket. Then she saw herself in the supermarket telling Matt Gagliardi to go to hell. Sophie again. Then herself again.

The scene could be played in two ways.

*

Matt opened his study door a moment or two after Leslie-Ann had waken up from her nap and begun to cry in her crib upstairs. "I'm coming, sweetheart!" he called with a radiant look of happiness on his face. He jogged ahead of Sophie, who was already climbing the stairs. "I'll get her," he grunted roughly. The pink nursery was dark and first thing he did was raise the blinds; Leslie-Ann was sitting in her crib and rubbed her eyes at the entering sunlight. He picked his daughter up and began to whisper in her ear. Snatches of the loving things he said came out in Italian. With considerable excitement he promised to take her to Venice in a few years. He'd just heard from Lorenza. She wasn't going away after all, and his world was safe.

*

Sophie dressed Leslie-Ann and tried some pleasant conversation with Matt at the breakfast table, and though he obliged her by sounding easy-going in return, she wondered while she watched him speak how much mortification or sadness she would feel that day. She momentarily relaxed when she heard his car pull out of the garage and knew she would not have to physically face him again for hours. When she'd cleaned up in the kitchen, showered, and dressed herself, however, she felt that earlier unnerved feeling creep back over her. It was as if she were holding back on an ugly and dismal secret. That secret was the knowledge that some part of herself was missing. Her future. She could no longer picture herself in the future. Now she was married to Matt and living in this house with him and Leslie-Ann, but where would she be in a year's time? She blindly intuited that everything would be very different.

"He's thinking about a divorce," she told Monique on the phone that afternoon, though she was only guessing. "He won't want to put up with me forever." Sophie understood she irritated him too profoundly for that.

"Do *you* want a divorce?"

"I don't have what it takes. He knows it. He'd walk all over me." A long while back, he had told her that if *she* tried to leave *him* it would be by herself—without Leslie Ann—and in a coffin. But of course that was just angry talk. Wasn't it?

If he *was* thinking of divorce, however, she had to think about it, too.

"Please tell me what to do," said Sophie unabashedly.

"I don't believe you just said that."

"Please. Just tell me what you would do," Sophie amended. "Whatever comes to your mind."

The rephrasing worked like the lock combination on Monique's old diary; Monique's talent for taking in panoramas really *was* indomitable.

"All I can tell you," she began, "is what you should try to end up with. I don't know how things are going to go for you. I'm not a fortune-teller. Maybe he won't get meaner and meaner, and more and more enraged, until the big blow-up. He could just find another woman, it happens all the time. Then it's S*o long, Sophie.* The big mansion gets sold, you lose you beautiful expensive things, you move into some hole. And I don't have to tell you what comes next; you know that you're going to be really depressed and dejected and not up to doing anything: you're going to come to me and I'm going to be worried but there'll be little I can do. How are you going to get by? You'll only have a bit of child support. Or worse." A keenly melodramatic but at the same time realistic turn of events came to Monique, and there was no holding it back. "He might keep Leslie-Ann, not let you see her, point to your near drowning as 'instability.'"

"No!"

The idea of losing Leslie-Ann really shook her; it entered her invasively and painfully. With this loathsome foreign object lodged inside her, Sophie stayed tense and vigilant for days.

*

It was around dinner time, and the five or six grills in the county-park picnic area reserved for hospital staff's Family Day were sizzling with bratwursts and hamburgers. When Sophie asked Matt to take care of Leslie-Ann for a bit while she got herself a plate of food, he made it clear that he didn't like her interrupting his lawn-chair conversation with his young interns; the "*fine*" that he muttered was even more arched and dismissive than usual as he thrust out his arms for Leslie-Ann to waddle into. "Has the baby eaten?" he asked sharply.

"Of course she has."

"Go, then. Go." He turned his back to her.

Dejectedly, she joined one of the lines by the grills, waiting behind three women in top-and-shorts outfits and with blonde ponytails like hers. Since dying her own hair she had stopped paying much attention to that of other women, the way someone who has purchased living room furniture ceases to study the living room choices of others, but something told her to pay attention to this similarity today. She carried her plate and hamburger over to a free corner of a picnic table of people she didn't recognize, and chomped her way through her meal in an uncommunicative state, knowing that Matt wouldn't be happy if she returned to eat in front of him and simultaneously suspecting he would be just as displeased if she brought him a platter of food he hadn't requested. The lady with short hair and glasses across from her asked if she knew where the condiments were, and as she shook her head, the woman's frosted gray-*blond* hair flagged her attention. Blondes everywhere. And why was she noticing this all of a sudden? As if it were a sign or revelation or something.

Then suddenly a possible reason came to her. She'd made a mistake by becoming blonde—maybe Matt disliked her, even hated her, that way. Dear God, was that it? She *had had brown hair* when they met. Maybe he preferred brunettes. It was strange, however, that she'd never suspected this. He'd never told her anything of the sort, not even in bed in a tender, opening moment of arousal, back in those days when they were still making love. And then, she reflected, he had said nothing nasty when she'd come home from the hairdresser's with her new blonde look two years ago. She remembered the moment clearly. That *'well, now'* comment of his.

"They just put out some yummy looking fruit salad." Back with her food and a ketchup bottle, the lady with the frosted hair leaned over the table towards Sophie. "Looks like you're ready for dessert."

Sophie came out of her distracted state with an automatic smile. Glad to have an excuse to leave the table, she stood up with her plate. "That does sound good. Can I get you some, too?"

Sophie circled the buffet tables laden with salads and desserts several times. She was simply too far into her thoughts about blondes and brunettes and Matt. There was something important to understand, but she had yet to grasp it. Could *this* be behind Matt's nastiness? In addition to all the other things that made him so mad, of course. Her stupidity. Passiveness. Silence. Lack of ideas. Lack of identity. An overwhelming list. And yet. Should she go to the hairdresser's tomorrow for brown hair? Would it make any difference, even a small one?

Her fruit salad eaten, she dumped her plate and cup into the trash can and made her way among the wooden tables and picnic blankets to rejoin Matt and Leslie-Ann. She knew that she'd been away for longer than she'd planned, for longer than was justified, and yet was genuinely puzzled to see that they weren't where she'd left them. Not only were their plastic chairs vacant but Leslie-Ann's necessity bag and even her own purse were gone. When she questioned the people who'd been sitting near them, all they could tell her was that they'd seen father and daughter "just a minute ago." Mystified and anxious, she went to the parking lot. The car wasn't there. Next to the now empty parking space, Matt's buddy, Phil, was unloading a cooler from his station wagon.

"Hi, Sophie. He shot her a knowledgeable look. "He didn't tell you, I take it."

"Did you see them leave, Phil?"

"I did, actually. Leslie Ann was tired and crying, and Matt was getting, well let's say, annoyed? So... ... yeah, he went home," said Phil, eyes on the white cooler top. "But I wouldn't be too sore, Sophie. You went off and were enjoying yourself, that's cool. And

Matt did maybe not a cool thing but a right thing in a way. He was just thinking of Leslie-Ann."

Just thinking of Leslie-Ann. Phil couldn't know how much panic he had made her feel.

Over the next two hours, until she saw someone leaving and could ask for a lift, her anguish over losing Leslie-Ann, of having her whisked away suddenly and unfairly—like today, only forever—mounted and mounted. She found a deserted stretch next to the pond, where she pretended to watch the ducks, shooing mosquitoes from her ears and letting the tears run down her cheeks. She turned round towards the parking lot every so often, hoping to see someone she knew walking towards a car, finally recognizing Matt's receptionist Betty, a thick-waisted woman with spiky hair, as she lumbered along with a fold-up chair under each arm; Sophie ran towards her, gave her a garbled story about Leslie-Ann getting feverish and Matt rushing her home, and obtained what she wanted, at the price of forty minutes of gossip about the medical office.

It was dark when Betty dropped her off. Sophie, who had her house keys in the pocket of her shorts, was able to let herself in because it was not yet ten o'clock, when Matt's alarm system came on. She found them in the family room: Matt intent on a crossword puzzle, with his bare feet up on the couch, and Leslie-Ann, still in her thin sleeveless picnic clothes soiled with ice cream and ketchup and grass, sitting in her plastic chair just a foot in front of the television set and absorbed in the floppy antics of her favorite Sesame Street puppets. Sophie noiselessly entered the room and swooped her up. Her little arms felt cold. "Hello, my baby!" Leslie-Ann's diaper was stone heavy and sopping wet. Behind her, presumably looking at her, Matt coughed harshly. She didn't know if it was involuntary or not. Since he didn't speak, she didn't either. In an instinctive and confused way, she understood that words would make the scene stranger, more frightening. She fled with Leslie-Ann out of the room.

Sophie did not know what this nasty business signified.

The idea of telling anyone about it was overwhelming. It upset her so much that she didn't even phone Monique. It was an infinitely intimate thing for Sophie. She worried herself into a stunned state, which lasted until the following Thursday evening, when it became apparent that Matt, who had his pager turned off, wasn't planning to come home; this mystery, which was potentially more than an insult, roused her from her numbness, and she lay in bed for hours trying in great anguish to decide if she should call the police.

In the end she reached for the phone and called someone else.

"Hello, Monique? It's me."

"What time is it?" mumbled Monique.

"It's almost four-thirty in the morning. He isn't home. Do you think something could have happened to him?"

"Alert the police." Monique's eyes stayed closed and her mind in the entranceway to sleep.

"Maybe I should wait."

"Then wait."

"It could be good to tell the judge about if this divorce happens."

Monique did not intend to wake up for speculation of this sort, which Sophie was totally inept at and only trying to get her attention with. "Concentrate on how life will be afterwards," she murmured, drawing in the right sort of breath to keep her in a half-sleep.

"I know but—."

Monique exhaled audibly and slowly, the way one did in yoga.

"Monique?"

"Don't ask me what I mean. I've already told you."

"But—I."

"No buts." Implacably, like the professor that she was, she recited dully from memory her description of how Sophie's next life would be: her going to live in a nice town of her choosing, with new friends and playmates for Leslie-Ann; her learning pottery-painting or jewelry-making or some such thing; her meeting friendly new men, maybe single fathers, at craft fairs. Completely plausible imaginings; nothing much different from Sophie's present life, except with Matt's long shadow removed.

"Good night, Sophie."

Monique breathed her way back into full slumber. The easy sleep of she who has done everything she can.

Famous last words.

*

Diane had prepared an elaborate Easter dinner with all the dishes that her mother had taught her to make—the coiled hand-made pasta called *fusilli,* lamb, *torta di melanzane,* braided Easter bread, and ricotta pie. Two year-old Leslie-Ann, in a lime-green spring dress that matched the two barrettes in her curly hair, was perched in her highchair next to Grandpa Gagliardi at the head of the long table. Her father spooned samples of various kinds of antipasto into her bowl, explaining about mozzarella *di bufala* and how to pickle eggplant and dry tomatoes in his most confidential, winning voice, as if she really might be enchanted by a good jolly papa into speaking more than the few monosyllables she had currently mastered.

Sophie was helping Diane carry platters to the table. As she set the salad bowl down by Matt's brother Tom and his companion Donna, who with her fair Irish looks and new engagement ring was attending her first Gagliardi family Easter dinner, Sophie saw that Matt was loading an alarmingly large portion of pasta with tomato sauce onto Leslie-Ann's plate.

"*Leezlie-Anna,*" crooned *Nonno* Gagliardi, hunched over his own portion. "*Mangia. Mangia.*"

Matt grated Parmesan cheese over her mound and speared the first fusilli for her. "*Brava, cosi!*" Gagliardi bobbed his head at her in approval, reeling into his mouth a few stray strands with lightning speed.

Leslie-Ann had already chewed her way through about half a plateful, and her face was smeared in red, when Sophie took her place at the table. No one had given her daughter a bib, she noticed.

"*Mangia! Mangia!*" *Nonno* Gagliardi personally piled a new coiled mass on the child's plate and urged her to eat.

One leg swinging and her head bouncing, Leslie-Ann showed him every forkful as she ate it. Matt glanced from the two of them to his wife. Sitting at the edge of her chair, her left hand in a worrying fist alongside her plate, she was taking tiny mincing bites with her front teeth, like someone bothered by taste and texture. What's wrong with her? he thought angrily. This was the best food in the world. The two of them just didn't have a damn thing in common, did they? Mind you, he'd never seen her *cringe* at Italian cooking before...But wait, what she was cringing at was Leslie-Ann. The bitch didn't like Leslie-Ann eating all she was eating and enjoying it. She didn't like her nodding at her *Nonno*'s question and flashing her big smile.

"More, Diana, we need more here," said Grandpa Gagliardi, gesturing to her to pass down the big pasta bowl from her end of the table. Wide-eyed with alarm, Sophie watched it go from Gagliardi brother to brother till it reached her father-in-law, who once again raised the fork and spoon solemnly into the air—you would have thought he was a priest with a host or something—and set this wallop in her daughter's bowl.

"*C'est trop!*" This protest in French, that enough was enough, burst from her spontaneously. They were Maman's words. Maman had taught her civilized limits, and that excess was to be shuddered at. For Leslie-Ann's sake she would insist.

"*Ma stai zitta!*" With his hand Gagliardi Senior made the Italian sign of disdain that is like a slow pantomimed slap.

"Daddy, Sophie's right. That's enough. The child's going to get sick," said Diane.

"*Ma stai zitta anche tu!*" he intimidated. "OH!" With a bizarre lop-sided smile, he banged a fist to show he really expected them to obey and keep quiet.

"Cool it, both of you," said Matt in a low voice through gritted teeth. First French against Italian. Then men against women. And culminating in husband against wife. It was all so clear to Matt.

"Leslie-Ann, honey, you eat," he added.

Looking immensely pleased, with herself and the attention she was getting, Leslie-Ann stuffed so much pasta into her mouth that both cheeks bulged. She resembled a red-smeared toad.

"Leslie-Ann, you'll choke!" Sophie rose and made her way to her daughter.

"You're out of your mind," Matt said callously. As Sophie came between Leslie-Ann and him, his intolerance of her flared. He would not have her there, blocking him off from his daughter. If there was going to be any wall erected, *he* would be the one to do it. With this diabolical energy he said, "Bad Mommy! Say it, Leslie-Ann, say 'bad Mommy!'" He gave Sophie's hip a demonstrative whack. "You show her. Like that. BAD MOMMY."

Leslie-Ann plummeted both fists into Sophie's stomach. "Badddd Mommmmmmmeeee!"

He is teaching my daughter to beat me, she had time to think, before Leslie-Ann pulled back her head and with a long agonizing snot-clogged gag, threw up five helpings of red mush all over the table.

*

An even more immense wall. That is what Matt Gagliardi erected when the stimulating idea occurred to him to *ignore his wife completely*.

He was walking out of a Mexican restaurant after lunch on a sunny day along with a group of other specialists from the hospital, when he saw Sophie's Garden Club group assembling to go in for lunch at the same place. He didn't think about not greeting or recognizing her, he just carried on talking about a patient case with a cardiologist, moving past her the way he would a tree in a clump of trees on a sunny day. How many times do we feign distraction or some other failure of perception (which does authentically happen every so often) so as to avoid the embarrassment or annoying necessity of having to acknowledge someone? Why, it occurs all the time, he reflected afterwards, so why not with a wife? And a few days later, when he was crossing the street by the post office in downtown Swarthmore and saw her getting out of their second car in a metered space by the same post office, he stared at the green traffic light, feeling her stare on his impassive face. His face was *not* all for her, no not for her these days by any means. When he ignored her, he didn't feel annoyance or irritation (which got whipped up so easily into rage) but indifference. She was a bearable presence, mother of his child after all, like a satellite orbiting him at a distance. The memory of his pursuing her, wanting her in Paris, nauseated him—it made him gag! She gave him nothing today, no vitality, no initiative, no counter-pressure to meet his. He couldn't remember what he'd seen in her and he didn't want to remember. How could he have thought she was wise? He'd realized something terrible seeing her hold Leslie-Ann in her arms. It had been an overpowering revelation: the baby was perfect and the woman was a sow.

She called his name.

He did not react.

She yelled, "Matt!"

Out of the corner of his eye, he noted her waving. He did not react. And walked rapidly out of earshot.

Matt Gagliardi knew he was choosing indifference, he knew it kept him as close as could be expected to his inner hot springs, to sweetness; he did not see it as rage gone underground.

Each time, having ignored his wife, Matt phoned Lorenza.

*

Sophie's astonishing request began as an exasperated retort. No doubt many plans hatch this way. She'd been crying; she described to Monique Matt's blank determination not to know her anymore: "And I can't do anything! I can't do anything! It's all going to happen like you said."

"Fight back," was Monique's reaction. "Treat *him* like a ghost in the house."

"No, no and no!" Sophie rebelled. "You always harp at me. It's always 'what I should have done.' Damn, if you were here instead of me, Monique, you'd feel in your bones how he has me pinned where he wants me. But it'd all end differently, wouldn't it? Because you wouldn't be me!"

She had always been strong and one of a kind; she had always managed to remain who she was even while becoming her sister. She was incapable of losing herself. The past had shown that she was the twin who could live for two. *Monique, prépare-toi.*

PART THREE

CHAPTER ELEVEN

This time of course it was dangerous. They weren't switching places for the length of a car ride into Philadelphia with their French relatives, nor even for the morning of a college-placement test. This was no lark. This was an arduous, thrilling undertaking. It depended on the one hand on Monique's resilience, cunning, and strength of character: and on the other, on Sophie's patience, acceptance of the temporary absence of her daughter, and ability to abide in a daily existence that was neither her own nor properly her sister's. (God forbid she should actually try to give a comparative lit lecture in Monique's place; for this reason Monique had taken a leave of absence). They foresaw that every now and then Sophie might have to impersonate Monique briefly but it wouldn't go beyond that. By contrast, Monique would not impersonate: Monique would become. Her inner walls of self would expand (as far as it was possible to do without going crazy) and envelop her sister's essence.

This was the plan. Aided by her sense of entitlement to Sophie's wealthy existence, guided by her theatrical abilities and nerves, Monique would find a way to make Matt Gagliardi bend. She would psychologically outwit him: and if not that, she would find the right tidbit for a lawyer; Sophie would have her daughter and the divorce settlement she deserved.

Yes, it was dangerous. But there was no need to be afraid. There was the advantage that Matt Gagliardi didn't suspect a thing. Also, Monique reasoned, one wife did so many of the same things as another wife—the cooking, cleaning, shopping, childcare—that already there was a natural human tendency to see them as interchangeable, at certain moments anyway, if only one closed his or her eyes.

Here there was no need to close one's eyes because she and Sophie were identical. The illusion could only gain in power. And she would enhance it further by talking, walking, thinking, and emoting like Sophie, as only she could.

Hard to detect, isn't she, this shadow wife?

*

When Manuel the hairdresser freed the two twin sisters of his smocks with a grin of relief, it was well past lunchtime. The ex-blonde paid. Without talking about what they would do next, the two red-headed sisters made their way from the gloomy corridor of Manuel's failing business venture to the bright hexagonal heart of the mall with its mirrors, busy see-through elevators, palms, and fountains. Under the blinking pink neon of a giant-cookie stand, Monique said with satisfaction, "We look gaudy, but it's because we're together. We're fine each on our own, I'd say."

People were looking at them. Three squat lady retirees, especially, were having a hey day. When Sophie coughed on a chocolate chip still other heads turned. After downing and gagging on a lot of water, she said, "What I was trying to say was that I forgot to give you the second secret code to my car. It's wired with another of Matt's weird security systems."

Monique took out her small special notebook and wrote this down. Her notes from the previous afternoon sessions at Sophie's house were already quite extensive, but any additional tidbit was welcome. Last Monday to Friday, she had driven over from their parents' place in New Jersey and spent three solid hours each time watching and observing. She followed Sophie's moves from room to room and imitated her walk; she noticed that her sister lifted Leslie Ann by hoisting her up by under the arms; she sang the same nursery rhymes as Sophie and smeared the diaper cream in the same way; she tried loading and unloading the dishwasher in the same fashion and putting all the contents in the right cupboards and drawers; she learned positions of everything in the master bath and made a note that Matt left the bathroom door unlocked but hated her barging in. She practiced the soft, slightly breathless, marveling "hello?" of Sophie answering the phone, as well as the modest, humble and rapid "This is Sophie. Is Matt free?" that her sister used when she phoned Matt's office.

When Monique got back to Maman's house, she shut herself in the old bedroom and practiced all these things in the mirror. As a small test, the last afternoon she phoned the housewife who babysat Leslie-Ann, Mrs. Korn, in Sophie's place. The woman seemed convinced that she was talking to the little girl's mother. The final thing she and Sophie did, before heading to the hairdresser, was to stand naked, side by side, in front of Sophie's long large dresser mirror. They scrutinized and compared shoulders, thighs, stretch marks, breasts, stomachs, hands, face wrinkles.

"You're no more of an athlete than I am. You had a baby and I baby my books, and so our bellies round a bit. Still, our arms are nice and thin. Forget the hair—that'll be the same soon enough," said Monique. "And forget this slight crease mark of mine between the eyes. It's not deep. We're only thirty-one. I have a special cream, and I can keep myself from scowling—when I do like this, there, it's gone. And look at my back—with your upright posture."

"Yes, yes." said Sophie happily. It was a moment for gloating. It was a moment of sisterhood as Sophie had always intended it.

And now even their hair was done... and they were two stunning redheads in the Ladies' room at the Mall putting on the white linen dresses they'd bought. Monique gave Sophie a kick under the partition between their toilet stalls to remind her to swap shoes with her. She finished first and waited for her sister out by the drinking fountain. In that moment of being alone, a peculiar energy pulsed through her—both her old power charge of superiority over her twin sister and something else too—the kind of over-extended lucidity that people expecting a radical change, or death perhaps, feel, which remains genuine if you let it pulse in silence.

"While I'm thinking of it..." Sophie muttered upon her reappearance. She slipped her gold wedding band onto Monique's finger. Then she handed Monique the shopping bag with her original clothes and took Monique's. "I'm giving it all up," she said abruptly, a change come over her too in her moment alone. "I'm walking into the ocean again."

"You're not going through anything. I am."

"I don't know about that. What if I can't handle my end of things?"

"Of course you can. Don't be stupid."

They left the mall by a perfectly normal, thronged exit inside J.C. Penney's. Sophie sniffled. "Be good," Monique told her warningly now. "Your daughter needs you."

"Now she'll need you."

Monique made a point of not answering that. She walked her sister through the parking lot to the red Toyota, and exhorted her not to go to any hotel but to stay with Maman and Dad tonight. She waved when Sophie finally pulled out onto the busy two-lane highway. Then, having worked all the fancy alarms to Sophie's silvery Mercedes Benz and slamming its door shut, Monique took obstinate mental possession of it and everything that wasn't hers. She sat there a while in a numb state with the air conditioning and engine running, her gaze tracing back and forth along the flat tar roof of the Mall as if it were a sightly example of castle crenellation. When enough of whatever it was that she half-fabricated and half-received from somewhere had entered her and sent her spirits soaring, she did it: she drove *home*.

*

The first day did not go at all smoothly; on the other hand, it went well.

Monique left Sophie's Mercedes Benz parked on the circular driveway. It was afternoon, and Leslie-Ann was still at her babysitter's house. Entering through the front door for the first time as the owner, Monique was enveloped by the immense idle silence typical of spacious homes with grandfather clocks in the foyer. Her footsteps echoed over wooden floors and on tiles, went dead on Persian rugs, and crinkled on bathroom linoleum. It being a mild September day, the window sashes were raised in the upstairs rooms and she could hear rustling trees and a distant sound of traffic, which only accentuated the house's illusion of sanctuary.

As was the case with other wealthy homes she'd seen, it looked as if a maid had just finished cleaning and left by the back door. Nothing was out of place: the beds were perfect under their frilly comforters; Leslie-Ann's crib was smartly draped with quilts and under the musical protection of a mobile carillon chiming in the light breeze; on the bed stands covered in tablecloths, there were dusted lamps, clocks, and water carafes. She noticed things that she hadn't had time to take in on her week-end visit last year nor during the two or three afternoons last week when she was here getting a feel for her part. My, this was a handsome house! To think of all the decorating hours that had been spent to achieve this lovely effect. To think that someone (Sophie? a paid decorator?) had taken all this to heart, spent time on colors, coordinated details, harmonized knick-knacks. Monique stopped for a second to wonder—in a fretful sort of way—about whether, in Sophie's place, she would have done it exactly the same. Then she roused herself and went back through the house to review what she believed were the important things.

She stepped into the pantry to check the food supplies for tonight, tomorrow, and the week; she investigated the adjacent laundry room in a more thorough way than before—right, here was where the vacuum cleaner was kept. She had a close look at Matt's desk in his den and at the supplies in her own office off the kitchen. In the living room, family room, and library (soon, she promised herself, she'd have a go at those books), she picked up curios, photos, coasters, small statues and plants, familiarizing herself with even their positions. She went through the music stored in the piano bench, to see what exactly Matt liked to play: Mozart, Schubert, "Arrivederci Roma," Christmas carols, ragtime. The piano bench, in addition to the toys and books in Leslie-Ann's room, and the top dresser drawers in Matt's and Sophie's master suite gave her more personal traces to draw inspiration from. The further she penetrated anywhere else, however, the more the house seemed like a resort hotel or an old college dorm, not properly private, not even its smell. And in this final short interval before the curtain went up on her performance, the lack of intimacy about the place bothered her soul, showed her how being mistress to a mansion was alien to her nature. Walking into her university-owned utilitarian flat in Chicago, one saw immediately all the space she had at her disposition; and eating a meal for her meant sharing the table with her spread of research notes. She liked it that way, she liked eating and thinking with nothing to keep them apart. For although she'd come round on her thinking regarding money, the sheer burden of property was another thing entirely. Yes, *burden*—she sensed it oppressing her body as she stood by the massive china cupboard in her sister's dining room.

Perhaps in response to this, she hungrily seized an apple from the fruit bowl in the kitchen. As she went to rinse it—pow!—a surge of water bursting a pipe made the door under the sink fly open.

Shutting off the tap didn't work, not even when she squeezed the handle more tightly, and still more tightly, unable to believe it. The geyser gushed angrily through the sink cabinet and poured in a fan-tail onto the floor. She ran for the bucket that she'd seen in the laundry room and stuck it under the break, despairing about how she could get help. To call a plumber she needed the phone book. Where was *that*? Behind her, the bucket overflowed and she watched the edges of the sheet of water roll forward like batter. Suddenly she remembered that she had a husband.

The number of his medical office was on the refrigerator door. Sophie had mentioned that Matt's receptionist was a friendly, self-sacrificing woman, *but what was her name?* Monique could only trust that the panic in her voice would explain away any etiquette slights that the other woman might notice. She picked up the phone and asked for Matt in her sister's rushed, mumbly way, only up an octave because it was an emergency.

"Oh dear me. Well, Dr. Gagliardi will be here from the hospital in less than an hour. Don't worry, Mrs. Gagliardi, you can count on Betty to tell him." Of course, *Betty*. Or was she referring to a co-worker? Monique held her tongue. "Or you can phone the hospital directly if you like," Betty added, ticking off the number by rote. A truly understanding woman. There was now an inch of water covering the entire kitchen floor. She opened the door to the patio and swept a small wave of it that way. Her feet sloshed in her shoes. She told herself, "It's *not really* my house." She called Matt's hospital and said it was an emergency. The nurse who answered managed to catch Matt on his way out of the X-ray lab. Monique felt the burden fall across her shoulders of 'playing the stupid woman' as the nurse muffled the receiver and told him it was his wife with a problem. Matt Gagliardi sounded tired. Mental fatigue. Monique recognized it. She couldn't tell him but she identified.

"Where's your address book of such things?" he asked.

"I—I can't find it, Matt. *There's water all over the floor.*"

"Go shut off the main in the cellar."

"Oh. Right. Good idea."

A short mean sound—a snicker?—escaped him. With precise instructions, he told her where to find the main and now to work the valve. He didn't ask if she could manage and she didn't ask him to phone back. He hung up before her, she heard the click.

After she mopped up all the water, it was time to go pick up Leslie-Ann. At the wheel of the silvery Mercedes, she cruised in a leisurely fashion out of the palatial end of town and, over past the state route, into a Medusan lair of modest housing developments. She wasn't concentrating properly and she knew it: her mind refused to settle attentively on Leslie-Ann, on how to mother her now that she was on her own, on how, too, to deal with Mrs. Korn in person. Instead, she mused on things as she was used to doing. *What a piece of luck* was her assessment of her first conversation with Matt. He hadn't been very understanding and he had practically hung up on her. *It was the stuff of a good argument.* She was going to make this sort of desire to pick a fight with Matt Gagliardi into an irrepressible urge. *He might ignore her, but she, Sophie, would not feel crushed and speechless; she would not lose her voice. Weren't there in the Eastern world three parts to every person, and not just two, body and soul? The invisible, the physical, and the vocal—or what we do with our voice, how it affects others, how it is recalled and re-evoked. The only way that we truly haunt others...* Oh yes, she would talk. Her Sophie would maintain the three parts of her nature; words would flow from her; they would start to obliterate some of his. The impression that she could trust herself to know how to do this was the foundation on which she, yes!, would build for days.

Mrs. Korn's face exercised its muscles in various sympathetic poses when she heard about the burst pipe, and as she took in the surprise of Mrs. Gagliardi's very short and mannish new red hairdo. She was clearly too stunned to think that the woman she'd opened the door to was anyone other than Sophie herself gone radical in her appearance and loquacious in her alarm. Leslie-Ann, on the other hand, seemed oblivious even to these changes. *Mama,* she'd said matter-of-factly, not even a smile for the magical disappearance of her mother's blond hair. *Mama!* –she complained when the two of them got home and lay on the big bed, followed by another *Mama,* for comfort. It was their first time alone. She took Monique's hand and showed her how she wanted her leg stroked as she drifted into her nap.

"How's that, sweetheart?"

The word *sweetheart* worked even nicer miracles; Sophie had told her this. Leslie-Ann turned towards her and kissed her cheek: "Love you." It was one of her few 'sentences.'

Sophie had described her as *good.* During their first afternoon together, Monique learned the profundity of the word. Leslie-Ann was the sort of toddler who resolved her own whining fit by going and pointing to a toy that she deemed she *could* keep by her side as she ate her snack, without fear of getting it dirty. Leslie-Ann was a child who managed after her nap to climb out of the crib where Monique had placed her (How had she done it?—Monique's heart leaped—though later she realized that she must have used her adjacent changing table as a sort of ladder) only to waddle, backwards and on her knees, down the stairs and into the family room to clamor: *more, more.* Where *more* was nothing but an ardent cuddle.

And so, the problem of how to lovingly deceive Leslie-Ann, did it exist? Oh it did all right. The challenge was not how to look like her mother to her but rather how to feel like Mama to her imploring fingers. It's easy to hug a child back but we hug all children except our own with a bit of timorous respect, with a concern that it might be too forceful or just too long. Her theatrical instinct told Monique that she should reach for Leslie-Ann on a deep relaxed breath, while common sense suggested that if she could find a temporary excuse for limiting the intensity of their contact she would be playing it safest. "Mama doesn't feel very well this afternoon. Mama's sick. If I lie here on the couch, will you play next to me and keep me company?"

For the next hour or maybe more, she lay grateful, and for the most part silent and still, while Leslie-Ann flitted back and forth through the room, carrying blocks, little cardboard books, stuffed animals. She had light-brown hair that ended in bouncing ringlets on her shoulders. Her sturdy broad chest recalled her father's. She also had his almond-shaped, nearly slanty eyes, though there was nothing sinister or exotic about them and they were French blue like Sophie's and hers. She pretended to doze. Leslie-Ann ran one of her plastic cars over her knee. She breathed regularly with her eyes shut. She began to wonder about how long Leslie-Ann could amuse herself; the time till Matt's coming home and her bedtime suddenly bothered her for its white noise of eternity, and she wished that she could pull it like a seashell away from her ear, then she said, "Are you hungry, Leslie-Ann?"

"Juice," said the child. The television clicked on. Monique raised her head. Leslie-Ann held the remote control in one fist. The toy commercials raced towards their top level of noise and promise like the engines of souped-up cars. The sound had the immediate effect of restoring the quick pulse of time as she knew it and wanted it, and her fit of intolerance subsided. Though Monique couldn't explain the connection, her certainty of Leslie-Ann's continuing ignorance and innocence, of things proceeding in a channeled course according to expectation, was reinforced. Leslie-Ann lowered herself into her small white rocking chair and became instantly enraptured by the TV again. Then the phone began to kazoo under the booming volume of the cartoons. On the other end of the line Sophie reminded her to pull the phone cord extension out to its full length and then step out through the French doors onto the gabled loggia.

"Is everything all right?"

Hearing that her daughter had asked for juice dispelled God knew what fears. Then Monique told her about the pipe, about having to shut off the water main, about Matt being unsympathetic on the phone. "Seems like a good opportunity to get a few things straight with him."

"Not yet. Let me give you the name of a plumber."

"You're impossible." But she wrote the number down.

"Don't push Matt, Monique. Not so soon…Do you want me to drive by later, around ten or so? You can leave a certain lamp on as a signal everything's all right."

"For God's sake, keep away. Where are you, by the way?"

She wasn't at their parents' yet, that's all she would say. "Don't get angry if I point out to you that for Leslie-Ann it's almost dinner time," she added. "Call the pizza place that delivers, the number's on the refrigerator, will you, please?"

"Yeah, all right." Monique allowed herself a laugh. "You should have seen the babysitter's face this afternoon when she saw this red hair."

"Wait till Matt sees you. Forget I said that. It just popped out. I don't mean anything by it. You know how it is with me. Remember to order the pizza. Bye, Moni—no, what am I saying?—bye, then, *just bye.*"

An hour later, Monique was in the kitchen cutting the hot pizza wedges still smaller for Leslie-Ann, with the phone tucked under her chin as she waited for the recorded message on the plumber's answering machine to finish, when Matt walked in. The white door between the mud room and the garage heaved, and with two steps he filled the threshold of the kitchen with the swell of chest that she remembered, which drew one's eyes to his smooth shirt and tie, that fitted trim armor over his chest and heart. He grasped the handle of his leather briefcase in one hand, as he unclipped his beeper from his belt with the other.

"Hi."

"Hi. Daddy's home, Leslie-Ann."

He frowned at her, his almond eyes painfully contracted. "What have you done to yourself?" he breathed.

She blinked the way Sophie would and said brightly, "I went to the hairdresser's."

He circled soundlessly around the kitchen island and her, set his briefcase on the counter by the toaster, took out the *Philadelphia Inquirer*, snapped the briefcase closed, and, still scowling, went with the same quiet, tired Indian tread into his den. She heard him empty his jacket pocket, the sounds of his unburdening: the wallet, pens, electronic calendar, coins, they jangled dully on his desk and desk pad. Leslie-Ann approached the door and she followed. Standing behind the little girl, she patted her head and smoothed her hair. He finished rolling up his shirt sleeves, then picked up Leslie-Ann. His hand ran through her curls as Monique's had. He glanced back at his wife. Almost, well, grief-stricken. "What have you done to yourself?"

Monique's impulse was to make a joke, to fling the seeds of a new principle: that what mattered was *her* amusement, *her* pleasure. (Once this territory was staked out, she would go on to bigger and better things). But the way he was taking it took her aback.

"I won't have it." He said this very slowly, savagely.

She watched him go into the bathroom and realize with a *'fuck it"* as he turned the faucet handle that the water main was still off. He returned to shut himself in his den to make phone calls, presumably one to a plumber, since he didn't ask her if she'd called one herself. He let Leslie-Ann in briefly to read her a story. Swinging open, the paneled door made a forty-five degree triangle of light, which receded to a flat line when the door clicked closed. He came out only once. She was in the kitchen still, in speechless vigilance. He accepted a piece of pizza on a plate. "You haven't answered my question. What have you done to yourself?" was all he said.

She took Leslie-Ann upstairs to bed after dinner and sang her the songs Sophie had said to put her to sleep by. The doorbell rang in the foyer. The plumber no doubt—the proof being that when she went to the bathroom after Leslie-Ann had fallen asleep, she found that the water had been turned back on.

Alone in her sister's master bedroom suite, Monique returned to herself. Foolish of her, she knew, but, honestly, she hadn't been able to get past brushing her teeth and removing her make-up for the first time in Sophie's marbled bathroom, without her, well, call them *old thoughts,* streaming back to her like a stubborn herd of work animals desirous of their pen. On this, her first night of false identity, she gazed at the woman with cropped scarlet hair in the wall mirror and mouthed her own name. *She saw herself riding the Paris metro, climbing its white-tiled stairs to the street, going into the softly-lit salle of the Bibliotèque Nationale and asking Madame, who recognized her, for accounting records relative to the musical fêtes given by Louis XIV. Which of the arts*—...but just as the threads of her real identity were coming together, she heard a toilet downstairs flushing. Matt the husband might be about to come up the stairs. Leslie-Ann might be stirring in the next room. This first night might contain any number of happenings. Lying rigidly at attention on Sophie's side of the bed, she make every mental effort to shrink herself back into her sister's life and wait apprehensively to see what came next. She had never play-acted her way through an entire night before, nor had she ever lay in a bed next to a man whom she didn't like but who had every right to touch her. Although his reaction to her red hair and his avoiding her all evening should have reassured her that Matt would *not* likely be coming to bed with any such thing on his mind, what she most dreaded was his eventual reaching for her. Sophie had told her to expect it. He had even gone for Sophie the night after he'd snubbed and ignored her in public. Monique had made up her mind not to push him away when it happened; that sort of change was to come later. But she was going to feel goose-bumps, an unquantifiable amount of aversion, and God only knew what else.

As things turned out, Leslie-Ann did not cry out even once, and Matt, who came to bed eventually in the grainy and blackest darkness—not even a filmy sheen of outside light through the blinds, for the curtains had been lined specially to allow for Sunday afternoon naps, Matt turned his back to her like a huge circus animal lying suddenly quiet, and slept till the sound of the alarm made him rise. They did not synchronize their breathing or extend their limbs (and she didn't know if that was good or bad, like or unlike Sophie in this bed). Every few hours Monique reassured herself that the long mummy radiating heat next to her lay dormant. After he left the house, in what seemed like the middle of the night but was just very early in the morning, a few hours prior to his first operation of the day, she finally had her first relaxed tuck of sleep. When she awoke, Leslie-Ann was next to her, elbows flapping as she moved two dolls at a gallop through the air. *I've done it, I've spent the night here*, she thought.

Leslie-Ann straddled her hips going downstairs, the child's head bouncing in time to the steps taken and to the squeezes and hugs; and when Mama finally with a pant dumped her into her high chair she cried a little. There was no finer antidote for intermittent sensations of unfamiliarity and strangeness than the bustling duties of childcare. For the next hour Monique was fully immersed in it, putting into practice the lessons she'd learned while taking care of her mentor's small children, following Sophie's instructions, and inventing the rest. Leslie-Ann was good, but she did have her morning fretting session, where she found herself missing a favorite toy and the like, the scene threatening at any minute to degenerate into a crying fit on account of her lack of words.

At last the moment came for Monique to get dressed herself. According to her notes, the one certainty of the day, a Tuesday, was that as of nine-thirty, Leslie-Ann could be dropped off at Mrs. Korn's. Inside the small square blind room which was her sister's closet, the closet with all the shoes from her dream, Monique delicately pulled a dress off a hanger as if it were a weightless, odorless body with its soul gone. Slipping into Sophie's panties brought electricity to her legs and when she smoothed the low elastic waistline over her hips, even a tickly shock to her crotch. "I am Sophie, SSSSSSophie." She exhaled and then inhaled deeply on that "*s*". She would not indulge in any more thoughts about her life in Chicago; she would not get distracted from her role.

She was happy strapping Leslie-Ann into her car seat. Happy driving to Mrs. Korn's. Happy stopping at the supermarket and frittering away a half hour on the purchase of some steak, salad, and milk.

Around noon, when she was back at the mansion and alone, she went through Matt's desk and read every slip of paper, every bill. Then she had a look at the strong box in the safe left ajar and in the file cabinets. After finishing in his study, she went down to the cellar, where she found labeled boxes from when he was single. When she had examined their contents, she climbed to the second floor and had a go at his bedroom closet and bureau. She found precious little, really: signed posters of high school theatre productions he'd starred in, a woman's pearl ring, a strange little black-iron statue of the devil; details that merely hinted of revelation. She tried looking in still other places -- the garage, his bathroom cabinet. Nothing. There were no shortcuts, not yet, to make her task of getting the better of him easier.

She decided she would provoke him at dinner by opening, without asking permission and pleading ignorance, a bottle of vintage Bordeaux he kept in a special wine refrigerator by his desk. She remembered how touchy he had been about that his wine during her first weekend in this house two and a half years ago. She would force him out of his indifference (feigned, she imagined) and make him show his ugly streak—that hint of violence that Sophie had once said alarmed the two of them. If he actually hit her—she breathed deeply—she'd go immediately to a lawyer. And if she then managed to enrage him a time or two after that, why Sophie would have her grounds for a divorce and a handsome settlement. This adventure would be over in record time.

There was just one problem. She couldn't know when Matt would get home in the evening. That evening or any evening. Sophie had forgotten to mention this. Boy, wasn't that just like Sophie! And it only emerged now because her sister, who sorely missed Leslie-Ann, impulsively telephoned the mansion, ready to hang up if Matt answered.

"If for some reason he wants to tell you his plans or movements, he'll phone," she explained in her unchagrined way. "But don't expect him to do that regularly."

It was after nine pm. Monique was drunk on a half bottle of Chateaux imbibed on a empty stomach and had not yet put Leslie-Ann to bed.

"You might not be awake in the same room with him very often, at least during the week," Sophie added.

"Great." Monique laughed hollowly. "Anything else?"

Maddening, simply maddening. Of course this lack of interaction with Matt put an incredible damper on her plans. What could she do in the hurried daytime encounters of that first week? What could she accomplish as she was passing through a room of the house where he happened momentarily to be? Sparking any argument was an arduous enterprise. She needed material to work with, and was disheartened at the prospects of obtaining it, for stockpiling up little five-minute scenes with the right kind of tension to them would surely take forever. He was very good at cold stoic sarcasm, at those nasty one-liners, delivered on his way out the door, the effect of which was a chill which lasted forever but never disturbed any one day's routine.

She found it hard to significantly increase the time they spent together; she literally didn't have access to him except for those hours at night when she lay next to his dark breathing bulk. Otherwise, the arrangement of the rooms in the large elaborate house, and his way of shutting himself up in one private space and then another, kept him from her sight...and vice versa. The moments where there was a bit of interaction with other people, on the other hand, had such a positive and engaging feel to them that she was bewildered by the contrast. Listening in on his phone conversations, when he let her, for instance, only reinforced her earliest impressions of him at his social best. She could tell from his voice that he was expecting to find a worthy person, the kind who could jog along in life at his own optimal pace, and should it be anyone else, he gave, generously, one final sprinkle of amicability in his "let me pass you to my wife." It might be anyone on the other end of the line: she tried to remember her lists, orient herself. He couldn't imagine how hard her mind was straining, using coughs or Sophie's faltering voice for cover, until she finally brought into focus the person she was talking to; he didn't know because he usually left the room.

A casual run-in with a neighbor one Saturday morning revealed even more to her; it afforded her a glimpse of the broad understanding over what was decent and civil which had once united Matt and Sophie: Matt talking in the driveway with an older neighbor astride his riding lawnmower; coming inside the house then to say to her—forgetting to grind his axe: "You know what? Mr. Pierce wanted to cut our swatch of property around the fire hydrant, too. He just apologized to me for not asking us first. What a guy—I think it was damn nice of him."

"How nice and thoughtful," she echoed. Warmly, unthinkingly Sophie, one-hundred percent Sophie. It both restored her faith in her own abilities, and gave her the flash truth that Monique would have laughed. Monique would have thought the fellow a Calvinist petit-bourgeois obsessed with neatness.

"I am Sophie, I start as Sophie, a quiet fish," she coached herself, "and in tiny increments of will and cunning, I will grow into a barracuda."

Meanwhile, she acquired knowledge about the stupid things that never got put on any list of a person's attributes but that had their relevance: how he favored after-dinner drinks to cocktails, how long he took to shower, how well he talked the jargon of medical tests when a colleague called, how business calls on the other hand made him serious and pondering, as, phone on his ear, he conspiratorially shut the door to his den.

Sophie fell into the pattern of phoning on weekdays in the late afternoon. "I'm at home with Maman and Dad," she announced into the second week. "Don't get mad, but they don't know. How could I tell them? Anyway, I'm leaving soon. I—well, you'll see," she promised lamely.

"You stay away from Chicago, if that's what you have in mind," said Monique. Her life there was on hold for four to six months; she was supposed to be off doing research in France and she wouldn't stand for Sophie messing that up by making an odd appearance at her apartment.

"How could I go that far away from my baby? How's my little girl?"

Twice already she'd begged to swap back temporarily with Monique, in a the ladies' room of a kiddie restaurant with a play area, say, so that she could be with Leslie-Ann an hour. "I want to hug her. I want to make her laugh."

"You want me to get caught?" Monique asked exasperatedly today.

Her sister gasped, "Oh no. Do you think that's going to happen?"

"Not if you keep out of it," retorted Monique. "Be good, because this isn't easy. I hardly see him. I'm trying to pick a fight, so far without success. I have to recalculate. By the way," she added, since she knew Sophie was dying to know, "he hasn't tried to touch me in bed yet."

"I bet he still asks you 'what you've done to yourself.'"

Frankly, Monique didn't see the importance of the red hair.

"You're never going to be able to answer,'" babbled Sophie for emphasis, still burdened with old, unsorted emotions about what had happened when she'd became a blonde.

"So what is he—hung up on virginal purity?"

"Oh no, Matt isn't crazy."

Maddening—truly maddening it was how Sophie could only tell you what a person was not, or didn't like, or couldn't do.

And yet what if the propelling motion to this marriage sprang precisely from these "isn't and aren't"s? Once Maman had repeated to her the odd but revealing claim that Sophie had made: she had sworn that she could read Matt's mind. "We don't need to talk," she maintained. With a soft snigger, Maman had told Monique that her reaction to this was to wonder if Sophie still believed in magic. Monique had enjoyed the joke at the time but now she was getting an faint inkling of what Sophie might have meant. True, the romance and good will had gone out of this marriage, and silence was no longer a means for communicating love. And yet perhaps it still allowed the passage of something every now and then. Nothing beautiful, but mysterious anyway. In its way even alluring. Monique got to feeling this towards the third week of her stay. In short, it was one very peculiar night that she spent with Matt Gagliardi.

It was a night when Matt was not supposed to be home until very late, and it began with the usual ritual of her giving Leslie-Ann a bath. Because she felt tired, and contemplating going to bed herself as soon as it was time for Leslie-Ann to be put down, she let the little girl have the long soak in the tub that delighted her, with bubbles and toys, while she herself relaxed by sitting on the lowered toilet seat and reading one of Sophie's glamour magazines. She scanned one of those articles on new make-up tricks for the eyes, the sort that were technical and beyond her. Then she came upon a letter from a woman who had suffered through the end of a love affair and wrote about it now with dignity and captivating honesty. It was marvelous, Monique thought, enjoying like wine the poetry the woman had made of her life. It was riveting how a stranger, in an exorcising account of something private, might suddenly move one, without trying to.

Little did she know that she would have cause in a few hours to feel moved a thousand times more intensely for the same reason.

The curious episode occurred at one or two in the morning, when she awoke for the first time and realized Matt was at home and lying next to her, moaning in his nightmare. As he rolled from his side to his back, his shoulder touched hers. After another moan, that shoulder contracted, twitched, went rigid. He drew a sharp breath, a man afraid, a man who gritted his teeth, a man who suddenly cried, "No!" She lay tense and alert, her eyes open to the darkness. One of his legs jerked at the knee and lifted the bedcovers. His torso shuddered with a fast epileptic tension. She listened in full alert for the fit to subside and his suffering—at her side—to stop, and when she realized that he wasn't going to moan himself awake unaided, she put a hand out and touched his upper arm. It was a rudimentary form of help, some ingrained tribal form of fraternity. The fact was that she had never voluntarily touched him before. She took him by both arms now; she pulled him from the grasp of the invisible force constraining his body to stiffness.

"Matt…," she whispered. It was too damn dark in the room with those lined curtains for her to see. When he didn't respond, she called him again. She pressed on his forearms, pressed on his wrists; without meaning to, her hands learned their shape, their warmth.

"OK," he breathed.

She withdrew her hands but they hovered in the dark ready for him again.

"Shipwrecked," he whispered. He sounded like a survivor.

"Everything all right now?" *Can I relax*?, she added silently to herself.

He grunted. "You had short hair because we were shipwrecked."

"You're incredible." It wasn't a very Sophie-like reaction but he didn't seem to notice.

He sat up then and jerked off his pajama top. "Are you there?" He reached out a hand, then suddenly stretched a bare arm with soft hair across her collarbone. So, she thought, it is finally happening. "Are you lying down?" he asked earnestly.

"Yes." She moved an inch away, staying flat on her back. Then she felt his pajama top—rolled as if he meant to wring it—on her forehead. He was up on his knees now, straddling her, in order to tuck it under her ear, turban style. He was breathing through his mouth, the sound of a man working, arranging. "Matt," she said, her heart beating faster.

"Shh. I'm showing you..." His body swayed—she could feel him, more than see him, and what for an instant seemed like the beginnings of male lovemaking, turned out to be strenuous pulls and caresses to right her turban, the way a doctor would an important new bandage. She presumed she had a head wound. He stroked her cheeks, too. Then the same back of his hand went hesitantly over her collarbone, her shoulders, the indentation of her waist. Every time he feared that the tunic around her head was slipping, his fingers flew up to check. His touch was strange; she felt as if she were being measured. Or as if in his mind she was someone else. Not Monique and not even Sophie. A Woman, a Female Body, maybe—who knew what a doctor might be fantasizing. Her flesh went cold and a complaint escaped her:

"I don't like this, Matt."

"Shh." Then, "I know you don't."

But he continued, laying a spread palm on her chest and then withdrawing it. Placing it, withdrawing it. Inside of making her cold now, it made her feel the heat of her own flesh and the working of her own heart.

"Matt," she said warningly, and rolled away. A slice of wind told her he'd reached out, found nothing, and withdrawn for the last time. He made a sigh. A strained one. Frustration? Ire? Her powers of comprehension were limited. In part she was moved by his struggle with his phantoms. In part she was forced to the queer realization that the silence in his marriage, which her sister believed fostered tenderness (in the absence of conflict and rancor), allowed the struggle to continue without interference from his wife.

He was a much more complicated man than she'd thought.

In a truce they slept.

*

The phone rang. By the time she got disentangled from Leslie-Ann (who wanted to keep her arms round Monique's neck in the sort of impossibly long show of gratitude she was capable of, kisses and nose-rubs and "love you, love, Mommy"'s, and all for pouring out a chocolatey cereal that Sophie had asked her to go easy with); by the time she managed to straighten up without upsetting her, the answering machine in Matt's study was responding and there followed the jerky typing-out of a fax. The words were in Italian and the sender, a certain Mario. She carefully ripped off the sheet from the machine and went back into the kitchen to sit with her coffee mug and Leslie-Ann, her mind lively to the possibilities of a mystery, which evaporated upon her remembering that Matt had a cousin in Italy named Mario: his name had made it onto the little family tree Sophie had drawn. A fascinating guessing game still remained. Her Italian was a pitiful mix of musical terms, Art History lingo, and French verb roots. Somehow she managed to form a narrowly circumscribed impression, the way professors of the humanities are trained to do in a pinch. It was a hot dispatch from Padua about Venice, giving a flight time and hotel number, and mentioning a certain "L". It talked of money, with many zeroes forming million and billions of *lires*. She read the fax again. Puzzling. She copied down the figures on a corner of the grocery list. Why was cousin Mario going into such financial detail? Was Matt deeply involved in these transactions? Was the money his?

The possibility that he was sending his fortune out of the country, foreseeing a messy divorce (why not?), took her breath away. She was sitting here like a duped idiot, every bit the guileless push-over as the real Sophie.

*

Ignorance makes bliss. But Ignorance also leads one to stumble onto clues that end the bliss. Monique decided to take the fax, with those figures and *contratti* and mention of "L"—which she photocopied, to Matt at his office. She would cancel Leslie- Ann's time at Mrs. Korn's and cart her along. It was a fairly complicated matter getting her ready. Sophie wanted her daughter to be toilet-trained: Monique was to take off her diaper during the day in the house and, every so often, ask Leslie-Ann if she had to do pee pee. The little girl, however, didn't realize yet that she made her own water, that it originated in her own body. Puzzled, she'd stare at the first, second, fifth puddle of the day to form on the floor under her and then—because she wasn't a child to hide anything—come tell Mommy.

Though they'd had three "accidents" that morning, she didn't want a diaper on. It was all Monique could do now to carry her writhing and howling (and even a bite—good grief! Leslie-Ann?) to her infant seat in the car. She had a diaper in her purse to stick on her when she calmed down. They made it to Matt's office shortly before noon. To trusty Betty behind her receptionist's window, her head turning with a look of warm surprise and a pivot away from the file cabinet, her big thighs doing their honest work under those white medical-office trousers, unaesthetically chopped at their widest point by the nurse's tunic—to Betty she said that she'd hopped in the car immediately just as soon as she received *this* from Venice.

The door to Matt's private office opened before Monique could touch it, and his swarthy, hairy father spread wide his arms. He exclaimed her name as if it were a good idea, then pressed her by the back of the head towards that smell of nicotine and cologne— her hair, mouth, and nose squeezed against his shoulder and her breasts against his chest. A moment later, his thick hands with their two nugget rings went for Leslie-Ann's waist, and he hoisted her up so that he could address her with tender respect. Monique imagined his enjoyment nowadays: poor man's fare. Card games and horse-betting, she supposed, knowing Matt paid for it, and meals out and maybe a topless bar or two.

In her best, controlled voice, she asked where Matt was.

John Gagliardi pushed at the door now behind him. "I'm waiting for him." To Leslie-Ann he added, "Come!" without calling her by any endearing nickname. In the office Monique saw Matt's leather-handled letter-opener, the showy silver-lidded beer mug, his framed degree certificates. There was an air of messiness to the side stack of papers and medical journals that paid tribute to a mind's hard work at the memorization of ideas, at assemblage and collage. She recognized the signs of inner life and reflection. She saw and willed herself to forget them because she couldn't afford to identify, to consider him her intellectual peer.

Leslie-Ann ran countless times around the desk then made a flying tangent and collided with a tall plant which, as it toppled, tipped a framed picture; it, too, would have fallen to the floor but Gagliardi Senior made a mid-air catch. The picture, a chalk sketch of a young woman in front of an arched bridge, looked like a kind of touristy souvenir, from Venice as a matter of fact. For a moment, it reminded Monique of Sophie and herself fifteen years before. She didn't ask Gagliardi Senior who the girl was because she warranted that she was supposed to already know such a thing; on the other hand, perhaps she was just a type, the room being full of other impersonal decorating touches. Leslie-Ann was fingering, for texture, the broad leaves of the potted plant she'd nearly upset. "Don't touch," Monique said automatically, though the toddler didn't turn around. After a moment, Leslie-Ann's hands, however, dropped away, and she seemed to be staring, immobile, into the foliage. She informed Monique softly: "Mama, pee pee." Two rivulets rolled down her legs. "What are you doing? *Madonna!*" guffawed her grandfather. Matt in his white lab coat appeared in the doorway, engrossed in conversation with the shorter man behind him, a brother who Monique dimly remembered from the wedding. His eyes weren't Turkish but wide, Roman, like their mother Frances's were in photographs, while his smile was nothing classier than the one a salesman hopes will convey good-natured decency. He had a general air of having time to take with all. "Every mall in America, bud" were his last words to Matt before Leslie-Ann said:

"Daddy, pee pee." Matt couldn't be bothered, couldn't be distracted until his brother had finished this reassuring point—something about Mario and Pete launching Venetian beads, colored goblets, and Murano-glass vanity mirrors to be sold in little kiosks licensed across the country. "Daddy, pee pee!"

"You're all wet, pumpkin? Where's your mother?"

"Where do you think?" Monique bent down at Leslie-Ann's feet with the new diaper and some tissues. "Leslie-Ann, step over there." She snapped at the child instead of the man. *Watch it, easy does it,* she told herself. She got the child to take off her shoes for her socks were wet. The clean-up job became messier and messier, the tissues continually breaking apart and left inside the puddle of piddle. None of the men cared in the least. And yet, damn it, Matt knew about this messy toilet-training stage; he was perfectly well aware of the fact that letting her go round without a diaper was a necessary step—not some impulsive decision or distracted act, the consequences of which her mother alone was responsible for. Willing herself to keep an indignant scowl off her face, Monique went to call Betty, who wordlessly brought her a bucket of soapy water from the bathroom. The three men still stood by the window, intent on each other's gesticulations. Their ignoring her was sexism of the lowest order, she concluded, but she bore in mind her sister's passive ways and didn't lash out. She picked up, instead, on what was passing between them. She'd seen it before, been fascinated before. There was an undercurrent of benevolent, mutual tolerance in the way they listened and spoke to each other, which not every brotherhood or sisterhood had but that this one seemed to. You could just feel how their divergences of opinion or interests could not come between them, and how, furthermore, this coexisting diversity was a frequent source of entertainment, prime material for jokes and puns which simply drew them closer together. To the Gagliardi men in the room with her, Leslie-Ann's peeing on herself was a happening beyond their magic circle. The men discussed their Venice, their Murano glass, their Pete, and Monique walked around them—unimportant in a way she hadn't been in years, led by Leslie-Ann in the circles she wanted to move in, brushing against their jackets.

"You're making me dizzy, Sophie" Matt remarked. "Stand still." He began patiently explaining that he had ten minutes before his next patient.

Monique quizzically raised her eyebrows. "Well, there's this fax," she said.

"Why did you go into my study? Why didn't you leave it there?" he said, suddenly riled. He didn't look at the paper she handed him; he just folded it in two and creased it possessively.

"I thought it was important," she said guardedly.

"Oh, so you can read it, can you?"

She realized the danger of admitting that. Her heart skipped a beat. Fortunately, a Sophie-like reply came to her: "It was because it came during the day, Matt. That's why I thought it could be urgent. Really, I was thinking of you."

"Don't think about me. Think about Leslie-Ann," he snapped.

She was only the mother of his child. Nothing more. How could she forget that for even one minute?

Stone-faced, he opened the door for her and Leslie-Ann but didn't close it tightly, for as she bent over to button up Leslie-Ann's jacket, it clicked metallically and reopened slightly behind her. She heard a guttural, half-retching voice say: "Awful. Red-haired punk."

A spitting sound.

Another.

"So put your foot down," Papa Gagliardi rumbled.

A red-haired punk. Those misogynistic bastards! As she left Matt's office, dissatisfied and piqued that there had not been any real martial clash and that she had found out nothing about that fax, Monique realized nevertheless that the Gagliardi family bond was the thing to cash in on.

Unfortunately at present she hadn't the faintest idea how to go about this. Never mind. It would be done! At home she looked at the calendar. She'd draw up a master schedule of nasty arguments to pick with Matt, that's what she'd do. She would adjust the power balance between husband and wife in this family, and bring the pre-divorce tension to a head, in a much more calculated and time-determined way now; no more improvising on a day's events. She began to jot down some small and big issues that could be used to spark a fight. They ranged from her refusing to go along with his ordering Chinese carry-out, to insisting on having the accountant's name and phone number (so that she could to go and hear the truth about their finances), to taking Leslie-Ann to see her parents in Jersey for a day without remembering to mention it to him. Her weekly goals, which she decided not to share with Sophie, ended up in a mysterious pencil code in all the calendar squares that said *Sunday.* They extended for two months.

*

As goals they were great. As achievements they were temporary. Remember the old saying about how you can lead a horse to water but you can't make him drink? Well, that was Matt Gagliardi—only worse because Matt actually did take a sip, really did seem to accept, without hostility, the perfect Conclusion that she found a way of offering him in an argument. But there was no satisfaction for her because she soon learned that it just meant that they were bound to have an argument at a later date about this argument not having convinced him. Yet this tendency of his to backslide was a small complication compared to the problems that sprang from Matt's perspective on any and all past happenings. The man *never* recounted any experience in the same terms twice, and *obviously* nothing ever happened on the day or at the hour or in the way she described them! She critically evaluated her own performance as Sophie. She was couching what she said in plain, even slightly ungrammatical talk, and asking for re-enforcement with "um"'s and "I guess"'s, and "isn't it?"'s, the way Sophie did. She took as much time as Sophie to get to the point but was a whole lot more stubborn. She was doing a good job in this regard, she concluded. She had changed things ever so slightly. Just enough. He didn't suspect a thing. And yet—had she ever seen anyone so impossible to throw off his inner clock as Matt Gagliardi? Anyone other than herself?

"Now what?" asked Sophie timidly on the phone.

"I don't know! And don't set me off!" Monique gave Leslie-Ann's stroller a couple of pushes, to keep her sleeping. She'd brought the stroller into the house at the end of their walk and set it in the kitchen.

"Don't get mad. Because I did tell Maman and D—well, Maman, anyway. She thought it was too much for Dad to handle. She didn't seem disturbed herself. She said something about how in a real war you have both enemies and people who help you. But in a private little war between husband and wife, others should stay out of it."

"Except me."

"Except you."

"I'm the shadow wife," Monique briskly said. "Maman doesn't seem to care much about whether you get a good settlement," she added.

"She's not phoning you up, she's not making it hard for you," Sophie pointed out. "So," her voice brightened, "when can I see Leslie-Ann? I miss her, I miss her *so* much."

As always, Monique roughly told her to forget it for now. She gave the little girl's stroller another roll, saw that her head was still resting on one shoulder. Sophie, Sophie would never change. "There are experts to see. You've got to get to a lawyer, hire a private detective! What are you doing? Nothing. My sabbatical's only for nine months, and we're already at the end of the second."

From the way Sophie didn't answer, Monique figured something was up. "Are you at Maman's now?... Sophie?" Not a sound, not a breath. "Are you *at my apartment!?*" she wailed.

"I, um, saw your friend Doug."

"I told you to stay away from there."

"He said hello first—it was downtown Chicago on State Street—so I had to stop and chat, I thought. I made up a good story. He's nice."

"I'm talking about my apartment. How—how did you manage to get in?" Monique was aghast: she was supposed to be in Europe, not traipsing around suburban Evanston with groceries.

"The keys were in your purse."

There was more: Sophie had impulsively answered the ringing phone and talked with the graphics designer that Monique had gone out with for a couple of evenings before coming East.

"He sounded kind of lonely. He asked me—you—out to dinner tomorrow night." She'd accepted.

Devastated, Monique angrily told her to stay out of her life—that *that* wasn't part of the deal. "Go back to New Jersey and stay *put* at Maman's. You can't run up a bill on my credit card at hotels and you *can't* stay in Chicago," she lectured. She told her to cancel that dinner—then changed her mind and asked for the number for she wanted to do it herself.

"He's away till late tonight, he said."

"Thank you very much," Monique yelled and hung up.

The damnedest sort of evening followed.

Her body played tricks on her. They'd had a surprise visit from Matt's two best buddies and business partners, each with family, out for a drive and an early dinner at a restaurant near their neighborhood. Monique wasn't unhappy to meet them—Phil with his blue bug eyes, and Mark with his Assyrian nose—but Matt generally hated a weekend going in a way he'd not envisioned and planned for. She had realized this over the past weeks: the Saturday when his sister asked if he could come over immediately and help her carry an old sofa out to the curb for the Salvation Army pickup; the Sunday when a doctor in his group of associates asked him at the last minute to cover him on hospital call; or those early morning wake-up calls when with a glance out the window he understood that the weather had disobeyed the meteorologists and his golfing or sailing weekend was spoiled. His customary reaction was to indulge in a muttering fit of foul humor, but today, by contrast, he had—or seemed to have—a good time, except for some strain on his nerves from the children.

When these people left, she put Leslie-Ann to bed, dropping her easily onto the sheets, without songs or stories or fuss, knackered as she was from her romp with a four-year-old boy, and returned downstairs. Before tackling the glasses, spilled Coke, scattered peanuts, olive pits in crumpled napkins, and toys, she indulged in a small barb: "You hid it well."

His expression was that of a Bedouin galloping after a stealthy traitor. "Not everything unscheduled and sudden has to be a problem, for God's sake!"

She barked back at him, trying not to lose all sense of being Sophie; she suddenly caught a glimpse of the top of that mountain she was climbing day by day and decided to precipitate things. She laid into him with the best she had. She stung him with the fact that when Leslie-Ann and two of the visiting toddlers had swarmed in upon him and Mark in his study he'd blown a fuse. "My Lord," she said, "you even shouted an obscenity, an *obscenity* at two-year-olds. And then—," she took a clever pause.

"Shut your mouth, Sophie. You're losing it."

So she had him. She'd managed it. "No, Matt, there's plenty more."

"THEN I'M LOSING IT, SOPHIE! That's enough."

As Monique had seen happen a long time ago, his face went red with blood rising through gnarly neck veins. One hand chopped at the other so that it couldn't make a fist. She couldn't guess what Sophie would have done in her place, and she knew that he had the trusty old example of his father, but she was too angry and victorious to be afraid. They stared each other down. His stare, of course, became instantly one of incredulity. He drew the ceremonious breath of the one with the final word. "What's made you this way?"

"I heard you with your father. If you can't have a blonde, what happens? You can't get it up?" Her own vulgarity was unforeseen.

He pursed his lips. "You're different," he purred.

It was then that her body failed her. She was powerless to the needles of fear breaking through her skin, the superficial epidermis of her imposture. "What do you mean?" she babbled.

"Oh stop it! Stop that shaking, *you sss--*...sow," he concluded the word reluctantly, not wanting the air to take it, whereas she was just astonished that he didn't go ahead and taunt her with *Monique*.

"I'm—I'm going to see if Leslie-Ann is still covered."

"Yeah, you do that."

Climbing the stairs, she told herself to stay calm. Why should he suspect anything? *He's bluffing*, she mumbled. *Bluffing, bluffing, bluffing.* By the light of the hall lamp, she pulled the blanket up over Leslie Anne, who lay with her hands raised over her head as if she were flying. Monique closed her eyes better for her; the darling girl didn't always shut them completely for some reason. Shutting the door with its dolly pom-pom, she stood in the darkness by the banister. She found, as Sophie might, that the peace was very soft in a house where a child slept soundly in flying position. She descended, an unhurried look at the family photos hung along the stairs, step by languid and carpet-muffled step, calmer, aware of her own defection from the inner tensions of Monique. Matt's grunted laugh and the rumpling of the newspaper that entertained him so came from the chair nearest to the family room fireplace. As she came in, he reached for the glass of red wine on the table by him, drained the rest of it with unguarded thirst, and went back with an excited smile to his paper. The last thing he appeared concerned about was the ugly scene of innuendo from ten minutes before. Because his wine glass sat precariously on the video-cassette she'd taped for Leslie-Ann, she moved it.

"What are you reading?" The question took a great deal of effort; her tongue was thick.

"The weather report for Europe." His face still shone.

She sat on the armchair near his. *Now that I am wearing it, this blanket of calm, let me relax, truly relax in his presence, and try again,* she thought. *I am Sophie.* After a moment she asked, "Italy?"

"Mmm."

Then the conversation took a peculiar turn. He folded the paper so that the last page he'd just read—the financial news and stock market reports—lay on top of the smudgy wine glass between them, and made a declaration: "It's flooding back to me how I used to collect checks when I was a paper boy. They had intimate facts on them, like people's middle names. I reasoned that if signatures, like on the checks, also served to validate wills, and wills were the voices of souls beyond the grave…well, I mixed the two ideas up, checks and wills, because I liked the feel in my pocket: half the people of the neighborhood in my pocket." Matt Gagliardi used that grunty laugh again.

He was her enemy but his candor was a most powerful weapon. Matt went to his wet bar in the corner for some more wine, brought her a glass without asking her if she wanted it. "I mean, my handling those checks anticipated, what?, a physician's interest in people."

He focused on a ceiling beam, on the fireplace mantle. Odd snatches they were, rather superficial, but one couldn't say completely unrevealing. She imaged that someone as closed-mouthed and self-satisfied as Matt had this extemporary fun only when the mood struck him. No matter what savagery may have come before. Matt Gagliardi, who considered her a big mistake, who would divorce her if and when for as little as possible and keep Leslie-Ann, Matt Gagliardi apparently *would talk if she stayed quiet, if she stayed his wife.*

"So, the way I see it…" he was gazing at the molding now, his eyes in a sort of open-lidded REM cycle, " *I* believe that, yes, we know what our fears are when we're young but we're pretty much in the dark about what pleasures are going to console us later on."

Didn't she make her own little grunt then? And didn't she, though not like before in their stare-down, didn't she meet his glance unguardedly, hold the eyes steady? The thought: *it's mostly Gagliardi's big ego anyway.* It took will power to keep her eyes still and receptive for this long; it had never been her modus operandi.

At least half an hour passed. He rambled on with his memories and aphorisms, rephrasing and clarifying his ideas as people do when they are listening closely to themselves. His truth hung in the air like smoke, and it was so thick, and he was so self-absorbed, that he didn't glance her way ever. Instead he looked at his lap, at his wine glass, at the ceiling, at nothing, talking and talking. Then at the end of this monologue, Matt Gagliardi stood, stretched, shut those eyes of his on a yawn, loosened his belt buckle, and matter-of-factly lumbered out of the room. It was asking too much of him to say 'good night', she presumed. Monique stayed in the armchair; she sat and sat and saw the family room at midnight, familiarizing herself more than ever before with the faint, pulsing particles spread in the air when there is silence. Then she said to herself, I've *learned not to talk*.

It was as if play-acting Sophie had this time taken her somewhere unexplored.

Silently, she made Matt breakfast in the morning. With a wordless nod, she responded to his "I'm leaving," as he headed out the door to the garage. She didn't sing to Leslie-Ann when she got her up. She maintained the outward quietness that was hers when she was alone in this house—and a glance in the mirror showed her that there was likewise the same serene look on her face.

She felt a strange contentment that day and over the next few days. She appreciated the pleasure one could take in choosing *not* to speak. How rewarding it could feel at times to be free of the straight-jacket of one's own uttered words! Certainly, she remained vigilant of the situation, the need to wrangle divorce terms from Gagliardi; and yet this strange unexpected mysticism had overtaken her and pushed her into an invisible territory. She found herself, for instance, adopting a slow Geisha-like way of retrieving dropped objects or fetching requested items for Leslie-Ann. "Mommy!" the little girl scolded, and once or twice she even kicked and kicked in her high-chair, passing on her best energy charge; *hating* to be helped in such a listless, dragged out way.

To complicate matters more, what Sophie had described finally happened to her that week: she got ignored by Matt in front of their bank. His not recognizing her was utterly phony, and yet because of the perfect, unbroken illusion of their being complete strangers which he maintained, a little whip of the truth—that you can never know another person—played over her sensibilities. When he dashed across the street to his parked car, her face did get warm for a moment and his arrogance did rile her, but her anger was brief. What remained with her after this bizarre travesty was the same thing that unsettled her the night he had his nightmare at her side, and that was not the arrogance but rather the enigma of the man.

Who had created this silent marriage.

Where her sister had found perfect understanding. And then disdain.

The sheer physicality of the silence between Matt and of Sophie. It was a silence that she, the shadow wife, had not foreseen having to deal with, having to enter, wanting to enter. She reflected, *I am going to go further and further into Sophie's silence*. It was her ocean wave.

She didn't know what was going to happen now.

*

Matt remained fairly communicative. He obviously took her silence for granted. Though his monologues in the library over a drink petered out, he had things to ask and say daily about his imminent trip to Italy. He was in a very up-beat mood, wondering one minute if his shirts and suits would get back from the cleaner's in time for his departure and then the next minute offering details (something he rarely did) as to his flight arrangements. He went so far as to mention something about the new company he was setting up in Padua. Most mornings the fax machine in the study spewed new pages in Italian about Mario, Pete, L., Murano, and plane times. It dawned on Monique that she should photocopy these in case they could be used against him by Sophie's divorce lawyer. Sometimes she actually made it to the post office where there was a coin-operated Zerox machine and made a copy or two. But she was disoriented and didn't feel the drive, consistency, and commitment to her sister's settlement that she'd had before. All her life she'd used words to force daily affairs to flow for a moment in the direction she desired. But there was no such daily movement of magma in the silent world. Instead, there was the light airiness of endlessly changing scenarios in one's head, which weighed nothing. Where was the driving tension of a week or so ago? Gone. And her original, two-month old intention of haunting Matt Gagliardi with her voice, as she'd studied in Eastern philosophy? It seemed to belong to some other woman entirely, not to her. Certainly, the things to resent Matt Gagliardi for were still there but they were like solids that had become gases. She found her own experience strange and slightly crazy.

Was she sure that she was still Monique inside Sophie?

One night in bed she placed a hand on his forearm, then, because her wordlessness accustomed her now to touch testing, patted it, its muscle and the hairs. He responded with a scratchy caress on her wrist. She gave him another of hers. He gave her one of his, using the same nail. It was all very egalitarian. Or was it like dog and master? It was wonderful that there could be no sure answer. She stopped and naturally he stopped. They slept.

*

Meanwhile, Sophie, who had declined to leave Chicago, went regularly out to dinner with Chris, the graphics designer, and an unspecified number of times 'did the whole evening.' Fortunately, she didn't run into any of the university crowd who knew Monique, or heaven only knew what would have happened. She was creating a problem that Monique would have to sort out later by frequenting St. John's Catholic church down the street, a place that Monique had always shied away from, having decided she was a humanist and agnostic in college. In addition to all this, there was the fact that the finances of the swap, having never been discussed in much detail, now began to show its ugly side. Sophie wrote a check on Monique's account to pay for the divorce lawyer's first consultation fee, and if Monique hadn't found out and had her sign an IOU, she probably would have written another, for the equivalent of half a month's salary, to a private eye. How natural it felt to be signing each other's name and administrating the other's money as one's own. How completely they had appropriated each other's life. With only Monique's academic career and Sophie's Leslie-Ann to keep them anchored to their right places...

It was Leslie-Ann who started to shake things up. Children have a way of doing that.

She grew curious, *very* curious, about the phone call which her mother was conducting out on the veranda, in a coat now that it was November. Leslie-Ann pantomimed such desperation at the window that she let her say hello to 'auntie.'

"I'm coming back," said Sophie in an emotional voice to Monique. "I want to take your place for that hour on the playground. I can't wait anymore, Mon--, I CAN'T."

"Where are you?"

"I'm packing. I'm going straight to O'Hare."

"With whose money are you buying that plane ticket?" Monique demanded to know.

"With mine. I mean yours. To be paid back with yours that's mine."

"All right," Monique said after a pause. "It's a good time for doing the playground bit. He's leaving for Italy the day after tomorrow."

"Matt's leaving? Great, I can stay with you! We'll all be together. Maybe we won't even be there when he gets back!"

"What do you mean, 'we won't be here'?" asked Monique in the strangest voice.

Sophie didn't like the 'no' that Monique went on to give her about staying at *her* house but her sister wouldn't relent.

"Ridiculous. Absurd," Monique sentenced. " I don't want to invite any suspicion by appearing together right now." She insisted: "I don't want you in the house." She noticed how possessive she sounded.

From silence to total absence.

Leslie-Ann was still upstairs asleep in her crib, and Matt hadn't had a chance to kiss her goodbye, because the airport limo had come early. He was gone. It was sunny in the kitchen, and the radio Matt had turned on before going was still announcing news. Her arms folded over her terrycloth robe, Monique watched for what if anything would happen next in the tree-lined street...what car would go by, what window move. She'd had similar moments since her arrival in this mansion, where she'd looked for an occurrence that could unfold into a larger one—expected it from the swaying branches on the block's expansive oaks and chestnuts. What drag this husband's absence, all of five minutes old, created. It wasn't like not knowing when he'd come home at night. This was to be three weeks of *living apart*—and not yet divorced or separated. Three weeks with the invisible master still solidly in control of the empire. She expelled one oppressed sigh after the other, dragged herself over to the dishwasher and opened it. How much additional lethargy it created inside a marriage that wasn't her marriage and that had just gone fully into the negative. She loaded a plate, then a saucer, then a plate, then a saucer.

She talked Leslie-Ann awake up in her nursery, she purposely chatted her up till she opened her eyes. Afterwards she rolled on the unmade bed in the master bedroom with her, still all sleepy-giggly. Then in the kitchen, they lined up four different boxes of cereal on the table and had breakfast. "Tomorrow Mommy's going to take you to the playground. The one by the school, remember? But not today. We have to decide about today. What would you like to do, honey?"

But of course the little girl said nothing one could call thoroughly comprehensible, and she was going on three years old now. Someone should really have her checked by a speech therapist. Who would it be? "Not me," she thought to herself. That was beyond the call of duty for a shadow wife. That was for her real mother to handle. If she didn't come up soon with some dirt to use against Matt Gagliardi, she'd skip out. She'd leave her sister to her life, divorce settlement or no divorce settlement. This morning she could only chide herself for her fascination with the silence in this marriage to this complicated man. Three weeks! How foolish she'd been to lose track of the fact that for three weeks she was going to be parked here, uselessly, while he was off in Italy! This was a tedious, rich breadwinner's absence, and it made her take one look at the calendar on the desk by the refrigerator and want to cry.

It was beyond her to foresee Matt's father stopping by the house to take Leslie-Ann for an ice cream in the late afternoon. He couldn't have picked a worse hour. They stood in the whirling sun dust of the front hall, and Monique felt like a lady debating with a prune-skinned dwarf over whether Leslie-Ann would ruin her supper, while Leslie-Ann herself fussed and jerked in Monique's arms, timorous and moody after her nap. John Gagliardi craned his neck to peer into his granddaughter's face. A look at the underside of certain cars had cost him less effort.

"*Bella!*" Since she would have nothing to do with him, he dug in his hand and—after a couple of soft pokes in his daughter-in-law's breast—found her chin to pat. "Leeezz…zleee-Anna?" he coaxed. "Leeezlee…" When she still refused his affection, he straightened up and replanted his feet. At sixty-eight, it felt good—and eased a pain—when a slightly bow-legged man like him took a little step in place; he regained his equilibrium and, walk, walk, he was himself again; a bit of elbow work did go into it now, but when he stood and took steps the world was right by him or promised to be so again soon. He didn't like thinking about himself much, but he was sure that his life was in his legs: the miles on foot to Palermo at age sixteen, all the standing on the ship voyage to America, and then the squatting as a mason pressing bricks onto globs of cement. All his choices, his few choices, were executed by his legs: into the building to sign his citizen papers, into the church for his wedding, into Newark during the Depression for the fresh eggs and oranges for his kids, into the court room where he was acquitted of stealing union funds, and out of that courtroom too, what a memorial walk that was, passing the table of his ex-friends who'd done what they could to frame him.

He knew his daughter-in-law was nettled by his presence but didn't care. He couldn't be instinctive with women; he'd never learned to be. One tried to read one's brother's mind every so often, or that of one's son. One's most profound loyalty was first to one's mother, and then to them, the brother or the son. In their absence, one became even more vigilant of what was in their best interest. Knowing Matt had left town drew him this afternoon to Matt's house: as if the house had something wrong with it now. His original plans for the day were to pickle some more garden peppers and stash the jars in the cellar of the townhouse Matt had bought for him, then get into the car and drive to the race track, but before he got started on the first pepper he'd already changed his mind.

With Matt gone, the big place just seemed to need a father's going to see it. He was very glad he'd come and it wasn't just for his granddaughter sprawled like a pint-sized Jesus in the Madonna's arms; he was also satisfied with the high hall with its curving staircase, whose thin banister posts seemed to radiate like spokes out of his daughter-in-law's head (kind of like she was a wordless Statue of Liberty with her eyeballs painted blue). He was satisfied with that the occupants of the house were still fully *Gagliardi* in Matt's absence. *Non si sa mai.* One never knows. He was there and breathing on them. The house had back what it'd been missing.

"Leezlee-Anna!" This time, on that joyous ring his call worked: she stretched towards Nonno and her mother poured the solid little girl into his arms. Throwing her over a shoulder, he freed a hand. "You know Matt doesn't like this red hair," he said kindly to her— kindness not being a quality she associated with him. He touched it softly, with *all* the fingers of one hand.

Fortunately, the child squirmed to get down, and his setting her there was a two-handed job. Through the front door still ajar, she saw a slim woman in tan bermudas and white sneakers jump out of a station wagon parked in the driveway. This familiar-looking woman made an enthusiastic, swooping wave, with a flopping pink something in hand. "Hi! Did you realize you forgot this?" It was one of those very rapid, neighborly acts that can be over before you rightly understand what's happening but, fortunately, it came to

Monique in time that this was Marianne, an acquaintance of Sophie's from the park, and she had brought back the pink hair band that Leslie-Ann had dropped the other day. Monique did not introduce Matt's father and was pleased to see him staring into space (but why did he keep eyeing the banister?), divested of the rights he seemed to think he had. After Marianne left, in mid-sentence and at a jog to stop the car horn one of her kids was sounding, the phone rang, and so Monique figured she was good as rid of John Gagliardi. "Going for ice cream?" she mouthed at him on her way to the phone, tapping her watch with an index finger to show it was getting late. He didn't take the hint; the man was incredibly thick. She heard his "hoopla!" and Leslie-Ann's finally happy squeal, as she picked up the receiver and it was *Maman*.

Maman called her 'Monique'. She loved her mother so much for that that tears came. Maman told her that Sophie had come back. Dad had picked her up at the airport knowing this time it was her; he'd said that he wouldn't call their switching despicable, no, but dishonorable, cowardly, and weird—"kinky!"; and that if Matt Gagliardi was not the man he thought he was but some ogre and wouldn't, if it came to divorce, give Sophie any money, "then that's tough for you, you live without money." And now Dad was in a real bind because they'd been disgraceful enough to inform him. Since this was far graver than their cheating on the S.A.T., he couldn't "just go off to Gettysburg." He said he wanted time alone to think what to do, and after about an hour in his arm chair, he called Maman and Sophie in to say that he wanted Sophie "or whoever you are" to stay on her own in the other half of the duplex, which was empty again after the junior manager from his insurance company who'd been renting it found a house to buy and moved out. 'Come and go, as you please, just so long as I don't have to watch.' Except for the word "kinky," Maman rendered Daddy in French, as she always had. *Voilà, c'est la vie,* for Dad's "well so that's life:" oh how the fatalism coming from her mother's lips was different. Pricked by that bleak amusement Monique wanted to ask her: *what do you think, Maman, of what we've done?* But she didn't, she couldn't. John Gagliardi's sudden re-entry into the kitchen made her say something garbled. For a man who couldn't understand French he certainly knew how to pick out Matt's name, and its mention promptly brought him closer. To Leslie-Ann, straddled around his hips, she said, "Say hi, it's Grand-mère," and Gagliardi transferred the little girl with her outstretched arms, fingering as he did Monique's hip, feigning concern that Leslie-Ann was really firmly anchored on it. She pulled her chin from the receiver: "Ex-CUSE me, it's my mother!"

Maman was so wise; she asked if she should call back. They parlayed the issue with lightning speed; afterwards, however, Monique wasn't sure what answer she gave. She was aching too much to be home—at Maman's house—as herself again to think straight. The one thing she remembered saying was, *'If only I could hand him (*her mother understood she meant John Gagliardi) *over to you, Maman. With the skills that Mrs. Vassalli attributes to you, I'm sure you could make mincemeat of him.'*

She was spared Gagliardi Senior's *amore* because the one thing that could stop him did: Matt phoned. The old man let her respond in peace. There were no background noises competing with Matt's voice, and she judged from the hour that he had to be at his hotel. He sounded fatigued, guarded, and even smaller than the geographical distance could account for. "So is Leslie-Ann there?" After he'd talked to his daughter, and Monique had translated everything the toddler had said about going for ice cream with Nonno, he yawned and said some disconnected but lengthy things about the weather. *Perhaps*, she reasoned, *this was her reward for the silence she'd given him in the days right before his departure?* He made a pause, which puzzled her, after the words 'sunny tomorrow.' "Well, have you had any news?" he blurted out.

News? "No *faxes*," she answered.

'Why should there be faxes?'

"Then what news?"

"Let me talk to my father."

John Gagliardi's pudgy brown hand didn't grasp the receiver so much as seem to restrain it, nailing it to his ear. "*Certo, certo,*" he concurred. Then he looked at Monique and attached a final curt "*certamente.*" What request was Matt making? But she knew, she knew! He was asking his father to keep an eye on things. Not on the house, which John Gagliardi positively coveted—she could see that, or on Leslie-Ann, and no, not on her, though he'd turned to look at her in his dirty way, but keep an eye, she thought, on the silent status quo which safe-guarded Matt's fortune. And which allowed him to do as he pleased.

Just as she had that night when he had his nightmare in bed by her side, once again she thought: *under the cover of this silence, God only knows what Matt is doing.*

The next morning she discovered what. Hearing odd noises— swings of a mallet on a stake, it seemed, she put down Leslie-Ann's cereal spoon and left the kitchen for the dining-room bay window and its full-length view of lawn, oaks and street. A workman in a fisherman's vest threw a tool into the back of his pickup parked not in the circular drive but along the curb. He wiped his hands on his vest, climbed in the cab, nosed his truck into the driveway, and hit the gas, rounding the curve of the semi-circle at the fantasy speed of a race track. He almost had an accident at the other end, pulling out into the road at the wrong moment, with a flare of red brake lights and a bounce on springs. Her eyes followed him, mystified. Then she saw, there in her lawn, the well-built colonial-style post with two brass hooks and a swinging shingle. *House for sale*, it read.

CHAPTER TWELVE

This time for him the Grand Canal beyond the glass front of the train station is not a framed proscenium of a waterway, the way it has seemed in the past. He parks his suitcase by the newsstand, and dedicates a minute to figuring out what sort of welcome Venice is giving him on this visit. It's a bright day and he feels marvelous, his duties dispensed with—the tour of two private clinics in Verona and the meeting with Mario in Padua behind him. The gothic points on the windows of the palazzi opposite wait like an honor guard for his review, but it is the luminous green water of the canal that receives his reverence. The ripples in the canal are like the folds of a garment in the expectant lap of a Madonna. This time Venice is more than the place where Lorenza lives; Venice is a woman, too.

Across the stone bridge with its fishy breeze, and around two damp turns of a *calle*, and *then* he is where he wants to be, on the small canal. A pressure on the top brass button between the door and a 500-year-old iron barred window, draws a "*Sì?*", staticky and just slightly feminine, from the intercom. He says—he confesses who he is: "*Sono io.*" He climbs the steep stairs, picks up with the life he could have had at its steep angle. She pulls the door open and leans out in greeting, gripping the doorframe; with those bony Venetian features, page-boy haircut, and shapely legs that never change, she grins as he puffs up towards the landing. "*Ciao, Matt...Ciao...Ciao*": her low, hoarse voice lights smoky fires of happy greeting again and again, till he finally stands before her and can kiss her. They hold hands crossing the threshold. The space is low and den-like, and those attic windows, giving onto roofs and potted terraces, seem once again, as they are every year, too large for it. There is no trace of anyone, not even him, no photo or memorabilia among the bookcases, by the couches, or on the plywood tables with sawhorse legs.

Keeping her place free of such presences is her gift to him, she's told him. It's supposed to make him feel like he's never left. But does she actually send a lover packing when he comes? Does she explain—has she ever explained to anyone—that she has a special, well, erotic friendship with this American once a year? He doesn't know, and doesn't want answers, though entertaining these questions upon his arrival is part of his mental hygiene. There is a settling-in phase that lasts for about a day, after which the apartment stops looking emptied on purpose. Then he always stops feeling like a doctor or even finished, for that matter, with college, and he sleeps with his arms wrapped around her, and lustfully deposits his semen and waste. He locks and unlocks that door, just to go for a walk or to see some art, but turning the key with the uncontestable sense of living in another dimension, while she tickles the small of his back and sings something about a sailor who drinks only for his lady. Yes, usually when the first day is over and done with, everything is always perfect.

The first day of this visit follows the happy rule. They stand in the low-ceilinged living room, running their hands up and down each other's body and re-finding the rhythm that they like to kiss by. Then they have tea and talk, "catching up on the year" as Lorenza puts it, side by side on the small couch, with their legs entwined. Everything they say to each other is a bridge over the differences in their cultures, families, and recent experiences. Lorenza (as passionate about her teaching as Monique his sister-in-law) tells him about the five-day trip with her high-school students to Paris, about her sister and her brother-in-law phoning from Algiers to recount how they got caught in a desert sandstorm with their caravan of tourists, about the books she's read on the advice of a bookseller named Stella, about how Stella has since become her friend, and how now the two of them often join a group from the University who meet regularly on Thursdays for a drink in a café. These details are the gangways into Lorenza's world, and Matt crosses them rapidly, holding her hand tenderly as she talks. When it's his turn, he offers a single bridge, an account of what his daughter Leslie-Ann has done this year as a two-year-old.

"The third time she got on that tricycle, she figured out what it meant to pedal and off she went," he brags happily. "She's great. She spent last Saturday morning making experiments with rubber bands, seeing what they can pull when attached to a door or a toy car." As he talks, the sweetness of his relationship with his daughter mixes with what he feels for Lorenza. "We have fun together, you know? I got out a flash light and waved it at the ceiling in her bedroom, and Leslie-Ann got so excited she started to dance."

Beyond these anecdotes about Leslie-Ann he is incapable of going. He knows this. The rest of his life is either too disappointing for him to want to discuss it, or too special and secret. Leslie-Ann represents the only thing in his life that he can openly declare to be perfect and imperfect at once. Being a father keeps him going round in an emotional circle of wonderment, interspersed by brief jolts of annoyance in those rare moments when she is being unreasonable or unmanageable. And while the delight he takes in her mere existence may be dampened suddenly in this way, it always—*always*—floods back over him again.

Lorenza asks many questions about Leslie-Ann this time. As Queen of Humanism, she mentally embraces his little girl and finds a way in which to love her long-distance, he thinks. Lorenza's questions continue even as she goes into the kitchenette to fix them lunch. *Do you want to phone her?* she calls to him.

He is pacing by the couch, jiggling the loose change in his trouser pockets. "No," he responds. His mind has turned from thoughts about Leslie-Ann to something else. He sees himself— alone—inside his house in Pennsylvania, its sun-dappled clapboard presence doing battle with what should be the stronger, shuttered and fortified one of Lorenza's palazzo. He sees the gingerbread mansion dialoguing with the hard new something in the front lawn: the '*for sale*' sign. He wonders when it went up, where they put it. He thinks about all the effort, work, and money he has sunk into that house. The central air-conditioning system alone cost a fortune. And then there is the ultra-sensitive alarm system, a source of pride to him; for a certain period after it was first installed, he often thought with immense satisfaction that he would never again come home to ransacked possessions vomited on the floor and against the walls (his entire world adulterated that spring when he turned nine and his parents' house was burglarized). And now he'll have even better—a penthouse on top of the building with the best security in downtown Philly. No lawn to care for, no neighbors. A view of the Delaware River, other people's lives adequately summed up in the winking lights for miles around, the dark rural stretches—so restful on the eyes—across the water in New Jersey.

He is tempted to describe all this to Lorenza, but Philadelphia is just too different from Venice; he is daunted by the conversational effort it would take to make her see both of his worlds clearly. He sits at the table—at the pine board resting on two sawhorses, and eats the pasta and drinks the wine she puts in front of him, while through the window drift the tinkling and clanging sounds of other Venetians doing the same across the narrow 600-year-old alley. The good red Cabernet begins to go to his head just enough now to block out thoughts of anything not in sight-range. He reaches across and fondles Lorenza's hand, the one grasping a chunk of bread. He tears a bit off the chunk and holds it up to her lips. She nibbles at it then kisses his fingers. He wants her badly. As soon as their meal is finished, he guides her urgently by the shoulders towards the bedroom. His senses are reeling thanks to the wine, which he usually doesn't drink at lunch. After they've made love, he naps.

It is a most restorative rest. When he wakes up around four, in a wonderful mood, Lorenza is on the couch marking student papers; her reading glasses have slipped down her nose, and she is making quick annotations with a red pen. A small transistor radio is propped on the end table next to her, and he can hear soft voices debating a political issue. *La sinistra. La destra. Il diritto di ogni cittadino. Il benessere.* Lorenza looks up with a smile and asks if he'd like to go for a walk. He says that he's dying for one. Borrowing the words of the political commentators on the radio, he quips that he's keen on asserting his right to well-being.

Yes, the first day works wonders on him. And the second day is a tonic as well. The weather is great and they get on a vaporetto and visit the island of Torricello. He gets so much sun and wind that he falls into bed like a log that night. Towards morning of the third day, however, a sudden shrill noise—like the cry of a seagull or the shriek of a tomcat—wipes out his dream and wakes him up. He is disoriented, without a clue as to what inward landscape he was wandering in merely a moment before. He squints at his watch on the nightstand but can't quite make out the hour. It's around dawn, in any case. He decides he'll get up and make coffee for Lorenza; he imagines sticking his head out the window, smelling the canal, hearing the plopping and plinking at the tiny quay and the whine and splosh of the next motorboat, a church bell chime, that sort of thing. Then, unbelievably, his mind travels at a tangent towards Sophie. Who he has *never* thought about in Venice. Now all of a sudden he has to think about her.

She has acted peculiar with him. In ways that his ignoring her publicly cannot explain. She's been coached and drilled by her twin sister Monique to challenge him, to obtain something. He's even thought, "wait a minute, this *is* Monique"... those moments in bed...But it is too outlandish to be true... Give it another six months and he'll be living in the poshest part of Philly, where when his little girl comes of age she will attend the best private school; he will finally buy or accept those season tickets he cares about; he'll get on the board at the Art Museum, the way he told himself he would as a boy: the time has come for these things on his life list. The list that no other eyes were privy to, the list that doesn't get thrown away—guaranteed by those hard years of medical training and the money he makes. *Let the rest be,* he tells himself, *let the sow be the lady of the house until I decide differently and*—and what? He is in Venice. He has his sweetness.

In the afternoon, Lorenza sits cross-legged on her couch, performs a neck roll: *Come, Matteo. Let's talk.* She pats the place next to her. He smiles back, happy to sit there. She talks about how miserable his marriage has become and how significant his move into Philadelphia seems to her, and he follows what she has to say in a silence of which he is proud, which is not in any way like the insignificant one Sophie gives him in their family room. For Lorenza, anything. He will fell a tree in his most intimate forest and offer it to her or else burn it.

"*Sei ad una svolta, Matteo.*" She adds that only he knows what this turning point in his life is precisely and when it must take place. The telephone on the end table rings, she makes plans for their going out to dinner with her closest friends, her eyes never leave him. After she hangs up, she swings her legs over his and whispers affectionately in his ear, "*Povero Matti, mi fai—,*" only to be interrupted by another phone call. By this hour even those of her fellow teachers with Saturday classes have finished their lessons and are free; Lorenza once told him that late Saturday afternoon is their favorite time for exchanging news, so he's not surprised when the phone rings yet a third and then a fourth time.

"I'm going out," he mouths at her.

She winks.

He winks back.

He spends the next several hours walking the passageways that she has taught him to take; the back alleys which run parallel or at a tangent to the broader pedestrian thoroughfares used by the tourists making a beeline from the train station to St. Mark's Square. Every so often he catches a glimpse of stampeding, noisy bodies in light-colored hats, shorts, and tennis shoes. In his quiet *calle*, he savors a feeling of privilege for being privy to information that the locals usually keep to themselves. Knowing how to navigate his way around Venice, he thinks, is like possessing a secret within a secret, the larger secret being the special, inexpressible nature of his feelings for Lorenza.

Once he returns to her apartment, which she only rents and fears, she tells him on this visit, she may soon be evicted from, he finds that she has already dressed for dinner. She is all in white and looks lithe. An hour and three foot-bridges later, they are at a pizzeria in Piazza San Stin, in the outside garden decorated with Chinese lanterns, where with reciprocal warmth and even a climatic surge of glee, he is hugging, and being hugged by, her best friend Vittoria and her husband Ernesto, both of them art teachers. Vittoria in her bright turquoise eyeglasses impishly props her elbows on the table and clamors for *Matti* at her side. She's wearing a large silver pendant with symbols in relief on it, which she pulls forward and looks at upside down, explaining how Ernesto designed and crafted it as a surprise for her birthday. She lets Matt finger it, turn it over—he's free to ask questions about the symbols but doesn't, believes it should stay private—and meanwhile she is beaming at him as if his arrival in town really were the wonderful event that she has claimed it is. *Matti,* she says, *it is good to see you. Now tell me about your year.* Though she's still smiling hard, her eyes are softly and gently receptive.

A breeze lifts the napkins on both their laps. He says a couple of things, knowing that she listens appreciatively; on past visits he's noticed how she keeps straight the dates and highlights gleamed from other people's accounts, weaving nothing into their story later—or at most a single, gold thread, reinforcing one that's already there. He is halting, that's just how he becomes with her, and sometimes she rewords what he says—they pretend it is to fine-tune his Italian but he knows that she renders him more personable and larger hearted. She is a positively good person. At the table she treats Lorenza and him reverentially, avoiding direct questions about how they have been spending their time together and in this way showing how much she respects their love; she reminds him a bit of an opera fan who is so thrilled to be viewing the singers this close-up that she can't put words to it.

When he returns from the bathroom there is commotion at the table and a third woman, with frizzy blond hair gone gray, flushed Nordic looks, and a set of house keys in one hand, some sort of accidentally encountered friend, is standing between Lorenza and Vittoria, shooting ping-pong glances from one to the other and wrinkling her nose on the edge of laughter. Certain that Vittoria will see and introduce him in a minute, he just watches, like Ernesto, their throaty happiness.

"And then, and then, and *then*," says Vittoria in that voice that caresses words as if they were packages to finger so that they'll betray the feel of what they protect, "just think. Every year he comes to Venezia, every year he comes to woo her. Even though he's married now and has a little girl. He returns because he can't forget her, his first and truest love."

They are talking about him.

He can just barely stand it, a glimpse, *di sfuggito*. He takes a sharp breath; he is in the stranglehold of his own humanity. They have told his story in three lines and think they know him, believe they had defined him! *His first and truest love.* Declared outright. Which makes it far too strong to seem true. The master logic of his life revealed—is that what they think? *He has returned to his first and truest love.* His heart begins to race. They must take back what they've said. Such a thing mustn't be put in words. An admission makes what is true *too true*, takes away all its strength and power. They must stop. He will lose all the sweetness; nothing will remain in his secret spiral.

Matt props his elbows on the table and covers his ears. They've all had so much to drink that no one notices what he's doing. When, still feeling wounded and vulnerable, he lowers his hands from his ears, they are talking about Vittoria's aunt who died two days ago. *It's hard to accept*, Vittoria says. Not for him. He can accept death—hard and impenetrable. His companions fall silent, acknowledge the mystery. That at least *this* secret goes undiscussed lessens his pain.

*

"He's done it, he's put the house up for sale."

"No!"

What was that hint of admiration for audacity doing in Sophie's voice on the phone? "We have to meet," Monique said. "Today, not tomorrow. We have to accelerate things." She had her voice back. The silence was definitively broken. "We need dirt. Something illegal or something he's ashamed of."

"First the hour with Leslie-Ann in the park!"

"There are more important things to think about."

"The park, Monique, the park!"

"Once he's sold the house, what happens?"

"He moves us into the terrible penthouse."

"Are you sure he moves *you* in there? I've been through every paper and file I could find in his study."

"The detective had someone look one night in his medical office, too."

"*And?*"

"Nothing. I mean the lawyer said it was nothing. You know, I don't like the divorce lawyer much, even if he's a friend of yours. He said that if Matt can prove we switched places he could probably win custody of Leslie-Ann and not give me a cent."

"You tell me *now*? And like that?"

Sophie made a contrite apology. After a little pause, however, she added, "You know, Monique, in church last Sunday the priest talked about humility. About waking up and starting the day with it—spray it on like a good perfume, he said. It's important to be humble and gentle with others. Not to mistreat or use people in order to put your own emotional needs first. He said a lot of things I've always felt until—," Sophie's voice trailed off. She took a sharp breath and said with anguish, "Why did Matt marry me?"

She was right to wonder, Monique thought. But she'd wondered it too often. "We've been through this, how many times? You can't have love from him. Get over it. Take the money."

Outwardly Sophie wasn't faltering. The transgressions she'd committed in Chicago, those stabs at being Monique and fooling a man or two in Monique's life, were behind her—not experiences that she had made sense of, but physiologically finished. Curiosity had been the impetus for all that; now, dutifully mindful of the scenario for her future life, she was learning decoupage. With Maman's help she had made a workplace for herself in the room in the other half of the duplex where she once did her lessons with Miss Fletcher. She was making a doll box for Leslie-Ann. She missed her more than any phone call to Monique could convey. If she saw young children or heard them she got weepy—consequently she didn't go out much. This made her a home recluse for the second time in her life. Looking at things from the outside, she was sticking to their plan; inwardly, she was tottering from the temptation to revert to her younger, convalescing self. Marriage to Matt had proved too much for her when his need for her suddenly ran dry—just as life with her sister had overwhelmed her when she was thirteen. Then as now, her family was there to sort things out, and so she escaped from the fray of daily existence—which she'd been tolerating for too long a while.

"Returning to our point," said Monique, "don't you think it's a good idea to file for divorce while you're still living in this house you like so much, so that you can keep it?'

"Sure. I'd like to keep the house. But things are going OK, aren't they?, now that Maman and even Dad know and with your being there to handle Matt."

Sophie's suggesting that the shadow wife stay on made Monique's spine tingle.

"I can't believe you," she scolded. "What about Leslie Ann?"

Leslie Ann, Leslie Ann.

Adults plodding on blindly with their plans because there are children to take care of. Children with small warm bodies and wide-eyed looks and needs.

Sophie plodding on because she is needed. When she remembers Leslie-Ann.

After nine complete descents of the slide, after nine smiles and pushes on Leslie-Ann's fanny to get her up those green plastic steps, Monique called over to Marianne, whose multiply-engaged hands made one trust her to look after one's child along with her own. If Marianne didn't mind, she was going to use the lavatory of the elementary school behind them. *"No problem! Take your time! BILLY, get BACK here!"*

Sophie was waiting for her at the dwarf sinks facing the kiddie toilets. She had let her red hairdo grow out a bit too much and Monique told her so—she hadn't seen her sister in two and a half months. "I haven't seen my baby in two and a half months—let me go, let me go!" Knees bent like a quarterback ready to hike, Sophie tossed Monique her purse with jubilant impatience, then nearly stumbled as she snatched it back to retrieve a box drink of fruit juice for Leslie-Ann, which Monique had forgotten to pack. She'd already slung her windbreaker up over the side wall of the little stall, and as soon as Monique was free of her own jacket, thrust her arms into it, running then so quickly out of the room that with three or four ticks of her shoes she was gone.

For a moment, for an infinitely quiet moment in front of those miniature sinks, Monique was on the verge of snatching back her own life and ending the charade *immediately*. Shutdown time. It suddenly felt so possible. It was hers if she wanted it. She could get into *her* Toyota, and instead of circling around like a zombie-Mom for an hour, drive to Chicago for her research notes and then hop a plane to Paris. Turning this attractive scenario over in her mind, she walked out to the car. The act of starting the engine of the Toyota brought back a sharp memory of driving to university for her classes. She cruised slowly past the school grounds where Sophie was racing Leslie-Ann's swing, and then at the first big intersection where she had to wait to make a left turn…she let the validity of the idea of escaping back to Chicago expire with the smart realignment of the steering wheel. *No*, she told herself firmly, *you're not going anywhere.* She wouldn't let him take the house. She was, and still had to be for a little while longer, Sophie Morton Gagliardi. She saw and heard again that derisive voice demanding to know, *"What have you done to yourself?"* She'd show him with the house. She needed only the tiniest of power levers to keep it; and *only she* could find that power lever. She had penetrated her sister's life, mind, everything because she could do this. She was over her moment of weakness. She would live up to the challenge and play out her role. She would deliver tangible bounty.

A car in the opposite lane of the residential street honked at her but she didn't know why until the police sedan with a flashing blue light but no siren forced her to the curb. The process of receiving a speeding ticket occurred in the drilled silence of the bureaucratic rote, except for when the officer requested her license and she passed it over with unvoiceable misgivings. By the time she tucked it and the ticket inside the purse she'd be handing back—soon enough—to Sophie along with the rest of her life, she felt no pangs whatsoever.

There were two children's birthday parties entering their cake-and-song phase at the ice cream parlor in the middle of the big deep parking lot. It was easy for her to go directly and unobserved to the restroom to wait for Sophie. She hadn't been long in position, with the windbreaker thrown over the stall, when she heard Sophie enter *with* Leslie-Ann, which was not how things were supposed to work; Marianne must have had a problem and gone home.

Sophie explained to her daughter about washing our hands really well, and as she raised her voice on *"our"* she could hear her sister writing something, the silk-stocking rubbing of a pencil and then a paper crinkle-cease and then a flush and a cough and the one-time sway of the draped windbreaker. "And now, sweetheart," she kissed her, getting in a whiff of her daughter's hair, "we're going to use the hand dryer…you're NOT AFRAID of the machine, are--." The dryer blasted the hot invisible ball that one's hands seemed to be rolling from palm to palm, and Leslie-Ann found it and danced her little hands there three or four times before Monique had finished coming quietly from the stall, into which Sophie then backed.

Sophie sat in that stall for over half an hour to be on the safe side, while Leslie-Ann ate her runny sundae in the restaurant dining room and didn't miss one of the openings of the birthday presents. But the wait was all right because, actually, Sophie just wanted to cry and stay doubled-over like that, her head suspended over the small well hole of water. It was better to be there than in the car. In one hand she clutched her sister's note (*Health spa. The one next to the Mall where we had our hair done. Ten-thirty tomorrow morning by yourself. YOUR husband comes home in two days)*, and she was startled enough when some stranger entered the bathroom that she almost sprang up and used it to vomit into, but fortunately she didn't.

*

First, Monique said, *a swim.* She shuffled in her plastic thongs along the mirror-lined spa pool, which was not bigger than the one at home but adorned by stone Greek nymphs caught in a mid-air pose as they clutched towels to their chests. A clomping Sophie obediently followed, her red hair stuffed up a bathing cap. Monique tossed her towel on a white chair, and dove into the water to swim a length of breaststroke and then one of backstyle, bumping twice into the wall. She was blind by choice, without contact lenses or corrective goggles, and everyone around her leveled to a blur, the way she'd always liked it. Naturally Sophie wore her lenses under her goggles, distinguishing the other swimmers in their fleshy oddity; when she'd chosen a lane with people that appealed to her, she dove in at an opportune, uncrowded moment and syncronized her speed and stroke with theirs.

Laps and laps of it. Monique didn't like to go swimming much, but today she wanted to push herself physically, swim until her muscles forgot what it was to flex and stayed clenched on their bones, pull herself up high enough at the edge so that she could flop over on her belly on the cement, and pant long breaths of corporal isolation, and know that she could outsmart Matt Gagliardi. Together she and Sophie were going to the divorce lawyer; she'd made an appointment for early this afternoon. This, she'd decided, was the first step. They'd take those photocopied faxes in Italian; they would ask if they represented grounds for stopping Matt from selling the house. If not, they would find out what grounds were needed. With luck the lawyer would be convinced and know what to do.

Monique swam yet another couple of laps in order to feel even luckier.

When all this swimming was finished, Sophie snapped off her cap, and plopped into the white chair alongside Monique's, facing the mirrored tiles. Over their heads hung slightly swaying ferns and the loudspeaker that played music. "Look at us," Sophie said, pointing to the spread of their dimpled laps where their thighs met. "Do you remember the Polaroid photos from eighth grade gym class?" The snap-shots labeled with their names, showing their little pot bellies and Monique's especially unflattering way of stretching forward her head.

Monique waved a hand, refusing even with her mind's eye to consider that old stuff. "We were just young girls. We thought we were different, and in that picture ugly even. But the truth was that anyone looking at us just saw two awkward teenagers on the verge of becoming women. You know, I've thought about that photo over the years, and while it used to mortify me it doesn't anymore. We're all the perfect embodiment of a physical cliché at least once in our life." She realized that her words were getting too complicated for Sophie, so she threw in an example. "A type. Like the touristy chalk drawing on the wall in your husband's office."

"The girl he fell in love with in Venice years ago?" She chuckled her big stupid chuckle, clearly never having given a thought to this old souvenir.

Monique would have shouted, but the beauty of what was happening laid a partial paralysis on her diaphragm. Of course she was from Venice. And her name?

"Lorenza, I believe."

"How charming!" was Monique's excited comment.

"Charming?"

"Sophie, she's just paid for your divorce."

It was over, all over, they had him now, it had been a question of translating poetry. Her beauty sung frequently by the fax machine.

L.L.L. *La! La! La!*

CHAPTER THIRTEEN

Life is often a matter of enduring other people's inopportune celebrations, thought Matt. Receiving the invitation card from Donna, his buddy Phil's engaging and indefatigable wife, was for Matt akin to being publicly exhorted to put a smile on his face. He'd been keeping to himself since his return from Italy, and Phil had noticed. When he phoned last week he said, "Boy, Matt, you sound flat. Are you down or what?" Matt glossed over what was troubling him, calling it "a bit of an early mid-life crisis, where you're forced to realize something about yourself." Phil wanted details, but Matt said that he frankly didn't want to get into it for the time being, and they'd talked about other things. Sending this invitation, however, was Phil's way, through Donna, of re-expressing his concern. "*In the spirit of reunion*", it read, "*between you and yours and us and ours.*" Of course, it was also a trumped up excuse for Phil and his wife to put on a weekend long bash, like the kind he and Sophie used to throw many moons ago. Donna wanted extended family, kids, grandparents, dogs and all, at the place on a small lake in Maryland that they'd rented.

Matt went into the kitchen to thrust the invitation under Sophie's nose and say with heavy irony, "So why don't you invite your sister?" If there were any funny business going on between Sophie and her sister, which he suspected there was, he'd make it even funnier, he would indeed. "Call Diane and then call Donna, too, because she wants to know today," he instructed her. "Tell her we're happy, we're goddamned ecstatic to come. Tell her we're all coming—your sister and parents, my sister and Papa. Here's the number. *Go on.*" Looking at his wife's blank, unresponsive expression, he felt suddenly so physically oppressed that he could scarcely breathe. And seeing that this passive inertia of hers was suddenly the rule again after months of belligerent, headstrong eruptions, it gave him to wonder if some conspiracy between Sophie and her sister was taking place against him. Clearly, they'd been discussing him, and yet he suspected there was more, that they sometimes traded places on him, those two perverts. He knew from the medical literature what twins were capable of doing and to what extent they could operate in cahoots with each other. How many wives was he to have, he'd wanted to sneer at the one standing in front of him sometimes. Oh, it was nothing he could prove, mind you. In any case, he was too clever and alert for them to try really pulling the wool over his eyes. He added a couple of cuss words of annoyance under his breath as he went back to his study.

Watching him retreat in this grotesquely dark mood, Monique wanted to let out a laugh but didn't because it might throw a monkey wrench in things. She herself felt so happy—*smugly* happy—about this weekend and everything else to boot. The lawyer had hammered out the divorce suit, all rather mechanical at this point, and soon there'd be photos from the detective…though if it were later rather than sooner, it didn't matter. At the lake, she and Sophie would switch back definitively; there was no sense in continuing now. As soon as the papers were served, Sophie would be in a position of absolute power over Matt, and this made Monique truly content. Sophie wouldn't have to talk to him, the lawyer could do that; she could just take Leslie-Ann and go wherever she wanted, or else order him to take down the for-sale sign and leave her the house. She, Monique, had pulled it off; and though she'd been through some weird, intense moments adrift in emotions that were not hers, in the end—with that stroke of luck of finding out L.'s real identity, and *then* stumbling on the fact, when an Italian translator made sense of it, that in the latest faxes Matt was getting one of his Italian cousins to buy an apartment as a surprise for her—Monique had maintained her promise. This was adultery *alla grande*. With what perfect timing, too, for Sophie had been getting hard to handle. Seeing Leslie-Ann for those few hours on the playground and at the ice cream parlor had started her moping and mooning as only she could do. Monique chose from Sophie's closet a favorite dress to wear one last time; come this time Sunday, she thought with a thrill of anticipated homecoming, she'd be heading to her parents' house, the first leg of her trip back to Chicago.

At his desk Matt agitatedly picked up the phone and made sure that his wife was really phoning his family and Donna on the kitchen extension. When he heard Diane's warm "Oh, neat!" he quietly replaced the receiver. Then he whacked his desk with both hands. On Saturday, he vowed, he'd tell his sister and Papa to keep up the party spirit, to cover for him because he just couldn't see himself having a good time. He felt paralyzed on all fronts, unable to cope with anything, beginning with the pressing questions in his life. How to get this house sold off; what to do about his moronic wife and her crafty sister. It was mind-boggling to have discovered in that restaurant in Venice that he could feel acute passion only far from the eyes of others. He'd received the startling lesson that all he apparently could handle were fugitive moments of a love so sweet and unadulterated that he couldn't stand being named in connection to it. Its integrity was preserved on the condition that it went untouched; as something pure, it was not possible to get too close to it, any more than it was possible to look directly at the sun. Though a couple of weeks had passed, the revelation still caused him surges of inward restlessness.

It had made him think hard about himself. He saw that he was driven in a peculiar way he hadn't fully grasped before. Though he'd always recognized how ambitious and goal-oriented he was in medicine and business, he'd been blind to how he'd been simultaneously straining towards certain *ideals*. Or that's he supposed they were called. The queer thing about these ideals of love and friendship was that while he was slowly—with his small actions—working his way towards achieving them, he didn't want witnesses. He didn't want to discuss what he cared about with anyone; he didn't want scrutiny. It occurred to him that he'd never liked attending church all these years for the same reason: he hated the people standing there and the priest with his sermon trying to hold sway over him while he attempted to take in the sublime. He got irascible—and, all right, even enraged, worked up into an extreme state of intolerance in a way that was reminiscent of his father—when people didn't respect his requirements. Or, and this was the new variation that had cropped up in Venice, he went into existential shock. He admitted it! And his perception of these intimate mental habits was tremendous: it brought him up against his nature and limits. His need to help others yet not have much direct contact with them, which he'd always acknowledged in his decision to specialize in radiology, appeared in a new light. So did his close friendships, which were exclusively with other doctors, likewise used to talking about life and death like body plumbers and letting the deeper emotions ride, die, or fester under the surface.

But in this new light he also had to reassess the charge of aloofness, of assuming a 'cool stud pose', that his first girlfriends had leveled against him. Had they really been so over-demanding or emotionally frail as he remembered them? He'd been maddened by their inability to accept that emotions could be passed back and forth between a man and woman in silence, and that a verbal confirmation of that sharing was absolutely unnecessary. He'd given a lot of importance to this shortcoming. The problem, he'd always thought, was theirs, not his. And though in time he was to meet Lorenza, and then even Sophie, for whom this wasn't true, the burden of blame had always belonged to the other in the relationship. For the first time in his life he could see that his own inner demands might be excess; he was judging them critically at last. Yet seeing that they constituted his identity, part of his worth as a man, what was he to do?! He felt despondent in a way he'd never experienced before, and possibly the worst thing was that although he was a doctor with a gamut of therapeutic tricks and treatments up his sleeve—the ones which doctors are trained to suggest to patients in similar turmoil, *he didn't know if he wanted to change.* No longer fully in charge of himself, he was going to Phil and Donna's bash to get drunk or go a bit crazy.

The Gagliardi-Morton clan arrived in a three-car caravan. Diane with Pete and their father. Matt with his little family. And Danielle and John and their daughter, who looked just like Matt's wife except she was wearing a set of pearl earrings. A long-ago present from Grand-mère Marinette, they had re-emerged the other day when Sophie happened upon her old toy safe in her parents' cellar, and out of fondness and nostalgia for her grandmother who she hadn't seen for some years, she'd put them on and found they became her.

The three Mortons pulled into the half-paved road last of all the guests. The lake shimmered behind the leafless trees, blue in its center, but in the slim finger extending to their left, creamy brown with mud and busy with ducks. By its edge, on the land where the dock and the long cabin stood, there was only sky and prairie glare; across the body of water, the trees were set like tight, upright bundles of kindling. The cabin's sturdy porch was already occupied by a crowd of people. They nodded and smiled from their chairs as the straggling line of Gagliardis passed into the church-like, cavernous interior of the cabin. The newcomers stowed their sleeping bags in the already cascading pile beside the shelves of yellow and red plates in the kitchen end. It was warm enough to be April rather than November, and the atmosphere of summertime partying hung in the air. There was a game of horse-shoes going on the grass, some kids were flying a kite, and two scrawny boys with their large broad-backed dads were trying to fish off the dock. Donna their hostess, who had braided her hair into pigtails for a girl-scout look which was disarmingly sexy, introduced her sister and brother-in-law to Matt's family by pointing to their backs in the rowboat that was pulling away from the dock. On the porch, as well as by the dock and at the rear of the cabin, stood tall white buckets with drinks, pop and beer and wine and even hard stuff, packed in ice water. Most of the adults were already doing brisk, serious drinking. Not to get to truths through a sudden rabbit hole, not that kind of drinking, but to lose the social awkwardness that afflicts acquaintances the way morning stiffness afflicts athletes.

"Matt!" called Phil, breaking away from a group of buddies, a few of whom Matt recognized from the golf field or squash court. "Want a beer?" Phil held up his bottle to show it was a brand Matt was partial to and at the same time gestured to Matt's family entourage standing in a compact group beside him. "You all help yourselves, OK?" The welcome formula worked like a charm: they broke up and went off in separate directions. Only Matt's father remained, restlessly shifting from leg to leg, his hands clasped behind his back, inspecting the lake with the air of a man practicing his patience.

"How you doing, man?" Phil asked Matt in a low voice.

"I'm all right. Nothing that's a matter or life or death." He was amicable but evasive, and looked at the ground before adding, "Did I tell you? Two more people came yesterday to look at the house." Phil gave him a pat of encouragement on the shoulder, his eyes likewise trained downwards. Then Matt flicked his head in his father's direction. "Can we get him some wine? *Red* wine," he specified.

As Phil was fetching a bottle and some paper cups, Matt brought a chair down from the porch and set it in the grass for his father. Except for his mother- and father-in-law, there didn't seem to be any other older people present. The "grandparents" in Donna's invitation hadn't showed up. So it had been a mistake to bring Dad, Matt rapidly concluded, as he and Phil and Dad made a toast with their first glassful. His father would be melancholic and in his cups by the afternoon, and because he didn't know in what state he himself would be in, Matt excused himself and went over to his sister. Diane, looking cheerful and prepared for the elements in her oversized windbreaker and hiking shoes, was making friends with some thirsty little kids for whom she was pouring soft drinks. He told her to keep an eye on Dad. "Where's Leslie-Ann?" he asked, looking around.

"Her Aunt Monique is following her around." Diane heaved a theatrically envious sigh. "Look, there they are. By the lake."

Matt saw Leslie-Ann throw a stone into the muddy brown shore water and wave her arms excitedly when it made a little splash. Her aunt clapped and handed her another pebble. Leslie-Ann made another good launch and this time they both raised their hands and made a little jump. Then her aunt caught her in her arms and gave her a big swing around in place, then another and another. When Leslie-Ann shrieked that she wanted to stop, her aunt set her down and cradled her against her chest. Tenderly swatting away the child's hand when she began to pull at one of her pearl earrings, she bent over her whispering things, and he called possessively across the lawn to Leslie-Ann that they would feed the ducks.

Turning around, Sophie didn't let the little girl go running but took her by the hand. He met her with a hard face: "I need just one wife, thank you. Come on, Leslie-Ann." He brusquely undid the child's hand from hers, watching her face. Sophie felt stinging grief, and blinked and blinked, as was her way when she was ousted from a better world. Seeing this fed his already strong suspicions. In another state of mind, and without his father to worry about, he would have made much more of it.

Because there were too many people astray at any given time with cups and open ears, and because she didn't want to call attention to the way Matt was treating her, Sophie prudently stayed away from him for the rest of the morning. As she was circling aimlessly in the grass around the cabin, thinking of how tomorrow night she would be tucking Leslie-Ann into her crib at home, her mother once again, a woman about her age set a chubby toddler and his ball down on the patch of ground in front of her. The little fellow crawled two steps, lifted a half-open fist, and reached for her ankle.

She bent over him, overjoyed. "You want to get me and pull me down, do you?" she teased.

"He's out to topple everything and anyone, just to see them go crash," his mother chuckled. "Was that your daughter I just saw going back into the cabin or are you the aunt, the twin sister?" She was nice and blunt in the way of people confined to the same party space.

Sophie confessed she was the aunt.

"Gee, twins, though. Are you married, too?"

Sophie nodded.

"And *your* husband? Is he here?"

"He's away in Venice." This just slipped out. But Sophie liked this vein of half-truths and imagined other particulars she could offer, if only Monique hadn't explicitly told her not to get personal. *Then he's going on to Paris, where our grandmother has a café. It's the café where he met me. And if I stop and tell you about that day, it'll become where he meets me again. For this new story is really the old story as it should have been told. It's about a man who has just come from Venice and from Lorenza. I know this now. I thought he hated me, that he found me stupid and worthless, but it's just that he already has Lorenza. Honestly, the first thing I felt was relief. I mean that!*

"I've never been to Venice," said the other covetously, as she scooped her son up in her arms. "But I think we'll take Jimmy there some day. My husband went a long time ago when he was in college," she added.

This sent a jolt of recognition and compassion plummeting down Sophie's spine.

There were shouts and whistles and waves to call bodies big and small to lunch at the massive table in the cabin, where platters were stacked with cold cuts, cheese, bread and fruit and paper plates. The drinking continued in stand-up fashion, with giggles or grunts about the simultaneous handling of plates and forks and cups, and around her Monique enjoyed hearing all the playful innuendo, which any successful party generates. There was a tall woman lawyer with a very strong jaw line, whose commanding voice grew louder and louder as she told increasingly funny stories about her Irish family, whom she claimed tried her patience, yet whom she seemed to love. Monique glanced over at her sister and saw she was enthralled. *Sophie hasn't changed at all*, she thought. *In her heart of hearts, she prefers happy endings of tolerant co-existence. Well, let's just hope that her inclinations will serve to make it a very civilly conducted divorce, at least on our end.* Monique knew that there was no counting on Matt to be anything but a sore loser.

When the lawyer's stock of tall tales had run out and people didn't know quite what to say or do next, John Morton got a fire started in the fireplace so that the kids could grill marshmallows and fix themselves "some-mores." While Danielle was circulating with a black trash bag for the throwaways, she noticed with concern that Matt's father was slumped over the chair he was straddling, looking glumly withdrawn from everyone around him. *To be expected, wasn't it?* she told herself. Despite Donna's good intentions and the polite ways of their fellow guests, this was a party for young married professionals and their children attending school or pre-school and taking dance or piano or karate. In spite of her own conversational skills and wealth of curiosity, Danielle too felt somewhat out of place.

The heat from the fireplace drove most people outside after lunch. In small clusters they stood on the porch or in the grass gazing at the lake as if it could give them all that the ocean did. A chill was lifting off the water as the short afternoon waned. Phil, their host, however, had a sailboat ride or two in mind; he began to drag the small banked Sunfish towards the water's edge. "Come on, people! Come on, kids! Who wants to go out with me first?" While the older children ran towards him immediately in excitement, most of the adults hung back. "It's starting to get cold, Phil," called one of his male buddies. "And it's not exactly relaxing on a full stomach," yelled another. "Guys?!" Phil pretended to be scandalized. Next to him Danielle Morton was standing. "Will you come, Danielle? *Allons-y, Madame?*" John urged her to go: "A new experience, right?" Of late she had been telling him that while she had reconciled herself to the idea that she would continue to live, and grow old, in this country, at the same time she perceived that her life had slowed to a standstill. She didn't know whether to blame that on America or not. One day she even confessed, "I have these uneasy moments when I begin to suspect that I am being prepared to die here before my time." He told her, then as now, that it was her attitude towards life that counted: Why didn't she just throw herself into new activities, take that plunge? "You've never once been sailing. Go for it, Danielle." He was glad when she agreed to go out with Phil and his pint-sized crew. *Forget everything—France and America are both on the Planet Earth. Try new things!*, he silently urged her yet another time. When she had her life jacket latched and was onboard, he gave her a smart wave and went back to the cabin to check on his fire.

The room was empty except for old Gagliardi, who was crouching down in front of the fireplace.

"Ah good, you're tending it," said John sociably. The other man didn't answer. When he came up alongside him, John Morton realized that Gagliardi was considerably more drunk than him. He kept stirring up the kindling flames flamboyantly and senselessly, with those red eyes and unstoppable yawn. It bothered John Morton to watch him hack at the fire so. He'd learned years ago how to make a fire anywhere, in Boy Scout conditions, with his brother Robert, and for a moment he tried to picture where this wrinkled and wine-reeking old Italian had been taught and by whom.

Suddenly Leslie-Ann and Monique rushed in, the plank door banging shut behind them. "There's Granddad, sweetie…oh and there's *Nonno* as well, how about that?" Monique raised her eyebrows at her father when her father-in-law didn't turn around to acknowledge them.

"I know, " murmured John Morton with mild disgust. "He's so out of it, he seems lost in another world."

Monique scrutinized John Gagliardi's slumped and trembling back. Cirrhosis of the liver would probably kill him off in a couple of years' time, she reflected, and she did not suppress the additional thought that her father would have and *deserved* a longer life, being a finer man.

"Mommy!" Leslie-Ann yanked on her hand, pulling away from the fireplace.

"We're here to go to the bathroom," Monique explained to him.

It was the furthest thing from her mind that her father would suddenly leave the cabin, and so after Leslie-Ann had had her tinkle, she let her out and locked herself in for a moment of privacy. Leslie-Ann found herself alone with her Nonno, who had returned to his chair and his cup of wine, in the big room with the rough springy floorboards that made interesting noises when she stomped on them and the equally fascinating fire that was popping and crackling with a new log. As she crouched down by it, the way she'd seen her grandfathers do, Leslie-Ann noticed that the flame turned green and blue at its center before it spat a red ember her way, which landed on her right shoe. On a shriek she shook and stomped her foot, then pressed her left shoe over the right one, wailing, "MOMMY!"

As Monique emerged from the bathroom with a loudly blurted "WHAT?!", a second ember came flying out from the fire towards Leslie-Ann. She covered her ears and instinctively span round to check her backside.

"Leslie-Ann, get away from there!" Running to the child, she lugged her quickly over to the table, where she rapidly checked for burn marks on the child's clothes and shoes. Catching her breath, she turned on John Gagliardi, who was squinting at them impassively. "Why didn't you do anything?! Are you crazy?" she shouted incredulously. The loathsome, self-engrossed old gizzard looked right through her. Bending back over Leslie-Ann, she shouted even more thunderously, "Naughty! Very naughty! You could have been burned. Didn't I tell you to stay away from the fire? BAD GIRL!" She meant this with all her heart and so she shook her.

"Esagerata!" Gagliardi hissed at Monique, jutting his chin in disdain. *"Ma va al diavolo!"*

Il diavolo was the Devil, so he was sending her to hell, making her out to be hysterical and overreacting, was he? But his granddaughter's clothes could have caught on fire! God in heaven, she wanted to have nothing to do with this jackass.

John Gagliardi banged a fist on the chair back.

"Stop that!" she said sharply, as Matt walked in.

"Matti, vieni qua!" The father gave a long, angry whistle. *"Matti, questa qui è una isterica, ma non si può. La bambina non si era fatta niente!"* She understood him saying that Leslie-Ann had not been hurt and the real problem was her, *questa qui*, literally *this one here*.

Matt responded in his own increasingly animated Italian, sticking by his father's side rather than coming around to the far end of the big table to her and Leslie-Ann, as old Gagliardi argued for a world free of women, especially ones who were not Italian, throwing his hand repeatedly in the air, smacking, smacking, smacking something invisible. Monique couldn't pick out a word now, and found the rising tone and repetitions maddening and histrionic. Was this going somewhere? The worst thing was that Matt's eyes were locked on those of his father. She recalled his strange, absorbed trance at his wedding reception when his father had got him to cut up the tie. He looked the same way now. She felt very uneasy when he suddenly made a few flicks of his right wrist, and the old man gave—or pantomimed—a spit. Monique tightened her grip protectively on Leslie-Ann's shoulder. Matt backed away from his father and towards her and Leslie-Ann, agreeing in a colorless voice: *"Va bene, Papà, va bene."*

What could that misogynistic old man be convincing Matt to do to them? Monique's heart jumped.

In burst Donna, John Morton, and three bantering women guests with their fingers in upside down stacks of dirty paper cups. Unable to breathe from her state of tension, Monique followed her father to the sink with Leslie-Ann's solid little body on her hip. "Here's Granddad! What's Granddad doing?" When she set the child in his arms, she felt a great swoon of peacefulness, as if reentering a safety zone.

"Why do you need to get as bombed as Daddy?" Diane asked Matt shortly afterwards, out on the porch. Feeling something touch her hair, she'd turned in her chair and found her brother's face peering into hers; he'd been aiming for her ear in order to whisper something, and instead here they were nose to nose. There was so much gin on Matt's breath that she reared her head back. "Why are you drinking like this?" she insisted. She'd give anything to get out of him why he looked so, well, *pained.* But that would mean using words like 'anguish' or 'hurt', and those had never cropped up in any conversation she could recall having with this brother. With Pete it was different. Pete told her what he felt, and what's more, he even showed her the short stories he wrote where the characters had feelings similar to his own, and once or two even like hers, at least as Pete imagined them. With brother Pete, in other words, there was some honest-to-goodness emotional sharing. In contrast, the closest she and Matt had come to sharing such things amounted to the time he copied a blues cassette and wrote out the titles for her; she still remembered those thrills of intimacy shooting through her as she read, "I love you so" or "Don't crush me tonight" in his handwriting.

"Diane, I have come here to tell you sssome-th-ing ssso will you lisss-sen to me?" Having embarrassingly slurred a bit of that question, he switched to short declarations, where he fared better.

"You're to take Leslie-Ann. This afternoon. Papa said so. Keep her safe at your house."

"Take her away from her mother?" Diane was incredulous.

"Her mother is a sow."

"Rubbish."

"She is!" replied Matt testily, his right hand swinging at the air.

"If I leave, it will be with Daddy and soon."

"NO."

"Stop drinking, Matt."

"NO."

A man and two women gave him a look as they passed, and he smiled at them devilishly.

A quarter of an hour later he was in a porch rocking chair asleep.

Dinner was simple—grilled hamburgers and bratwursts—and smoothly choreographed, as mothers and fathers came and went from outside fire to inside fire with their children's plates. Danielle, who'd enjoyed her sailboat ride immensely and hoped there might be another one tomorrow, served her granddaughter and daughters, who sat next to each other, looking all the more like each other in this light. Matt, whose stomach after his nap couldn't handle the rest of the table's questions nor any more drink, got up on a pretext and went out onto the lawn where in the half-darkness his father was having a cigarette and scratching his upper thigh, or then again, maybe it was his balls.

"Eat something, *Papi*," Matt urged gently.

His father made a rapid hand-roll in the air, which meant *dopo*. Later. He said he hadn't been outside at night in the middle of nature—*la campagna*, not in a city or at the Jersey shore—for over sixty years. They didn't have time to reconsider the distant lake shore in light of this, however (what a pity, Matt would reflect later), for Donna came up behind them suddenly and said, "There's a guitar, Matt. Will you play?" He felt sober enough to agree to this; after all, it was something Phil expected him to do, something he'd done at many of their get-togethers over the years. He gave one of her braids a playful pull, and then leaning forward till his cheek brushed hers, he added, "Just see that my dad gets something to eat, will you? Thanks."

With only one small lurch to testify to the still considerable level of alcohol in his bloodstream, he found his way back to the cabin. Ducking into the neck strap they held waiting for him, Matt settled the guitar under an arm: she was warm, and his fingers instantly made a feathery lacework of notes for their ears. He took his time tuning the strings, and their mellow sounds worked reciprocal changes on him. When finally they were in tune, so was he. He was free of his emotional extremes: disapproval of himself, intense love for his father, scornful intolerance of his wife.

He took their requests. They wanted folksongs and the kind of upbeat spirituals that if you don't want to sing you can chant. He didn't fix on anyone as he played, and while they were deciding what they wanted next, his fingers picked out, as if it were the way home, the song about the sailor who only drank for his lady. The image of Lorenza entered the cabin as he sang the word "lady"; and at the end of each verse she made it clear she was staying. She had escaped from his inner forest. The sweet presence of Lorenza grew stronger and stronger; surely everyone in the room must have detected that there was passion breaking free of the music. He was letting them see, letting them scrutinize! He shut his eyes in joy. Only to find when he strummed his last chord and looked at his audience again that heads were turned away from him. They were straining to catch a conversation.

Her hands darting across the table in excitement to tap those of John and Danielle, Donna was quizzing the pair with a raw eagerness that stemmed from a newfound desire to spend Christmas in Paris. "Did you meet your wife there?" she asked, certain of the answer, hanging on the details.

"We met," John Morton cleared his throat so he could say it more loudly and matter-of-factly, "We met during the liberation of Paris. I rescued my wife. She was in danger, being in the Underground."

"The Underground?!" exclaimed Donna, letting the rescuing part go.

It had been a long time since Danielle had last been asked. She talked about *Système D*; about the English pilots in the cellar; about hiding a code once in her bra; about going on bikes into the countryside with her brother to scrounge for mushrooms and berries. It was Donna's face that somehow helped her find the words: she had never seen the same kind of interest, this desire to follow the full story of the complicated compromises that those times had forced on her and everyone she knew in France. She'd never glimpsed this on the faces of her American neighbors in Southern New Jersey in the 1950s and 1960s. It had been a question of waiting out a generation, she saw that now. With Donna, and— look, Donna's sister too, and even Diane, with these younger women for confidantes, she recounted the Louise Vassalli fiasco, her two daughters watching the show in admiration. Her body performed jerks it had waited for years to perform again, and soon she was standing up and doing a vengeful imitation of the French *madame* those women had considered her to be, sticking out her breasts, and wiggling her hips and crooking her finger to sexually conspire with John her husband and John the dirty old man Gagliardi, with Phil, even with dark-faced Matt, collapsing then with laughter, as her husband barked in a good-humored stage voice: "Danielle, that's enough! Somebody cut off her wine!"

As Danielle's new young friends were begging her to parlay with them in their rusty French from college days, the line in front of the bathroom grew longer and longer, and even the old outhouse across the lawn had its pretenders. People were unrolling sleeping bags, and there was already a padded patchwork behind the tiny couch where the older children were camped.

"Matt, what are we going to do about Papa?" Diane demanded, one sleeping bag thrown over one arm and another over her shoulder. She'd brought an extra one for their father but he wouldn't have anything to do with it. Matt, moreover, didn't seem to be listening to her.

Donna made the offer of a camp bed, but John Gagliardi refused that, too.

"He can't sit up at the table all night!" Donna trilled at her husband Phil as half the room tried to get to sleep, including John Morton, who rolled over on his back and let out a "jeez!", half sign and half exclamation of annoyance. Nobody was concerned about him and Danielle bedding down in sleeping bags, and they were only six or seven years younger than Gagliardi.

"Like on a train, you know." John Gagliardi reassured Donna stubbornly. "A long train across America, across Italy." He smiled briefly at his hostess for the first time since the party began. Then he took a chair, turned it backwards and straddled it, folding his arms over the top of its back and resting his head there for a demonstrative moment. He gave her a second cordial and inebriated smile. "Buona notte."

Bodies shifted and covers rustled and eyes adjusted to the light of both the coals and, on the opposite end of the room, the smudge of white that the full moon was sending through the kitchen window. Most families occupied a rectangular patch of space, the children lying in between their parents. The Mortons and Gagliardis, however, stretched out in a straight row from wall to wall: Diane, Sophie, Danielle and John, Monique, and Leslie-Ann. Next to Leslie-Ann was an empty sleeping bag that Matt would go to in a moment. Monique patted Leslie-Ann's arm soothingly.

Propping herself up on one arm, Sophie could make out old Gagliardi five feet away in his chair. She wondered what he was thinking as he stared at the table in front of him. Ten minutes or so later, after the final bathroom noises had ceased and a general silence, broken only by the first snores and strangled breathing, had settled over the large room, Sophie lifted her head quietly again. John Gagliardi had not moved or shifted position in his chair. His head was bowed and his hands were clasped over the back of his chair. She watched him a long time, keenly and earnestly. He was with them but not with them. It had been true all day, while everyone was ignoring him. John Gagliardi wasn't a troublesome guest stubbornly set on sitting up all night; he was in the land of loss. He had been there on the day of his wife's funeral too, she was his witness, only then his grief had been fresh and now it was something else—not faded, not dried, not gone, but literally a different thing. As Sophie watched him, and felt along with him, she picked up on the unruffled, thorough way in which he was engrossed by the past. In the middle of this cabin and this night, nothing distracted him from this private expanse. Surely, there were scenes and landscapes that he'd never forgotten, and words, too, that his inner ear had captured and kept chained for him, till he was ready, as he appeared to be tonight, to let them resound and echo. It was only right that old people had the privilege of reliving their past while at the same time living and breathing the present. In the end, whether it was meditation, anxiety, strong drink, or chance to make the past kaleidoscope with the present had no importance. She knew from her own brush with death that she too would have this vision in its entirety someday. From her brief glimpse she understood there was more to come. The sensation of the past and the present all mixed up together was nothing to be afraid of. She hadn't told anyone but it was a certainty.

After a long while, Sophie lowered her head and went respectfully to sleep... in an old drunk's cathedral.

*

Sunday divided the drivers from the drinkers. There were those who were having coffee and those downing Bloody Marys at the big brunch in the light-filled cabin, all five of its windows opened to air out the human night smells. The guests spilled all over the property, some of them absorbed in rituals from yesterday and others looking for new activities. The undecided and the lake-gazers kept to the porch and contended for chairs. Sophie happened to catch a glimpse of Matt as he parted a bush to make a short-cut to the water. The ground sloped downwards and he vanished. *But he's still there*, she thought. It was an idle, even silly thought but it seemed to mean something extra today. A moment later Matt reappeared into view, dockside. *Bodies don't evaporate, do they?* she said to herself. *If death doesn't obliterate the sense you have of another person (it hasn't for John Gagliardi), then neither does divorce.* And though, overpowered by the terrible conviction it was otherwise, she'd called her sister Monique in to right the ghastly wrong of his looking through her on the street, the truth was that no one disappeared from anyone in life. As she had already a number of times this week, she fantasized this morning at the lake about Matt's Italian mistress, Lorenza. She pictured a woman who looked like a Morton in a tiny apartment overlooking a canal. Matt walked in the door and they kissed. Matt loved her. She pictured this, and it did her no harm. Matt's love for Lorenza didn't erase her, Matt's wife, from the face of the earth. Not at all! Each time she indulged in this fantasy, joy surged through Sophie. Because she looked like Lorenza in that drawing, Matt had found Lorenza in her, Sophie. No one disappeared from anyone. She wanted to laugh and cry tears of gladness.

To be jealous, one had to have a center-heavy self. Sophie had no such self. Sophie was made in such a way that she could only find this overlapping with Lorenza illuminating, beautiful, stunning. Though she was presently in a position to divorce Matt for a lot of money, it was hard to maintain the sense of being so grievously wronged. Even his insults, his ignoring her, his scorn which had made her desperate —even this had an explanation now: the fact that he had both Lorenza and her in his life was too much for him to handle. He needed supreme help and compassion from her, being incapable of either himself.

As if by association, the memory came flooding back to her of how she had felt in the hospital after her accident. She had reopened her eyes to life—all of life—then. Though the choice facing her now was much smaller, it was similar enough to the one made on instinct in the hospital to show her a pattern, a story line to her existence, and she felt a prick of excitement. It was as if she had decoded something…made sense of her destiny as her mother had intuited she could. *Starting over was something she instinctively knew how to do.*

Emerging from the bathroom, where he'd finally managed to get a shower, John Morton ran into one of his daughters. He didn't want to know which. "Your mother wants another boat ride before we leave. Do you think that can be arranged?"

"Why not?" said Monique neutrally, feeling in reality thwarted in her plans for she'd been on the verge of calling Sophie into the bathroom for their big swap. She checked through the doorway. "The rowboat's there. Why don't you just take her out?"

"She wants the *sail*boat like yesterday. Matt and Phil are the only ones who know how to sail."

"Well, Dad, can't you handle it yourself and ask one of them?" she said impatiently and walked off.

"Matt! Maaaaaatt!" Danielle herself spotted him. He was tromping up from the lake in muddy sneakers and had a cloud of children around him. They stood on the balls of their feet and chanted that they wanted a sailboat ride, too. "Go ask your parents," Danielle told them. "Then we'll all go out together."

Their swarm lifted immediately, leaving only Leslie-Ann by Matt's side, her curly head against his thigh, her arms clasped around it. "Daddy, my Daddy," she said.

"Haven't got all day. We're leaving after lunch, you know," Matt told his mother-in-law perfunctorily. "Where are John and my father?"

It has gotten in the way of his plans, thought Danielle, without answering.

"Well, Danielle? Let's go find your husband and my dad, shall we?"

That ugliness of his, the inability to lay aside resentment at the inconvenience you were causing him, had crept into his voice.

John Gagliardi stood by the white bucket at the rear of the cabin, the one that many guests overlooked, silently scrounging for another bottle of red wine. He'd spent most of the morning smoking his cigarettes in the grass a little way off from everyone else, every so often taking his small step in place, and not so much gazing at the lake as staring it down with the squinting, unflinching sort of melancholy of old Italian men. His daughter Diane pulled on his sleeve and said, "Come, *Papi*, Matt wants to take you out on the lake." He was being so uncharacteristically asocial that she hardly knew him. "Then we're all going to leave," she underlined.

He didn't come. She knew he wouldn't until Matt himself waved and called from the dock, which wouldn't be for a while, because Phil was taking the Schultz family, with the longest drive home of all, out for a sail first. The Gagliardi-Morton clan was left to watch with about as much interest as stranded train passengers.

Though John Morton wasn't confessing it to anyone—wasn't even making one of his stoic sighs because he was mindful of being a guest—all the same his nerves were getting tenser and tenser. The way they were all catering to Matt's father and continuing to excuse his rude behavior was beyond belief. When finally Matt took the sailboat rope from Phil and hollered for them all to be helped into the pitching and bobbing boat, and when on top of that Matt's father refused, gruffly muttering that he would throw up if he went out on that sailboat and would only, to make Matt happy, go in the rowboat, which led to Matt assigning his father with him and Soph—well, that protesting daughter of his without the pearl earrings who was going by the name Sophie and muttering angrily about not wanting to go near the old man, to that other boat—when this had taken place, John Morton's peevishness crested like beer foam and he said, "Sorry, I've had it, I'll go wait by the car." He assumed his defection would be enough for Matt to give up on the rowboat idea, but no.
"SOPHIE, YOU HEAR ME?!" Matt roared from the water, exasperated. "Get in that boat with my father! Row it! DO SOMETHING FOR ONCE!"
Because it was for the last time, Monique acquiesced.

Danielle kept her arm around Leslie-Ann, the only one in a life jacket. Though there was little wind by the dock, the current immediately nudged both the rowboat and sailboat away from the shore. Both Monique and Matt began to paddle strenuously, and the boats stayed together until a small gust caught in the sail by Matt's head and the Starfish began to move and move over the brown brothy surface. Left behind to go at a snail's pace, and with no sail to protect her eyes from the sun blazing down from between the clouds, Monique rowed blindly on. Every so often she managed a squint at wheezing old Gagliardi, on the wooden plank opposite her with his elbows on his knees and his head locked in the half-raised position of a man straining his bowel on the toilet.

Perched by the rudder bar on the swiftly moving Starfish, Sophie followed what was going on in the rowboat with some concern. As her sister continued with her jerky pulls on the oars, old John Gagliardi went from a humped-over stance to suddenly upright; he twisted round and pulled free the cushion stowed under the prow, passing it to Monique, who must have asked for it for she sat on it immediately. He planted his fists on his thighs and eyed her in a fixed and interested way. Though Sophie couldn't make out his precise look, she presumed it was, as Monique had put it once, "the way a horse breeder with a sick imagination would a horse." Her sister barked something at him and vigorously shook her head, rising from her seat with the oars and making the boat rock. As sorry as Sophie felt for old Gagliardi at times, she was glad she was not in that rowboat.

Suddenly the sailboat veered sharply to the right, and the hull lifted on one side, nearly spilling Sophie, Danielle, and Leslie-Ann into the water. Matt rapidly pulled the three of them toward him, yanking with insistence on their shoulders so that they were sitting precariously on the raised edge, Danielle's heart beating fast with a sense of danger for her little granddaughter. "I love it," said Diane, the only one still sitting on the dipped side, treating her face to the wind as if it were the facial beauty treatment she never had time for. By the rudder Matt had his eyes raised to the sail and his mouth open for an order, which suddenly came: "Watch the boom, watch its swing, DUCK!" And they all ducked. The swift breeze held, whereas the sun began come and go from behind the clouds now, and they rode on the crest of the boat to the far side of the dark chilled lake. "See anyone?" asked Matt, with a backwards jerk of his head, and Danielle looked past his shoulder and said, "I saw John before standing on the shore, but then he left."

"The row boat is there to the left. I can barely see them. They're going way over towards the finger," Diane reported.

"Headed for the mud," muttered Matt sarcastically, catching the boom just in time. "Shift positions!" He let go of the struggling aluminum beam and its sail. "DUCK!"

Monique rowed with her face crooked against a shoulder, watching the ducks, the flat deserted shoreline as they entered the lake's side branch, the water's nearly black, silty patches, watching everything but John Gagliardi, who was gasping or belching or else doing something even more disgusting like swallowing his vomit. "Do you want to lean over and throw up?" she asked testily. He said 'no' on a hiccup, and stopped his awful noises. Without meaning to, she turned the boat in a circle, then in another, her left arm not working the oar the way it should, not scooping a heavy weight of water. She was tiring. There was no sign of the sailboat, and she couldn't see the far shore clearly enough to pick out the cabin. Gagliardi started talking to himself in Italian, gesturing in the direction that both of them supposed the cabin to be. The lake was deep and gelatin-like. Rowing back into the main basin and homewards meant going into the wind. The wooden oar clanged this way and that against its metal ring. The boat didn't seem to want to go more than a few feet in the direction she desired. For the most part it bobbed in place, and when she gave up rowing completely, the wind and current lurched them backwards. They'd been out for a good half an hour and it was getting colder. There were no voices nor even birdcalls in the air. There was only the thumping of the small waves against the hull, the oars turning like old bones in their sockets, and Gagliardi's sick breathing.. She was stranded out here with *this person*. His red cloudy eyes opened and shut in time with the lurches the boat made. The wind showed no letting up. Her hands began to sweat and she could no longer get a proper grip. Try as she might, she just couldn't get the oars to dig into the water. As she continued to flex and strain her arms and wrists, she told herself that it was a question of falling into the rhythm, of getting one's shoulders and pelvis moving automatically. In the meantime they were moving in half-completed and reversing circles.

John Gagliardi did not see the water: he saw some flat gleamings that came and went with the sunlight. He wasn't in his son's car yet, he wasn't home yet, but he wasn't with all those strangers anymore. In this peaceful if chilly boat, his son's wife, one of *la famiglia*, did the repetitive actions that women do and men find distracted comfort in: she was rowing but she could have been rolling pie dough. He felt sick and she knew it. He considered telling her, asking her, if such a bad burning in the chest could be from the wine—if the wine of their host, a wealthy doctor, could be so bad, *cattivo*, as that. But he didn't ask her, because she wasn't Frances, his wife, and because it eased a bit.

Monique gave little grunts now as she heaved her uncooperative left shoulder. She had rowed once or twice in her girlhood, in a lot of wind too, without any problem. She refused to believe that this lake was navigable to everyone but her! *Stay calm*, she ordered herself. *Try harder*.

As she made her mightiest and most desperate pull of the morning, her bent knees in her plaid trousers thrashed back and forth, brushing his. John Gagliardi saw the slim thighs move and reached for the nearest. She jerked, her head tipping back so far that it was almost horizontal with the water, the boat swaying violently. "Don't you DARE!"

Her shriek made his upper torso heave, and suddenly there was so much new burning inside it that he just had to spring to his feet and take a step to feel alive. Monique saw him rise and lunge at her. She let go of the frustrating, nearly useless oars and kicked, kicked—how to stop him from throwing himself on top of her was her only thought, as she sent his arms and then his chin sideways, over the edge, the boat in its mad jerk dumping both of them in the lake.

When she surfaced in the thick and freezing muddy water, she found the overturned boat bucking slightly in the current but not going anywhere, like a tied up colt. John Gagliardi did not reappear. She trod water for a moment, waiting for the lecherous little man to balloon up from the depths, barely able to stand the cold, which felt numbing on her legs, like icy lava. After a few more minutes passed, and the old Italian had still not bobbed to the surface, she took hold of the edge of the boat and felt this way and that with her feet for his body. A tremendous, involuntary strangling sensation rose in her throat as she imagined his agony. When she hit upon nothing soft, nothing human, she wondered if he was pinned at the bottom, with his jacket, say, caught onto something. She submerged her face in the stinging cold, completely opaque lake water, but without a search light there was no way she could locate him. She raised her head toward the unbroken line of trees contouring both the main lake and side channel. Could he have swum to shore? She remembered his labored breathing, that of a man incapable of any sort of physical exertion. Then she saw him lunge towards her again, his broad bulk toppling her way. *Tackling and pinning her*…this was why she'd kicked. But as she relived it in her mind, he suddenly became a man keeling over from a heart attack.

Dead. Dead even before he hit the water. Dead because it was his moment to die. She was blameless. The pleasure of this conclusion lasted for one or two seconds, and then the commandments instilled in her since childhood made her do, with an anxiously beating heart, what she had decided was pointless to do: she turned a somersault in the water and went a yard or two underwater in a yielding wall of blackness, the cold like a leaden cylinder around her chest. Her mind raced in a voice that was not hers, the all-knowing composite voice of the generation that had taught her right from wrong. *Even a repellent old man, even a repellent old man.* The words repeated over and over, revolving like a drill that opened blind tunnels for her underwater. When she could no longer bear the cold and those vertiginous channels, she surfaced, panting. Then as if her life depended on it, and it probably did, she swam a fast breast stroke to the shore.

In her smeared, sopping wet clothes and jacket she ran down a rutted path and crossed the lawn, in sight of the Schultz family, who were now loading their car for departure, but they barely noticed her, and because she was running did not realize her clothes were wet. She had the very good fortune of finding Phil in the cabin.

"Call the police," she told him breathlessly and explained about Matt's father. "We capsized, Phil. Then suddenly I was under water."

He went white. "Christ. Where's Matt?" He dialed the emergency number on his cell phone as he jogged towards the lake, shouting to his wife and her friends in the grass that there'd been an accident, calling and waving and beckoning to Matt. When the people on the sailboat started waving back, he thrust his phone in the hands of one of the boys fishing on the dock, and leaped into the water.

Favored by the wind, the sailboat rapidly see-sawed its way over a stretch of choppy water to where he was swimming and picked him up. Hoisting himself up over the hull, Phil flopped onto his belly in their midst, his legs kicking in the air as the trickling water from his drenched clothes wetted their knees and formed a puddle under their feet.

"Rowboat overturned. Your dad's missing, Matt," he gasped.

The boat raced along with its two grim captains (Matt swallowing his saliva, aborting sobs) while Leslie-Ann dozed with her head in her grandmother's lap. Danielle remembered her first encounter with John Gagliardi at Diane's house. His wife was already dead, and he looked vulnerable and damageable to her, like most widows or widowers. Even when they were younger than Gagliardi and more or less about her age (upper fifties), they seemed closer to their death than she was to hers for the fact that their wife or husband was already gone, whereas she still had John. *The partnerless seem to be waiting for something bad to suddenly happen, don't they?*, Danielle acknowledged with a pang to her heart. Their sailboat was galloping over to verify how freakish— how mortal—John Gagliardi's accident had turned out to be.

Alone in the cabin, Monique had burst into sobs of relief. It had taken her but a second to lock herself in the bathroom. She was safe. She was chilled to the bone but alive. With contracted shoulders, rigid knocking knees, and trembling gray and blue arms, she reached into the shower stall to turn on the hot water. She stood shaking, her teeth chattering violently until the little cubicle began to emit mists of steam, which thickened and whitened like the vapors of a hot spring. She stripped down then, got under, and finally got warm. She ran her hands over her head, face, and eyes, letting the pounding water work the numbness out in her fingers. There was nothing the water could do, however, to relieve the hollow emptiness inside her.

Wrapped in her towel, she cracked the door open and bounded out to find some clothes. No one was there, although now there were voices outside, the sound of shouting in the grass by the cars. She wondered how the rescue efforts were going, if John Gagliardi had been found yet.

Crossing the room to the small fire that was still burning, she saw out the window that an ambulance had arrived. It stood abandoned, its orange lights revolving slowly and the rear doors flung open; a stretcher, blanket, and oxygen tanks lay ready on the ground. Nearby, a subdued-looking family—people whose names she couldn't remember—were packing their car, the father heaving the last bags into the trunk as the mother lifted her son from his stroller and deftly aimed a kick at its back bar to fold it up. In the meantime, another family of three (the Rathmans, if she remembered rightly) had appeared with their bags alongside their sedan, and while the wife dealt with her child and stroller, the two men exchanged a few words, each with a hand gripping the edge of the roof of his car. Both were still at an age when any death seemed a ghastly surprise and when a fatal accident put the fear of God into their hearts that they could lose their children in a similarly unforeseen way.

Suddenly the second man, Rathman, pointed towards the water. Whatever he saw was of enough interest to him to make him back away from his car and go in that direction. Monique opened the cabin door a crack. A scraggly crowd had gathered by the dock— among them she caught a glimpse of her father, and a yellow rescue truck was turned with its nose to the cabin, its boat trailer empty. On the horizon, a motorboat slapped the water impatiently at high speed. Divers would be going down to look on the lake bottom, she thought. If necessary, after dark they would work with floodlights.

A vision of the coming hours gripped her, with Diane crying her eyes out and Matt consumed by a grief that would gravitate towards rage. Would he go for her this time, do as his father once did? She would be the object of his wrath—she had been out there in the rowboat with his father, so it was all her fault. But Daddy wouldn't let Matt touch a hair on her head. She hugged herself—and so remembered she was naked under the towel. Damn, but she didn't want to put on Sophie's clothes again! *God, I don't want to be here*, she said aloud, then suddenly started to blubber. These tears were accompanied by the most heartless thoughts (*the old man is a dead old leech, I wish the funeral were tomorrow, I wish the divorce were the day after tomorrow, I wish Matt Gagliardi would fall off the face of the earth, I want to be home in Chicago, home!*). Another attack of the chills overtook her, her shoulders and upper arms convulsed and goose bumps pimpled her arms. Life could be sinister. She wanted Matt Gagliardi, her intellectual equal, to understand this—for it was this lesson which made her body shake this time. Life could deny and deprive you, plans worked out only in part and in unforeseen ways, you could only be sure that you would learn the astonishing, the bitter.

Outside, the driver of the police car pulling up to the cabin accidentally set the siren going in its wail-and-honk mode for a second. She only just had time to snatch up her bag of clothes, and Sophie's as well, and dash back into the bathroom. A minute later, the two troupers in their high black boots lumbered into the cabin at Donna's heels.

"Sophie?" Donna called, going immediately to the bathroom door. "You all right?"

There was a snuffle and a cough. Then, "Yeah, I guess."

"Then please come talk to the police," Donna said, not meaning to sound brusque and feeling inwardly very distraught. "*Please!*" she insisted. No one seemed to fathom how much she had to do as hostess.

Matt and Phil exclaimed at the same time, "There!"

Nudged up against the shore of the peninsula, the capsized rowboat looked like the shell of a giant sea turtle. Matt had the sick feeling that his father's body was wedged inside that shell as he dropped the sailboat's anchor and dived off the side, followed by Phil. The two men swam to either side of the boat and prepared to heave it in the air. The engine drone of the rescue boat announced its approach as they raised one side of the green hull. The planks where Monique and John Gagliardi had sat were exposed like wet ribs, but the only thing to spill out was the cushion stowed under the bow. The carcass was empty.

To his shock and dismay, Matt was not allowed to take part in any of the professional search efforts. The head of the rescue crew would not let Matt help in their operations.

"But I need to. I'm his son!" Matt protested angrily to the head of the rescue crew. "And I'm a doctor!"

"I don't think we need a doctor out here, do we, guys?" the other man asked his two suited-up divers, who were too occupied with their masks and mouthpieces to pay him any heed. "But an extra one waiting for us on shore, now that's a different matter, " he reassured Matt. Deeply tanned and gray-haired, he spoke with the sort of twangy West Virginian accent that can make just about any rebuke sound down-home and wry. "Is that your little girl on the sailboat? Jeez, get your kid back to the cabin, doc. You know this ain't going to be pretty."

The policemen had just finished with their questions to a pale, sniffling Monique by the fireplace when Diane, Sophie, and Danielle dragged themselves in, Leslie-Ann sucking her thumb in Sophie's arms, bleary-eyed from the sun, wind, and emotion of the last two hours. When one of the officers cleared his throat to signal his presence, Diane gasped, "Dear God, there're troopers here." She swung round towards the fireplace towards the woman whom she took to be her sister-in-law and exclaimed imploringly, "Sophie!? Oh!" with tears glistening in her eyes. If Sophie would just break down in front of her and bawl her eyes out in sorrow and regret for *Papi*, instead of standing there looking numb as she was, it would provide Diane with a small consolation.

But Danielle's maternal instinct was aroused. "Diane? Let Sophie be."

The mention of Diane's name had an instant effect on the two Maryland police officers.

"Ma'am, I'd like to ask you some questions about your father, the presumed victim," said the beefier and blonder of the two, looking politely at Diane.

"Of course." Her voice wobbled. "But don't you want my brother, too?"

"Where is your brother?" asked the officer, as his colleague finished his circling past the windows and looked out the door, more out of restlessness and curiosity.

He pulled the door wide open to let Donna and John Morton in. Donna spared Diane the trouble of answering the officer. "They've just pulled the boat out of the water. Matt's coming," she tersely informed all of them and no one in particular, leaning over her overnight bag and energetically rummaging through it. Rising a moment later with her retrieved cell phone, Donna gave a glance to the people at the table. Her eyes rested on Leslie-Ann. "What is Leslie-Ann doing here?" she exclaimed agitatedly. Sophie was cut to the quick; how powerless she was to decide for her child and how she longed to be identified in the eyes of all as the mother again.

Donna plucked the startled little girl from Sophie's arms and took her outside.

For a half minute or so after the heavy door shut there was an abrupt drop in energy and noise in the room. As they waited for Matt Gagliardi, even the two policemen looked momentarily spellbound, staring opaquely at the toes of their shiny black boots.

The only one untouched by this physiological lethargy was Danielle. Her maternal instinct went into red alert. Matt would come rushing in and things would get nasty and ugly, and yet she wasn't as alarmed about this as one might think—she could count on John and the policemen to protect her girls after all. What really caused her anxiety was how to save-guard the twins' final swapping back. The final *coup*. *Mes enfants*, she thought with a lump in her throat. Doing this all on their own. And what ingenuity and method they'd showed over these past months! She felt a mother's audacious pride that she would never, could never confess. Her girls' *Sistème D.*, their alibis, disguises, and subterfuges, coming to an end. If they kept their nerve, they would obtain what they were after. Not the defeat of the Nazis—this was her and their generational divide—but a rightly chunk of money to live on after such unhappiness. Her daughters had taken to heart the lesson that you don't get something for nothing in life. Courage was courage. Taking Sophie quietly by the hand, she passed behind Diane and the two policemen, joining Monique by the fireplace

Lock yourselves in, Danielle told her daughters. Into Monique's ear she murmured, "*Prépare-toi*', and into Sophie's the same.

John Morton—still listening empathetically to Diane at the table—wondered what was going on, why the three women in his family were huddled together by the fireplace, their backs to the room.

Suddenly Danielle gave both twins a little shoulder push in the direction of the bathroom.

The moment was now!

"Maybe it was his heart," Diane was saying listlessly to the police officers and John Morton. "I don't understand otherwise why he would have started to topple over on Sophie."

Neither John or the police officers had a chance to show agreement, sympathy, or any other reaction. As the bathroom door closed behind Monique and Sophie, Matt Gagliardi bellowed his way into the cabin, his face gone burgundy, "SOPHIE!!!!!!"

Silence.

"BITCH!" he yelled, going over to the closed door and plummeting it with a fist.

There was still no response from inside the bathroom but this time the bigger of the two officers said sharply, "Better calm down there, buddy!"

Matt gave the two policemen a look of hatred which they didn't see because their walkie talkies had come alive; they pulled them out of their breast pockets and held them up to their ears, exchanging nods and glances as they repeated after the crackling voice and moved towards the door: "We got a search boat coming in…about to land now….We've got a body…get the ambulance down to the water for the body."

The word *body* echoed in their ears.

With a fierce sob, Matt flung his hands and head on his sister's shoulders and cried against her neck. "I couldn't find Papa...couldn't save Papa."

The two embraced, Diane cradling his head against her chest. "Matt, Matt, I'm here," she said softly.

When she'd rocked him three or four times, Matt abruptly pulled free. His eyes were swollen into two red slits, like a rabid and wounded animal. "Are they both in that bathroom?" he seethed at his in-laws.

John was so taken aback by this savage tone that he didn't answer. Matt stalked over to the kitchen stove and pulled down the garden scissors that hung on a hook, and Danielle grabbed John's forearm in alarm. John cried out, "You break down that door and I'll go call the officers back!"

Matt gave him a wild stare. "Sophie, get out here! JUST Sophie!" he shouted with his scissors. "I'm going to BRAND her, by CHOPPING OFF A FRONT LOCK OF HAIR. Imagine that—a man needing to *identify* his wife!"

"I've seen this already, long before you were born," replied John scornfully, adding in a menacing voice of his own, "and I did something about it, buster."

Matt hadn't the faintest idea what he was talking about. "SOPHIE!" he shouted at the bathroom door again.

"Sophie!" called Danielle nervously. She was going on instinct that Matt's rage would subside rather than peak when he saw his wife, if only because he wanted the ugly details from her.

This time the door opened. His wife emerged. "Yes, Matt."

He was inches from her, waving the scissors at her and roaring, "YOU KILLED MY FATHER!"

"No, Matt. He was drunk. He lost his balance and fell in."

"You didn't rescue him!"

"I looked for him, I did my best," she said, all honesty and sincerity. "How could I do more, Matt? You know how I hate to put my head underwater. But I did it."

Her mother could see that it really *was* Sophie.

"You sow!" he hissed at her. He threw the scissors on the floor.

She came towards him wordlessly all the same. No insult could stop her. Her spread fingers grasped his right shoulder. "I know you don't hate me... Matt, I realized--," she started, eager to explain.

"What the— (his voice dropped and he whispered ferociously) *hell are you talking about?*"

"*Lorenza,* Matt--."

He raised the side of his hand. "Don't you dare say her name." His inner forest was ablaze and nothing could be saved. He lowered his hand only to raise it again. Everything was burning and his father was dead.

"DOCTOR GAGLIARDI! DOCTOR MATT GAGLIARDI!" boomed an amplified voice outside. "Doctor Gagliardi to the dock, please!!" The search squad leader's West Virginian accent was thick enough to make it even through a megaphone.

With the cold realization that he wasn't where he should be, wasn't where the search team and police and Phil and Leslie-Ann were, where the things that were left him in life –his friend and his daughter—would brace him for that view of his father's dead face, Matt dashed outside. His heart rose in his throat when he saw the bulky form covered by the white sheet on the stretcher that the paramedic was pushing along the dock. Then he heard her behind him, matching his footsteps in the grass, and he turned.

"Don't follow me!" he commanded coldly.

But Sophie continued. She was sure of herself and of what she was doing.

"DON'T!"

She persisted. Her eyes were downcast, her face radiant.

"Don't."

But she continued and he didn't say anything. She walked a step behind him, processing with the dignity and savvy of her bridal walk, towards her daughter Leslie-Ann and towards the scene of death: the finest and fullest that life had to offer.

CHAPTER FOURTEEN

The autopsy report was the only reason Matt tolerated Sophie's presence at his father's funeral, which was held two days later back in Pennsylvania: it concluded that he'd most likely suffered a massive heart attack before drowning. Because it was, medically-speaking, his only option, he made no further allusions to her presumed responsibility in his father's death. He would put up with his saccharine and self-effacing spouse until his father was laid in the ground.

Stroking and patting Diane's hand throughout Mass, he was able to withstand his sense of aversion on the church steps when he found her advising his brothers alongside the loaded hearse as to how best to organize the car procession to the cemetery. He didn't intervene a few hours later either when Sophie helped to serve the cold cuts, bread, and wine that Diane had thought necessary to offer their father's old cohorts at her house. He kept out of the way; in return, however, he had demanded two things from the start. First, he wanted her to make sure that Leslie-Ann did not get frightened at anything she saw or heard during those days—Mrs. Korn should be contacted. Second, he had her tell her parents and her sister to stay home in New Jersey—he did not want them pretending to feel grief.

Though it was sunny with a stunning blue sky the day they buried *Papi,* the next afternoon it snowed. Snow was normal for the end of November, but the fact that it was falling and accumulating on their father's fresh grave made it anything but normal.

"*Snow*, Matt," moaned Diane in a phone message left on the answering machine of his private line at the office. Apparently, she'd called him just to say this.

And that night it snowed again. Around midnight he woke up on the sofa in his home study, where he'd been sleeping since coming home from the lake, and through the window he saw the thick white splotches emerge from the darkness and into range of the spotlights on the lawn. It would be an abundant snowfall, he thought. When he was a boy he used to love snow. The same peaceful feeling from years ago was his again for a moment. That white blanketing softened everything. He closed his eyes. The whiteness enhanced his inner landscape, too, flat and treeless as it was.

Towards the end of that week, he received a call from the real estate agent, Jean Parker, who was handling both the sale of the mansion and his bid on the city penthouse suite. Since she had a couple who were ready to sign on the Swarthmore place, pending the imminent approval of their financing by the bank, she proposed going to have another look at the city pad, on which his "option to buy" contract was about to expire.

"You're lucky to have such an option, Doctor Gagliardi," she emphasized over the phone in the fawning way of a salesperson who wants to convince you that there is a karma to buying and selling which she or he keeps a close watch over. "The timing is such that you can go ahead and buy it or else withdraw your offer without paying an penalty. You just have to decide how much you want it."

He rode into Philly with Jean on the late side of one cold sunny afternoon and toured the apartment again. This time he hated it. It felt like an all-glass multi-roomed prison suspended in the air, without the possibility of opening a window. And those triple security doors that left you for a moment trapped in a vault as they slid open and shut—awful, ghastly! How could he have cared about and *wanted* such a thing? If he had once believed in protective security and blindage, if he had thought that both the physical and psychological versions were not only good but possible, he certainly didn't anymore.

When they exited the climatically sealed building on the ground floor, the outside world blasted them with an oceanic wave of smelly, rejected air. Real life was like that, wasn't it?

"I've decided against it, Jean. I'm pulling out of the deal."

"Pardon me?"

"It's not for me, sorry."

She squinted at him, trying to make sense of this abrupt decision. They'd toured the penthouse rapidly and silently; it had seemed like a finalized visit. "And where are you and your family moving to, if the house gets sold?" Jean Parker asked. She suspected there was another real estate agent, one of her cut-throat competitors, behind this cool disinterest. Not even a "Well, I'll think it over for another day." This didn't seem like Doctor Gagliardi.

"Let me rephrase that," Jean said in a somewhat darker voice. "Do you have a back-up plan as to a place to live when the Snegons buy your house as they almost certainly are?"

Matt eyed her as if she were testing him, as if under it all she'd like to make him acknowledge that life was simultaneously the stirring personal question of where one lived and the larger social question of who lived where and with whom. Life was *especially* that second question.

"My wife and I are divorcing, " he revealed.

He was a pioneer standing on a snowy deserted plain.

"Doctor Gagliardi?! I'm sorry!" From how she said this, he knew that perfect strangers would hear about this before his own family.

*

Bill Steinfeld, the lawyer who had defended Matt once in a trumped up malpractice suit, could not get over the coincidence when Matt phoned, asking for an appointment and stating the reason. Just that morning he'd received a copy of the tentative pre-divorce agreement, along with very compromising photos to prove the 'cruel and unusual punishment *cum* adultery' angle, from a colleague representing Sophie Gagliardi, his client's wife. He had the papers there on his desk and glanced at them repeatedly as he listened to Matt spontaneously offer to give his wife just about everything itemized on the last page. If the sale of the big house they had in Swarthmore didn't do through, Matt told Steinfeld, she and their daughter could keep that as well.

He did not give any sign of knowing that his wife had already proceeded against him. It was a very cut and dried, run-of-the-mill presentation of a wealthy professional who wanted to get rid of his wife and whose only concern was for his little girl. Presumably, he was leaving Sophie Gagliardi for the Venetian woman, his mistress in the photos, Bill Steinfeld mused. They were both consulting their date books for a good appointment time (out of professional courtesy, Steinfeld did this himself, rather than passing the line to one of his secretaries), when the youngest girl on his staff entered with a quiet knock and set a fax by the phone.

Gagliardi, he read from the fax. The wife had decided not to file for divorce after all.

"How does next Tuesday at 2 pm suit you?" he asked Matt, reaching across his desk for a pencil. "Very good, see you next Tuesday, Doctor." When Steinfeld got off the phone, he picked up the draft that his colleague had sent and, shaking his head over the second coincidence, inverted the names at the top, Sophie *Gagliardi vs. Matt Gagliardi*, with a double arrow.

*

The Chicago-Philadelphia night flight was an alarmingly bumpy ride through a great deal of turbulence, and though Monique had been looking forward to seeing her parents and sister and niece for Christmas, she spent numerous ten-minute stretches battling with the queasy feeling—just shy of panic—that the elements would manage to rip open the plane's belly under her vibrating feet. At least she knew what awaited her at the end of this trip, however. There was none of the trepidation that had gripped her as she'd landed in Chicago a month ago, finally herself again and yet wondering if everyone in her old world would recognize her as such, as the Monique Morton they used to know, and not that eccentric imitation that Sophie had provided them with.

"Well, HELLO! Paris was good, then, was it?" beamed Cheryl Wares, the associate professor of French whose faculty office was adjacent to hers, on her first day back at university. "Gosh, you really went all out, with that short French waif hair cut. Henna, is it? You tempt me, you know," added Cheryl, whose own hair had gone completely gray. "Now tell me something about all the good stuff that I'm sure you unearthed. Which libraries did you get to work in this time?"

Monique was still standing there with her key inserted in the door, offering Cheryl one of the small intriguing tidbits that she'd prepared to give the impression that she had truly gotten ahead on her Christine de Pizan project, when Marion, one of the secretaries on their floor, popped out of her own office to offer the same enthusiastic welcome.

Evidently no one knew, no one had found her out. They were all too genuinely surprised by her red hairdo for it to be otherwise. *But no*, Monique realized on second thought, remembering an old phone conversation with Sophie, *Mike from Rochester must suspect something*. He and Sophie spent more than one evening together in her apartment. Well, never mind, it was a blessing that he was from out of town. And when she put all these impressions together, she felt certain that Sophie hadn't dared to show her face on campus.

When she went home at the end of the day, she inspected her apartment closely, down to the last bookshelf. She discovered that all her shoes had been rearranged according to color in her little closet (only Sophie would have bothered to do that) and there was an opened letter from Mike, stuck behind the napkins in the napkin holder on the kitchen counter, asking her to Rochester for Christmas. Poor man. She couldn't help it that the very idea of seeing him again physically repulsed her. She couldn't have anything to do with him now that Sophie had.

He called the next evening. She'd expected that he would of course. Because she couldn't let him back into her life, because her old life was perfectly intact if she cut this contaminated part out of it, she told him that unfortunately, well, while she had been away in Paris she'd fallen in love. *Her new man was a silent type but she was learning the beauty of silence, too, and things were going so well, everything seemed so right between them.*

Was she mistaken, she wondered when she hung up, or did Mike gag at those words?

Both her parents had come to meet her at the airport gate. Her father had on a ridiculous fur-lined plaid cap with ear covers that made him look like a hunter whereas Maman looked elegant and happy in her red belted overcoat. That they were hand in hand tonight in those incongruous outfits made Monique smile. Maman had warned her not to ask him what he knew about Sophie's divorce, or even make a comment about being glad that she had indeed been able to keep the house. "Wait for him to bring it up—if he does," she'd said in their last phone conversation. "You know he finds it ignoble to talk too openly about other people's money." Dad didn't know that it had been Matt who asked Sophie for the divorce and not vice versa. Seeing that he was still incensed at the rough and offensive treatment Matt had given his daughters at the lake, it had seemed best just to let this fact slide. After all, what mattered in the end was that she had ended up with a fortune, the lot, everything they'd hoped for. Yet she and Maman had to keep an eye on Sophie all the same. By the way she acted one would have thought that Matt had not merely stunned her with his move but in the most profound way betrayed her—by *divorcing* her, mind you, *not* by going to bed with Lorenza. Sophie confided to Maman that recently she had told a new mother on the playground that *although Leslie-Ann's father was alive, her husband was dead*. In short she was a widow. Oh yes, they were going to have to watch her very closely. Christmas vacation would provide them with plenty of time for that.

"Hi, sweetie," said John Morton as he hugged her. "Got any more luggage than the one you have with you?"

"No, that's it, Dad." She gave both her parents a fond kiss. It was going to be a nice quiet family Christmas.

Walking out to the car she asked if Sophie and Leslie-Ann had arrived yet.

"This morning, " said Danielle gaily. "Sophie decorated the Christmas tree and then Leslie-Ann accidently pulled it down. They're at home now working at it." She added in a softer and yet still light voice, "They're a little behind in getting it done because Matt phoned for Leslie-Ann about an hour ago from Venice."

After they had pulled out of the over-illuminated airport parking lot and entered the twilight zone of curving access roads to the expressway, Monique closed her eyes. After ten minutes of sleep in her father's dark car, somewhere on the way home, she opened them again, feeling rested. Daddy was hunched over his steering wheel and getting on with the unpleasant task of night driving, and Maman, who seemed more contented this December and doing things like square-dancing with Dad on Saturday nights in Woodbury, was quietly contemplating the distantly placed houses with their roofs and bushes lined with Christmas lights. Matt Gagliardi crossed Monique's mind, probably because Maman had mentioned his call. So he'd capitulated to his overpowering feelings for Lorenza, had he? Well, well. Either he was doing it for the mere sex or if he wasn't (unlikely), then it must be that he was obsessed with her body-and-soul. And what was the food for all obsession? Memories. Traced and retraced memories. Not that Matt Gagliardi was alone in his fantasticating. There was half the human race keeping him company, she thought. She imagined them asleep in their beds at night; didn't they look just like huge beached fish with those big wads of memories engorging their mouths?

Memories could and should be kept in check. It was easier said than done, but one had to make the effort and get on with life. Of course, indulging in private nostalgia every so often didn't do any harm, but, personally, she'd much rather explore *archetypes*. There were certain fascinating theories uniting Eastern and Western traditions…so fascinating that she closed her eyes and fell back into a half doze. She didn't wake up (why should she, when she was in her Grandmère Marinette's café?) until her father exchanged "good evening"s with the toll attendant through his open car window. Five minutes more of pitch-black county highway and then their duplex came into view.

"You left a light on in the other half," she rebuked her parents on a yawn.

"That's the new renter," said Maman. "He's just separated from his wife and needs a place to live."

"A guy from around here?"

"That's right, a local boy." Dad's joshing voice. "*Prepare-toi, Monique,*" he said in his awful French accent.

"Don't tease. Just tell her, John," murmured Maman.

"We've got an old acquaintance of yours from middle school, Daughter. Name is Jim Toth."

**

"But let me hasten to assure you that not all marriages are conducted with such spite, for there are those who live together in great peacefulness, love, and loyalty because the partners are virtuous, considerate, and reasonable. And although there are bad husbands, there are also very good ones, truly valiant and wise, and the women who meet them were born in a lucky hour, as far as the glory of the world is concerned, for what God has bestowed on them."

Christine de Pizan, ***The Book of the City of Ladies***

**

"... Sweetness defies description; it can't be extended past itself by metaphor, nor can it reduce the world to itself the way pain or pleasure can. It adds a dimension to our dreams and 'shows' us that our most ardent desire is, in truth, not for immortality but for a full exploration of our own nature. Intimacy reveals how closely our bodies resemble our minds, in that our physical nature, too, never seems to come to a definitive configuration but remains open, ready for us to unlock it time and time again. This form of closeness is something worthy of marvel and meditation, not only on account of the unrepeatable wonder we feel when others give themselves to us, but also because of how each of these occasions of intimacy eludes us when we return to the outside world, becoming just one of the many forms of experience and pleasure... While the mounting and dissolving of enthusiasm during our intimacy can't be rendered

in any of the words we use in public, its initial freshness nevertheless frees us from the sense of conclusions and ending inevitably re-enforced by our 'public language'—a sense or thrust which at the same time confers on this public language the cohesion of a work of art in its own right, that of discourse capable of going without a falter to its logical end."

Roberto Bordiga, "The Absolute Shortening of Distances"

www.ingramcontent.com/pod-product-compliance
Lightning Source LLC
Chambersburg PA
CBHW030114180626
46812CB00002B/419